THE LOEB CLASSICAL LIBRARY

FOUNDED BY JAMES LOEB 1911

EDITED BY

JEFFREY HENDERSON

GREEK EPIC FRAGMENTS

LCL 497

GREEK EPIC FRAGMENTS

FROM THE SEVENTH TO THE FIFTH CENTURIES BC

EDITED AND TRANSLATED BY

MARTIN L. WEST

HARVARD UNIVERSITY PRESS
CAMBRIDGE, MASSACHUSETTS
LONDON, ENGLAND
2003

S/O M-W 5/03 21.50

Library of Congress Catalog Card Number 2002031808
CIP data available from the Library of Congress

ISBN 0-674-99605-4

CONTENTS

PREFACE

In the old Loeb Classical Library edition by H. G. Evelyn-White, which originally appeared in 1914, the poems and fragments of Hesiod were coupled with the Homeric Hymns and Epigrams, the remains of the Epic Cycle and other poems associated with Homer's name (including the *Battle of Frogs and Mice*), and the *Contest of Homer and Hesiod.* This material is now being distributed across three new volumes, each of which will contain a considerable amount of additional matter. In the present one the section dealing with the Epic Cycle has been expanded to take in more or less all the remains of early epic down to and including Panyassis.

Dealing with fragmentary works is never as satisfactory as having complete ones. The fragments of the early epics, however, are in one way more rewarding than (say) those of the lyric poets. This is because most of them are cited for their mythological content rather than to illustrate some lexical usage, and often this helps us to build up an idea of the larger whole. For most of the poems of the Epic Cycle, at least, we are able to get a fair notion of their structure and contents.

I have edited and arranged the texts according to my own judgment, but relied on existing editions for information about manuscript readings. The nature of the Loeb

series precludes the provision of the fullest philological detail about the sources of fragments, variant readings, or scholars' conjectures. I have nevertheless tried to ensure that the reader is alerted to the significant textual uncertainties, and, in the case of fragments quoted by ancient authors, supplied with sufficient context to appreciate the purpose for which each one is adduced.

I owe a particular debt of gratitude to Dr. Dirk Obbink for allowing me to see and cite the forthcoming second volume of his monumental edition of Philodemus, *On Piety*, a work well known as an important source of poetic fragments.

Martin L. West
Oxford, May 2002

ABBREVIATIONS AND SYMBOLS

CAG	M. Hayduck and others, Commentaria in Aristotelem Graeca (Berlin, 1882–1909)
CEG	P. A. Hansen, *Carmina Epigraphica Graeca* (Berlin and New York, 1983–1989)
CQ	*Classical Quarterly*
FGrHist	Felix Jacoby, *Die Fragmente der griechischen Historiker* (Berlin and Leiden, 1923–1958)
FHG	Carolus et Theodorus Müller, *Fragmenta Historicorum Graecorum* (Paris, 1841–1873)
GRBS	*Greek, Roman and Byzantine Studies*
HSCP	*Harvard Studies in Classical Philology*
JHS	*Journal of Hellenic Studies*
LIMC	*Lexicon Iconographicum Mythologiae Classicae* (Zurich and Munich, 1981–1999)
Mus. Helv.	*Museum Helveticum*
NGG	*Nachrichten der Gesellschaft der Wissenschaften zu Göttingen*
OCD[3]	*The Oxford Classical Dictionary,* third edition (Oxford, 1996)
PMG	*Poetae Melici Graeci,* ed. D. L. Page (Oxford, 1962)

PMGF	*Poetarum Melicorum Graecorum Fragmenta*, ed. M. Davies (Oxford, 1991)
RE	*Paulys Real-Encyclopädie der classischen Altertumswissenschaft* (Stuttgart, 1894–1980)
Rh. Mus.	*Rheinisches Museum*
SVF	H. von Arnim, *Stoicorum Veterum Fragmenta* (Leipzig, 1903–1905)
TAPA	*Transactions of the American Philological Association*
ZPE	*Zeitschrift für Papyrologie und Epigraphik*

[ ]	words restored where the manuscript is damaged
⟦ ⟧	letters deleted by scribe
⟨ ⟩	editorial insertion
{ }	editorial deletion
† †	corruption in text
*	(attached to a fragment number) uncertain attribution

GREEK EPIC FRAGMENTS

INTRODUCTION

The term "epic" has sometimes been applied to all early hexameter poetry, including, for example, the works of Hesiod and Empedocles. It is now usual to restrict it to narrative poetry about events some distance in the past. Within this category there is a distinction to be made between poetry that is primarily concerned with the narration of a particular heroic episode or series of episodes and poetry concerned with the long-term history of families or peoples, their affiliations and relationships. In the first type, which we may call heroic poetry, the action extends over a few days, a few weeks, or at most a period of years. In the second, which we may call genealogical and antiquarian poetry, it extends over many generations.

The distinction is one of convenience, and it is not absolute, as poems of either sort may contain elements of the other. In Homer we find here and there genealogies going back for six or eight generations, and in the pseudo-Hesiodic *Catalog of Women*, the prime example of genealogical–antiquarian poetry, we find summary heroic narratives attached to individuals as they appear in the genealogies.

Because the archaic epics were redactions of traditional material, there was not always such a clear-cut sense of authorship as there was with lyric, elegy, or iambus. A

few of the later epics, such as Eugammon's *Telegony* and Panyassis' *Heraclea*, were firmly associated with a specific author, but most tended to be cited anonymously by title, and there was often real uncertainty about the author's identity. Many writers throughout antiquity preferred not to opt for a name but to use expressions such as "the poet of the *Cypria*."

HEROIC POEMS. THE EPIC CYCLE

The identifiable poems of the heroic category either belonged to one of the two great cycles, the Theban and the Trojan, or were concerned with the exploits of one of the two great independent heroes, Heracles and Theseus. Other epics—for example a self-contained *Argonautica*—must once have existed at least in oral tradition, but if they were ever written down they seem to have disappeared at an early date.

Sometime in the fourth century BC an "epic cycle" (ἐπικὸς κύκλος) was drawn up, probably in Peripatetic circles. It was in effect a reading list, comprising at least the Trojan epics, and perhaps a wider collection. The poems were to be treated as a corpus which could be read in sequence to yield a more or less continuous story (though in fact some of them overlapped in subject matter). The Epic Cycle that Proclus described in his *Chrestomathy* began with a theogony, so that its narrative extended from the beginning of the world to the end of the heroic age.[1]

The epics were well known in the classical period, and poets such as Stesichorus, Pindar, and the tragedians drew

[1] Photius, *Bibl.* 319a21–30.

on them extensively. Later they fell out of favor. The Hellenistic artists who depicted scenes from Troy and who named Cyclic poems and poets on their works were probably already using prose summaries, not the originals.[2] Yet some of the poems appear to have been still available in the second century AD to certain bookish writers such as Pausanias and Athenaeus.

The Theban Cycle

The Theban and Trojan Wars were the two great military enterprises of the mythical age, the wars which according to Hesiod (*Works and Days* 161–165) brought to an end the race of the heroes who are called demigods. The poet of the *Iliad* knows of the earlier war and refers to it in several places.

The legend tells in fact of two separate Theban wars: the failed assault on Thebes by the Seven, and the successful assault by their sons, the so-called Epigoni. The first, which resulted from the quarrel between the sons of Oedipus, was the more famous and the deeper rooted in tradition. It was the subject of the *Thebaid*. The second, the subject of the *Epigoni*, was a later invention, a pallid re-

[2] The works in question are the mass-produced Macedonian "Homeric cups," dating from the third to second centuries BC, and the miniature relief plaques from the Roman area, such as the Borgia and Capitoline tablets, which are from the time of Augustus or Tiberius. On the cups see U. Sinn, *Die homerischen Becher* (Berlin, 1979); on the plaques A. Sadurska, *Les tables Iliaques* (Warsaw, 1964); Nicholas Horsfall, "Stesichorus at Bovillae?" *JHS* 99 (1979), 26–49.

flection of the first war, on which some of its details were clearly modelled. If we can trust the information given in the *Contest of Homer and Hesiod*, each of these epics was about 7,000 lines in length, something under half the size of the *Iliad*.

There were two others on associated subjects. The *Oedipodea*, said to have been of 6,600 lines, told the story of Oedipus; the *Alcmeonis*, of unknown length, told of Alcmaon, son of the seer Amphiaraus.[3] Alcmaon became notorious (like Orestes) for killing his mother, which he did because of her role in the first Theban war.

To judge by what we know of their contents, the poems of the Theban cycle breathed a different spirit from the *Iliad* and *Odyssey*. With their emphasis on family quarrels and killings, vengeful exiles, and grimly ruthless women and warriors, they have reminded more than one scholar of the world of Germanic saga.

Oedipodea

The Borgia plaque attributes this poem to Cinaethon. Of its contents we know only two details: that the Sphinx was represented as a devouring monster, to whom even the regent Creon's son fell victim, and that Oedipus' children, Polynices, Eteocles, and their two sisters, were not the product of his incestuous union with his mother (as in the tragedians) but of a previous marriage to one Euryganea. We do not even know what his mother was called in the poem, whether Epicaste as in the earliest reference to the

[3] Alcmaon is the epic form of the name, Alcmeon the Attic, Alcman the Doric; Alcmaeon is a false spelling. The poem was anciently cited as the *Alcmeonis* (Ἀλκμεωνίς), though later manuscripts generally give Ἀλκμαιωνίς.

story (*Odyssey* 11.271), Iocaste (Jocasta) as in tragedy, or something else again.

Thebaid

The opening line is preserved (fr. 1), and it indicates that the war was seen from the Argive viewpoint rather than (as in Aeschylus' *Seven Against Thebes*) from the Theban. It was thus a story of disastrous failure, not of salvation from peril.

Polynices and Eteocles were doomed to their fatal dispute by curses which their father laid on them. The fragments of the poem describe two occasions of his wrath and two versions of the curse (frs. 2 and 3): the first, that the brothers should be forever quarrelling, the second, more specific, that they should die at one another's hand. According to later authors they initially made an amicable arrangement that each would rule Thebes in alternate years while the other went away. But then Eteocles refused to relinquish power or allow Polynices back into the city.

Polynices made his way to Argos, where Adrastus was king. He arrived at the same time as Tydeus, a fierce Aetolian who was in exile after a domestic killing. The two got into a dispute, whereupon Adrastus recognized them as the boar and the lion that a seer had advised him to make his sons-in-law. He accordingly gave them his two daughters. He agreed to help Polynices recover his rightful throne at Thebes, and the military expedition was prepared.

It is not quite certain, but it is likely, that there were already in the epic seven commanders to correspond to the fabled seven gates of Thebes. The probable list is: Adrastus, Polynices, Tydeus, Capaneus, Parthenopaeus,

Mecisteus, and Amphiaraus. This last hero, who was a wise seer as well as a doughty warrior (fr. 6), knew from the omens that the enterprise was destined to fail, and he tried to avoid enlistment. But he was married to Adrastus' sister Eriphyle; Adrastus had given her to him in settlement of a quarrel, and it had been agreed that in the event of any disagreement between the two of them her arbitration would be final (fr. 7*). On this occasion, bribed by Polynices with a priceless heirloom, the necklace given by Cadmus to Harmonia, she decreed that Amphiaraus must go to the war. As he prepared to set out, knowing that he would not return alive, he gave advice to his sons, Alcmaon and Amphilochus, on how they should conduct themselves when he was no longer there (fr. 8*). He may have charged Alcmaon with the duty of taking revenge on Eriphyle.

For most details of the campaign we have to turn to other authors, who may or may not give an accurate reflection of the narrative of the *Thebaid*.[4] On reaching Nemea the expedition paused to honor with funeral games the boy Opheltes, also called Archemoros, who had been fatally bitten by a snake: this was the mythical origin of the Nemean Games.[5] If the episode occurred in the *Thebaid*, the poem must date from after 573, when the Nemean Games in fact began.

[4] See especially *Iliad* 4.372–398, 5.801–808, 10.285–290; Pindar, *Ol.* 6.13–17, *Nem.* 9.13–27; Bacchylides 9.10–20; Diodorus 4.65.5–9; Apollodorus 3.6.3–8; Pausanias 9.5.12, 8.7–9.3; Hyginus, *Fabulae* 68; Gantz, *Early Greek Myth*, 510–519.

[5] Bacchylides 9.10–24; Euripides, *Hypsipyle*; Hypotheses to Pindar's *Nemeans*; Apollodorus 3.6.4; Hyginus, *Fabulae* 74, 273.6. For a parallel myth about a heroic origin for the Isthmian Games see below on Eumelus' *Corinthiaca*.

At the river Asopus, a few miles from Thebes, the army halted, and Tydeus was sent ahead to deliver an ultimatum. In the version known to the poet of the *Iliad* he was entertained at a banquet in Eteocles' house, after which he challenged the Cadmeans to athletic trials and easily beat them all. When he departed they set fifty men to ambush him, but he overcame them all, leaving only one alive to tell the tale.

The Argive attack then went forward. After fierce fighting outside the walls the Thebans were driven back into the city. Capaneus mounted the wall on a ladder, and it seemed that nothing could stop him, until Zeus struck him down with a thunderbolt. This gave the defenders new courage, and the issue was again in the balance. It was agreed that Eteocles and Polynices should fight a duel to settle which was to be king, but it resulted in their both being killed. The battle resumed. One by one the Argive champions were killed, Tydeus showing his savage nature to the last (fr. 9*). The good Amphiaraus was saved from this ignominy: as he fled in his chariot, the earth opened up and swallowed him. He remains alive underground to issue prophecies at his oracular site. Only Adrastus escaped with his life, thanks to the marvellous horse Arion (fr. 11).

The elegiac poet Callinus in the mid seventh century associated this subject matter with "Homer," and no alternative author is ever named. Herodotus surely has the *Thebaid* in mind when he speaks of "Homeric" poetry that Cleisthenes of Sicyon banned because of its celebration of Argos and Argives (5.67.1). He goes on to tell that Cleisthenes reduced the honor in which Adrastus was held at Sicyon and introduced the cult of Melanippus, who had killed Mecisteus and Tydeus in the Theban war.

Pseudo-Herodotus in his *Life of Homer* does not mention the *Thebaid* as such among Homer's compositions, but he represents the poet as reciting in the cobbler's at Neonteichos, at an early stage in his career, "*Amphiaraus' Expedition to Thebes*, and the Hymns that he had composed to the gods." The circumstances imply that the *Expedition* was a relatively short poem, not a full-length epic, not therefore the whole *Thebaid*, but a partial narrative covering perhaps Eriphyle's machinations and the seer's instruction of his sons. We should not suppose that this existed as a poem distinct from the *Thebaid*, as Bethe thought. The author imagines the young Homer trying out a specimen of the *Thebaid* that he was working on.[6]

Epigoni

The opening line of the *Epigoni* (fr. 1) proclaims it to be a continuation of the *Thebaid*. It may have been attached to it in some ancient texts, though at least from the time of Herodotus (4.32) it had the status of a separate poem.

The Epigoni and their expedition are known to the *Iliad* poet (4.405–408), although in other passages, such as 5.115–117 and 14.111–127, he seems to forget that Diomedes has proved himself in a previous war.[7] If we trust the mythographers' accounts,[8] the sons of the Seven were led not by Adrastus' son Aegialeus, as we might have expected, but (on the advice of Apollo's oracle) by Alcmaon. After laying waste the villages in the surrounding country

[6] Carl Robert, *Oidipus*, i.219.

[7] Robert, *Oidipus*, i.186, 195.

[8] See especially Pindar, *Pyth.* 8.39–56; Diodorus 5.66; Apollodorus 3.7.2–4; Pausanias 9.5.13, 8.6, 9.4–5; Hyginus, *Fabulae* 71; Gantz, *Early Greek Myth*, 522–525.

they met the Cadmean army at Glisas, five miles northeast of Thebes. Aegialeus was killed by Laodamas, the son of Eteocles,[9] but the Thebans were routed and fled back to the city. Their seer Teiresias advised them to abandon it, and a stream of refugees departed. He went with them as far as Tilphusa, where he died. Some of them went and founded Hestiaea in Thessaly, others settled among the Encheleis, an Illyrian tribe. The victorious Epigoni sacked Thebes and captured Teiresias' daughter Manto, whom they sent to Delphi as a thanks offering to Apollo (fr. 4). She ended up at Claros in Asia Minor, and established Apollo's sanctuary there. The famous seer Mopsus was said to be her son.

Herodotus (4.32) expresses doubt about Homer's authorship of the *Epigoni*, and a scholiast on Aristophanes (fr. 1) ascribes it to Antimachus, presumably meaning Antimachus of Teos, a poet who was supposed to have seen a solar eclipse in 753 BC.[10] On the strength of this a verse quoted from Antimachus of Teos may be assigned to the *Epigoni* (fr. 2), and we may also infer that the epic contained a portent in which the sun turned dark. The interest in Claros would be appropriate for a poet from nearby Teos. But he probably wrote long after the eighth century.

Alcmeonis

We may guess that the major event narrated in this poem was Alcmaon's murder of his mother Eriphyle for having sent Amphiaraus to his doom. This made a natural sequel

[9] He was the only one of the Epigoni to lose his life, as his father had been the only one to escape with his in the earlier conflict.

[10] Plutarch, *Life of Romulus*, 12.2.

to the first expedition against Thebes, but it does not combine easily with the second expedition, which Alcmaon led.[11] The story may therefore predate the development of the Epigoni legend.

It was popular with the tragedians, and their treatments have influenced the later mythographers, so that it is hard to know how much goes back to the epic. The motif of Alcmaon's being driven mad by his mother's Erinyes, for example, may have been worked up by the tragedians on the analogy of the Orestes story. But they will not have invented the tradition of his travels through Arcadia and Aetolia to Acarnania. The reference to Tydeus' exile from Aetolia (fr. 4) suggests that the *Alcmeonis* may have told how Alcmaon went there with Tydeus' son Diomedes and helped him to rout the enemies of his family.[12] It is likely also to have related how Alcmaon found absolution from his bloodguilt, in accordance with an oracle of Apollo, by finding a place to live that had not existed under the sun when he killed his mother. He found it in land newly created by silting at the mouth of the Achelous.[13] The poet's interest in those western regions is confirmed by fr. 5.

The work is never ascribed to a named author. The importance it gives to the Delphic oracle, its concern with Acarnania, which was an area of Corinthian settlement in the time of Cypselus and Periander, and its mention of Zagreus (fr. 3, otherwise first heard of in Aeschylus) suggest a sixth-century or even early fifth-century date.

[11] See Gantz, *Early Greek Myth*, 525.

[12] Ephorus *FGrHist* 70 F 123; Apollodorus 1.8.6.

[13] Thucydides 2.102.5–6; Apollodorus 3.7.5; Pausanias 8.24.8–9.

The Trojan Cycle

The Trojan cycle comprised eight epics including the *Iliad* and *Odyssey*. For the six lost ones we are fortunate to possess plot summaries excerpted from the *Chrestomathy* of Proclus; that for the *Cypria* is found in several manuscripts of the *Iliad*, while the rest are preserved in a single manuscript (Venetus A). For each epic Proclus states its place in the series, the number of books it contained, and an author's name.

It is disputed whether the Proclus who wrote the *Chrestomathy* was the famous fifth-century Neoplatonist (as was believed at any rate by the sixth century) or a grammarian of some centuries earlier.[14] It makes little practical difference, as agreements with other mythographic sources, especially Apollodorus, show that Proclus was reproducing material of Hellenistic date.

His testimony is in some respects defective. It appears from other evidence that Ajax's suicide has been eliminated from the end of the *Aethiopis*, and the whole sack of Troy from the end of the *Little Iliad*, because these events were included in the next poems in the series. Evidently he (or rather his Hellenistic source) was concerned to produce a continuous, nonrepetitive narrative based on the Cyclic poems rather than a complete account of their individual contents. There are other significant omissions too,

[14] He is the Neoplatonist in the *Suda*'s life of Proclus (from Hesychius of Miletus). For the other view see Michael Hillgruber, "Zur Zeitbestimmung der Chrestomathie des Proklos," *Rh. Mus.* 133 (1990), 397–404.

as the fragments show. It is attested, for instance, that the *Returns* contained a descent to Hades, but there is no hint of it in Proclus. It is probably legitimate to fill out his spare summary with some details from the parallel narrative of Apollodorus, and so I have done, giving the additions between angle brackets. Caution is needed, as Apollodorus has sometimes incorporated material from other sources such as tragedy.

Cypria

The title means "the Cyprian epic" and implies that it came from Cyprus. It was usually ascribed to a Cypriot poet, Stasinus or Hegesias (or Hegesinus); there was a story, apparently already known to Pindar, that Homer composed it but gave it to Stasinus as his daughter's dowry.[15] Nothing is known of this Stasinus, or indeed of the other poets named in connection with the Cycle such as Arctinus of Miletus and Lesches of Pyrrha.

The poet set himself the task of telling the origin of the Trojan War and all that happened from then to the point where the *Iliad* begins. The resulting work lacked organic unity, consisting merely in a long succession of episodes. Many of them were traditional, and are alluded to in the *Iliad*. But the *Cypria* must have been composed after the *Iliad* had become well established as a classic. The language of the fragments (especially fr. 1) shows signs of lateness. The poem can hardly be earlier than the second half of the sixth century.

[15] See the Testimonia. Herodotus (at fr. 14) argues against Homer's authorship without indicating that there was any other named claimant.

Aethiopis

The *Iliad* poet started with a scheme in which, after killing Hector, Achilles was to chase the rest of the Trojans into the city by the Scaean Gate and there meet his fate in accordance with Thetis' warning (18.96). But he changed it, deferring Achilles' death to an indeterminate moment after the end of the poem, and giving to Patroclus the funeral games that would have been Achilles'. A subsequent poet who wished to narrate the death of Achilles had to create another situation in which he killed a champion and pursued the mass of the enemy to the city. On the *Iliad*'s terms the Trojans had no suitable champion left after Hector. But younger poets spun out the story by having a succession of new heroes arrive unexpectedly from abroad to help the Trojans. There was the Thracian Rhesus in the interpolated tenth rhapsody of the *Iliad*; in the *Aethiopis* there were successively the Amazon Penthesilea and the Ethiop Memnon; in the *Little Iliad* there was Eurypylus the son of Telephus. It was Memnon who took the place of Hector as the hero whose death led swiftly to that of Achilles.

Achilles' death was the climax of the *Aethiopis,* as Hector's is of the *Iliad*. It was followed by funeral games in his honor. The awarding of his armor to the bravest warrior went with the games. Hence it was natural for Arctinus (if that was the poet's name) to tell of Odysseus' victory over Ajax in that contest and, at least briefly in conclusion, of Ajax's suicide.

He used an existing account of Achilles' death, the Nereids' laments for him, and the funeral games, an account very like the one known to the *Iliad* poet. But the hero's

translation to the White Island is post-Iliadic, as are the Amazon and Ethiop interventions. The *Odyssey* poet knows of Memnon (4.188, 11.522), the battle for Achilles' body, the Nereids' and Muses' laments, and the funeral games (24.36–94), but he shows no awareness of the Penthesilea episode, which was perhaps the last addition to the structure. She first appears in artistic representations around 600 BC.

The *Amazonia* listed before the *Little Iliad* and *Returns* in the Hesychian *Life of Homer* was presumably the same as the *Aethiopis*, not a separate work.

The Little Iliad

This poem, ascribed to Lesches from Pyrrha or Mytilene in Lesbos, is cited by Aristotle together with the *Cypria* to illustrate the episodic nature of some of the Cyclic poems. But it had a more coherent structure than may appear from Proclus' summary. It began with the Achaeans facing a crisis: with Achilles and Ajax both dead, how were they to make further progress against Troy? Odysseus' capture of the Trojan seer Helenus unlocked the information they needed. They learned of three essential steps that they had to take. They had to bring Heracles' bow to Troy; that meant fetching Philoctetes from Lemnos, and it led to the death of Paris, the man whose desire for Helen had caused and sustained the war. They had to bring Neoptolemus from Scyros to take Achilles' place; he was able to defeat the Trojans' new champion Eurypylus and end their capability of fighting outside their walls. And they had to steal the Palladion, the divine image that protected the city.

When all that was accomplished, it remained to breach

the Trojan defences. The building of the Wooden Horse provided the means to achieve this. The epic concluded with an account of the sack.

The *Odyssey* poet shows an extensive acquaintance with the subject matter of the *Little Iliad*,[16] and must have known, if not that very poem, something quite similar. The *Iliad* poet knew the Philoctetes story (2.716–725), and of course some version of the sack of Troy; the passages referring to Achilles' son Neoptolemus, however, are suspect (19.326–337, 24.467). The *Little Iliad* may have been composed about the third quarter of the seventh century.

The Sack of Ilion

This poem, ascribed to the same poet as the *Aethiopis*, gave an alternative account of the sack that diverged in some details from that in the *Little Iliad*. In Proclus' summary of the Cycle the corresponding portion of the *Little Iliad* is suppressed in favor of the *Sack*.

As he represents it, Arctinus' poem began with the Trojans wondering what to do with the Wooden Horse, the Achaeans having apparently departed. This has been thought an implausible point at which to take up the story; but it corresponds remarkably well to the song of Demodocus described in *Odyssey* 8.500–520, and we may again suspect that the *Odyssey* poet knew an epic similar to the Cyclic poem as current in the classical period.

[16] Ajax's defeat over the armor (11.543 ff.); Deiphobus as Helen's last husband (compare 4.276, 8.517); Neoptolemus and Eurypylus (11.506 ff., 519 f.); Odysseus' entry into Troy disguised as a beggar (4.242 ff.); Epeios' building of the horse (8.492 ff.).

The Returns

The *Odyssey* poet was also familiar with "the return of the Achaeans" as a subject of epic song (1.326, 10.15), and he composed his own epic against that background. His references to the other heroes' returns are in fair agreement with the content of the Cyclic *Returns.* The Cyclic poem, on the other hand, seems to have made only one brief allusion to Odysseus' return (Neoptolemus' path crossed with his at Maronea)—no doubt because a separate *Odyssey* was already current.

Many of the heroes had uneventful homecomings. The major return stories were (*a*) the drowning of the Locrian Ajax as punishment for his sacrilege at Troy, and (*b*) the murder of Agamemnon when he arrived home, followed after some years by Orestes' revenge. There was no place in this story for Menelaus, whose return had therefore to be detached from his brother's and extended until just after Orestes' deed. The return of the two Atreidai formed the framework of the whole epic: it began with the dispute that separated them, and ended with Menelaus' belated return. Athenaeus in fact cites the poem as *The Return of the Atreidai*.

Of the other stories incorporated in it, the death of Calchas at Colophon is connected with the foundation of the oracle at Claros,[17] while Neoptolemus' journey to the Molossian country implies the legends of his founding a kingdom there and the claims of local rulers to descend

[17] Compare *Epigoni* fr. 4. The poet's interest in this region lends some color to Eustathius' belief that he was a Colophonian, though other sources attribute the work to Agias of Troezen.

from him. What is completely obscure is the place occupied in the epic by the account of "Hades and the terrors in it," attested by Pausanias (at fr. 1) and the probable context of a whole series of fragments (2–8). The least unlikely suggestion is perhaps that the souls of Agamemnon and those killed with him were described arriving in the underworld, like the souls of the Suitors in *Odyssey* 24.1–204.

Telegony

The final poem of the Cycle, intended as a sequel to the *Odyssey*, was an ill-assorted bundle of legends about the end of Odysseus' life,[18] in which the number of his sons was raised from one to four or possibly five, born of three different mothers.

Teiresias in the *Odyssey* (11.121–137) had told Odysseus that after returning to Ithaca he should journey inland until he found a people ignorant of the sea, and there dedicate an oar and make sacrifice to Poseidon. Then he should go back home and govern his subjects in peace. Eventually in old age he would succumb to a mild death coming from the sea. Eugammon, the poet of the *Telegony*, developed these prophecies. Odysseus not only travelled into Thesprotia but married a local queen there and stayed until her death, leaving their son to rule the kingdom. On his return to Ithaca he found that Penelope had borne him another son. Meanwhile his earlier year-long sojourn with Circe had also borne fruit in a son, Telegonus, "Faraway-born." Telegonus' role was to introduce into epic the folktale of the son who unknowingly kills his father in combat, a motif

[18] On these see especially Albert Hartmann, *Untersuchungen über die Sagen vom Tod des Odysseus* (Munich, 1917).

familiar from the stories of Hildebrand and Hadubrand, Sohrab and Rustum, and others.[19] His use of a sting ray spear made for a somewhat forced fulfilment of the prophecy about Odysseus' death from the sea. The ending in which everyone married each other and lived happily ever after was pure novelette.

The author of this confection is identified as a Cyrenaean active in the 560s. That seems corroborated by the information (fr. 4) that Odysseus' second son by Penelope was called Arcesilaus. In its Doric form, Arcesilas, this was a dynastic name of the Battiad kings of Cyrene; Arcesilas II was reigning in the 560s. By giving Odysseus a son of this name Eugammon was lending credence to a claim that the Battiads were descended from Odysseus. The Thesprotian part of his story, which may have existed earlier, was likewise constructed to bolster the pretensions of a local nobility.[20]

Poems on Exploits of Heracles

Myths of Heracles may go back to Mycenaean times.[21] At any rate poems about his deeds were current before 700 BC. Hesiod was familiar with them, as appears from a se-

[19] See M. A. Potter, *Sohrab and Rustem. The Epic Theme of a Combat between Father and Son* (London, 1902).

[20] Clement's allegation that Eugammon stole it from Musaeus (see the Testimonia) may imply that it had some independent currency under another name. Pausanias (at fr. 3) cites a *Thesprotis*, but this may be identical with the *Telegony*.

[21] See M. P. Nilsson, *The Mycenaean Origin of Greek Mythology* (Berkeley, 1932), 187–220.

ries of allusions in the *Theogony* (287–294, 313–318, 327–332, 526–532; compare also 215 f., 334 f., 518), and there are many references to him also in the *Iliad* and *Odyssey*. Heracles' fight with the Hydra is already represented on a Boeotian fibula of the late eighth or early seventh century. Considerably earlier is a terracotta centaur with a knee wound, found at Lefkandi in Euboea and dating from the late tenth century: it is perhaps to be connected with the story of Heracles shooting Chiron in the knee.[22]

The early poems may in most cases have been concerned with single exploits, as in the *Capture of Oichalia* attributed to Homer or Creophylus and the pseudo-Hesiodic *Shield of Heracles* and *Wedding of Ceyx*. But the myth of Heracles' subjugation to Eurystheus, who laid a series of tasks on him, presupposes narratives in which his successful accomplishment of all these tasks was described, and this myth is already alluded to in the *Iliad* and *Odyssey*.[23] There must therefore have been a poem or poems covering "the Labors of Heracles," even if it is uncertain how many or which Labors were included.[24]

The only archaic epic on this subject that survived to be read by Alexandrian scholars was the *Heraclea* of Pisander of Camirus. (Clement mentions one Pisinous of Lindos from whom, he alleges, Pisander's poem was plagiarized,

22 Apollodorus 2.5.4; M. R. Popham and L. H. Sackett, *Lefkandi* i (London, 1980), 168–170, 344 f., pl. 169, and frontispiece.

23 *Iliad* 8.362–365, 15.639 f., 19.95–133; *Odyssey* 11.617–626.

24 The number varies in later accounts. The tally of twelve is not documented earlier than the metopes on the temple of Zeus at Olympia (around 460 BC) and perhaps Pindar fr. 169a.43.

but this may have been no more than a variant attribution found in some copies.) In the second quarter of the fifth century Panyassis of Halicarnassus, a cousin or uncle of Herodotus, wrote a much longer *Heraclea*; this may be counted as the last product of the old epic tradition, as Choerilus' *Persica*, from the late fifth century, represents a self-conscious search for new paths, and Antimachus' *Thebaid* even more so. Both Pisander and Panyassis are included in a canon of the five major epic poets, first attested in its complete form by Proclus but perhaps Alexandrian in origin.[25]

"Creophylus," The Capture of Oichalia

Creophylus of Samos appears in Plato and various later authors as a friend of Homer's who gave him hospitality and was rewarded with the gift of this poem; the effect of the story was to vindicate as Homer's a work generally current under Creophylus' name.[26] However, Creophylus seems not to have been a real person but the fictitious eponym of a Samian rhapsodes' guild, the Creophyleans, one of whom, Hermodamas, was said to have taught Pythagoras.[27]

Oichalia was the legendary city of king Eurytus.[28] Its

[25] See Quintilian 10.1.54. The other three in the canon are Homer, Hesiod, and Antimachus. The absence of Eumelus, Arctinus, and the other Cyclic poets is noteworthy.

[26] Callimachus, *Epigram* 6 Pf., inverts the relationship, saying that it was really by Creophylus but became known as Homer's.

[27] See Walter Burkert, *Kleine Schriften I: Homerica* (Göttingen, 2001), 141–143; Filippo Càssola, *Inni omerici* (Milan, 1975), xxxvii.

[28] *Iliad* 2.596, 730; *Odyssey* 8.224; [Hesiod] fr. 26.28–33.

location was disputed in antiquity, some placing it in Thessaly (as in the *Iliad*), some in Euboea (as in Sophocles' *Trachiniae*), and others in the Peloponnese (Arcadia or Messene). Pausanias (in fragment 2) implies that Creophylus' poem favored the Euboean claim, but Strabo (also in fragment 2) indicates that it was ambivalent.

Heracles visited Oichalia and was entertained by Eurytus, but presently a quarrel arose between them and Heracles was driven away, perhaps after winning an archery contest in which Eurytus' daughter Iole was the prize. Heracles then stole Eurytus' horses, killed his son Iphitus when he came looking for them, and finally attacked Oichalia, sacked it, and took Iole by force. The story possibly continued, as in Sophocles' play, with Heracles' wife Deianeira sending him the poisoned robe that killed him.[29]

Pisander

Theocritus, in an epigram composed for a bronze statue of Pisander, celebrates him as the first poet to tell the story of Heracles and all his Labors. The fragments of the poem show that it dealt not only with the Labors performed at Eurystheus' behest but also with other exploits such as Heracles' encounter with Antaios and his assault on Troy. If the *Suda*'s statement that it was in two books is correct, it was quite a compact work.

The same source tells us that some dated Pisander earlier than Hesiod (presumably on account of Hesiod's references to the Heracles myths), while others put him in the

[29] For the various versions of the legend see Gantz, *Early Greek Myth*, 434–437.

mid seventh century. The only real clue is that he represented Heracles as wearing a lion skin and armed with a bow and a club. In art he is portrayed in this garb only from about 600; before that he is shown like a normal hoplite, with shield, spear, and sword.

Panyassis

Panyassis' *Heraclea* was much more extensive, a work of some 9,000 lines, divided into fourteen books: the longest of pre-Alexandrian epics after the *Iliad*, *Odyssey*, and Antimachus' *Thebaid*. The length is accounted for by an ample narrative style which had room for some leisurely dialog scenes (see fragments 3, 13, 18–22).

The Nemean Lion was mentioned in book 1 (fr. 6), a drinking session which may have been that with the centaur Pholos in book 3 (fr. 9), and the crossing of Oceanus, presumably to Erythea to get the cattle of Geryon, in book 5 (fr. 13). The Geryon exploit usually comes towards the end of the Labors for Eurystheus; if this was the case in Panyassis, the implication will be that a large portion of his poem was taken up with adventures recounted after the conclusion of the Eurystheus cycle. But we have little reliable evidence as to the sequence of episodes. In default of it, it is convenient to take Apollodorus' narrative as a guide in ordering the fragments, though his principal source appears to have been Pherecydes, who wrote a few years after Panyassis and introduced complications of his own.[30]

Besides the *Heraclea*, Panyassis is said to have com-

[30] The three modern editors of Panyassis, Matthews, Bernabé, and Davies, all differ in their numbering of the fragments, and I have not felt it necessary to follow any one of them.

posed an elegiac poem in 7,000 lines on the legendary colonization of Ionia. As with similar long antiquarian elegies attributed to Semonides (*Samian Antiquities*) and Xenophanes (*Foundation of Colophon*, *Colonization of Elea*), there is no clear trace of the poem's currency or influence in antiquity, and some doubt remains as to whether it ever really existed.

Theseis

Aristotle in his *Poetics* criticizes "all those poets who have composed a *Heracleis*, a *Theseis*, and poems of that kind" for their mistaken assumption that the career of a single hero gives unity to a mythical narrative. We have just two citations from an epic referred to as "the *Theseid*," no author being identified.

Theseus is an Attic hero with only a marginal place in the older epic tradition. He and his family are unknown to the *Iliad* except in interpolated lines (1.265, 3.144). The *Odyssey* mentions the Ariadne story (11.321–325; compare Sappho fr. 206), and the Cyclic poems incorporated the tale that Theseus' sons Acamas and Demophon went to fight at Troy for the sole purpose of rescuing their grandmother Aethra, who had been captured by the Dioscuri and enslaved to Helen.[31] But Theseus' emergence as a sort of Attic Heracles, who overcame a series of monsters and brigands and had various other heroic achievements to his credit, appears on artistic evidence to have occurred only

[31] *Cypria* fr. 12*; *Little Iliad* fr. 17; *Sack of Ilion* Argum. 4 and fr. 6; compare Alcman *PMGF* 21, and the interpolation at *Iliad* 3.144.

around 525 BC.[32] It probably reflects the circulation of an epic *Theseis* at this time, perhaps the work from which our citations come. But a *Theseis* is also ascribed to one Nicostratus, who lived in the fourth century.[33]

GENEALOGICAL AND ANTIQUARIAN EPICS

Pausanias tells us that, wishing to settle a point of mythical genealogy, he read "the so-called *Ehoiai* and the *Naupaktia*, and besides them all the genealogies of Cinaethon and Asius."[34] The *Ehoiai*, that is, the pseudo-Hesiodic *Catalog of Women*, was the most widely current of the early poems that dealt with this kind of subject matter, and an obvious place to turn for information of the sort that Pausanias wanted. There was also a *Great Ehoiai* under Hesiod's name. But there were various other poems of this category dating from the fifth century BC or earlier, some of them ascribed to particular authors, others anonymous. They were not widely read, but they existed. The quantity is surprising. The explanation is to be sought, not in the archaic Greeks' insatiable urge to write verse, but rather in the desire of clans and cities to construct a prehistory for themselves, or to modify current assumptions about their prehistory. Sometimes the citizenship of the poet is reflected in the emphasis of the poem. Eumelus is creating a prehis-

32 See Emily Kearns and K. W. Arafat in *OCD*3 s.v. Theseus.

33 Diogenes Laertius 2.59. The choliambic *Theseis* of Diphilus (schol. Pind. *Ol.* 10.83b, uncertain date) was presumably a burlesque.

34 Paus. 4.2.1 = Cinaethon fr. 5.

tory for Corinth and Sicyon; Asius is creating one for Samos. This does not represent the entirety of their ambitions, to be sure. There are many fragments that we cannot relate to the poets' national interests, or see how they fitted into the overall structure.

Eumelus

Eumelus of Corinth, according to Pausanias, was the son of Amphilytus and belonged to the Bacchiad family, who ruled Corinth up to the time of Cypselus (about 657 BC); he is dated in the generation before the first Messenian War, so sometime in the mid eighth century.[35] He was credited with the authorship of a processional song (*PMG* 696) that the Messenians performed for Apollo on Delos, and in Pausanias' opinion this was his only genuine work. Five other titles are associated with him: *Titanomachy*, *Corinthiaca*, *Europia*, *Return of the Greeks*, and *Bougonia*. The last two are mentioned in only one source each. *Bougonia* suggests a poem about cattle-breeding, but it is difficult to imagine such a work. The *Return of the Greeks* is presumably identical with the Cyclic *Returns*, which is otherwise ascribed to Agias of Troezen: its attribution to Eumelus may be an isolated error.

The three remaining titles are more regularly associ-

35 Paus. 2.1.1; 4.4.1. Eusebius in his *Chronicle* dated Eumelus similarly to 760/759 or 744/743, while Clement (*Strom.* 1.131.8) says he overlapped with Archias, another Bacchiad, who founded Syracuse around 734. See A. A. Mosshammer, *The* Chronicle *of Eusebius and the Greek Chronographic Tradition* (Lewisburg, 1979), 198–203.

ated with Eumelus, even if many authors prefer to cite them without an author's name.[36] As they are bound together by certain links of subject matter, they may be considered as forming a sort of Corinthian epic cycle transmitted under the name "Eumelus," and kept together under that name, whether or not they are in fact by one poet. It may be that Eumelus' name was remembered in connection with the processional and then attached to the epics because no other name of a Corinthian poet was available.

Titanomachy

This poem was divided into at least two books (fr. 14). The war in which the younger gods defeated the Titans must have bulked large in it, but the fragments show that it had a wider scope. It began with some account of the earlier generations of gods (fr. 1). Both this divine genealogy and the account of the war diverged from Hesiod's *Theogony*.

The poem shows points of contact with the *Corinthiaca* in the interest shown in the Sun god (frs. 10–11) and in the many-handed sea deity Aigaion or Briareos (fr. 3); see frs. 16–17. The prominence of the sons of Iapetos (frs. 5*, 7*) may also be significant in view of Ephyra's connection with Epimetheus in the *Corinthiaca* (fr. 15). It appears that the *Titanomachy* supplied the divine prehistory to the Corinthian dynastic history.

Corinthiaca

This composition was valued more for its content than for its poetry, and the poetic text was largely displaced from

[36] For the *Titanomachy* Athenaeus mentions Arctinus as a claimant besides Eumelus. On these works see my study listed in the Bibliography.

circulation by a prose version, still under Eumelus' name, that told the same story in what was perhaps felt to be a more accredited format. Hence Clement can associate Eumelus with Acusilaus as a prose writer who used material of the Hesiodic type, and Pausanias can refer to the *Corinthian History*, using a form of title that definitely suggests a prose work. It may have been from a preface prefixed to the prose version that he obtained his biographical details about Eumelus.[37] Fragments 17 and 21, however, and 16 if rightly assigned to Eumelus, show that some people still had access to the poetic version.

The work was concerned with the origins of Corinth and the history of its kingship, but it also took account of its western neighbor Sicyon. These cities rose to prominence only after about 900 BC, and they had no standing in traditional epic myth; they are hardly mentioned in Homer. Mythical histories had to be constructed for them in the archaic period. For Corinth the first step was to identify it with the Homeric Ephyra, the city of Sisyphus, which lay "in a corner of the Argolid" (*Iliad* 6.152) but whose location was not firmly established. The name was explained as being that of an Oceanid nymph who was the first settler in the area of Corinth (fr. 15). She was married to Epimetheus, who in Hesiod is the husband of the first woman, Pandora.

The royal line was traced from Helios, the Sun god, who had been awarded the site in a dispute with Poseidon (fr. 16*), down to Sisyphus and Glaucus. We do not know how much further the tale went. It can hardly have omit-

[37] Clem. *Strom.* 6.26.7; Paus. 2.1.1 (fr. 15).

ted Glaucus' son Bellerophon, who went to Lycia and started a new royal line there (*Iliad* 6.168–211). It may be that Eumelus was the source for Pindar's myth of the golden bridle which Bellerophon obtained from Athena and which enabled him to capture Pegasus.[38]

Europia

The title *Europia* implies that the story of Europa had a prominent place in the work, which Pausanias indeed (at fr. 30) calls "the Europa poem." It apparently recorded her abduction by Zeus in the form of a bull (fr. 26), presumably also the birth of her sons Minos, Rhadamanthys, and Sarpedon, and perhaps some of their descendants.

The story of Europa led also towards Boeotia. The *Europia* of Stesichorus included the story of Cadmus' foundation of Thebes (*PMGF* 195), no doubt after he had searched in vain for his vanished sister Europa and received advice from Delphi. If the Europa story was developed similarly in the Eumelian poem, this suggests possible contexts for the Delphic reference of fr. 28 and for Amphion and his lyre (fr. 30). Europa herself had Boeotian connections, as did one of her sons.

Does the *Europia* show any signs of connection with the *Corinthiaca* or with Corinth or Sicyon? We may note firstly that the story of Dionysus and Lycurgus (fr. 27) is dragged oddly into the *Iliad* in the episode where Glaucus relates to Diomedes the history of Sisyphus of Ephyra and his descendants (6.130–140, 152–211). Nowhere else in the *Iliad* or *Odyssey* does Dionysus have such prominence. But he was the patron deity of the Bacchiadai, as

[38] Pindar, *Ol.* 13.63–92, cf. Paus. 2.4.1.

their name implies; the Bacchis from whom they claimed descent was a son of the god.[39]

Secondly, Amphion and Zethus (fr. 30) have a direct connection with Sicyon, as there was a tale that their mother Antiope, a daughter of Asopus, had been abducted from Hyria in Boeotia by the Sicyonian Epopeus, and that he was actually their father.[40] Epopeus played a part in the narrative of the *Corinthiaca*, and an Antiope figured there as his grandmother, the consort of Helios.

It seems likely that fr. 29, as it deals with another daughter of Asopus abducted from Hyria, should also be assigned to the *Europia*. This Asopid is Sinope, the eponym of the Milesian colony on the Black Sea, founded (to judge by the archaeological evidence) in the mid seventh century. The interest in this area parallels the Argonautic element in the *Corinthiaca*.[41]

There is, then, some reason to treat the *Titanomachy*, *Corinthiaca*, and *Europia* as a group, apart from their common attribution to Eumelus. That they were really the work of an eighth-century Bacchiad is excluded on chronological grounds. The *Titanomachy* is not likely to antedate the later seventh century, as the motifs of the Sun's chariot and his floating vessel are not attested earlier than that. The *Corinthiaca* must date from sometime after the foundation of the Isthmian Games (582) and probably af-

[39] Sch. Ap. Rhod. 4.1212/1214a.

[40] See Paus. 2.6.1–4, who quotes Asius (fr. 1); Apollodorus 3.5.5.

[41] Alternatively, if fr. 29 is from the *Corinthiaca*, the two poems are linked by the interest in Asopids abducted from Hyria.

ter the first Greek settlement in Colchis (mid sixth century). Orpheus and the race in armor (fr. 22*) are also late elements. As for the *Europia*, if the Sinope fragment is rightly assigned to it, that poem too reflected a fairly advanced stage in Greek penetration of the Black Sea, in this case after about 650.

Cinaethon, Asius, and Others

Among his texts of first recourse on questions of mythical genealogy Pausanias names the poems of Cinaethon and Asius, and the *Naupaktia*. None of these was widely read in the Roman period, and for Cinaethon and Asius Pausanias himself is the source of nearly all the fragments. Cinaethon is described as a Lacedaemonian, but we can say nothing else about him; Eusebius' dating to 764/3 BC is of no more value than any of the other datings assigned to epic poets by ancient chronographers. There is a puzzling randomness in the titles occasionally associated with Cinaethon: *Oedipodea*, *Little Iliad*, *Telegony*. The actual fragments cannot be ascribed to any of these. They are from a genealogical work which contained (appropriately for a Spartan poet) information about descendants of Agamemnon and Menelaus, but also about Cretan figures and about the children of Medea and Jason.

Asius of Samos seems somewhat more a figure of flesh and blood. He has a father's name as well as a city, and he does not appear among the claimants for authorship of any of the Cyclic poems. His genealogies showed a healthy concern with the history of his native island (frs. 7, 13), though they also took in heroes from Boeotia (frs. 1–4),

Phocis (fr. 5), Aetolia (fr. 6), the Peloponnese (frs. 8–10), and Attica (fr. 11). Besides hexameter poetry, Asius is also quoted for an enigmatic elegiac fragment.[42]

We have one fragment each from two obscure poets whom Pausanias had found quoted by an earlier author, Callippus of Corinth, and who were no longer current in his own time. These were Hegesinous, author of an *Atthis* (the fragment, however, concerns Boeotia), and Chersias of Orchomenos. Callippus was a writer of the early imperial period, perhaps an epideictic orator rather than a historian. It is often maintained that the two poets and their fragments, which he quoted in what was perhaps an oration to the Orchomenians, were his own inventions.[43] There seems no strong ground for the suspicion; if he had wanted to forge testimonies of old poets, he would surely have come up with verses of a less humdrum character. Chersias' existence at least is recognized by Plutarch, who makes him a contemporary of Periander and Chilon and an interlocutor in the *Banquet of the Seven Sages* (156e, 163f); he alludes to some incident which had caused him to fall out of favor with Periander. This may be a novelistic fiction, but some record of a poet Chersias seems to lie behind it.

42 Douglas E. Gerber, *Greek Elegiac Poetry* (Loeb Classical Library), p. 426.

43 Carl Robert, "De Gratiis Atticis," in *Commentationes philologae in honorem Th. Mommseni scripserunt amici* (Berlin, 1877), 145–146; Felix Jacoby, commentary on *FGrHist* 331 (IIIB Supplement, 609).

Anonymous Poems

The "Naupactus epic" (*Naupaktia* or *Naupaktika*), although regularly cited by its title alone, or with the phrase "the author of the *Naupaktika*," is not wholly anonymous, as Pausanias tells us that Charon of Lampsacus, an author of about 400 BC, ascribed it to a Naupactian named Carcinus, whereas most people credited it to a Milesian. He implies that the title was not accounted for by any particular concentration on Naupactian matters. That being so, the title would imply a poem that was current in the Naupactus area or believed to originate from there.[44]

Pausanias describes it as being "on women," which suggests a structure similar to that of the Hesiodic *Ehoiai*, with a succession of genealogies taking their starting point from various heroines. But it contained at least one ample narrative of the heroic type: the story of the Argonauts. More than half of the fragments come from the scholia to Apollonius Rhodius, which contrast details of Apollonius' narrative with that of the older poem. It is a sign of Naupactian interest in the northwest that Jason was represented as migrating to Corcyra after the death of Pelias (fr. 9). This was no doubt the Corcyraean legend of the time, as was the affiliation to Jason of the Epirotic figure Mermerus.[45]

The *Phoronis* told of Phoroneus, the first man in Argive myth, and his descendants. The Argive focus is clear in fr. 4, less so in other fragments, such as those on the Phrygian

[44] The clearest parallel is the title *Cypria*; perhaps also *Phocais* and *Iliad*, *Little Iliad*.

[45] See the note to the translation.

Kouretes and Idaean Dactyls (2–3). It is not apparent whether the poem told of Io's journey to Egypt and her progeniture of an Egyptian family that eventually returned to Argos. That story was related in another anonymous poem, the *Danais* or *Danaides*. This is classified here as a genealogical rather than a heroic (single-episode) poem because of the nature of the myth, which leads on ineluctably to the Danaids' slaughter of their bridegrooms, the sons of Aegyptus, and the dynasty that descended from the one who was spared, Lynceus. The remarkable length of the poem, reported as 6,500 verses, also suggests a broad scope. Like the *Phoronis*, it found occasion to speak of the Kouretes (fr. 3), and of myth about the gods (fr. 2) whose relevance to the Danaid saga is obscure.

Also assigned to this section are the fragments of the *Minyas*. The Minyans were the legendary inhabitants of Orchomenos, and the poem may perhaps have begun with genealogies covering that part of Boeotia; there were no particular myths about the Minyans as such,[46] or about their eponym Minyas. The fragments, however, come exclusively from an account of Theseus' and Pirithous' descent to the underworld, and of various people whom they met there or observed undergoing punishment. How this was connected with Minyan matters is entirely obscure.

It may be that the *Minyas* was the same as the poem on the descent of Theseus and Pirithous to Hades which Pausanias (9.31.5) mentions in his list of poems that some people (wrongly, in his view) attributed to Hesiod. If they were two different poems, then the papyrus fragment here

46 The identification of the Argonauts as Minyans was a secondary development.

given as fr. 7 of the *Minyas* might be from either.[47] But the *Minyas* has the stronger claim, as the poem for which there is actual evidence of currency; and what Meleager says about his own death in fr. 7.1–2 corresponds exactly to the information in fr. 5.

UNPLACED FRAGMENTS

A number of authors quote from "Homer" lines or phrases that do not occur in the poems known to us. In some cases this must be put down to confusion or corruption, or the distortion of genuine Homeric lines through misrecollection. Of the residue that cannot be so accounted for, a part probably came from poems of the Epic Cycle, which we know tended to be attributed wholesale to Homer, especially in the fifth century. Sometimes we can guess at a likely context in one or other of these poems.

Other epic fragments are quoted with no attribution. Here the editor must try to decide whether they have a claim to be old rather than Hellenistic or later. I have restricted myself to a few quoted by pre-Hellenistic authors or by Homeric commentators who are probably citing what they think are early poems.

There are many hexameter fragments on papyrus that do not show clear signs of late composition and might in theory be from archaic epic. But in view of the limited currency that the early epics had in later times, the chances are not high, and their subject matter is generally doubtful. There would have been little advantage in including them in the present volume.

[47] It is also Hesiod fr. 280 Merkelbach–West.

SELECT BIBLIOGRAPHY

Editions

Kinkel, Gottfried. *Epicorum Graecorum Fragmenta.* Leipzig, 1877.

Allen, Thomas W. *Homeri Opera,* v. Oxford Classical Texts, 1912.

Bethe, Erich. *Homer. Dichtung und Sage. Zweiter Band* (as below): 149–200.

Matthews, Victor J. *Panyassis of Halikarnassos. Text and Commentary.* Leiden, 1974.

Bernabé, Albertus. *Poetas Epici Graeci,* pars i. Leipzig, 1987.

Davies, Malcolm. *Epicorum Graecorum Fragmenta.* Göttingen, 1988.

General

Davies, Malcolm. *The Epic Cycle.* Bristol, 1989.

Gantz, Timothy. *Early Greek Myth. A Guide to Literary and Artistic Sources.* Baltimore, 1993.

Huxley, G. L. *Greek Epic Poetry from Eumelos to Panyassis.* London, 1969.

Rzach, Alois. "Kyklos," in *RE* xi (1922): 2347–2435.

Severyns, Albert. *Le cycle épique dans l'école d'Aristarque*. Liége and Paris, 1928.
Welcker, F. G. *Der epische Cyclus, oder die homerischen Dichter.* Bonn, i^2 1865, ii 1849.

Theban Cycle

Bethe, Erich. *Thebanische Heldenlieder.* Leipzig, 1891.
Robert, Carl. *Oidipus. Geschichte eines poetischen Stoffs im griechischen Altertum.* Berlin, 1915.

Trojan Cycle

Bethe, Erich. *Homer. Dichtung und Sage. Zweiter Band: Odyssee. Kyklos. Zeitbestimmung.* Leipzig and Berlin, 1922.
Griffin, Jasper. "The Epic Cycle and the Uniqueness of Homer," *JHS* 97 (1977): 39–53.
Kullmann, Wolfgang. *Die Quellen der Ilias* (Hermes Einzelschriften, 14). Wiesbaden, 1960.
Monro, D. B. "Homer and the Cyclic Poets," in *Homer's Odyssey, Books XIII–XXIV* (Oxford, 1901): 340–384.

Eumelus

Marckscheffel, Guilelmus. *Hesiodi, Eumeli, Cinaethonis, Asii et Carminis Naupactii Fragmenta.* Leipzig, 1840.
West, M. L. "'Eumelos': a Corinthian Epic Cycle?" *JHS* 122 (2002).
Will, Édouard. *Korinthiaka. Recherches sur l'histoire et la civilisation de Corinthe des origines aux guerres médiques.* Paris, 1955.

THE THEBAN CYCLE

ΟΙΔΙΠΟΔΕΙΑ

TESTIMONIUM

IG 14.1292 ii 11 = Tabula Iliaca K (Borgiae) p. 61 Sadurska

τ]ὴν Οἰδιπόδειαν τὴν ὑπὸ Κιναίθωνος τοῦ [Λακεδαιμονίου λεγομένην πεποιῆσθαι παραλιπόν]τες, ἐπῶν οὖσαν ͵ϝχ΄, ὑποθήσομεν Θηβαΐδα [

[Λακεδαιμονίου - παραλιπόν]τες e.g. suppl. Wilamowitz.

FRAGMENTA

1 Paus. 9.5.10–11

παῖδας δὲ ἐξ αὐτῆς οὐ δοκῶ οἱ γενέσθαι, μάρτυρι Ὁμήρωι χρώμενος, ὃς ἐποίησεν ἐν Ὀδυσσείαι (11.271–274)· "μητέρα τ' Οἰδιπόδαο ἴδον, καλὴν Ἐπικάστην, | ἣ μέγα ἔργον ἔρεξεν ἀϊδρείῃσι νόοιο | γημαμένη ὧι υἱεῖ· ὃ δ' ὃν πατέρ' ἐξεναρίξας | γῆμεν· ἄφαρ δ' ἀνάπυστα θεοὶ θέσαν ἀνθρώποισιν." πῶς οὖν ἐποίησαν ἀνάπυστα ἄφαρ, εἰ δὴ τέσσαρες ἐκ τῆς Ἐπικάστης ἐγένοντο παῖδες τῶι Οἰδίποδι; ἐξ Εὐρυγανείας <δὲ> τῆς Ὑπέρφαντος ἐγεγόνεσαν·

THE THEBAN CYCLE

OEDIPODEA

TESTIMONIUM

Borgia plaque

. . . passing over t]he *Oedipodea*, which [they say was composed] by Cinaethon the [Lacedaemonian] in 6,600 verses, we will put down the *Thebaid* [. . .

FRAGMENTS

1 Pausanias, *Description of Greece*

That he had children by his mother, I do not believe; witness Homer, who wrote in the *Odyssey*, "And I saw Oedipus' mother, fair Epicaste, who unwittingly did a terrible thing in marrying her own son, who had killed his father; and the gods soon made it known among people." How did they *soon* make it known, if Oedipus had four children by Epicaste? No, they had been born from Euryganea, the daughter of Hyperphas.

δηλοῖ δὲ καὶ ὁ τὰ ἔπη ποιήσας ἃ Οἰδιπόδια ὀνομάζουσι.

Cf. Pherec. fr. 95 Fowler; Apollod. *Bibl.* 3.5.8; schol. Eur. *Phoen.* 13, 1760.

2* Asclepiades *FGrHist* 12 F 7a

"ἔστι δίπουν ἐπὶ γῆς καὶ τετράπον, οὗ μία φωνή,
καὶ τρίπον, ἀλλάσσει δὲ φυὴν μόνον, ὅσσ' ἐπὶ γαῖαν
ἑρπετὰ κινεῖται καὶ ἀν' αἰθέρα καὶ κατὰ πόντον.
ἀλλ' ὁπόταν πλείστοισιν ἐρειδόμενον ποσὶ βαίνηι,
ἔνθα μένος γυίοισιν ἀφαυρότατον πέλει αὐτοῦ."

Ath. 456b; *Anth. Pal.* 14.64; Argum. Aesch. *Sept.*, Soph. *O.T.*, Eur. *Phoen.*; schol. Eur. *Phoen.* 50; schol. et Tzetz. in Lyc. 7.

Variae lectiones: 1 φωνή] μορφή 2 φυὴν] φύσιν 3 κινεῖται] γίνηται, γίνονται καὶ ἀν'] ἀνά τ' 4 πλείστοισιν] τρισσοῖσιν, πλεόνεσσιν ἐρειδόμενον] ἐπειγόμενον 5 μένος] τάχος.

3 Schol. Eur. *Phoen.* 1760

ἀναρπάζουσα δὲ μικροὺς καὶ μεγάλους κατήσθιεν, ἐν οἷς καὶ Αἵμονα τὸν Κρέοντος παῖδα . . . οἱ τὴν Οἰδιποδίαν γράφοντες †οὐδεὶς οὕτω φησὶ† περὶ τῆς Σφιγγός·

This is made clear also by the poet of the epic that they call *Oedipodea*.

2* Asclepiades, *Tragedians' Tales*

"There is on earth a two-footed and four-footed creature with a single voice, and three-footed, changing its form alone of all creatures that move in earth, sky, or sea. When it walks on the most legs, then the strength of its limbs is weakest."[1]

3 Scholiast on Euripides, *Phoenician Women*

(The Sphinx) seized and devoured great and small, including Haemon the son of Creon . . . The authors of the *Oedipodea* say of the Sphinx:

[1] This hexameter version of the Sphinx's riddle is quoted by various sources which go back to Asclepiades of Tragilus (late fourth century BC). There is a good chance that he took it from the *Oedipodea*. The solution of the riddle is "man," who starts by crawling on all fours and ends by using a stick as a third leg.

ἀλλ' ἔτι κάλλιστόν τε καὶ ἱμεροέστατον ἄλλων
παῖδα φίλον Κρείοντος ἀμύμονος, Αἵμονα δῖον.

Cf. Apollod. *Bibl.* 3.5.8.

ΘΗΒΑΪΣ

TESTIMONIA

IG 14.1292 ii 11, see above.

Paus. 9.9.5

ἐποιήθη δὲ ἐς τὸν πόλεμον τοῦτον καὶ ἔπη Θηβαΐς. τὰ δὲ ἔπη ταῦτα Καλλῖνος ἀφικόμενος αὐτῶν ἐς μνήμην ἔφησεν Ὅμηρον τὸν ποιήσαντα εἶναι· Καλλίνωι δὲ πολλοί τε καὶ ἄξιοι λόγου κατὰ ταὐτὰ ἔγνωσαν. ἐγὼ δὲ τὴν ποίησιν ταύτην μετά γε Ἰλιάδα καὶ τὰ ἔπη τὰ ἐς Ὀδυσσέα ἐπαινῶ μάλιστα.

Ps.-Herod. *Vita Homeri* 9

κατήμενος δὲ ἐν τῶι σκυτείωι, παρεόντων καὶ ἄλλων, τήν τε ποίησιν αὐτοῖς ἐπεδείκνυτο, Ἀμφιάρεώ τε τὴν ἐξελασίαν τὴν ἐς Θήβας, καὶ τοὺς ὕμνους τοὺς ἐς θεοὺς πεποιημένους αὐτῶι.

But also the handsomest and loveliest of all, the dear son of blameless Creon, noble Haemon.[2]

THEBAID

TESTIMONIA

Borgia plaque, see above.

Pausanias, *Description of Greece*

There was also an epic composed about this war, the *Thebaid*. Callinus in referring to this epic said that Homer was its author, and many worthy critics have agreed with Callinus. I myself rate this poem the best after the *Iliad* and the Odysseus epic.

Pseudo-Herodotus, *Life of Homer*

As he sat in the cobbler's shop, with others also present, he would perform his poetry for them, *Amphiaraus' Expedition to Thebes*, and the Hymns that he had composed to the gods.

[2] Sophocles makes Haemon the fiancé of Antigone.

THEBAN CYCLE

FRAGMENTA

1 *Certamen Homeri et Hesiodi* 15

ὁ δὲ Ὅμηρος ἀποτυχὼν τῆς νίκης περιερχόμενος ἔλεγε τὰ ποιήματα, πρῶτον μὲν τὴν Θηβαΐδα, ἔπη ,ζ, ἧς ἡ ἀρχή·

Ἄργος ἄειδε, θεά, πολυδίψιον, ἔνθεν ἄνακτες.

2 Ath. 465e

ὁ δὲ Οἰδίπους δι' ἐκπώματα τοῖς υἱοῖς κατηράσατο, ὡς ὁ τὴν κυκλικὴν Θηβαΐδα πεποιηκώς φησιν, ὅτι αὐτῶι παρέθηκαν ἔκπωμα ὃ ἀπηγορεύκει, λέγων οὕτως·

αὐτὰρ ὁ διογενὴς ἥρως ξανθὸς Πολυνείκης
πρῶτα μὲν Οἰδιπόδηι καλὴν παρέθηκε τράπεζαν
ἀργυρέην Κάδμοιο θεόφρονος· αὐτὰρ ἔπειτα
χρύσεον ἔμπλησεν καλὸν δέπας ἡδέος οἴνου.
αὐτὰρ ὅ γ' ὡς φράσθη παρακείμενα πατρὸς ἑοῖο
τιμήεντα γέρα, μέγα οἱ κακὸν ἔμπεσε θυμῶι,
αἶψα δὲ παισὶν ἑοῖσι μετ' ἀμφοτέροισιν ἐπαράς
ἀργαλέας ἠρᾶτο, θεὰν δ' οὐ λάνθαν' Ἐρινύν,
ὡς οὔ οἱ πατρώϊ' ἐνηέϊ <ἐν> φιλότητι
δάσσαιντ', ἀμφοτέροισι δ' ἀεὶ πόλεμοί τε μάχαι τε . . .

8 θεὰν Robert: θεὸν codd. 9 πατρώϊ' ἐνηέϊ ἐν Ribbeck: πατρωιαν εἴη cod. 10 δάσσαιντ' Hermann: δάσαντο cod.: δάσσοντ' Wackernagel.

THEBAID

FRAGMENTS

1 *The Contest of Homer and Hesiod*

Homer, after his defeat in the contest, went about reciting his poems: firstly the *Thebaid* (7,000 lines), which begins

> Sing, goddess, of thirsty Argos, from where the lords
> . . .

2 Athenaeus, *Scholars at Dinner*

Oedipus cursed his sons on account of cups, as the author of the Cyclic *Thebaid* says, because they set before him a cup that he had forbidden. These are his words:

But the highborn hero, flaxen-haired Polynices, firstly set beside Oedipus the fine silver table of Cadmus the godly; then he filled his fine gold cup with sweet wine. But when he became aware that his father's precious treasures had been set beside him, some great evil invaded his heart, and at once he laid dreadful curses on both his sons, which the divine Erinys did not fail to note: that they should not divide their patrimony in friendship, but the two of them ever in battle and strife . . .

3 Schol. Soph. *Oed. Col.* 1375

οἱ περὶ Ἐτεοκλέα καὶ Πολυνείκην, δι' ἔθους ἔχοντες τῶι πατρὶ Οἰδίποδι πέμπειν ἐξ ἑκάστου ἱερείου μοῖραν τὸν ὦμον, ἐκλαθόμενοί ποτε, εἴτε κατὰ ῥαιστώνην εἴτε ἐξ ὁτουοῦν, ἰσχίον αὐτῶι ἔπεμψαν· ὃ δὲ μικροψύχως καὶ τελέως ἀγεννῶς, ὅμως δ' οὖν ἀρὰς ἔθετο κατ' αὐτῶν, δόξας κατολιγωρεῖσθαι. ταῦτα ὁ τὴν κυκλικὴν Θηβαΐδα ποιήσας ἱστορεῖ οὕτως·

ἰσχίον ὡς ἐνόησε χαμαὶ βάλεν εἶπέ τε μῦθον·
"ὤι μοι ἐγώ, παῖδες μὲν ὀνειδείοντες ἔπεμψαν . . ."

εὖκτο Διὶ βασιλῆϊ καὶ ἄλλοις ἀθανάτοισιν,
χερσὶν ὕπ' ἀλλήλων καταβήμεναι Ἄϊδος εἴσω.

4*

Ἄδρηστον μελίγηρυν

Plat. *Phaedr.* 269a

τί δὲ τὸν μελίγηρυν Ἄδραστον οἰόμεθα ἢ καὶ Περικλέα, εἰ ἀκούσειαν ὧν νῦν δὴ ἡμεῖς διῇμεν τῶν παγκάλων τεχνημάτων, κτλ.

5 Apollod. *Bibl.* 1.8.4

Ἀλθαίας δὲ ἀποθανούσης ἔγημεν Οἰνεὺς Περίβοιαν τὴν Ἱππονόου. ταύτην δὲ ὁ μὲν γράψας τὴν Θηβαΐδα πολε-

3 Scholiast on Sophocles, *Oedipus at Colonus*

Eteocles and Polynices, who customarily sent their father Oedipus the shoulder as his portion from every sacrificial animal, omitted to do so on one occasion, whether from simple negligence or for whatever reason, and sent him a haunch. He, in a mean and thoroughly ignoble spirit, but all the same, laid curses on them, considering he was being slighted. The author of the Cyclic *Thebaid* records this as follows:

When he realized it was a haunch, he threw it to the ground and said, "Oh, my sons have insultingly sent . . ." . . . He prayed to Zeus the king and to the other immortals that they should go down into Hades' house at each other's hands.

4*

Adrastus the honey-voiced

Plato, *Phaedrus*

How do we imagine the honey-voiced Adrastus or even Pericles would react, if they could hear of the wonderful rhetorical devices we were just going through, etc.

5 Apollodorus, *The Library*

When Althaea died, Oineus married Periboia the daughter of Hipponoos. The writer of the *Thebaid* says that Oineus got her

μηθείσης Ὠλένου λέγει λαβεῖν Οἰνέα γέρας· Ἡσίοδος δὲ (fr. 12 M.–W.) . . . ἐγεννήθη δὲ ἐκ ταύτης Οἰνεῖ Τυδεύς.

6

ἀμφότερον μάντίς τ᾽ ἀγαθὸς καὶ δουρὶ μάχεσθαι.

Pind. *Ol.* 6.15

ἑπτὰ δ᾽ ἔπειτα πυρᾶι νεκρῶν τελεσθέντων Ταλαϊονίδας | εἶπεν ἐν Θήβαισι τοιοῦτόν τι ἔπος· "ποθέω στρατιᾶς ὀφθαλμὸν ἐμᾶς, | ἀμφότερον μάντίν τ᾽ ἀγαθὸν καὶ δουρὶ μάρνασθαι." Schol. ad loc. ὁ Ἀσκληπιάδης φησὶ ταῦτα εἰληφέναι ἐκ τῆς κυκλικῆς Θηβαΐδος.

Versum heroicum restituit Leutsch; item *CEG* 519.2 (Attica, s. iv).

7* Schol. Pind. *Nem.* 9.30b

διαφορὰ δὲ ἐγενήθη τοῖς περὶ Ἀμφιάραον καὶ Ἄδραστον, ὥστε τὸν μὲν Ταλαὸν ὑπὸ Ἀμφιαράου ἀποθανεῖν, τὸν δὲ Ἄδραστον φυγεῖν εἰς Σικυῶνα . . . ὕστερον μέντοι συνεληλύθασι πάλιν, ἐφ᾽ ὧι συνοικήσει τῆι Ἐριφύληι ὁ Ἀμφιάραος, ἵνα εἴ τι

μέγ᾽ ἔρισμα μετ᾽ ἀμφοτέροισι γένηται,

αὐτὴ διαιτᾶι.

as a prize from the sack of Olenos, whereas Hesiod says . . . From her Tydeus was born to Oineus.

6

(Amphiaraus), both a good seer and good at fighting
with the spear.

Pindar, *Olympian Odes*

Then after the seven dead were hallowed on the pyre, the son of Talaos[3] at Thebes said something like this: "I miss my army's seeing eye, both a good seer and good at fighting with the spear." Scholiast: Asclepiades (of Myrlea) says Pindar has taken this from the Cyclic *Thebaid*.

7* Scholiast on Pindar

A quarrel came about between Amphiaraus and Adrastus, with the consequence that Talaos was killed by Amphiaraus and Adrastus fled to Sicyon . . . But later they came to terms, it being provided that Amphiaraus should marry Eriphyle,[4] so that if any

great dispute should arise between the two of them,

she would arbitrate.

[3] Adrastus.
[4] Adrastus' sister.

8*

"πουλύποδός μοι, τέκνον, ἔχων νόον, Ἀμφίλοχ' ἥρως,
τοῖσιν ἐφαρμόζειν, τῶν κεν κατὰ δῆμον ἵκηαι,
ἄλλοτε δ' ἀλλοῖος τελέθειν καὶ χροιῆι ἕπεσθαι."

1–2 Ath. 317a ὁμοίως ἱστορεῖ καὶ Κλέαρχος, ἐν δευτέρωι περὶ παροιμιῶν (fr. 75 Wehrli) παρατιθέμενος τάδε τὰ ἔπη, οὐ δηλῶν ὅτου ἐστί· "πουλύποδός—ἵκηαι". Antig. Caryst. *Mirab.* 25 ὅθεν δῆλον καὶ ὁ ποιητὴς τὸ θρυλούμενον ἔγραψεν· "πουλύποδός—ἐφαρμόζειν".

3 Zenob. vulg. 1.24 "ἄλλοτε—ἕπεσθαι"· ὅτι προσήκει ἕκαστον ἐξομοιοῦν ἑαυτὸν τούτοις ἐν οἷς ἂν καὶ γένηται τόποις· ἐκ μεταφορᾶς τοῦ πολύποδος. Item fere Diogenian. 1.23.

1–2 cum 3 coniunxit Bergk 1 ἔχων ἐν στήθεσι θυμόν Antig. 2 ἐφαρμόζων vel -ζου Ath. codd. τῶν κεν κατὰ Schweighäuser: ὧν καὶ vel κε Ath. codd. 3 ἀλλοῖος Bergk: -ον codd. χροιῆι West: χώρα codd.

9* Schol. (D) *Il.* 5.126

Τυδεὺς ὁ Οἰνέως ἐν τῶι Θηβαϊκῶι πολέμωι ὑπὸ Μελανίππου τοῦ Ἀστακοῦ ἐτρώθη, Ἀμφιάρεως δὲ κτείνας τὸν Μελάνιππον τὴν κεφαλὴν ἐκόμισεν. καὶ ἀνοίξας αὐτὴν ὁ Τυδεὺς τὸν ἐγκέφαλον ἐρρόφει ἀπὸ θυμοῦ. Ἀθηνᾶ δέ, κομίζουσα Τυδεῖ ἀθανασίαν, ἰδοῦσα τὸ μίασμα ἀπεστράφη αὐτόν. Τυδεὺς δὲ γνοὺς ἐδεήθη τῆς θεοῦ ἵνα κἂν

8*

"Pray hold to the octopus' outlook, Amphilochus my son,[5] and adapt it to whatever people you come among; be changeable, and go along with the color."

1–2 Athenaeus, *Scholars at Dinner:* Clearchus records likewise in the second book of his work *On Proverbs*, quoting these verses without declaring whose they are: "Pray hold—come among."

Antigonus of Carystus, *Marvels:* Hence the Poet[6] wrote the much-quoted words "Pray hold—adapt it."

3 Zenobius, *Proverbs:* "Be changeable—color": meaning that one should assimilate himself to the surroundings he finds himself in. It is a metaphor from the octopus.

9* Scholiast on the *Iliad*

Tydeus the son of Oineus in the Theban war was wounded by Melanippus the son of Astacus. Amphiaraus killed Melanippus and brought back his head, which Tydeus split open and gobbled the brain in a passion. When Athena, who was bringing Tydeus immortality, saw the horror, she turned away from him. Tydeus on realizing this begged the goddess at least

[5] The speaker is Amphiaraus.
[6] Perhaps meaning "Homer."

τῶι παιδὶ αὐτοῦ παράσχηι τὴν ἀθανασίαν.

Similiter schol. (AbT), ubi additur *ἱστορεῖ Φερεκύδης* (3 F 97): *ἡ ἱστορία παρὰ τοῖς κυκλικοῖς* G m.rec. suo Marte ut videtur.

10 Paus. 9.18.6

καὶ ὁ Ἀσφόδικος οὗτος ἀπέκτεινεν ἐν τῆι μάχηι τῆι πρὸς Ἀργείους Παρθενοπαῖον τὸν Ταλαοῦ, καθὰ οἱ Θηβαῖοι λέγουσιν, ἐπεὶ τά γε ἐν Θηβαΐδι ἔπη τὰ ἐς τὴν Παρθενοπαίου τελευτὴν Περικλύμενον τὸν ἀνελόντά φησιν εἶναι.

11 Schol. (D) *Il.* 23.346

Ποσειδῶν ἐρασθεὶς Ἐρινύος καὶ μεταβαλὼν τὴν αὑτοῦ φύσιν εἰς ἵππον ἐμίγη κατὰ Βοιωτίαν παρὰ τῆι Τιλφούσηι κρήνηι· ἣ δὲ ἔγκυος γενομένη ἵππον ἐγέννησεν, ὃς διὰ τὸ κρατιστεύειν Ἀρίων ἐκλήθη. Κοπρεὺς Ἁλιάρτου βασιλεύων πόλεως Βοιωτίας ἔλαβεν δῶρον αὐτὸν παρὰ Ποσειδῶνος· οὗτος δὲ αὐτὸν Ἡρακλεῖ ἐχαρίσατο γενομένωι παρ' αὐτῶι. τούτωι δὲ διαγωνισάμενος ὁ Ἡρακλῆς πρὸς Κύκνον τὸν Ἄρεως υἱὸν καθ' ἱπποδρομίαν ἐνίκησεν ἐν τῶι τοῦ Παγασαίου Ἀπόλλωνος ἱερῶι, ὅ ἐστι πρὸς †Τροιζῆνι. εἶθ' ὕστερον αὖθις ὁ Ἡρακλῆς Ἀδράστωι τὸν πῶλον παρέσχεν· ὑφ' οὗ μόνος ὁ Ἄδραστος ἐκ τοῦ Θηβαϊκοῦ πολέμου διεσώθη, τῶν ἄλλων ἀπολομένων. ἡ ἱστορία παρὰ τοῖς κυκλικοῖς.

Cf. schol. (T) 347; Apollod. *Bibl.* 3.6.8.

to bestow the immortality on his son.[7]

Some manuscripts add "The story is in Pherecydes"; in one a late hand adds "The story is in the Cyclic writers."

10 Pausanias, *Description of Greece*

And this Asphodicus in the battle against the Argives killed Parthenopaeus the son of Talaos, according to what the Thebans say; the verses about Parthenopaeus' death in the *Thebaid* make Periclymenus the one who slew him.

11 Scholiast on the *Iliad*

Poseidon fell in love with Erinys, and changing his form into a horse he had intercourse with her by the fountain Tilphousa in Boeotia. She conceived and gave birth to a horse, which was called Arion because of its supremacy.[8] Copreus, who was king at Haliartus, a town in Boeotia, received him from Poseidon as a gift. He gave him to Heracles when the latter stayed with him. Heracles used him to compete against Ares' son Cycnus in a horse race at the shrine of Pagasaean Apollo, which is near Troezen,[9] and won. Then Heracles gave the foal in turn to Adrastus, and thanks to him Adrastus alone was saved from the Theban war when all the others perished. The story is in the Cyclic poets.

[7] Diomedes.

[8] The name suggested *aristos*, "best."

[9] Perhaps an error for "Trachis." Heracles has Arion in his fight against Cycnus in pseudo-Hesiod, *Shield of Heracles* 120. It is mentioned as Adrastus' steed, a byword for swiftness, at *Il.* 23.346.

Paus. 8.25.7–8

τὴν δὲ Δήμητρα τεκεῖν φασιν ἐκ τοῦ Ποσειδῶνος θυγατέρα ... καὶ ἵππον τὸν Ἀρίονα ... ἐπάγονται δὲ ἐξ Ἰλιάδος ἔπη καὶ ἐκ Θηβαΐδος μαρτύριά σφισιν εἶναι τοῦ λόγου, ἐν μὲν Ἰλιάδι (23.346–347) ἐς αὐτὸν Ἀρίονα πεποιῆσθαι· . . . ἐν δὲ τῆι Θηβαΐδι ὡς Ἄδραστος ἔφευγεν ἐκ Θηβῶν

εἵματα λυγρὰ φέρων σὺν Ἀρίονι κυανοχαίτηι.

αἰνίσσεσθαι οὖν ἐθέλουσι τὰ ἔπη Ποσειδῶνα Ἀρίονι εἶναι πατέρα.

εἵματα codd.: σήματα Beck.

ΕΠΙΓΟΝΟΙ

1 *Certamen Homeri et Hesiodi* 15

ὁ δὲ Ὅμηρος ἀποτυχὼν τῆς νίκης περιερχόμενος ἔλεγε τὰ ποιήματα, πρῶτον μὲν τὴν Θηβαΐδα . . . εἶτα Ἐπιγόνους, ἔπη ͵ζ, ὧν ἡ ἀρχή·

Νῦν αὖθ᾽ ὁπλοτέρων ἀνδρῶν ἀρχώμεθα, Μοῦσαι.

φᾶσι γάρ τινες καὶ ταῦτα Ὁμήρου εἶναι.

---

10 Or, with Beck's emendation (*Mus. Helv.* 58 (2001), 137–139), "bearing the sad symbols," that is, tokens that the Seven had attached to Adrastus' chariot before they started, as keepsakes for their heirs if they perished. See Aeschylus, *Seven Against Thebes* 49–51.

Pausanias, *Description of Greece*

They say that Demeter bore a daughter by Poseidon . . . and the horse Arion . . . And they adduce verses from the *Iliad* and from the *Thebaid* as evidence of their tale, saying that in the *Iliad* it is written of Arion himself . . . and in the *Thebaid* that Adrastus fled from Thebes,

> his clothes in sorry state,[10] with Arion the sable-haired.

So they want the verse to hint that Poseidon was father to Arion.[11]

EPIGONI

1 *The Contest of Homer and Hesiod*

Homer, after his defeat in the contest, went about reciting his poems: firstly the *Thebaid* . . . and then the *Epigoni* (7,000 lines), which begins

> But now, Muses, let us begin on the younger men.

(For some say that this too is Homer's work.)

[11] Because "sable-haired" is usually an epithet of Poseidon. Later poets hint at Arion uttering prophetic speech at the Games for Archemoros at Nemea (Propertius 2.34.37) or when Adrastus fled from the war at Thebes (Statius, *Thebaid* 11.442). Their source may be Antimachus, but it is possible that the motif appeared in the Cyclic epic; compare the speech of Achilles' horse Xanthus in *Iliad* 19.404 ff.

Schol. Ar. *Pac.* 1270, "*νῦν αὖθ' ὁπλοτέρων ἀνδρῶν ἀρχώμεθα*"

ἀρχὴ δὲ τῶν Ἐπιγόνων Ἀντιμάχου.

2 Clem. *Strom.* 6.12.7

Ἀντιμάχου τε τοῦ Τηΐου εἰπόντος

ἐκ γὰρ δώρων πολλὰ κάκ' ἀνθρώποισι πέλονται,

Ἀγίας ἐποίησεν· (*Nosti* fr. 7).

3* Phot., *Et. Gen.*, *Suda* s.v. Τευμησία

περὶ τῆς Τευμησίας ἀλώπεκος οἱ τὰ Θηβαϊκὰ γεγραφηκότες ἱκανῶς ἱστορήκασι, καθάπερ Ἀριστόδημος (*FGr Hist* 383 F 2)· ἐπιπεμφθῆναι μὲν γὰρ ὑπὸ θεῶν τὸ θηρίον τοῦτο τοῖς Καδμείοις, διότι τῆς βασιλείας ἐξέκλειον τοὺς ἀπὸ Κάδμου γεγονότας. Κέφαλον δέ φασι τὸν Δηϊόνος, Ἀθηναῖον ὄντα καὶ κύνα κεκτημένον ὃν οὐδὲν διέφευγεν τῶν θηρίων, ὡς ἀπέκτεινεν ἄκων τὴν ἑαυτοῦ γυναῖκα Πρόκριν, καθηράντων αὐτὸν τῶν Καδμείων, διώκειν τὴν ἀλώπεκα μετὰ τοῦ κυνός· καταλαμβανομένους δὲ περὶ τὸν Τευμησὸν λίθους γενέσθαι τόν τε κύνα καὶ τὴν ἀλώπεκα. εἰλήφασι δὲ οὗτοι τὸν μῦθον ἐκ τοῦ ἐπικοῦ κύκλου.

Scholiast on Aristophanes, "But now, Muses, let us begin on the younger men"

It is the beginning of the *Epigoni* of Antimachus.

2 Clement of Alexandria, *Miscellanies*

And where Antimachus of Teos had said

For from gifts much ill comes to mankind,[12]

Agias wrote: [see *Returns*, fr. 7.]

3* Photius, *Lexicon*

Concerning the Teumesian Fox the writers of Theban history have given a sufficient account, for example Aristodemus. They say that the animal was sent upon the Thebans by the gods because they were excluding the descendants of Cadmus from the kingship. They say that Cephalus the son of Deion, an Athenian who had a hunting dog that no animal could escape, after accidentally killing his wife Procris and being purified by the Cadmeans, hunted the fox with his dog; and that just as it was catching it near Teumesos, both the dog and the fox were turned to stone. These writers have taken the myth from the Epic Cycle.[13]

[12] Probably an allusion to the bribing of Eriphyle.

[13] The story was presumably told in one of the Theban epics. It is assigned to the *Epigoni* on the hypothesis that it was after the death of Eteocles that the Thebans excluded Cadmus' descendants from the kingship.

4 Schol. Ap. Rhod. 1.308b

οἱ δὲ τὴν Θηβαΐδα γεγραφότες φασὶν ὅτι ὑπὸ τῶν Ἐπιγόνων ἀκροθίνιον ἀνετέθη Μαντὼ ἡ Τειρεσίου θυγάτηρ εἰς Δελφοὺς πεμφθεῖσα· καὶ κατὰ χρησμὸν Ἀπόλλωνος ἐξερχομένη περιέπεσε Ῥακίωι τῶι Λέβητος υἱῶι, Μυκηναίωι τὸ γένος. καὶ γημαμένη αὐτῶι (τοῦτο γὰρ περιεῖχε τὸ λόγιον, γαμεῖσθαι ὧι ἂν συναντήσηι), ἐλθοῦσα εἰς Κολοφῶνα καὶ ἐκεῖ δυσθυμήσασα ἐδάκρυσε διὰ τὴν τῆς πατρίδος πόρθησιν· διόπερ ὠνομάσθη Κλάρος ἀπὸ τῶν δακρύων. ἐποίησεν δὲ Ἀπόλλωνι ἱερόν.

5 Herod. 4.32

ἀλλ' Ἡσιόδωι μέν ἐστι περὶ Ὑπερβορέων εἰρημένα (fr. 150.21 M.–W.), ἔστι δὲ καὶ Ὁμήρωι ἐν Ἐπιγόνοισι, εἰ δὴ τῶι ἐόντί γε Ὅμηρος ταῦτα τὰ ἔπεα ἐποίησε.

ΑΛΚΜΕΩΝΙΣ

1 Schol. Eur. *Andr.* 687

καὶ ὁ τὴν Ἀλκμαιωνίδα πεποιηκώς φησι περὶ τοῦ Φώκου·

> ἔνθά μιν ἀντίθεος Τελαμὼν τροχοειδέϊ δίσκωι
> πλῆξε κάρη, Πηλεὺς δὲ θοῶς ἀνὰ χεῖρα
> ταυύσσας
> ἀξίνηι εὐχάλκωι ἐπεπλήγει μέσα νῶτα.

1 *μιν* Schwartz: *κεν* codd.

4 Scholiast on Apollonius of Rhodes

The writers of the *Thebaid*[14] say that Teiresias' daughter Manto was sent to Delphi by the Epigoni and dedicated as a tithe; and she went out in obedience to an oracle of Apollo and encountered Rhakios the son of Lebes, a Mycenaean by blood. She married him—this was part of the oracle, that she should marry the first man she met—and went to Colophon, and there, overcome by sorrow, she wept for the sack of her native city. Hence the place was named Claros, from her tears.[15] And she established a shrine for Apollo.

5 Herodotus, *History*

But Hesiod has mention of the Hyperboreans, and so does Homer in the *Epigoni*, if Homer really composed this poem.

ALCMEONIS

1 Scholiast on Euripides

And the author of the *Alcmeonis* says about Phocus:

There godlike Telamon hit him on the head with a wheel-shaped discus, and Peleus quickly raised his arm above his head and struck him in the middle of his back with a bronze axe.[16]

14 Assumed to be an error for the *Epigoni*, unless this is here taken to be part of the *Thebaid*.

15 The implied etymology is from *klao*, "I weep."

16 Phocus (ancestor of the Phocians), Telamon, and Peleus were the three sons of Aeacus. After the murder Telamon went to live on Salamis and Peleus to Thessaly.

2 Ath. 460b

καὶ ὁ τὴν Ἀλκμαιωνίδα δὲ ποιήσας φησίν·

νέκυς δὲ χαμαιστρώτου ἔπι τείνας
εὐρείης στιβάδος προέθηκ᾽ αὐτοῖσι θάλειαν
δαῖτα ποτήριά τε, στεφάνους τ᾽ ἐπὶ κρασὶν ἔθηκεν.

3 *Et. Gud.* s.v. Ζαγρεύς

ὁ μεγάλως ἀγρεύων, ὡς·

"πότνια Γῆ, Ζαγρεῦ τε θεῶν πανυπέρτατε πάντων",

ὁ τὴν Ἀλκμαιωνίδα γράψας ἔφη.

Cf. Ἐκλογαὶ διαφόρων ὀνομάτων, *Anecd. Ox.* ii 443.8.

4 Apollod. *Bibl.* 1.8.5

Τυδεὺς δὲ ἀνὴρ γενόμενος γενναῖος ἐφυγαδεύθη κτείνας, ὡς μέν τινες λέγουσιν, ἀδελφὸν Οἰνέως Ἀλκάθοον, ὡς δὲ ὁ τὴν Ἀλκμαιωνίδα γεγραφώς, τοὺς Μέλανος παῖδας ἐπιβουλεύοντας Οἰνεῖ, Φηνέα Εὐρύαλον Ὑπέρλαον Ἀντίοχον Εὐμήδην Στέρνοπα Ξάνθιππον Σθενέλαον.

5 Strab. 10.2.9

ὁ δὲ τὴν Ἀλκμεωνίδα γράψας Ἰκαρίου τοῦ Πηνελόπης

2 Athenaeus, *Scholars at Dinner*

The author of the *Alcmeonis* says too:

And laying the bodies out on a broad pallet spread on the ground, he set before them a rich banquet and cups, and put garlands on their heads.

3 *Etymologicum Gudianum*

Zagreus: the one who greatly hunts, as the writer of the *Alcmeonis* said:

"Mistress Earth, and Zagreus highest of all the gods."[17]

4 Apollodorus, *The Library*

Tydeus grew into a gallant man, but was forced into exile after killing, as some say, Oineus' brother Alcathous, but as the writer of the *Alcmeonis* says, the sons of Melas, who were plotting against Oineus: Pheneus, Euryalus, Hyperlaus, Antiochus, Eumedes, Sternops, Xanthippus, and Sthenelaus.

5 Strabo, *Geography*

But the writer of the *Alcmeonis* says that Icarius, Penelope's

[17] The etymologist falsely explains Zagreus' name from *za-* "very" and *agreuein* "hunt." In Aeschylus (frs. 5, 228) he is a god of the underworld. The line perhaps comes from a prayer in which Alcmaon called upon the powers of the earth to send up his father Amphiaraus.

πατρὸς υἱεῖς γενέσθαι δύο, Ἀλυζέα καὶ Λευκάδιον, δυναστεῦσαι δὲ ἐν τῆι Ἀκαρνανίαι τούτους μετὰ τοῦ πατρός.

6 Schol. Eur. *Or.* 995

ἀκολουθεῖν ἂν δόξειεν τῶι τὴν Ἀλκμαιωνίδα πεποιηκότι εἰς τὰ περὶ τὴν ἄρνα, ὡς καὶ Διονύσιος ὁ κυκλογράφος φησί (15 F 7). Φερεκύδης δὲ (fr. 133 Fowler) οὐ καθ᾽ Ἑρμοῦ μῆνίν φησι τὴν ἄρνα ὑποβληθῆναι ἀλλὰ Ἀρτέμιδος. ὁ δὲ τὴν Ἀλκμαιωνίδα γράψας τὸν ποιμένα τὸν προσαγαγόντα τὸ ποίμνιον τῶι Ἀτρεῖ Ἀντίοχον καλεῖ.

7 Philod. *De pietate* B 6798 Obbink

κα[ὶ τῆς ἐ]π̣ὶ Κρόνου ζω[ῆς εὐ]δαιμονεστά[της οὔ]σ̣ης, ὡς ἔγραψ[αν Ἡσί]οδος καὶ ὁ τὴν [Ἀλκμ]εωνίδα ποή[σας, καὶ] Σοφοκλῆς κτλ. (fr. 278 R.).

father, had two sons, Alyzeus and Leucadius,[18] and that they ruled with their father in Acarnania.

6 Scholiast on Euripides, *Orestes*

Euripides would appear to be following the author of the *Alcmeonis* in regard to the story about the lamb,[19] as Dionysius the Cyclographer also says. Pherecydes says that it was not from Hermes' wrath that the lamb was put into the flock, but from Artemis'. And the writer of the *Alcmeonis* calls the shepherd who brought the lamb to Atreus Antiochus.

7 Philodemus, *On Piety*

And the life in the time of Kronos was most happy, as [Hesi]od and the author of the [*Alcm*]*eonis* have written, and Sophocles etc.

18 Mythical eponyms of the Acarnanian town Alyzea and the nearby island of Leucas.

19 A golden lamb was discovered in Atreus' flocks, and on the strength of this he claimed the kingship. His brother Thyestes seduced his wife and got possession of the lamb, but was banished. The story may have been told in the *Alcmeonis* as a parallel to Eriphyle's fatal betrayal of her husband.

THE TROJAN CYCLE

ΚΥΠΡΙΑ

TESTIMONIA

Ael. *V.H.* 9.15

λέγεται δὲ κἀκεῖνο πρὸς τούτοις, ὅτι ἄρα ἀπορῶν ἐκδοῦναι τὴν θυγατέρα (Ὅμηρος) ἔδωκεν αὐτῆι προῖκα ἔχειν τὰ ἔπη τὰ Κύπρια· καὶ ὁμολογεῖ τοῦτο Πίνδαρος (fr. 265 Sn.–M.).

Cf. Hesych. Mil. *Vita Homeri* 5; Tzetz. *Hist.* 13.631–4.

Arist. *Poet.* 1459a37, see below, Testimonia to the *Little Iliad.*

Merkelbach–Stauber, *Steinepigramme aus dem griechischen Osten* 01/12/02 (de Halicarnasso)

ἔσπειρεν Πανύασσιν ἐπῶν ἀρίσημον ἄνακτα,
Ἰλιακῶν Κυπρίαν τίκτεν ἀοιδοθέτην.

THE TROJAN CYCLE

CYPRIA

TESTIMONIA

Aelian, *Historical Miscellany*

This too is said in addition, that when Homer had no means of giving his daughter in marriage, he gave her the epic *Cypria* to have as her dowry; and Pindar agrees on this.

Aristotle, *Poetics*: see below, Testimonia to the *Little Iliad*

Halicarnassian inscription (second century BC)

(This city) sowed the seed of Panyassis, famous master of epic verse; it gave birth to Cyprias, the poet of Trojan epic.

Phot. *Bibl.* 319a34

λέγει δὲ (Πρόκλος) καὶ περί τινων Κυπρίων ποιημάτων, καὶ ὡς οἱ μὲν ταῦτα εἰς Στασῖνον ἀναφέρουσι Κύπριον, οἱ δὲ Ἡγησῖνον τὸν Σαλαμίνιον αὐτοῖς ἐπιγράφουσιν, οἱ δὲ Ὅμηρον γράψαι, δοῦναι δὲ ὑπὲρ τῆς θυγατρὸς Στασίνωι, καὶ διὰ τὴν αὐτοῦ πατρίδα Κύπρια τὸν πόνον ἐπικληθῆναι. ἀλλ' οὐ ‹προσ›τίθεται ταύτηι τῆι αἰτίαι, μηδὲ γὰρ Κύπρια προπαροξυτόνως ἐπιγράφεσθαι τὰ ποιήματα.

Schol. Clem. *Protr.* 2.30.5, "Κυπριακὰ ποιήματα"

Κύπρια ποιήματά εἰσιν τὰ τοῦ κύκλου· περιέχει δὲ ἁρπαγὴν Ἑλένης. ὁ δὲ ποιητὴς αὐτῶν ἄδηλος· εἷς γάρ ἐστι τῶν κυκλικῶν.

Schol. Dion. Thr. i.471.34 Hilgard, see the Testimonia to the *Margites*.

ARGUMENTUM

Proclus, *Chrestomathia*, suppleta ex Apollod. epit. 3.1–33

ἐπιβάλλει τούτοις τὰ λεγόμενα Κύπρια ἐν βιβλίοις φερόμενα ἕνδεκα, ὧν περὶ τῆς γραφῆς ὕστερον ἐροῦμεν, ἵνα μὴ τὸν ἑξῆς λόγον νῦν ἐμποδίζωμεν. τὰ δὲ περιέχοντά ἐστι ταῦτα·

---

[1] Proclus was wrong. *Kypria* was proparoxytone, being the neuter plural adjective, "Cyprian," agreeing with *poiemata* or *epea*, "verses." The Halicarnassians, however, to appropriate the

Photius, *Library*

(Proclus) also speaks of some poetry called *Cypria*, and of how some attribute it to Stasinus of Cyprus, while some give the author's name as Hegesinus of Salamis, and others say that Homer wrote it and gave it to Stasinus in consideration of his daughter, and that because of where he came from the work was called *Cypria*. But he does not favor this explanation, as he says the poem's title is not *Kypria* with proparoxytone accent.[1]

Scholiast on Clement of Alexandria

"The Cyprian poem" is the one belonging to the Cycle; it deals with the rape of Helen. Its poet is uncertain, being one of the Cyclics.

ARGUMENT

Proclus, *Chrestomathy*, with additions and variants from Apollodorus, *The Library*[2]

This[3] is succeeded by the so-called *Cypria*, transmitted in eleven books; we will discuss the spelling of the title[4] later, so as not to obstruct the flow of the present account. Its contents are as follows.

work for themselves (see the inscription above, and below, frs. 5 and 10), claimed that *Kypria* was to be read paroxytone, that is, "by Cyprias," this being supposedly the name of a Halicarnassian poet. Proclus apparently accepted this.

[2] Enclosed in angle brackets; see Introduction, pp. 12 f.

[3] We do not have what preceded this excerpt in Proclus' work, but it was no doubt an account of the Theban cycle.

[4] See the note above on the Photius passage.

(1) Ζεὺς βουλεύεται μετὰ τῆς Θέμιδος[1] περὶ τοῦ Τρωϊκοῦ πολέμου. παραγενομένη δὲ Ἔρις εὐωχουμένων τῶν θεῶν ἐν τοῖς Πηλέως γάμοις νεῖκος περὶ κάλλους ἐνίστησιν Ἀθηνᾶι, Ἥραι καὶ Ἀφροδίτηι· αἳ πρὸς Ἀλέξανδρον ἐν Ἴδηι κατὰ Διὸς προσταγὴν ὑφ' Ἑρμοῦ πρὸς τὴν κρίσιν ἄγονται. <αἳ δὲ ἐπαγγέλλονται δῶρα δώσειν Ἀλεξάνδρωι· Ἥρα μὲν οὖν ἔφη προκριθεῖσα δώσειν βασιλείαν πάντων, Ἀθηνᾶ δὲ πολέμου νίκην, Ἀφροδίτη δὲ γάμον Ἑλένης. Ap.> καὶ προκρίνει τὴν Ἀφροδίτην ἐπαρθεὶς τοῖς Ἑλένης γάμοις Ἀλέξανδρος. ἔπειτα δὲ Ἀφροδίτης ὑποθεμένης ναυπηγεῖται. <πηξαμένου ναῦς Φερέκλου Ap.> καὶ Ἕλενος περὶ τῶν μελλόντων αὐτοῖς προθεσπίζει. καὶ ἡ Ἀφροδίτη Αἰνείαν συμπλεῖν αὐτῶι κελεύει. καὶ Κασσάνδρα περὶ τῶν μελλόντων προδηλοῖ.

(2) ἐπιβὰς δὲ τῆι Λακεδαιμονίαι Ἀλέξανδρος ξενίζεται παρὰ τοῖς Τυνδαρίδαις, καὶ μετὰ ταῦτα ἐν τῆι Σπάρτηι παρὰ Μενελάωι <ἐπὶ ἐννέα ἡμέρας Ap.>· καὶ Ἑλένηι παρὰ τὴν εὐωχίαν δίδωσι δῶρα ὁ Ἀλέξανδρος. καὶ μετὰ ταῦτα Μενέλαος εἰς Κρήτην ἐκπλεῖ <κηδεῦσαι τὸν μητροπάτορα Κατρέα Ap.>, κελεύσας τὴν Ἑλένην τοῖς ξένοις τὰ ἐπιτήδεια παρέχειν, ἕως ἂν ἀπαλλαγῶσιν. ἐν τούτωι δὲ Ἀφροδίτη συνάγει τὴν Ἑλένην τῶι Ἀλεξάνδρωι. καὶ μετὰ τὴν μίξιν τὰ πλεῖστα κτήματα ἐνθέμενοι νυκτὸς ἀποπλέουσι. <ἣ δὲ ἐνναέτη Ἑρμιόνην καταλιποῦσα, ἐνθεμένη τὰ πλεῖστα τῶν χρημάτων, ἀνάγεται τῆς νυκτὸς σὺν αὐτῶι. Ap.> χειμῶνα δὲ αὐτοῖς ἐφίστησιν Ἥρα, καὶ προσενεχθεὶς

(1) Zeus confers with Themis about the Trojan War. As the gods are feasting at the wedding of Peleus, Strife appears and causes a dispute about beauty among Athena, Hera, and Aphrodite. On Zeus' instruction Hermes conducts them to Alexander on Ida for adjudication. <They promise Alexander gifts: Hera said that if she were preferred she would give him kingship over all, Athena promised victory in war, and Aphrodite union with Helen.> Alexander, excited by the prospect of union with Helen, chooses Aphrodite. After that, at Aphrodite's instigation, ships are built <by Phereclus>. Helenus prophesies what will happen to them. Aphrodite tells Aeneas to sail with Alexander. And Cassandra reveals what will happen.

(2) On landing in Lacedaemon, Alexander is entertained by the Tyndarids, and subsequently in Sparta by Menelaus, <for nine days>. While receiving this hospitality Alexander gives Helen presents. After this, Menelaus sails off to Crete <for the funeral of his maternal grandfather, Catreus>, instructing Helen to look after the visitors until their departure. Then Aphrodite brings Helen together with Alexander, and after making love they put most of Menelaus' property on board and sail away in the night. <Helen left behind her nine-year-old daughter Hermione.> But Hera sends a storm upon them, and after being

---

[1] Θέμιδος Heyne, cf. P. Oxy. 3829 ii 11: θέτιδος codd.

Σιδῶνι ὁ Ἀλέξανδρος αἱρεῖ τὴν πόλιν. <εὐλαβούμενος δὲ Ἀλέξανδρος μὴ διωχθῆι, πολὺν διέτριψε χρόνον ἐν Φοινίκηι καὶ Κύπρωι. Ἀρ.> καὶ ἀποπλεύσας εἰς Ἴλιον γάμους τῆς Ἑλένης ἐπετέλεσεν.

(3) ἐν τούτωι δὲ Κάστωρ μετὰ Πολυδεύκους τὰς Ἴδα καὶ Λυγκέως βοῦς ὑφαιρούμενοι ἐφωράθησαν. καὶ Κάστωρ μὲν ὑπὸ τοῦ Ἴδα ἀναιρεῖται, Λυγκεὺς δὲ καὶ Ἴδας ὑπὸ Πολυδεύκους. καὶ Ζεὺς αὐτοῖς ἑτερήμερον νέμει τὴν ἀθανασίαν.

(4) καὶ μετὰ ταῦτα Ἶρις ἀγγέλλει τῶι Μενελάωι τὰ γεγονότα κατὰ τὸν οἶκον· ὁ δὲ παραγενόμενος <εἰς Μυκήνας Ἀρ.> περὶ τῆς ἐπ' Ἴλιον στρατείας βουλεύεται μετὰ τοῦ ἀδελφοῦ. καὶ πρὸς Νέστορα παραγίνεται Μενέλαος, Νέστωρ δὲ ἐν παρεκβάσει διηγεῖται αὐτῶι ὡς Ἐπωπεὺς φθείρας τὴν Λυκούργου[2] θυγατέρα ἐξεπορθήθη, καὶ τὰ περὶ Οἰδίπουν, καὶ τὴν Ἡρακλέους μανίαν, καὶ τὰ περὶ Θησέα καὶ Ἀριάδνην.

(5) ἔπειτα τοὺς ἡγεμόνας ἀθροίζουσιν ἐπελθόντες τὴν Ἑλλάδα. <ὁ δὲ πέμπων κήρυκα πρὸς ἕκαστον τῶν βασιλέων τῶν ὅρκων ὑπεμίμνησκεν ὧν ὤμοσαν, καὶ περὶ τῆς ἰδίας γυναικὸς ἕκαστον ἀσφαλίζεσθαι παρήινει, ἴσην λέγων γεγενῆσθαι τὴν τῆς Ἑλλάδος καταφρόνησιν καὶ κοινήν. Ἀρ.> καὶ μαίνεσθαι προσποιησάμενον Ὀδυσσέα ἐπὶ τῶι μὴ θέλειν συστρατεύεσθαι ἐφώρασαν, Παλαμήδους ὑποθεμένου τὸν υἱὸν Τηλέμαχον ἐπὶ κόλασιν ἐξαρπάσαντες. <ἁρπάσας δὲ Τηλέμαχον ἐκ τοῦ Πηνελόπης κόλπου ὡς κτενῶν ἐξι-

carried to Sidon, Alexander takes the city. <As a precaution, in case he was pursued, he stayed for a long time in Phoenicia and Cyprus.> And he sailed off to Ilion and celebrated a wedding with Helen.

(3) Meanwhile Castor and Polydeuces were caught stealing the cattle of Idas and Lynceus. And Castor was killed by Idas, but Lynceus and Idas were killed by Polydeuces. And Zeus awarded them immortality on alternate days.

(4) After this, Iris brings Menelaus the news of what has happened back home. He goes <to Mycenae> and confers with his brother about the expedition against Ilion. And Menelaus goes to Nestor, and Nestor in a digression relates to him how Epopeus seduced the daughter of Lycurgus[5] and had his city sacked; also the story of Oedipus, and the madness of Heracles, and the story of Theseus and Ariadne.

(5) Then they travel round Greece assembling the leaders. <Agamemnon sent a herald to each king reminding them of the oaths they had sworn; and he advised each one to make sure of his wife, as this contempt shown to Greece was an equal threat to all.> Odysseus feigned insanity, as he did not want to take part in the expedition, but they found him out by acting on a suggestion of Palamedes' and snatching his son Telemachus for a beating. <Palamedes snatched Telemachus from Penelope's bosom and drew his

[5] Perhaps a mistake for "Lycus," the brother of Nycteus, whose daughter Antiope was seduced by Epopeus and recovered by Lycus. See Asius, fr. 1.

---

[2] Λύκου Heyne.

φούλκει. Ap.><Μενέλαος σὺν Ὀδυσσεῖ καὶ Ταλθυβίωι πρὸς <Κινύραν εἰς> Κύπρον ἐλθόντες συμμαχεῖν ἔπειθον. ὃ δὲ Ἀγαμέμνονι μὲν οὐ παρόντι θώρακα{ς} ἐδωρήσατο· ὀμόσας δὲ πέμψειν πεντήκοντα ναῦς, μίαν πέμψας ἧς ἦρχεν < > ὁ Πυγμαλίωνος[3] καὶ τὰς λοιπὰς ἐκ γῆς πλάσας μεθῆκεν εἰς τὸ πέλαγος. Ap.>

(6) καὶ μετὰ ταῦτα συνελθόντες εἰς Αὐλίδα θύουσι. καὶ τὰ περὶ τὸν δράκοντα καὶ τοὺς στρουθοὺς γενόμενα δείκνυται, καὶ Κάλχας περὶ τῶν ἀποβησομένων προλέγει αὐτοῖς.

(7) ἔπειτα ἀναχθέντες Τευθρανίαι προσίσχουσι, καὶ ταύτην ὡς Ἴλιον ἐπόρθουν. Τήλεφος δὲ ἐκβοηθεῖ, Θέρσανδρόν τε τὸν Πολυνείκους κτείνει καὶ αὐτὸς ὑπὸ Ἀχιλλέως τιτρώσκεται. <τοὺς Μυσοὺς καθοπλίσας ἐπὶ τὰς ναῦς συνεδίωκε τοὺς Ἕλληνας καὶ πολλοὺς ἀπέκτεινεν, ἐν οἷς καὶ Θέρσανδρον τὸν Πολυνείκους ὑποστάντα. ὁρμήσαντος δὲ Ἀχιλλέως ἐπ᾽ αὐτὸν οὐ μείνας ἐδιώκετο· καὶ διωκόμενος ἐμπλακεὶς εἰς ἀμπέλου κλῆμα τὸν μηρὸν τιτρώσκεται δόρατι. Ap.>[4] ἀποπλέουσι δὲ αὐτοῖς ἐκ τῆς Μυσίας χειμὼν ἐπιπίπτει καὶ διασκεδάννυνται. Ἀχιλλεὺς δὲ Σκύρωι προ<σ>σχὼν γαμεῖ τὴν Λυκομήδους θυγατέρα Δηϊδάμειαν. ἔπειτα Τήλεφον κατὰ μαντείαν παραγενόμενον εἰς Ἄργος ἰᾶται Ἀχιλλεὺς ὡς ἡγεμόνα γενησόμενον τοῦ ἐπ᾽ Ἴλιον πλοῦ. <Τήλεφος δὲ ἐκ τῆς Μυσίας, ἀνίατον τὸ τραῦμα ἔχων, εἰπόντος αὐτῶι τοῦ Ἀπόλλωνος τότε

3 Πυγμαλίωνος West: μυγδαλίωνος cod.

sword as if to kill him.› ‹Menelaus went with Odysseus and Talthybius to ‹Cinyras in› Cyprus and urged him to join the expedition. He made the absent Agamemnon a present of a cuirass; and after promising on oath to send fifty ships, he sent one, under the command of ‹ › the son of Pygmalion, but the rest he shaped out of clay and launched them to sea.›

(6) After this they gather at Aulis and make sacrifice. And the episode of the snake and the sparrows is set forth,[6] and Calchas prophesies to them about the future outcome.

(7) Then they put to sea and land at Teuthrania, and they were setting out to sack it thinking it was Ilion. Telephus comes out to defend it, kills Polynices' son Thersander, and is himself wounded by Achilles. ‹He armed the Mysians and pursued the Greeks to their ships and killed many of them, including Polynices' son Thersander, who had made a stand. But when Achilles charged at him, he did not stand fast but fled from him, and in his flight he became entangled in a vine branch, and got a spear wound in his thigh.› As they are sailing away from Mysia, a storm catches them and they become dispersed. Achilles lands on Scyros and marries Lycomedes' daughter Deidamea. Then Telephus comes to Argos on the advice of an oracle and Achilles heals him on the understanding that he will be their guide when they sail against Ilion. ‹Telephus, his wound refusing to heal, and Apollo having told him that he would be cured when the one who caused

[6] The episode recalled at *Iliad* 2.301–329.

---

[4] Similar information is attributed to "post-Homeric poets" by schol. (D) *Il.* 1.59.

τεύξεσθαι θεραπείας ὅταν ὁ τρώσας ἰατρὸς γένηται, τρύχεσιν ἠμφιεσμένος εἰς Ἄργος ἀφίκετο, καὶ δεηθεὶς Ἀχιλλέως καὶ ὑπεσχημένος τὸν εἰς Τροίαν πλοῦν δεῖξαι θεραπεύεται ἀποξύσαντος Ἀχιλλέως τῆς Πηλιάδος μελίας τὸν ἰόν. θεραπευθεὶς οὖν ἔδειξε τὸν πλοῦν, τὸ τῆς δείξεως ἀσφαλὲς πιστουμένου τοῦ Κάλχαντος διὰ τῆς ἑαυτοῦ μαντικῆς. Ap.>[5]

(8) καὶ τὸ δεύτερον ἠθροισμένου τοῦ στόλου ἐν Αὐλίδι Ἀγαμέμνων ἐπὶ θήρας βαλὼν ἔλαφον ὑπερβάλλειν ἔφησε καὶ τὴν Ἄρτεμιν· μηνίσασα δὲ ἡ θεὸς ἐπέσχεν αὐτοὺς τοῦ πλοῦ χειμῶνας ἐπιπέμπουσα. Κάλχαντος δὲ εἰπόντος τὴν τῆς θεοῦ μῆνιν καὶ Ἰφιγένειαν κελεύσαντος θύειν τῆι Ἀρτέμιδι, ὡς ἐπὶ γάμον αὐτὴν Ἀχιλλεῖ μεταπεμψάμενοι θύειν ἐπιχειροῦσιν. <Κάλχας δὲ ἔφη οὐκ ἄλλως δύνασθαι πλεῖν αὐτούς, εἰ μὴ τῶν Ἀγαμέμνονος θυγατέρων ἡ κρατιστεύουσα κάλλει σφάγιον Ἀρτέμιδος παραστῆι . . . πέμψας Ἀγαμέμνων πρὸς Κλυταιμήστραν Ὀδυσσέα καὶ Ταλθύβιον Ἰφιγένειαν ᾔτει, λέγων ὑπεσχῆσθαι δώσειν αὐτὴν Ἀχιλλεῖ γυναῖκα μισθὸν τῆς στρατείας. Ap.> Ἄρτεμις δὲ αὐτὴν ἐξαρπάσασα εἰς Ταύρους μετακομίζει καὶ ἀθάνατον ποιεῖ, ἔλαφον δὲ ἀντὶ τῆς κόρης παρίστησι τῶι βωμῶι.[6]

(9) ἔπειτα καταπλέουσιν εἰς Τένεδον. <ταύτης

[5] Similar information is attributed to "post-Homeric poets" by schol. (D) *Il.* 1.59.

[6] The story is told in similar terms in schol. (D) *Il.* 1.106 = (A) 1.108–9b, and attributed to "many of the post-Homeric writers."

the wound tended it, came from Mysia to Argos, clothed in rags, and after begging Achilles and undertaking to show the way to Troy, he was treated as Achilles scraped the verdigris off his ashwood spear from Pelion.[7] So he was cured and showed the ships the way, the reliability of his guidance being guaranteed by Calchas through his own gift of prophecy.>

(8) When the expedition was assembled at Aulis for the second time, Agamemnon killed a deer while hunting and claimed to surpass Artemis herself. The goddess in her wrath stopped them from sailing by sending wild weather. When Calchas told them of the goddess's wrath and said they should sacrifice Iphigeneia to Artemis, they sent for her as if she was to marry Achilles, and set about to sacrifice her. <Calchas said they would only be able to sail if the most beautiful of Agamemnon's daughters was offered as a sacrifice to Artemis . . . Agamemnon sent Odysseus and Talthybius to Clytaemestra to ask for Iphigeneia, saying he had promised her to Achilles as payment for his participation in the expedition.> But Artemis snatches her away and conveys her to the Tauroi[8] and makes her immortal, setting a deer by the altar in place of the girl.

(9) Then they sail in to Tenedos. <Its king was Tennes,

[7] The head of the spear was of bronze. The verdigris was applied to the wound. Apollodorus' narrative may be colored by Euripides' treatment of the story in his *Telephus*, in which Telephus' appearance in rags was a notorious spectacle.

[8] A fierce people living in the Crimea. This is the setting of Euripides' *Iphigeneia among the Tauroi*.

ἐβασίλευε Τέννης ὁ Κύκνου καὶ Προκλείας, ὡς δέ τινες Ἀπόλλωνος . . . προσπλέοντας οὖν Τενέδωι τοὺς Ἕλληνας ὁρῶν Τέννης ἀπεῖργε βάλλων πέτρους· καὶ ὑπὸ Ἀχιλλέως ξίφει πληγεὶς κατὰ τὸ στῆθος θνήισκει, καίτοι Θέτιδος προειπούσης Ἀχιλλεῖ μὴ κτεῖναι Τέννην, τεθνήξεσθαι γὰρ ὑπὸ Ἀπόλλωνος αὐτόν, ἐὰν κτείνηι Τέννην. Ap.> καὶ εὐωχουμένων αὐτῶν Φιλοκτήτης ὑφ᾽ ὕδρου πληγεὶς διὰ τὴν δυσοσμίαν ἐν Λήμνωι κατελείφθη. καὶ Ἀχιλλεὺς ὕστερος κληθεὶς διαφέρεται πρὸς Ἀγαμέμνονα. <τελούντων δὲ αὐτῶν Ἀπόλλωνι θυσίαν, ἐκ τοῦ βωμοῦ προσελθὼν ὕδρος δάκνει Φιλοκτήτην . . . Ὀδυσσεὺς αὐτὸν εἰς Λῆμνον μεθ᾽ ὧν εἶχε τόξων Ἡρακλείων ἐκτίθησι, κελεύσαντος Ἀγαμέμνονος. Ap.>

(10) ἔπειτα ἀποβαίνοντας αὐτοὺς εἰς Ἴλιον εἴργουσιν οἱ Τρῶες, καὶ θνήισκει Πρωτεσίλαος ὑφ᾽ Ἕκτορος· ἔπειτα Ἀχιλλεὺς αὐτοὺς τρέπεται ἀνελὼν Κύκνον τὸν Ποσειδῶνος. <Ἀχιλλεῖ δὲ ἐπιστέλλει Θέτις, πρώτωι μὴ ἀποβῆναι τῶν νεῶν· τὸν γὰρ ἀποβάντα πρῶτον, πρῶτον μέλλειν καὶ τελευτᾶν. πυθόμενοι δὲ οἱ βάρβαροι τὸν στόλον ἐπιπλεῖν, σὺν ὅπλοις ἐπὶ τὴν θάλασσαν ὥρμησαν καὶ βάλλοντες πέτροις ἀποβῆναι ἐκώλυον. τῶν δὲ Ἑλλήνων πρῶτος ἀπέβη τῆς νηὸς Πρωτεσίλαος, καὶ κτείνας οὐκ ὀλίγους ὑφ᾽ Ἕκτορος θνήισκει. τούτου <ἡ> γυνὴ Λαοδάμεια καὶ μετὰ θάνατον ἤρα, καὶ ποιήσασα εἴδωλον Πρωτεσιλάωι παραπλήσιον, τούτωι προσωμίλει . . . Πρωτεσιλάου δὲ τελευτήσαντος ἐκβαίνει

son of Cycnus and Proclea, or as some say of Apollo . . . When Tennes saw the Greeks approaching Tenedos, he tried to repel them by throwing stones; and he was struck in the chest by Achilles with his sword and died, despite Thetis having warned Achilles not to kill Tennes, because if he did so he would be killed by Apollo.› And Philoctetes was bitten by a water snake while they were feasting and left behind on Lemnos on account of the foul smell of his wound. And Achilles quarrels with Agamemnon because he received a late invitation. ‹As they were making sacrifice to Apollo, a water snake came up from the altar and bit Philoctetes . . . On Agamemnon's instructions Odysseus put him out on Lemnos with the bows of Heracles that he had.›

(10) Then they disembark at Ilion and the Trojans try to repel them, and Protesilaus is killed by Hector. But then Achilles turns them back by killing Cycnus, son of Poseidon. ‹Thetis told Achilles not to be the first to disembark from the ships, as the first to disembark would be the first to die. When the barbarians learned that the expedition was approaching, they armed themselves and made for the sea, and tried to prevent them from disembarking by throwing stones. The first of the Greeks to disembark was Protesilaus, and after killing no small number he was slain by Hector. His wife Laodamea loved him even after death, and making an image in his likeness she would have intercourse with it . . . After Protesilaus' death Achilles disem-

μετὰ Μυρμιδόνων Ἀχιλλεὺς καὶ λίθον <βα>λὼν εἰς τὴν κεφαλὴν Κύκνου κτείνει. ὡς δὲ τοῦτον νεκρὸν εἶδον οἱ βάρβαροι, φεύγουσιν εἰς τὴν πόλιν, οἱ δὲ Ἕλληνες ἐκπηδήσαντες τῶν νεῶν ἐνέπλησαν σωμάτων τὸ πεδίον· καὶ κατακλείσαντες τοὺς Τρῶας ἐπολιόρκουν· ἀνέλκουσι δὲ τὰς ναῦς. Ap.> καὶ τοὺς νεκροὺς ἀναιροῦνται. καὶ διαπρεσβεύονται πρὸς τοὺς Τρῶας, τὴν Ἑλένην καὶ τὰ κτήματα ἀπαιτοῦντες· <καὶ πέμπουσιν Ὀδυσσέα καὶ Μενέλαον τὴν Ἑλένην καὶ τὰ χρήματα αἰτοῦντες. συναθροισθείσης δὲ παρὰ τοῖς Τρωσὶν ἐκκλησίας οὐ μόνον τὴν Ἑλένην οὐκ ἀπεδίδουν, ἀλλὰ καὶ τούτους κτείνειν ἤθελον. τούτους μὲν οὖν ἔσωσεν Ἀντήνωρ. Ap.> ὡς δὲ οὐχ ὑπήκουσαν ἐκεῖνοι, ἐνταῦθα δὴ τειχομαχοῦσιν.

(11) ἔπειτα τὴν χώραν ἐπεξελθόντες πορθοῦσι καὶ τὰς περιοίκους πόλεις. καὶ μετὰ ταῦτα Ἀχιλλεὺς Ἑλένην ἐπιθυμεῖ θεάσασθαι, καὶ συνήγαγεν αὐτοὺς εἰς τὸ αὐτὸ Ἀφροδίτη καὶ Θέτις. εἶτα ἀπονοστεῖν ὡρμημένους τοὺς Ἀχαιοὺς Ἀχιλλεὺς κατέχει. κἄπειτα ἀπελαύνει τὰς Αἰνείου βοῦς. <παραγίνεται εἰς Ἴδην ἐπὶ τὰς Αἰνείου {τοῦ Πριάμου} βόας. φυγόντος δὲ αὐτοῦ τοὺς βουκόλους κτείνας καὶ Μήστορα τὸν Πριάμου τὰς βόας ἐλαύνει. Ap.> καὶ Λυρνησσὸν καὶ Πήδασον πορθεῖ καὶ συχνὰς τῶν περιοικίδων πόλεων, καὶ Τρωΐλον φονεύει. <ἐνεδρεύσας Τρωΐλον ἐν τῶι τοῦ Θυμβραίου Ἀπόλλωνος ἱερῶι φονεύει. καὶ νυκτὸς ἐλθὼν ἐπὶ τὴν πόλιν Λυκάονα λαμβάνει. Ap.> Λυκάονά τε Πάτροκλος εἰς Λῆμνον ἀγαγὼν ἀπεμπολεῖ.

barked with the Myrmidons, and threw a stone at Cycnus' head and killed him. When the barbarians saw that he was dead, they fled towards the city, while the Greeks leaped out of their ships and filled the plain with corpses; and shutting the Trojans in, they laid siege to them, and hauled the ships ashore.> And they take up their dead. And they send negotiators to the Trojans to demand the return of Helen and the property. <And they sent Odysseus and Menelaus, demanding Helen and the property. But when the Trojan assembly was convoked, not only did they refuse to surrender Helen, but they even wanted to kill the envoys; but they were saved by Antenor.> When they did not agree to the demands, then they began a siege.

(11) Next they go out over the country and destroy the surrounding settlements. After this Achilles has a desire to look upon Helen, and Aphrodite and Thetis bring the two of them together. Then when the Achaeans are eager to return home, Achilles holds them back. And then he drives off Aeneas' cattle. <He comes to Mount Ida after Aeneas' cattle. Aeneas himself escapes, but he kills the cowherds and Priam's son Mestor and drives off the cattle.>[9] And he sacks Lyrnessus and Pedasus and many of the surrounding settlements, and he slays Troilus. <Ambushing Troilus at the shrine of Thymbraean Apollo he slays him. And he gets into the city in the night and captures Lycaon.> And Patroclus takes Lycaon to Lemnos and sells him into slavery.[10]

[9] See *Iliad* 20.90–93, 188–194.
[10] See *Iliad* 21.34–44, 23.746–747.

(12) *καὶ ἐκ τῶν λαφύρων Ἀχιλλεὺς μὲν Βρισηΐδα γέρας λαμβάνει, Χρυσηΐδα δὲ Ἀγαμέμνων. ἔπειτά ἐστι Παλαμήδους θάνατος· καὶ Διὸς βουλὴ ὅπως ἐπικουφίσηι τοὺς Τρῶας Ἀχιλλέα τῆς συμμαχίας τῆς Ἑλλήνων ἀποστήσας· καὶ κατάλογος τῶν τοῖς Τρωσὶ συμμαχησάντων.*

(1) Cf. P. Oxy. 3829 ii 9 *ὁ Ζεὺς ἀσέβειαν καταγνοὺς τοῦ ἡρωϊκοῦ γένους βουλεύεται μετὰ Θέμιδος ἄρδην αὐτοὺς ἀπολέσαι. θύων δὲ ἐν τῶι Πηλίωι ὄρει παρὰ Χείρωνι τῶι Κενταύρωι τοὺς Θέτιδος καὶ Πηλέως γάμους τοὺς μὲν ἄλλους θεοὺς ἐπὶ τὴν ἑστία<σι>ν παρεκάλει, μόνην δὲ τὴν Ἔριν εἰσιοῦσαν Ἑρμῆς κωλύει Διὸς κελεύσαντος· ἡ δὲ ὀργισθεῖσα χρυσοῦν μῆλον προ[σ]έρριψεν τῶι συμποσίωι, ὑπὲρ οὗ φιλονικίας γενομένης Ἥρας και Ἀθηνᾶς καὶ Ἀφροδίτης ὁ Ζεὺς ἔπαθλον προύθηκεν τῆι καλλίστηι.*

FRAGMENTA

1 Schol. (D) *Il.* 1.5, "*Διὸς δ' ἐτελείετο βουλή*"

ἄλλοι δὲ ἀπὸ ἱστορίας τινὸς εἶπον εἰρηκέναι τὸν Ὅμηρον. φασὶ γὰρ τὴν Γῆν βαρουμένην ὑπὸ ἀνθρώπων πολυπληθίας, μηδεμιᾶς ἀνθρώπων οὔσης εὐσεβείας, αἰτῆσαι τὸν Δία κουφισθῆναι τοῦ ἄχθους· τὸν δὲ Δία πρῶτον μὲν εὐθὺς ποιῆσαι τὸν Θηβαϊκὸν πόλεμον, δι' οὗ πολλοὺς πάνυ ἀπώλεσεν, ὕστερον δὲ πάλιν τὸν Ἰλιακόν, συμβούλωι τῶι Μώμωι χρησάμενος, ἣν Διὸς βουλὴν Ὅμηρός φησιν, ἐπειδὴ οἷός τε ἦν κεραυνοῖς ἢ κατακλυσμοῖς ἅπαντας διαφθείρειν· ὅπερ τοῦ Μώμου κωλύσαντος, ὑποθεμένου δὲ αὐτῶι γνώμας δύο, τὴν Θέτιδος

(12) And from the spoils Achilles gets Briseis as his prize, while Agamemnon gets Chryseis. Then comes the death of Palamedes; and Zeus' plan to relieve the Trojans by removing Achilles from the Greek alliance; and a catalog of the Trojans' allies.

(1) Oxyrhynchus papyrus (second century): Zeus, finding the race of heroes guilty of impiety, conferred with Themis about destroying them completely. When he was celebrating the wedding of Thetis and Peleus on Mount Pelion with the Centaur Chiron, he invited the other gods to the feast, but Strife alone was stopped at the door by Hermes on Zeus' orders. She was angry, and threw a golden apple into the party. A quarrel arose over it between Hera, Athena, and Aphrodite, and Zeus offered it as a prize for the most beautiful of them.

FRAGMENTS

1 Scholiast on the *Iliad*, "and Zeus' plan was being fulfilled"

Others have said that Homer was referring to a myth. For they say that Earth, being weighed down by the multitude of people, there being no piety among humankind, asked Zeus to be relieved of the burden. Zeus firstly and at once brought about the Theban War, by means of which he destroyed very large numbers, and afterwards the Trojan one, with Cavil as his adviser, this being what Homer calls the plan of Zeus, seeing that he was capable of destroying everyone with thunderbolts or floods. Cavil prevented this, and proposed two ideas to him, the marriage of Thetis to a mortal and the birth of a

θνητογαμίαν καὶ θυγατρὸς καλῆς γένναν, ἐξ ὧν ἀμφοτέρων πόλεμος Ἕλλησί τε καὶ βαρβάροις ἐγένετο, ἀφ' οὗ συνέβη κουφισθῆναι τὴν γῆν πολλῶν ἀναιρεθέντων. ἡ δὲ ἱστορία παρὰ Στασίνωι τῶι τὰ Κύπρια πεποιηκότι, εἰπόντι οὕτως·

ἦν ὅτε μυρία φῦλα κατὰ χθόνα πλαζόμενα <αἰεί
ἀνθρώπων ἐ>βάρυ<νε βαθυ>στέρνου πλάτος αἴης.
Ζεὺς δὲ ἰδὼν ἐλέησε, καὶ ἐν πυκιναῖς πραπίδεσσιν
κουφίσαι ἀνθρώπων παμβώτορα σύνθετο γαῖαν,
ῥιπίσσας πολέμου μεγάλην ἔριν Ἰλιακοῖο,
ὄφρα κενώσειεν θανάτωι βάρος. οἱ δ' ἐνὶ Τροίηι
ἥρωες κτείνοντο, Διὸς δ' ἐτελείετο βουλή.

1 suppl. Ebert, 2 Peppmüller 4 *σύνθετο κουφίσαι παμβώτορα γαῖαν (γαίης) ἀνθρώπων* codd.: corr. Ribbeck 5 *ῥιπίσσας* Wolf: *ῥιπίσαι* codd. 6 *θανάτωι* Lascaris: *-του* codd.

Cf. schol. Eur. *Or.* 1641.

2 Philod. *De pietate* B 7241 Obbink

ἔτι δὲ ὁ τ]ὰ Κύπ[ρια γράψας τῆι Ἥ]ραι χαρ[ιζομένη]ν φεύγειν αὐ[τὴν τὸ]ν γάμον Δ[ιός· τὸν δ' ὀ]μόσαι χολω[θέντ]α διότι θ̣νη[τῶι συ]νοικίσει.

Cf. Apollod. *Bibl.* 3.13.5.

beautiful daughter. From these two events war came about between Greeks and barbarians, resulting in the lightening of the earth as many were killed. The story is found in Stasinus, the author of the *Cypria*, who says:

There was a time when the countless races <of men> roaming <constantly> over the land were weighing down the <deep->breasted earth's expanse. Zeus took pity when he saw it, and in his complex mind he resolved to relieve the all-nurturing earth of mankind's weight by fanning the great conflict of the Trojan War, to void the burden through death. So the warriors at Troy kept being killed, and Zeus' plan was being fulfilled.

2 Philodemus, *On Piety*

And the author of t]he *Cyp[ria* says that it was to pl]ease Her[a that Thetis] shied away from the union with Z[eus; and he was angry, and swore to make her live with a mortal man.

3* Schol. (T) *Il.* 18.434a, "*καὶ ἔτλην ἀνέρος εὐνὴν πολλὰ μάλ' οὐκ ἐθέλουσα*"

ἐντεῦθεν οἱ νεώτεροι τὰς μεταμορφώσεις αὐτῆς φασιν.

Cf. Apollod. *Bibl.* 3.13.5 *Χείρωνος οὖν ὑποθεμένου Πηλεῖ συλλαβεῖν καὶ κατασχεῖν αὐτὴν μεταμορφουμένην, ἐπιτηρήσας συναρπάζει, γινομένην δὲ ὁτὲ μὲν πῦρ, ὁτὲ δὲ ὕδωρ, ὁτὲ δὲ θηρίον, οὐ πρότερον ἀνῆκε πρὶν ἢ τὴν ἀρχαίαν μορφὴν εἶδεν ἀπολαβοῦσαν.*

4 Schol. (D) *Il.* 16.140

κατὰ γὰρ τὸν Πηλέως καὶ Θέτιδος γάμον οἱ θεοὶ συναχθέντες εἰς τὸ Πήλιον ἐπ' εὐωχίαι ἐκόμιζον Πηλεῖ δῶρα, Χείρων δὲ μελίαν εὐθαλῆ τεμὼν εἰς δόρυ παρέσχεν. φασὶ δὲ Ἀθηνᾶν μὲν ξέσαι αὐτό, Ἥφαιστον δὲ κατασκευάσαι. τούτωι δὲ τῶι δόρατι καὶ Πηλεὺς ἐν ταῖς μάχαις ἠρίστευσεν καὶ μετὰ ταῦτα Ἀχιλλεύς. ἡ ἱστορία παρὰ τῶι τὰ Κύπρια ποιήσαντι.

Cf. Apollod. *Bibl.* 3.13.5 *γαμεῖ δὲ ἐν τῶι Πηλίωι, κἀκεῖ θεοὶ τὸν γάμον εὐωχούμενοι καθύμνησαν. καὶ δίδωσι Χείρων Πηλεῖ δόρυ μείλινον, Ποσειδῶν δὲ ἵππους Βαλίον καὶ Ξάνθον· ἀθάνατοι δὲ ἦσαν οὗτοι.*

5 Ath. 682d–f

ἀνθῶν δὲ στεφανωτικῶν μέμνηται ὁ μὲν τὰ Κύπρια ἔπη πεποιηκὼς Ἡγησίας ἢ Στασῖνος ‹ἢ καὶ Κυπρίας›· Δημοδάμας γὰρ ὁ Ἁλικαρνασσεὺς ἢ Μιλήσιος ἐν τῶι περὶ Ἁλικαρνασσοῦ (*FGrHist* 428 F 1) *Κυπρία Ἁλικαρ-*

3* Scholiast on the *Iliad*, "and I endured a man's bed much against my will"

Hence post-Homeric authors tell of her metamorphoses.

Compare Apollodorus, *The Library*: So Chiron advised Peleus to catch her and hold her as she changed her shape, and he kept watch and seized her, and though she turned now into fire, now into water, now into an animal, he did not let go until he saw her resume her original form.

4 Scholiast on the *Iliad*

For at the wedding of Peleus and Thetis the gods gathered on Pelion to feast, and brought gifts for Peleus, and Chiron cut down a fine ash and gave him it for a spear. They say that Athena planed it and Hephaestus fashioned it. With this spear Peleus was supreme in battle, and afterwards Achilles. The story is found in the author of the *Cypria*.

Compare Apollodorus, *The Library*: He had his wedding on Pelion, and there the gods made the wedding feast and sang his praises. And Chiron gave Peleus an ashen spear, while Poseidon gave him the horses Balius and Xanthus, who were immortal.

5 Athenaeus, *Scholars at Dinner*

Flowers in garlands are mentioned by the author of the *Cypria*, Hegesias or Stasinus ‹or Cyprias›; for Demodamas of Halicarnassus or Miletus in his work on Halicarnassus says

νασσέως αὐτὰ εἶναί φησι ποιήματα. λέγει δ' οὖν ὅστις ἐστὶν ὁ ποιήσας αὐτὰ ἐν τῶι α´ οὑτωσί·

εἵματα μὲν χροῒ ἕστο, τά οἱ Χάριτές τε καὶ Ὧραι
ποίησαν καὶ ἔβαψαν ἐν ἄνθεσιν εἰαρινοῖσιν
ὅσσα φέρουσ' ὧραι, ἔν τε κρόκωι ἔν θ' ὑακίνθωι
ἔν τε ἴωι θαλέθοντι ῥόδου τ' ἐνὶ ἄνθεϊ καλῶι
ἡδέϊ νεκταρέωι ἔν τ' ἀμβροσίαις καλύκεσσιν
†ἄνθεσι ναρκίσσου καλλιρρόου δ' οια† Ἀφροδίτη
ὥραις παντοίαις τεθυωμένα εἵματα ἕστο.

οὗτος ὁ ποιητὴς καὶ τὴν τῶν στεφάνων χρῆσιν εἰδὼς φαίνεται δι' ὧν λέγει·

3 *ὅσσα φέρουσ'* Hecker: *οἷα φοροῦσ'* cod.

6

ἡ δὲ σὺν ἀμφιπόλοισι φιλομμειδὴς Ἀφροδίτη
‹ ›
πλεξάμεναι στεφάνους εὐώδεας, ἄνθεα γαίης,
ἂν κεφαλαῖσιν ἔθεντο θεαὶ λιπαροκρήδεμνοι,
Νύμφαι καὶ Χάριτες, ἅμα δὲ χρυσῆ Ἀφροδίτη,
καλὸν ἀείδουσαι κατ' ὄρος πολυπιδάκου Ἴδης.

2 lac. stat. Kaibel 3 *ἄνθεα ποίης* Hecker.

7* Naevius(?), *Cypria Ilias* fr. 1 Courtney (ex libro I)

collum marmoreum torques gemmata coronat.

that it is a composition by Cyprias of Halicarnassus. Anyway, whoever the author is, he says in Book 1:

Her body was dressed in garments that the Graces and Horai had made for her and steeped in all the spring flowers that the seasons bring forth, in crocus and hyacinth, and springing violet, and the rose's fair, sweet, nectarine bloom, and the ambrosial buds of narcissus . . .[11] So Aphrodite was dressed in garments scented with blossoms of every kind.

This poet is clearly also acquainted with the use of garlands, when he says:

6

And she with her attendants, smile-loving Aphrodite ‹ . . . › They wove fragrant garlands, the flowers of the earth, and put them on their heads, those goddesses with glossy veils, the Nymphs and Graces, and golden Aphrodite with them, as they sang beautifully on Mount Ida of the many springs.

7* Naevius(?), *The Cyprian Iliad*, Book 1

Her gleaming neck was encircled by a jewelled torque.

[11] Text corrupt.

8 Schol. (D) *Il.* 3.443

Ἀλέξανδρος υἱὸς Πριάμου Τροίας βασιλέως, ὁ καὶ Πάρις ἐπικαλούμενος, Ἀφροδίτης ἐπιταγῆι ναυπηγήσαντος αὐτῶι ναῦς Ἁρμονίδου ἢ κατά τινας τῶν νεωτέρων Φερέκλου τοῦ τέκτονος, μετὰ Ἀφροδίτης ἦλθεν εἰς Λακεδαίμονα τὴν Μενελάου πόλιν.

Cf. schol. (A) *Il.* 5.60a (Aristonici); schol. Nic. *Ther.* 268; Apollod. epit. 3.2 (supra in Argumento).

9 Clem. *Protr.* 2.30.5

προσίτω δὲ καὶ ὁ τὰ Κυπριακὰ ποιήματα γράψας·

Κάστωρ μὲν θνητός, θανάτου δέ οἱ αἶσα πέπρωται,
αὐτὰρ ὅ γ' ἀθάνατος Πολυδεύκης, ὄζος Ἄρηος.

10 Ath. 334b

ὁ τὰ Κύπρια ποιήσας ἔπη, εἴτε Κυπρίας τίς ἐστιν ἢ Στασῖνος ἢ ὅστις δή ποτε χαίρει ὀνομαζόμενος, τὴν Νέμεσιν ποιεῖ διωκομένην ὑπὸ Διὸς καὶ εἰς ἰχθὺν μεταμορφουμένην διὰ τούτων·

τοὺς δὲ μέτα τριτάτην Ἑλένην τέκε, θαῦμα βροτοῖσιν·
τήν ποτε καλλίκομος Νέμεσις φιλότητι μιγεῖσα
Ζηνὶ θεῶν βασιλῆϊ τέκε κρατερῆς ὑπ' ἀνάγκης.
φεῦγε γάρ, οὐδ' ἔθελεν μιχθήμεναι ἐν φιλότητι

8 Scholiast on the *Iliad*

Alexander, son of Priam the king of Troy, also known as Paris, after ships had been built for him on Aphrodite's instructions by Harmonides, or according to some of the post-Homeric writers by the joiner Phereclus, went with Aphrodite to Lacedaemon, the city of Menelaus.

9 Clement of Alexandria, *Protreptic*

Let the author of the *Cypria* also come forward:

Castor mortal, with death his destined lot, but Polydeuces immortal, scion of the War-god.

10 Athenaeus, *Scholars at Dinner*

The author of the epic *Cypria*, whether he is one Cyprias or Stasinus, or whatever he likes to be called, has Nemesis chased by Zeus and turning herself into a fish in these verses:

Third after them she (he?) gave birth to Helen, a wonder to mortals; whom lovely-haired Nemesis once bore, united in love to Zeus the king of the gods, under harsh compulsion. For she ran away, not wanting to unite in love with

πατρὶ Διὶ Κρονίωνι· ἐτείρετο γὰρ φρένας αἰδοῖ
καὶ νεμέσει· κατὰ γῆν δὲ καὶ ἀτρύγετον μέλαν ὕδωρ
φεῦγε, Ζεὺς δ' ἐδίωκε—λαβεῖν δ' ἐλιλαίετο θυμῶι—
ἄλλοτε μὲν κατὰ κῦμα πολυφλοίσβοιο θαλάσσης
ἰχθύϊ εἰδομένην, πόντον πολὺν ἐξοροθύνων,
ἄλλοτ' ἀν' Ὠκεανὸν ποταμὸν καὶ πείρατα γαίης,
ἄλλοτ' ἀν' ἤπειρον πολυβώλακα· γίνετο δ' αἰεί
θηρί', ὅσ' ἤπειρος αἰνὰ τρέφει, ὄφρα φύγοι μιν.

(Ath.) Κυπρίας Severyns: Κύπριος cod.
(fr.) 1 τοὺς Meineke: τοῖς cod. 9 ἐξοροθύνων Wakefield: ἐξορόθυνεν cod. 12 νιν cod.

11 Philod. *De pietate* B 7369 Obbink

Νέμε]σίν τ' ὁ τὰ Κύ[πρια γ]ράψας ὁμοιωθέ[ντ]α χηνὶ κα[ὶ] *αὐτ[ὸν] δ̣ιώκειν, καὶ μιγέ̣ν[το]ς ὠ̣ι̣ὸν τεκεῖν, [ἐξ] ο̣ὗ γενέσθαι τὴν* [Ἑλ]*ένην.*

Apollod. *Bibl.* 3.10.7

λέγουσι δὲ ἔνιοι Νεμέσεως Ἑλένην εἶναι καὶ Διός· *ταύτην γὰρ τὴν Διὸς φεύγουσαν συνουσίαν εἰς χῆνα τὴν μορφὴν μεταβαλεῖν, ὁμοιωθέντα δὲ καὶ Δία †τῶι κύκνωι† συνελθεῖν· τὴν δὲ ὠιὸν ἐκ τῆς συνουσίας ἀποτεκεῖν. τοῦτο δὲ ἐν τοῖς ἄλσεσιν εὑρόντά τινα ποιμένα Λήδαι κομίσαντα δοῦναι, τὴν δὲ καταθεμένην εἰς λάρνακα φυλάσ-*

father Zeus the son of Kronos, tormented by inhibition and misgiving: across land and the dark, barren water she ran, and Zeus pursued, eager to catch her; sometimes in the noisy sea's wave, where she had the form of a fish, as he stirred up the mighty deep; sometimes along Ocean's stream and the ends of the earth; sometimes on the loam-rich land; and she kept changing into all the fearsome creatures that the land nurtures, so as to escape him.

11 Philodemus, *On Piety*

And the author of the *Cy[pria]* says that Zeus pursued [Neme]sis after changing himself too into a goose, and when he had had union with her she laid an egg, from which Helen was born.

Apollodorus, *The Library*

But some say that Helen was the daughter of Nemesis and Zeus. For Nemesis, fleeing from intercourse with Zeus, changed her form into a goose, but Zeus too took the likeness of †the swan† and had congress with her, and as a result she laid an egg. A shepherd found this among the trees and brought it and gave it to Leda, who put it away in a chest and

σειν· καὶ χρόνωι γεννηθεῖσαν Ἑλένην ὡς ἐξ αὑτῆς θυγατέρα τρέφειν.

Cf. Sappho fr. 166; schol. Call. *Hymn.* 3.232; schol. Lyc. 88; ps.-Eratosth. *Catast.* 25.

12* Schol. (D) *Il.* 3.242

Ἑλένη . . . πρότερον ὑπὸ Θησέως ἡρπάσθη, καθὼς προείρηται (ad 3.144, = Hellanicus fr. 168c Fowler). *διὰ γὰρ τὴν τότε γενομένην ἁρπαγὴν Ἄφιδνα πόλις Ἀττικῆς πορθεῖται, καὶ τιτρώσκεται Κάστωρ ὑπὸ Ἀφίδνου τοῦ τότε βασιλέως κατὰ τὸν δεξιὸν μηρόν. οἱ δὲ Διόσκουροι Θησέως μὴ τυχόντες λαφυραγωγοῦσιν τὰς Ἀθήνας. ἡ ἱστορία παρὰ †τοῖς πολεμωνίοις†* (*Πολέμωνι* Fabricius) *ἢ τοῖς κυκλικοῖς, καὶ ἀπὸ μέρους παρὰ Ἀλκμᾶνι τῶι λυρικῶι* (*PMGF* 21).

13* Naevius(?), *Cypria Ilias* fr. 2 Courtney (ex libro II)

penetrat penitus thalamoque potitur.

14

εὐαεῖ τ᾽ ἀνέμωι λείηι τε θαλάσσηι.

Herod. 2.116.6–117

ἐν τούτοισι τοῖσι ἔπεσι (*Il.* 6.289–292) *δηλοῖ* (*Ὅμηρος*) *ὅτι ἠπίστατο τὴν ἐς Αἴγυπτον Ἀλεξάνδρου πλάνην· ὁμουρεῖ γὰρ ἡ Συρίη Αἰγύπτωι, οἱ δὲ Φοίνικες, τῶν ἐστι ἡ*

kept it; and when in time Helen was born from it, she raised her as her own daughter.

12* Scholiast on the *Iliad*

Helen . . . was previously carried off by Theseus, as mentioned above. For it was because of that abduction that the Attic town of Aphidna was sacked, and Castor was wounded in the right thigh by Aphidnus, the king of the time. The Dioscuri, not finding Theseus, plundered Athens. The story is found in Polemon(?) or the Cyclic writers, and in part in Alcman the lyric poet.

13* Naevius(?), *The Cyprian Iliad*, Book 2

He penetrated to the inner rooms and gained her bedroom.

14 Herodotus, *History*

a fair wind and a smooth sea

In these lines (*Iliad* 6.289–292) Homer shows that he knew of Alexander's diversion to Egypt, since Syria borders Egypt, and

Σιδών, ἐν τῆι Συρίηι οἰκέουσι. κατὰ ταῦτα δὲ τὰ ἔπεα καὶ τόδε τὸ χωρίον οὐκ ἥκιστα ἀλλὰ μάλιστα δηλοῖ ὅτι οὐκ Ὁμήρου τὰ Κύπρια ἔπεά ἐστι ἀλλ᾽ ἄλλου τινός· ἐν μὲν γὰρ τοῖσι Κυπρίοισι εἴρηται ὡς τριταῖος ἐκ Σπάρτης Ἀλέξανδρος ἀπίκετο ἐς τὸ Ἴλιον ἄγων Ἑλένην, εὐαέϊ τε πνεύματι χρησάμενος καὶ θαλάσσηι λείηι· ἐν δὲ Ἰλιάδι λέγει ὡς ἐπλάζετο ἄγων αὐτήν.

15 Paus. 3.16.1

πλησίον δὲ Ἱλαείρας καὶ Φοίβης ἐστὶν ἱερόν· ὁ δὲ ποιήσας τὰ ἔπη τὰ Κύπρια θυγατέρας αὐτὰς Ἀπόλλωνός φησιν εἶναι.

16 Schol. Pind. *Nem.* 10.110, "ἀπὸ Ταϋγέτου πεδαυγάζων ἴδεν Λυγκεὺς δρυὸς ἐν στελέχει ἥμενος"

ὁ μὲν Ἀρίσταρχος ἀξιοῖ γράφειν "ἥμενον," ἀκολούθως τῆι ἐν τοῖς Κυπρίοις λεγομένηι ἱστορίαι· ὁ γὰρ τὰ Κύπρια συγγράψας φησὶ τὸν Κάστορα ἐν τῆι δρυὶ κρυφθέντα ὀφθῆναι ὑπὸ Λυγκέως. τῆι δὲ αὐτῆι γραφῆι καὶ Ἀπολλόδωρος κατηκολούθησε (*FGrHist* 244 F 148) πρὸς οὓς φησι Δίδυμος . . . παρατίθεται δὲ καὶ τὸν τὰ Κύπρια γράψαντα οὕτω λέγοντα·

αἶψα δὲ Λυγκεύς
Τηΰγετον προσέβαινε ποσὶν ταχέεσσι πεποιθώς,
ἀκρότατον δ᾽ ἀναβὰς διεδέρκετο νῆσον ἅπασαν
Ταντολίδεω Πέλοπος· τάχα δ᾽ εἴσιδε κύδιμος ἥρως

the Phoenicians to whom Sidon belongs live in Syria. And not least in these lines and this passage, but especially in them, he makes plain that the *Cypria* is not by Homer but by someone else. For in the *Cypria* it is stated that Alexander arrived from Sparta at Ilion with Helen on the third day, having had a fair wind and a smooth sea, whereas in the *Iliad* he says that he went on a diversion with her.

15 Pausanias, *Description of Greece*

Nearby is a shrine of Hilaeira and Phoibe. The author of the epic *Cypria* says they were daughters of Apollo.

16 Scholiast on Pindar, "gazing from Taygetus Lynceus saw (them) sitting in the trunk of an oak"

Aristarchus thinks one should write *ἥμενον* [i.e. "saw him sitting"], in accordance with the story told in the *Cypria*. For the writer of the *Cypria* says that Castor had hidden in the oak and was seen by Lynceus. Apollodorus too followed this reading. Against them Didymus says . . . And he quotes the author of *Cypria* as saying:

At once Lynceus climbed Taygetus, relying on his swift legs, and going up to the summit he surveyed the whole island of Pelops the Tantalid.[12] And with his formidable eyes

[12] That is, the Peloponnese.

δεινοῖς ὀφθαλμοῖσιν ἔσω κοίλης δρυὸς ἄμφω,
Κάστορά θ' ἱππόδαμον καὶ ἀεθλοφόρον Πολυδεύκεα.
νύξε δ' ἄρ' ἄγχι στὰ<ς> μεγάλην δρῦν <ὄβριμος Ἴδας>

καὶ τὰ ἑξῆς.

5 *δρυὸς ἄμφω κοίλης* codd.: corr. Gerhard 7 *ὄβριμος Ἴδας* e.g. suppl. West.

17 Philod. *De pietate* B 4833 Obbink

Κάστο[ρα δ]ὲ ὑπὸ Ἴδα τοῦ [Ἀφα]ρ̣έως κατη[κοντ]ί̣σθαι γέγραφεν ὁ [τὰ Κύπρια] ποήσα[ς καὶ Φερεκύ]δης ὁ Ἀ[θηναῖος (fr. 127A Fowler).

18 Ath. 35c

οἶνόν τοι, Μενέλαε, θεοὶ ποίησαν ἄριστον
θνητοῖς ἀνθρώποισιν ἀποσκεδάσαι μελεδῶνας·

ὁ τῶν Κυπρίων τοῦτό φησι ποιητής, ὅστις ἂν εἴη.

19 Schol. (D) *Il.* 19.326

Ἀλεξάνδρου Ἑλένην ἁρπάσαντος Ἀγαμέμνων καὶ Μενέλαος τοὺς Ἕλληνας κατὰ Τρώων ἐστρατολόγησαν. Πηλεὺς δὲ προγινώσκων ὅτι μοιρίδιον ἦν ἐν Τροίαι θανεῖν Ἀχιλλέα, παραγενόμενος εἰς Σκῦρον πρὸς Λυκομήδην τὸν βασιλέα παρέθετο τὸν Ἀχιλλέα, καὶ γυναι-

the glorious hero soon spotted them both inside a hollow oak, Castor the horse-tamer and prize-winner Polydeuces. And ‹doughty Idas› stood up close and stabbed the great oak,

and so on.

17 Philodemus, *On Piety*

That Castor was speared by Idas the son of [Apha]reus has been written by the author of [the *Cypria* and Pherecy]des of A[thens.

18 Athenaeus, *Scholars at Dinner*

"Wine, Menelaus, is the best thing the gods have made for mortal men for dispelling cares."

The poet of the *Cypria* says so, whoever he may be.[13]

19 Scholiast on the *Iliad*

When Alexander stole Helen, Agamemnon and Menelaus recruited the Greeks against the Trojans. Peleus, knowing in advance that it was fated that Achilles should die at Troy, went to Scyros, to king Lycomedes, and placed Achilles in his care,

[13] The lines were perhaps spoken by Nestor when Menelaus went and told him of Helen's disappearance.

κεῖαν ἐσθῆτα ἀμφιέσας ὡς κόρην μετὰ τῶν θυγατέρων ἀνέτρεφεν. χρησμοῦ δὲ δοθέντος μὴ ἁλώσεσθαι τὴν Ἴλιον χωρὶς Ἀχιλλέως, πεμφθέντες ὑφ᾽ Ἑλλήνων Ὀδυσσεύς τε καὶ Φοίνιξ καὶ Νέστωρ, Πηλέως ἀρνουμένου παρ᾽ αὐτῶι τὸν παῖδα τυγχάνειν, πορευθέντες εἰς Σκῦρον καὶ ὑπονοήσαντες μετὰ τῶν παρθένων τὸν Ἀχιλλέα τρέφεσθαι, ταῖς Ὀδυσσέως ὑποθήκαις ὅπλα καὶ ταλάρους ἔρριψαν σὺν ἱστουργικοῖς ἐργαλείοις ἔμπροσθεν τοῦ παρθενῶνος. αἱ μὲν οὖν κόραι ἐπὶ τοὺς ταλάρους ὥρμησαν καὶ τὰ λοιπά, Ἀχιλλεὺς δὲ ἀνελόμενος τὰ ὅπλα κατάφωρος ἐγένετο· καὶ συνεστρατεύσατο. πρότερον δὲ ταῖς παρθένοις συνδιατρίβων ἔφθειρε Δηϊδάμειαν τὴν Λυκομήδους, ἥτις ἐξ αὐτοῦ ἐγέννησε Πύρρον τὸν ὕστερον Νεοπτόλεμον κληθέντα· ὅστις τοῖς Ἕλλησι νέος ὢν συνεστρατεύσατο μετὰ θάνατον τοῦ πατρός. ἡ ἱστορία παρὰ τοῖς κυκλικοῖς.

Paus. 10.26.4

τὰ δὲ Κύπρια ἔπη φησὶν ὑπὸ Λυκομήδους μὲν Πύρρον, Νεοπτόλεμον δὲ ὄνομα ὑπὸ Φοίνικος αὐτῶι τεθῆναι, ὅτι Ἀχιλλεὺς ἡλικίαι ἔτι νέος πολεμεῖν ἤρξατο.

Cf. schol. (T) *Il.* 9.668b.

20 Schol. Soph. *El.* 157, "*οἵα Χρυσόθεμις ζώει καὶ Ἰφιάνασσα*"

ἢ Ὁμηρωι ἀκολουθεῖ εἰρηκότι τὰς τρεῖς θυγατέρας τοῦ Ἀγαμέμνονος (*Il.* 9.144) *ἤ, ὡς ὁ τὰ Κύπρια, δ̄ φησιν,*

and he dressed him in female clothing and brought him up as a girl with his daughters. But as an oracle had been issued that Ilion would not be captured without Achilles, the Greeks sent Odysseus, Phoenix, and Nestor, and when Peleus denied that his son was with him, they travelled to Scyros. Suspecting that Achilles was being raised among the girls, at Odysseus' suggestion they scattered some weapons, together with work baskets and weaving implements, in front of the girls' chamber. The girls made for the baskets and the other things, but Achilles took up the weapons, and so was caught out, and he joined the expedition. But before that, while he was living with the girls, he had seduced Lycomedes' daughter Deidamea, and by him she gave birth to Pyrrhus, who was later named Neoptolemus; he went to fight with the Greeks as a young man after his father's death. The story is found in the Cyclic writers.

Pausanias, *Description of Greece*

The epic *Cypria* says that he was given the name of Pyrrhus by Lycomedes, but that of Neoptolemus by Phoenix, because Achilles was still young (*neos*) when he began to make war (*polemein*).

20 Scholiast on Sophocles, *Electra*, "as Chrysothemis lives, and Iphianassa"

Alternatively he is following Homer, who named Agamemnon's three daughters, or, like the author of the *Cypria*, he is

Ἰφιγένειαν καὶ Ἰφιάνασσαν.

21* Chrysippus, *SVF* ii.57.11

εἰ Ἀγαμέμνων οὕτως ἀπέφασκεν·

οὐκ ἐφάμην Ἀχιλῆϊ χολωσέμεν ἄλκιμον ἦτορ
ὧδε μάλ᾽ ἐκπάγλως, ἐπεὶ ἦ μάλα μοι φίλος ἤην,

ἀξίωμά ἐστιν κτλ.

22 Paus. 4.2.7

ὁ δὲ τὰ ἔπη ποιήσας τὰ Κύπρια Πρωτεσιλάου φησίν, ὃς ὅτε κατὰ τὴν Τρωιάδα ἔσχον Ἕλληνες ἀποβῆναι πρῶτος ἐτόλμησε, Πρωτεσιλάου τούτου τὴν γυναῖκα Πολυδώραν μὲν τὸ ὄνομα, θυγατέρα δὲ Μελεάγρου φησὶν εἶναι τοῦ Οἰνέως.

23 Schol. (T) *Il.* 16.57b, "πόλιν εὐτείχεα πέρσας"

τὴν Πήδασον οἱ τῶν Κυπρίων ποιηταί, αὐτὸς δὲ Λυρνησσόν (*Il.* 2.690).

24 Schol. (bT) *Il.* 1.366c

εἰς Θήβας δὲ ἤκουσα ἡ Χρυσηῒς πρὸς Ἰφινόην τὴν Ἠετίωνος ἀδελφήν, Ἄκτορος δὲ θυγατέρα, θύουσαν Ἀρτέμιδι, ἥλω ὑπὸ Ἀχιλλέως.

saying there were four, Iphigeneia as well as Iphianassa.[14]

21* Chrysippus, *On Negation*

If Agamemnon made this negative statement:

I did not think I would anger Achilles' brave heart so very greatly, as he was my good friend,

there is a positive proposition, etc.

22 Pausanias, *Description of Greece*

The author of the epic *Cypria* says about Protesilaus, who was the first to venture to disembark when the Greeks put in at the Troad, that this Protesilaus' wife was named Polydora, and he says she was a daughter of Meleager the son of Oineus.

23 Scholiast on the *Iliad*, "when I sacked her well-walled town"[15]

The poets of the *Cypria* say it was Pedasus, but Homer himself says Lyrnessus.

24 Scholiast on the *Iliad*

When Chryseis came to Thebes to Iphinoe, the sister of Eetion and daughter of Actor, who was sacrificing to Artemis, she was captured by Achilles.

14 That is, in addition to Chrysothemis and Electra.
15 The reference is to Briseis.

Eust. *Il.* 119.4

ἱστοροῦσι δέ τινες ὅτι ἐκ τῶν Ὑποπλακίων Θηβῶν ἡ Χρυσηῒς ἐλήφθη, οὔτε καταφυγοῦσα ἐκεῖ οὔτ' ἐπὶ θυσίαν Ἀρτέμιδος ἐλθοῦσα, ὡς ὁ τὰ Κύπρια γράψας ἔφη, ἀλλὰ πολῖτις ἤτοι συμπολῖτις Ἀνδρομάχης οὖσα.

25* Schol. (A) *Il.* 24.257b (Aristonici)

ὅτι ἐκ τοῦ εἰρῆσθαι ἱππιοχάρμην τὸν Τρωΐλον οἱ νεώτεροι ἐφ' ἵππου διωκόμενον αὐτὸν ἐποίησαν. καὶ οἱ μὲν παῖδα αὐτὸν ὑποτίθενται, Ὅμηρος δὲ διὰ τοῦ ἐπιθέτου τέλειον ἄνδρα ἐμφαίνει· οὐ γὰρ ἄλλος ἱππόμαχος λέγεται.

26

Οἰνώ τε Σπερμώ τε καὶ <ἀγλαόκαρπος> Ἐλαΐς.

Schol. Lyc. 570

τοῦτον δὲ (Ἄνιον) Ἀπόλλων ἤνεγκεν εἰς Δῆλον. ὃς γήμας Δωρίππην ἐγέννησε τὰς Οἰνοτρόπους, Οἰνώ, Σπερμώ, Ἐλαΐδα, αἷς ὁ Διόνυσος ἐχαρίσατο, ὁπότε βούλονται σπέρμα λαμβάνειν. Φερεκύδης δέ φησιν (fr. 140 Fowler) ὅτι Ἄνιος ἔπεισε τοὺς Ἕλληνας παραγενομένους πρὸς αὐτὸν αὐτοῦ μένειν τὰ θ′ ἔτη· δεδόσθαι δὲ αὐτοῖς παρὰ τῶν θεῶν τῶι δεκάτωι ἔτει πορθῆσαι τὴν Ἴλιον· ὑπέσχετο δὲ αὐτοῖς ὑπὸ τῶν θυγατέρων αὐτοῦ τραφήσεσθαι. ἔστι δὲ τοῦτο καὶ παρὰ τῶι τὰ Κύπρια πεποιηκότι. μέμνηται

Eustathius, commentary on the *Iliad*

But some relate that Chryseis was taken from Hypoplacian Thebes, not having taken refuge there or gone for a sacrifice to Artemis, as the writer of the *Cypria* said, but being a fellow-citizen of Andromache.

25* Scholiast on the *Iliad* (Aristonicus)

(The critical sign is) because, from Troilus' being called a "cavalry warrior," the post-Homeric writers have represented him as being pursued on horseback. And they take him to be a boy, whereas Homer indicates by the epithet that he was a grown man, for no one else is called a cavalry warrior.

26

Oino, Spermo, and Elaiis ‹of splendid fruit›.[16]

Scholiast on Lycophron

Apollo brought Anios to Delos. He married Dorippe, and fathered the Oinotropoi, Oino, Spermo, and Elaiis, to whom Dionysus granted the boon of becoming fertile at will. Pherecydes says that Anios persuaded the Greeks when they visited him to stay there for the nine years, it having been granted to them by the gods to sack Ilion in the tenth year; and he promised them that they would be fed by his daughters. This is also in the author of the *Cypria*. Callimachus too men-

[16] Reconstructed verse.

δὲ καὶ Καλλίμαχος τῶν Ἀνίου θυγατέρων ἐν τοῖς Αἰτίοις (fr. 188 Pf.).

Cf. ib. 580 αὗται καὶ τοὺς Ἕλληνας λιμώττοντας ἐλθοῦσαι εἰς Τροίαν διέσωσαν· μαρτυρεῖ δὲ ταῦτα καὶ Καλλίμαχος; 581 Ἀγαμέμνων γὰρ τῶν Ἑλλήνων λιμῶι συνεχομένων μετεπέμψατο αὐτὰς διὰ τοῦ Παλαμήδους, καὶ ἐλθοῦσαι εἰς τὸ Ῥοίτειον ἔτρεφον αὐτούς; Simon. *PMG* 537; Apollod. epit. 3.15; Dictys 1.23.

27 Paus. 10.31.2

Παλαμήδην δὲ ἀποπνιγῆναι προελθόντα ἐπὶ ἰχθύων θήραν, Διομήδην δὲ τὸν ἀποκτείναντα εἶναι καὶ Ὀδυσσέα, ἐπιλεξάμενος ἐν ἔπεσιν οἶδα τοῖς Κυπρίοις.

28 Paus. 10.26.1

Λέσχεως δὲ (*Il. Parva* 19) καὶ ἔπη τὰ Κύπρια διδόασιν Εὐρυδίκην γυναῖκα Αἰνείαι.

29 Plat. *Euthyphro* 12a

λέγω γὰρ δὴ τὸ ἐναντίον ἢ ὁ ποιητὴς ἐποίησεν ὁ ποιήσας·

Ζῆνα δὲ τόν τ' ἔρξαντα καὶ ὃς τάδε πάντ' ἐφύτευσεν
οὐκ ἐθέλει νεικεῖν· ἵνα γὰρ δέος, ἔνθα καὶ αἰδώς.

tions Anios' daughters in his *Aetia*.

They also went to Troy and saved the Greeks when they were suffering from famine. Callimachus too attests this. For when the Greeks were in the grip of famine, Agamemnon sent for them by Palamedes, and they came to Rhoiteion and kept them fed.

27 Pausanias, *Description of Greece*

That Palamedes was drowned on a fishing expedition, and that Diomedes was the one who killed him with Odysseus, I know from reading it in the epic *Cypria*.

28 Pausanias, *Description of Greece*

Lescheos and the epic *Cypria* give Aeneas Eurydice as wife.

29 Plato, *Euthyphron*

For I say the contrary of the poet who wrote

"But as for Zeus, the agent responsible, who sowed the seeds of all this, he (she?) is unwilling to criticize him; for where there is fear, there is inhibition."

Schol. ad loc. εἴρηται δὲ ἐκ τῶν Στασίνου Κυπρίων; item Stob. 3.31.12; cf. *Mantiss. proverb.* 1.71. 2 ἵνα - αἰδώς laudant etiam Plut. *Agis et Cleom.* 30.6, *Mor.* 459d; Diogenian. 5.30; Apostol. 9.6.

2 ἐθέλει νεικεῖν Burnet ex schol.: ἐθέλειν vel -εις εἰπεῖν codd., Stob., *Mantissa*.

30 Herodian. περὶ μονήρους λέξεως 9 (ii.914.15 L.)

καὶ (Σαρπηδὼν) ἡ νῆσος ἰδίως ἐν Ὠκεανῶι Γοργόνων οἰκητήριον οὖσα, ὡς ὁ τὰ Κύπριά φησι·

τῶι δ' ὑποκυσαμένη τέκε Γοργόνας, αἰνὰ πέλωρα,
αἳ Σαρπηδόνα ναῖον ἐπ' Ὠκεανῶι βαθυδίνηι
νῆσον πετρήεσσαν.

1 αἰνὰ Dindorf: δεινὰ cod. 2 αἳ Heinrichsen: καὶ cod.

31 Clem. *Strom.* 6.19.1

πάλιν Στασίνου ποιήσαντος

νήπιος, ὃς πατέρα κτείνας παῖδας καταλείπει,

Ξενοφῶν λέγει κτλ.

Versum laudant etiam Arist. *Rhet.* 1376a6 (v.l. υἱοὺς), 1395a16 (v.l. κτείνων); Polyb. 23.10.10 (υἱοὺς).

Scholiast: It is a quotation from Stasinus' *Cypria*.

30 Herodian, *On Peculiar Words*

And Sarpedon in the special sense of the island in Oceanus, where the Gorgons live, as the author of the *Cypria* says:

And she conceived and bore him the Gorgons, dread creatures, who dwelt on Sarpedon on the deep-swirling Oceanus, a rocky island.

31 Clement of Alexandria, *Miscellanies*

Again, where Stasinus had written

He is a fool who kills the father and spares the sons,

Xenophon says, etc.

ΑΙΘΙΟΠΙΣ

TESTIMONIA

IG 14.1284 i 10 = Tabula Iliaca A (Capitolina) p. 29 Sadurska

Αἰθιοπὶς κατὰ Ἀρκτῖνον τὸν Μιλήσιον.

Hesychius Milesius, *Vita Homeri* 6

ἀναφέρεται δὲ εἰς αὐτὸν καὶ ἄλλα τινὰ ποιήματα· Ἀμαζονία, Ἰλιὰς Μικρά, κτλ.

Clem. *Strom.* 1.131.6

Φανίας δὲ (fr. 33 Wehrli) πρὸ Τερπάνδρου τιθεὶς Λέσχην τὸν Λέσβιον Ἀρχιλόχου νεώτερον φέρει τὸν Τέρπανδρον, διημιλλῆσθαι δὲ τὸν Λέσχην Ἀρκτίνωι καὶ νενικηκέναι.

Euseb. *Chron.*

Ol. 1.2: Arctinus Milesius uersificator florentissimus habetur.

Ol. 5.1: Eumelus poeta . . . et Arctinus qui Aethiopidam conposuit et Ilii Persin agnoscitur.

Cf. Cyrill. *Contra Iulian.* 1.12 (Patrol. Gr. lxxvi. 520D).

AETHIOPIS

TESTIMONIA

Capitoline plaque

The *Aethiopis* according to Arctinus of Miletus.

Hesychius of Miletus, *Life of Homer*

Certain other poems are also attributed to him: the *Amazonia*, the *Little Iliad*, etc.

Clement of Alexandria, *Miscellanies*

Phanias[17] places Lesches of Lesbos before Terpander, makes Terpander younger than Archilochus, and says that Lesches had a contest with Arctinus and was victorious.

Eusebius, *Chronicle*

Ol. 1.2 (775/774): Arctinus the Milesian poet is reckoned at his peak.

Ol. 5.1 (760/759): the poet Eumelus . . . is recognized, and Arctinus who composed the *Aethiopis* and *Sack of Ilion*.

[17] The Peripatetic Phanias or Phaenias of Eresos.

Suda α 3960

Ἀρκτῖνος Τήλεω τοῦ Ναύτεω ἀπογόνου, Μιλήσιος, ἐποποιός, μαθητὴς Ὁμήρου, ὡς λέγει ὁ Κλαζομένιος Ἀρτέμων ἐν τῶι περὶ Ὁμήρου (*FGrHist* 443 F 2), γεγονὼς κατὰ τὴν θʹ Ὀλυμπιάδα, μετὰ υιʹ ἔτη τῶν Τρωϊκῶν.

ARGUMENTUM

Proclus, *Chrestomathia*, suppleta ex Apollod. epit. 5.1–6

ἐπιβάλλει δὲ τοῖς προειρημένοις {ἐν τῆι πρὸ ταύτης βίβλωι} Ἰλιὰς Ὁμήρου· μεθʼ ἥν ἐστιν Αἰθιοπίδος βιβλία πέντε Ἀρκτίνου Μιλησίου περιέχοντα τάδε·

(1) Ἀμαζὼν Πενθεσίλεια παραγίνεται Τρωσὶ συμμαχήσουσα, Ἄρεως μὲν θυγάτηρ, Θρᾶισσα δὲ τὸ γένος, <ἀκουσίως Ἱππολύτην κτείνασα καὶ ὑπὸ Πριάμου καθαρθεῖσα. μάχης γενομένης πολλοὺς κτείνει, ἐν οἷς καὶ Μαχάονα. Ap.> καὶ κτείνει αὐτὴν ἀριστεύουσαν Ἀχιλλεύς, οἱ δὲ Τρῶες αὐτὴν θάπτουσι. καὶ Ἀχιλλεὺς Θερσίτην ἀναιρεῖ λοιδορηθεὶς πρὸς αὐτοῦ καὶ ὀνειδισθεὶς τὸν ἐπὶ τῆι Πενθεσιλείαι λεγόμενον ἔρωτα. καὶ ἐκ τούτου στάσις γίνεται τοῖς Ἀχαιοῖς περὶ τοῦ Θερσίτου φόνου. μετὰ δὲ ταῦτα Ἀχιλλεὺς εἰς Λέσβον πλεῖ, καὶ θύσας Ἀπόλλωνι καὶ Ἀρτέμιδι καὶ Λητοῖ καθαίρεται τοῦ φόνου ὑπʼ Ὀδυσσέως.

(2) Μέμνων δὲ ὁ <Τιθωνοῦ καὶ Ap.> Ἠοῦς υἱὸς ἔχων ἡφαιστότευκτον πανοπλίαν <μετὰ πολλῆς Αἰθιόπων

AETHIOPIS

The *Suda* (from Hesychius of Miletus, *Index of Famous Authors*)

Arctinus, son of Teleas the descendant of Nautes, Milesian, epic poet, a pupil of Homer, as Artemon of Clazomenae says in his work *On Homer*; flourished about the ninth Olympiad (744/741), 410 years after the Trojan War.

ARGUMENT

Proclus, *Chrestomathy*, with additions and variants from Apollodorus, *The Library*

The aforesaid material[18] is followed by Homer's *Iliad*, after which are the five books of the *Aethiopis* of Arctinus of Miletus, with the following content:

(1) The Amazon Penthesilea arrives to fight with the Trojans, a daughter of the War god, of Thracian stock. <She had involuntarily killed Hippolyta, and was purified by Priam. When a battle was fought she killed large numbers, including Machaon.> She dominates the battlefield, but Achilles kills her and the Trojans bury her. And Achilles kills Thersites after being abused by him and insulted over his alleged love for Penthesilea. This results in a dispute among the Achaeans about the killing of Thersites. Achilles then sails to Lesbos, and after sacrificing to Apollo, Artemis, and Leto, he is purified from the killing by Odysseus.

(2) Memnon, the son of <Tithonus and> the Dawn, wearing armor made by Hephaestus <and accompanied by

[18] The contents of the *Cypria*.

δυνάμεως Ap.> παραγίνεται τοῖς Τρωσὶ βοηθήσων· καὶ Θέτις τῶι παιδὶ τὰ κατὰ τὸν Μέμνονα προλέγει. καὶ συμβολῆς γενομένης Ἀντίλοχος ὑπὸ Μέμνονος ἀναιρεῖται, ἔπειτα Ἀχιλλεὺς Μέμνονα κτείνει· καὶ τούτωι μὲν Ἠὼς παρὰ Διὸς αἰτησαμένη ἀθανασίαν δίδωσι.

(3) τρεψάμενος δ' Ἀχιλλεὺς τοὺς Τρῶας καὶ εἰς τὴν πόλιν συνεισπεσὼν ὑπὸ Πάριδος ἀναιρεῖται καὶ Ἀπόλλωνος. <πρὸς ταῖς Σκαιαῖς πύλαις τοξεύεται ὑπὸ Ἀλεξάνδρου καὶ Ἀπόλλωνος εἰς τὸ σφυρόν. Ap.> καὶ περὶ τοῦ πτώματος γενομένης ἰσχυρᾶς μάχης Αἴας <Γλαῦκον ἀναιρεῖ, καὶ τὰ ὅπλα δίδωσιν ἐπὶ τὰς ναῦς κομίζειν· τὸ δὲ σῶμα Ap.> ἀνελόμενος ἐπὶ τὰς ναῦς κομίζει, Ὀδυσσέως ἀπομαχομένου τοῖς Τρωσίν.

(4) ἔπειτα Ἀντίλοχόν τε θάπτουσι καὶ τὸν νεκρὸν τοῦ Ἀχιλλέως προτίθενται. καὶ Θέτις ἀφικομένη σὺν Μούσαις καὶ ταῖς ἀδελφαῖς θρηνεῖ τὸν παῖδα· καὶ μετὰ ταῦτα ἐκ τῆς πυρᾶς ἡ Θέτις ἀναρπάσασα τὸν παῖδα εἰς τὴν Λευκὴν νῆσον διακομίζει. οἱ δὲ Ἀχαιοὶ τὸν τάφον χώσαντες ἀγῶνα τιθέασι, <ἐν ὧι νικᾶι Εὔμηλος ἵπποις, Διομήδης σταδίωι, Αἴας δίσκωι, Τεῦκρος τόξωι. τὴν δὲ Ἀχιλλέως πανοπλίαν τιθεῖσι τῶι ἀρίστωι νικητήριον. Ap.> καὶ περὶ τῶν Ἀχιλλέως ὅπλων Ὀδυσσεῖ καὶ Αἴαντι στάσις ἐμπίπτει.

a large force of Ethiopians>, arrives to assist the Trojans. Thetis prophesies to her son about the encounter with Memnon. When battle is joined, Antilochus is killed by Memnon, but then Achilles kills Memnon. And Dawn confers immortality upon him after prevailing on Zeus.

(3) Achilles puts the Trojans to flight and chases them into the city, but is killed by Paris and Apollo. <At the Scaean Gates he is shot by Alexander and Apollo in the ankle.> A fierce battle develops over his body, in which Ajax <kills Glaucus. He hands over Achilles' armor to be taken to the ships; as for the body, he> takes it up and carries it towards the ships, with Odysseus fighting the Trojans off.

(4) Then they bury Antilochus, and lay out the body of Achilles. Thetis comes with the Muses and her sisters, and laments her son.[19] And presently Thetis snatches her son from the pyre and conveys him to the White Island.[20] When the Achaeans have raised the grave mound, they organize an athletic contest, <in which Eumelus wins in the chariot race, Diomedes in the sprint, Ajax in the discus, Teucer in the archery. They offer Achilles' armor as the prize for the outstanding hero.> And a quarrel arises between Odysseus and Ajax over the arms of Achilles.

[19] Thetis' sisters are the Nereids. Achilles had probably been lamented also by Briseis (like Patroclus in *Iliad* 19.282–302); see Propertius 2.9.9–14.

[20] In the Black Sea opposite the mouth of the Danube, the modern Ostrov Zmeinyy.

FRAGMENTA

1 Schol. (T) *Il.* 24.804a

τινὲς γράφουσιν·

ὣς οἵ γ' ἀμφίεπον τάφον Ἕκτορος· ἦλθε δ' Ἀμαζών,
Ἄρηος θυγάτηρ μεγαλήτορος ἀνδροφόνοιο.

2 Ὀτρήρ[η]‹ς› *θυγάτηρ εὐειδὴς* Πενθεσẹ́λ‹ε›ια P. Lit. Lond. 6 xxii 43.

2 P.Oxy. 1611 fr. 4 ii 145

["τίς πόθεν εἰς] σύ, γύναι; τίνος ἔκγον[ος] ẹὔχ̣[ε]αι ẹἶναι̣;"

καὶ τ[ὰ ἑ]ξῆς, καὶ ὡς ἐκτίθετ[αι Ἀρκτῖ]ṿος ὅλον αὐτῆ[ς τὸν] θάνατον.

3 Schol. (A, Aristonici) *Il.* 17.719

ὅτι ἐντεῦθεν τοῖς νεωτέροις ὁ βασταζόμενος Ἀχιλλεὺς ὑπ' Αἴαντος, ὑπερασπίζων δὲ Ὀδυσσεὺς παρῆκται. εἰ δὲ Ὅμηρος ἔγραφε τὸν Ἀχιλλέως θάνατον, οὐκ ἂν ἐποίησε τὸν νεκρὸν ὑπ' Αἴαντος βασταζόμενον, ὡς οἱ νεώτεροι.

Cf. schol. *Od.* 11.547.

AETHIOPIS

FRAGMENTS

1 Scholiast on the last line of the *Iliad*

Some write:

> So they busied themselves with Hector's funeral. And an Amazon came,
> a daughter of Ares the great-hearted, the slayer of men.[21]

2 Oxyrhynchus papyrus[22]

> ["Who and whence are] you, lady? Whose child do you claim to be?"

and what follows, and how [Arcti]nus relates her whole death.

3 Scholiast on the *Iliad* (Aristonicus)

(The critical sign is) because from this passage [*Iliad* 17.719] post-Homeric writers have derived Achilles being carried by Ajax with Odysseus defending him. But if Homer had been describing the death of Achilles, he would not have had the body carried by Ajax, as the later writers do.

21 A papyrus source gives the variant "and an Amazon came, the daughter of Otrera, the fair Penthesilea." The lines are not properly part of the *Aethiopis*, but were devised to make the *Iliad* lead on to it.

22 The text is a scholarly commentary or the like; the author and context are unknown. The verse quoted was probably spoken to Penthesilea by Priam or Achilles.

4* Schol. (D) *Il.* 23.660

Φόρβας ἀνδρειότατος τῶν καθ' ἑαυτὸν γενόμενος, ὑπερήφανος δέ, πυγμὴν ἤσκησεν, καὶ τοὺς μὲν παριόντας ἀναγκάζων ἀγωνίζεσθαι ἀνῄρει· ὑπὸ δὲ τῆς πολλῆς ὑπερηφανίας ἠβούλετο καὶ πρὸς τοὺς θεοὺς τὸ τοιοῦτο φρόνημα ἔχειν. διὸ Ἀπόλλων παραγενόμενος καὶ συστὰς αὐτῶι ἀπέκτεινεν αὐτόν. ὅθεν ἐξ ἐκείνου καὶ τῆς πυκτικῆς ἔφορος ἐνομίσθη ὁ θεός. ἡ ἱστορία παρὰ τοῖς κυκλικοῖς.

5 Diomedes, *Gramm. Lat.* i.477.9

Alii a Marte ortum Iambum strenuum ducem tradunt, qui cum crebriter pugnas iniret et telum cum clamore torqueret, ἀπὸ τοῦ ἰεῖν καὶ βοᾶν Iambus appellatur. Idcirco ex breui et longa pedem hunc esse compositum, quod hi qui iaculentur ex breui accessu in extensum passum proferuntur, ut promptiore nisu telis ictum confirment. Auctor huius librationis Arctinus Graecus his uersibus perhibetur: {ὁ Ἴαμβος}

ἐξ ὀλίγου διαβὰς προφόρωι ποδί, γυῖά οἱ ὄφρα
τεινόμενα ῥώοιτο καὶ εὐσθενὲς εἶδος ἔχησιν.

1 γυῖά οἱ ὄφρα West: *ofra oi gya* vel *gria* codd.

6 Schol. Pind. *Isth.* 4.58b

ὁ γὰρ τὴν Αἰθιοπίδα γράφων περὶ τὸν ὄρθρον φησὶ τὸν Αἴαντα ἑαυτὸν ἀνελεῖν.

4* Scholiast on the *Iliad*

Phorbas, the manliest man of his time, but an arrogant one, practised boxing, and he used to force passersby to compete with him and then destroy them. In his great arrogance he was prepared to take this attitude even towards the gods. So Apollo came and squared up to him, and killed him. Hence after that the god was recognized as the patron of boxing. The story is in the Cyclic poets.[23]

5 Diomedes, *The Art of Grammar*

Others relate that Iambus was a son of Mars, a vigorous chieftain, who because he constantly went into battle and hurled [Greek *hiein*] his spear with a shout [Greek *boân*] was named "Iambus"; and that the iambic foot is made up of a short and a long because those throwing a javelin take a short step forward and then a long stride, to put their weight into the shot and give it greater force. The authority for this throwing method is said to be the Greek Arctinus in these verses:

With legs slightly apart and one foot forward, so that his limbs should move vigorously at full stretch and have a good appearance of strength.[24]

6 Scholiast on Pindar

For the author of the *Aethiopis* says that Ajax killed himself towards dawn.

23 The boxing match in the funeral games for Achilles is a possible context.

24 The verses suggest not a man throwing a spear but one getting set for a foot race, or perhaps for wrestling. The original context may therefore have been the funeral games for Achilles.

TROJAN CYCLE

ΙΛΙΑΣ ΜΙΚΡΑ

TESTIMONIA

Arist. *Poet.* 1459a37

οἱ δ᾽ ἄλλοι περὶ ἕνα ποιοῦσι καὶ περὶ ἕνα χρόνον καὶ μίαν πρᾶξιν πολυμερῆ, οἷον ὁ τὰ Κύπρια ποιήσας καὶ τὴν Μικρὰν Ἰλιάδα. τοιγαροῦν ἐκ μὲν Ἰλιάδος καὶ Ὀδυσσείας μία τραγωιδία ποιεῖται ἑκατέρας, ἢ δύο μόναι, ἐκ δὲ Κυπρίων πολλαὶ καὶ τῆς Μικρᾶς Ἰλιάδος πλέον ὀκτώ, οἷον Ὅπλων κρίσις, Φιλοκτήτης, Νεοπτόλεμος, Εὐρύπυλος, Πτωχεία, Λάκαιναι, Ἰλίου πέρσις, καὶ Ἀπόπλους καὶ Σίνων καὶ Τρωιάδες.

Poculum Homericum MB 31 (cf. 32) (p. 97 Sinn)

κατὰ ποιητὴν Λέσχην ἐκ τῆς Μικρᾶς Ἰλιάδος· ἐν τῶ(ι) Ἰλίω(ι) οἱ σύμ(μ)α[χοι] μείξαντες πρὸς τοὺς Ἀχαιοὺς μάχην.

IG 14.1284 i 10 = Tabula Iliaca A (Capitolina) p. 29 Sadurska

Ἰλιὰς ἡ Μικρὰ λεγομένη κατὰ Λέσχην Πυρραῖον.

Εὐρύπυλος, Νεοπτόλεμος, Ὀδυσσεύς, Διομήδης, Παλ(λ)άς, δούρηος ἵππος. Τρωάδες καὶ Φρύγες ἀνάγουσι τὸν ἵππον. Πρίαμος, Σίνων, Κασσάνδρα, Σκαιὰ πύλη.

THE LITTLE ILIAD

TESTIMONIA

Aristotle, *Poetics*

But the others[25] tell the story of one person or one time or one action made up of many parts, like the author of the *Cypria* and the *Little Iliad*. Hence with the *Iliad* and *Odyssey* a single tragedy can be made from each, or no more than two, whereas from the *Cypria* many can be made, and from the *Little Iliad* more than eight, for example *The Award of the Armor*, *Philoctetes*, *Neoptolemus*, *Eurypylus*, *The Beggar's Expedition*, *The Laconian Women*, *The Sack of Ilion*, and *The Sailing Away* and *Sinon* and *Trojan Women*.[26]

Caption to vase relief (third–second century BC)

After the poet Lesches, from the *Little Iliad*: the allies at Ilion joining battle with the Achaeans.

Capitoline plaque

The *Iliad* known as *Little*, after Lesches of Pyrrha.

Eurypylus, Neoptolemus, Odysseus, Diomedes, Pallas, the wooden horse. Trojan women and Phrygians are taking the horse up. Priam, Sinon, Cassandra, the Scaean Gate.

25 The poets other than Homer.

26 Some regard the list of titles as interpolated. Most of them, perhaps all, are taken from actual tragedies. Sophocles' *Laconian Women* dealt with the theft of the Palladion.

Cf. Tabulam Iliacam Ti (Thierry) p. 52 Sadurska Ἰλιὰς Μεικρὰ κα[τὰ Λέσχην Πυρραῖον.

Clem. *Strom.* 1.131.6, v. supra ad *Aethiopidem*.

Euseb. *Chron.*

Ol. 30.3: Alcmeon clarus habetur et Lesches Lesbius qui Paruam fecit Iliadem.

Hesychius Milesius, *Vita Homeri* 6

ἀναφέρεται δὲ εἰς αὐτὸν καὶ ἄλλα τινὰ ποιήματα· Ἀμαζονία, Ἰλιὰς Μικρά, κτλ.

ARGUMENTUM

Proclus, *Chrestomathia*, suppleta ex Apollod. epit. 5.6–16

ἑξῆς δ' ἐστὶν Ἰλιάδος Μικρᾶς βιβλία τέσσαρα Λέσχεω Μυτιληναίου περιέχοντα τάδε·

(1) ἡ τῶν ὅπλων κρίσις γίνεται καὶ Ὀδυσσεὺς κατὰ βούλησιν Ἀθηνᾶς λαμβάνει. Αἴας δ' ἐμμανὴς γενόμενος τήν τε λείαν τῶν Ἀχαιῶν λυμαίνεται καὶ ἑαυτὸν ἀναιρεῖ. <Ἀγαμέμνων δὲ κωλύει τὸ σῶμα αὐτοῦ καῆναι· καὶ μόνος οὗτος τῶν ἐν Ἰλίωι ἀποθανόντων ἐν σορῶι κεῖται. ὁ δὲ τάφος ἐστὶν ἐν Ῥοιτείωι. Ap.>

(2) μετὰ ταῦτα Ὀδυσσεὺς λοχήσας Ἕλενον λαμβάνει, καὶ χρήσαντος περὶ τῆς ἁλώσεως τούτου Διομήδης <Ὀδυσσεὺς μετὰ Διομήδους Ap.> ἐκ Λήμνου Φιλοκτήτην ἀνάγει. ἰαθεὶς δὲ οὗτος ὑπὸ Μαχάονος καὶ

Clement of Alexandria, *Miscellanies*: see above on the *Aethiopis*.

Eusebius, *Chronicle*

Ol. 30.3 (658/657): Alcman is famous, and Lesches of Lesbos who composed the *Little Iliad*.

Hesychius of Miletus, *Life of Homer*

Certain other poems are also attributed to him: the *Amazonia*, the *Little Iliad*, etc.

ARGUMENT

Proclus, *Chrestomathy*, with additions and variants from Apollodorus, *The Library*

Next are the four books of the *Little Iliad* by Lesches of Mytilene, with the following content:

(1) The awarding of the armor takes place, and Odysseus gets it in accord with Athena's wishes. Ajax goes insane, savages the Achaeans' plundered livestock, and kills himself. <Agamemnon prevents his body being cremated; he is the only one of those who died at Ilion to lie in a coffin. His tomb is at Rhoiteion.>

(2) After this Odysseus ambushes Helenus and captures him. Following a prophecy he makes about the taking of the city, <Odysseus with> Diomedes brings Philoctetes back from Lemnos.[27] He is healed by

[27] The prophecy was that the city could only be taken with Heracles' bow, which was in Philoctetes' possession.

μονομαχήσας Ἀλεξάνδρωι κτείνει· καὶ τὸν νεκρὸν ὑπὸ Μενελάου καταικισθέντα ἀνελόμενοι θάπτουσιν οἱ Τρῶες. μετὰ δὲ ταῦτα Δηΐφοβος Ἑλένην γαμεῖ.

(3) καὶ Νεοπτόλεμον Ὀδυσσεὺς ἐκ Σκύρου ἀγαγὼν τὰ ὅπλα δίδωσι τὰ τοῦ πατρός· καὶ Ἀχιλλεὺς αὐτῶι φαντάζεται. Εὐρύπυλος δὲ ὁ Τηλέφου ἐπίκουρος τοῖς Τρωσὶ παραγίνεται <πολλὴν Μυσῶν δύναμιν ἄγων Ap.>, καὶ ἀριστεύοντα αὐτὸν ἀποκτείνει Νεοπτόλεμος. καὶ οἱ Τρῶες πολιορκοῦνται.

(4) καὶ Ἐπειὸς κατ᾽ Ἀθηνᾶς προαίρεσιν <ἀπὸ τῆς Ἴδης ξύλα τεμὼν Ap.> τὸν δούρειον ἵππον κατασκευάζει. Ὀδυσσεύς τε αἰκισάμενος ἑαυτὸν <καὶ πενιχρὰν στολὴν ἐνδὺς Ap.> κατάσκοπος εἰς Ἴλιον παραγίνεται· καὶ ἀναγνωρισθεὶς ὑφ᾽ Ἑλένης περὶ τῆς ἁλώσεως τῆς πόλεως συντίθεται, κτείνας τέ τινας τῶν Τρώων ἐπὶ τὰς ναῦς ἀφικνεῖται. καὶ μετὰ ταῦτα σὺν Διομήδει τὸ Παλλάδιον ἐκκομίζει ἐκ τῆς Ἰλίου.

(5) ἔπειτα εἰς τὸν δούρειον ἵππον τοὺς ἀρίστους ἐμβιβάσαντες, τάς τε σκηνὰς καταφλέξαντες οἱ λοιποὶ τῶν Ἑλλήνων <καὶ καταλιπόντες Σίνωνα, ὃς ἔμελλεν αὐτοῖς πυρσὸν ἀνάπτειν, τῆς νυκτὸς Ap.> εἰς Τένεδον ἀνάγονται. οἱ δὲ Τρῶες τῶν κακῶν ὑπολαβόντες ἀπηλλάχθαι τόν τε δούρειον ἵππον εἰς τὴν

---

[28] According to Apollodorus' narrative Machaon had been killed by Penthesilea, and it was Podalirius who healed Philoctetes.

[29] Compare the scholiast on *Odyssey* 8.517, "and it is this pas-

Machaon,[28] and fights alone against Alexander and kills him. His body is mutilated by Menelaus, but then the Trojans recover it and give it burial. After this Deiphobus marries Helen.[29]

(3) And Odysseus[30] fetches Neoptolemus from Scyros and gives him his father's armor; and Achilles appears to him. Eurypylus the son of Telephus arrives to help the Trojans, ‹bringing a large force of Mysians,› and dominates the battlefield, but Neoptolemus kills him. The Trojans are penned in the city.

(4) Epeios, following an initiative of Athena's, ‹fells timber from Ida› and constructs the wooden horse. Odysseus disfigures himself ‹and puts on pauper's clothes› and enters Ilion to reconnoitre. He is recognized by Helen, and comes to an agreement with her about the taking of the city. After killing some Trojans, he gets back to the ships. After this he brings the Palladion[31] out of Ilios with Diomedes.

(5) Then they put the leading heroes into the wooden horse. The rest of the Greeks burn their huts and ‹leaving Sinon behind, who was to light a torch signal for them, in the night› they withdraw to Tenedos. The Trojans, believing themselves rid of their troubles, take the wooden horse

sage that led the later writers to say that Helen also married Deiphobus."

30 Accompanied by Phoenix, according to Apollodorus.

31 The statue of Pallas Athena, on which Troy's safety depended. According to Apollodorus and the first-century papyrus Rylands 22, it was Helenus again who revealed this secret. The papyrus narrative puts the theft of the Palladion before the fetching of Neoptolemus from Scyros.

πόλιν εἰσδέχονται διελόντες μέρος τι τοῦ τείχους, καὶ εὐωχοῦνται ὡς νενικηκότες τοὺς Ἕλληνας.

3–4 cf. P. Rylands 22 (saec. i).

FRAGMENTA

1 Ps.-Herod. *Vita Homeri* 16

διατρίβων δὲ παρὰ τῶι Θεστορίδηι ποιεῖ Ἰλιάδα τὴν ἐλάσσω, ἧς ἡ ἀρχή·

Ἴλιον ἀείδω καὶ Δαρδανίην εὔπωλον,
ἧς πέρι πόλλα πάθον Δαναοὶ θεράποντες Ἄρηος.

Versus ex parte exhibent testae duae in regione Pontica repertae, saec. v a.C.: Jurij G. Vinogradov, *Pontische Studien* (Mainz, 1997), 385, 419.

2 Schol. Ar. *Eq*. 1056a

διεφέροντο περὶ τῶν ἀριστείων ὅ τε Αἴας καὶ ὁ Ὀδυσσεύς, ὥς φησιν ὁ τὴν Μικρὰν Ἰλιάδα πεποιηκώς· τὸν Νέστορα δὲ συμβουλεῦσαι τοῖς Ἕλλησι πέμψαι τινὰς ἐξ αὐτῶν ὑπὸ τὰ τείχη τῶν Τρώων ὠτακουστήσοντας περὶ τῆς ἀνδρείας τῶν προειρημένων ἡρώων. τοὺς δὲ πεμφθέντας ἀκοῦσαι παρθένων διαφερομένων πρὸς ἀλλήλας, ὧν τὴν μὲν λέγειν ὡς ὁ Αἴας πολὺ κρείττων ἐστὶ τοῦ Ὀδυσσέως, διερχομένην οὕτως·

Αἴας μὲν γὰρ ἄειρε καὶ ἔκφερε δηϊοτῆτος
ἥρω Πηλείδην, οὐδ᾿ ἤθελε δῖος Ὀδυσσεύς.

into the city by breaching a portion of the wall, and start celebrating their supposed victory over the Greeks.

FRAGMENTS

1 Pseudo-Herodotus, *Life of Homer*

While staying with Thestorides he composed the *Lesser Iliad*, which begins

Of Ilios I sing, and Dardania land of fine colts, over which the Danaans suffered much, servants of the War god.

2 Scholiast on Aristophanes, *Knights*

There was a dispute over the prize for valor[32] between Ajax and Odysseus, as the author of the *Little Iliad* says, and Nestor advised the Greeks to send some men to below the Trojans' wall to eavesdrop concerning the bravery of the heroes in question. They heard some girls arguing, one of whom said that Ajax was much better than Odysseus, explaining:

Ajax, after all, lifted up the warrior son of Peleus and carried him out of the fighting, but noble Odysseus would not.

[32] The armor of Achilles.

τὴν δὲ ἑτέραν ἀντειπεῖν Ἀθηνᾶς προνοίαι·

πῶς ἐπεφωνήσω; πῶς οὐ κατὰ κόσμον ἔειπες;

(Ar. *Eq.* 1056–1057)

καί κε γυνὴ φέροι ἄχθος, ἐπεί κεν ἀνὴρ ἀναθείη,
ἀλλ᾽ οὐκ ἂν μαχέσαιτο.

4 cit. Plut. *De Alex. fort.* 337e 5 χέσαιτο γάρ, εἰ μαχέσαιτο add. Aristophanes: χάσαιτο κτλ. Lesches? (von Blumenthal).

3 Porph. (*Paralip.* fr. 4 Schrader) ap. Eust. 285.34

ὁ τὴν Μικρὰν Ἰλιάδα γράψας ἱστορεῖ μηδὲ καυθῆναι συνήθως τὸν Αἴαντα, τεθῆναι δὲ οὕτως ἐν σορῶι διὰ τὴν ὀργὴν τοῦ βασιλέως.

Cf. Apollod. epit. 5.7 (supra in Argumento).

4 Schol. (T) *Il.* 19.326, "ὃς Σκύρωι μοι ἐνιτρέφεται"

ὁ δὲ τὴν Μικρὰν Ἰλιάδα ἀναζευγνύντα αὐτὸν ἀπὸ Τηλέφου προσορμισθῆναι ἐκεῖ·

Πηλείδην δ᾽ Ἀχιλῆα φέρε Σκῦρόνδε θύελλα·
ἔνθ᾽ ὅ γ᾽ ἐς ἀργαλέον λιμέν᾽ ἵκετο νυκτὸς ἐκείνης.

Cf. schol. (b) et Eust. ad loc.

But the other retorted, by providence of Athena,

What did you say? How can you be so wrong? Even a woman could carry a load, if a man put it onto her, but she couldn't fight.[33]

3 Porphyry, commentary on Homer

The writer of the *Little Iliad* records that Ajax was not cremated in the usual way either, but placed in a coffin as he was, because of the king's anger.[34]

4 Scholiast on the *Iliad*, "the son I have growing up in Scyros"

The author of the *Little Iliad* says that he landed there on leaving Telephus:

As for Achilles the son of Peleus, the storm carried him to Scyros; there he made the harbor with difficulty that night.

[33] The last sentence is supplied from the text of Aristophanes, who adds, "for if she'd fight, she'd shite." This is unlikely to be a genuine part of the quotation, though it might be a humorous adaptation of an original "for if she'd fight, she'd retreat," with *chesaito* substituted for *chasaito*.

[34] Agamemnon was angry because Ajax had intended to kill the Achaean leaders. Because Athena made him insane, he had attacked the animals instead.

5 Schol. (T) *Il.* 16.142, "ἀλλά μιν οἶος ἐπίστατο πῆλαι Ἀχιλλεύς"

οἱ δὲ πλάττονται λέγοντες ὡς Πηλεὺς μὲν παρὰ Χείρωνος ἔμαθε τὴν χρῆσιν αὐτῆς, Ἀχιλλεὺς δὲ παρὰ Πηλέως, ὃ δὲ οὐδένα ἐδίδαξεν. καὶ ὁ τῆς Μικρᾶς Ἰλιάδος ποιητής·

ἀμφὶ δὲ πόρκης
χρύσεος ἀστράπτει, καὶ ἐπ' αὐτῶι δίκροος αἰχμή.

2 ἄστραπτεν?

Schol. Pind. *Nem.* 6.85b, "ἔγχεος ζακότοιο"

δίκρουν γάρ, ὥστε δύο ἀκμὰς ἔχειν . . . καὶ Αἰσχύλος (fr. 152) . . . καὶ Σοφοκλῆς (fr. 152) . . . μετάγουσι δὲ τὴν ἱστορίαν ἀπὸ τῆς Λέσχου Μικρᾶς Ἰλιάδος λέγοντος οὕτως· ἀμφὶ δὲ - δίκροος †δίη.

6 Schol. Eur. *Tro.* 822

τὸν Γανυμήδην . . . Λαομέδοντος νῦν εἶπεν ἀκολουθήσας τῶι τὴν Μικρὰν Ἰλιάδα πεποιηκότι, ὃν οἱ μὲν Θεστορίδην Φωκ<αι>έα φασίν, οἱ δὲ Κιναίθωνα Λακεδαιμόνιον, ὡς Ἑλλάνικος (fr. 202c Fowler), οἱ δὲ Διόδωρον Ἐρυθραῖον. φησὶ δὲ οὕτως·

ἄμπελον, ἣν Κρονίδης ἔπορεν οὗ παιδὸς ἄποινα
χρυσείην, φύλλοισιν ἀγαυοῖσιν κομόωσαν
βότρυσί θ', οὓς Ἥφαιστος ἐπασκήσας Διὶ πατρί
δῶχ', ὃ δὲ Λαομέδοντι πόρεν Γανυμήδεος ἀντί.

5 Scholiast on the *Iliad*, "only Achilles knew how to wield it"[35]

Some tell the fictitious tale that Peleus learned the use of it from Chiron, and Achilles from Peleus, and that he taught nobody else. The poet of the *Little Iliad* says:

About it a collar of gold flashes, and on it a forked blade.[36]

Scholiast on Pindar, "his malignant spear"

It was forked, so as to have two points . . . Witness Aeschylus . . . and Sophocles . . . They are borrowing the story from the *Little Iliad* of Lesches, who says "About it—a forked blade."

6 Scholiast on Euripides, *Trojan Women*

Here he makes Ganymede the son of Laomedon, following the author of the *Little Iliad*, who some say was Thestorides of Phocaea, others Cinaethon of Lacedaemon, as Hellanicus has it, and others Diodorus of Erythrae. He says:

The vine that Zeus gave in compensation for his son; it was of gold, luxuriant with splendid foliage and grape clusters, which Hephaestus fashioned and gave to father Zeus, and he gave it to Laomedon in lieu of Ganymede.[37]

[35] The subject is Achilles' great ash-wood spear.

[36] If the present tense is correct, the fragment must come from a speech. Compare Quintus of Smyrna, 7.195 ff.

[37] Zeus had abducted Ganymede for his own purposes; see *Hymn to Aphrodite* 202–217. The golden vine was inherited by Priam, who sent it to Eurypylus' mother to overcome her objections to her son's going to fight at Troy.

Cf. schol. Eur. *Or.* 1391; *Od.* 11.520–522 cum schol. (Acusil. fr. 40c Fowler).

7 Paus. 3.26.9

Μαχάονα δὲ ὑπὸ Εὐρυπύλου τοῦ Τηλέφου τελευτῆσαί φησιν ὁ τὰ ἔπη ποιήσας τὴν Μικρὰν Ἰλιάδα.

8 Schol. Lyc. 780

ὁ δὲ τὴν Μικρὰν Ἰλιάδα γράψας φησὶ τρωθῆναι τὸν Ὀδυσσέα ὑπὸ Θόαντος ὅτε εἰς Τροίαν ἀνήρχοντο.

9 Schol. *Od.* 4.248, "δέκτηι"

ὁ κυκλικὸς τὸ ΔΕΚΤΗΙ ὀνοματικῶς ἀκούει· παρ᾽ οὗ φησι τὸν Ὀδυσσέα τὰ ῥάκη λαβόντα μετημφιάσθαι . . . Ἀρίσταρχος δὲ δέκτηι μὲν ἐπαίτηι.

10 Schol. *Od.* 4.258, "κατὰ δὲ φρόνιν ἤγαγε πολλήν"

οἱ δὲ νεώτεροι φρόνιν τὴν λείαν ἀπεδέξαντο.

11 Hesych. δ 1881

Διομήδειος ἀνάγκη· παροιμία. Κλέαρχος μέν φησι (fr. 68 Wehrli) . . . ὁ δὲ τὴν Μικρὰν Ἰλιάδα φησὶν ἐπὶ τῆς τοῦ Παλλαδίου κλοπῆς γενέσθαι.

7 Pausanias, *Description of Greece*

Machaon died at the hands of Eurypylus son of Telephus, according to the poet of the *Little Iliad*.

8 Scholiast on Lycophron

The writer of the *Little Iliad* says that Odysseus was wounded by Thoas when they went up to Troy.[38]

9 Scholiast on the *Odyssey*

The Cyclic poet takes DEKTES as the name of a man, from whom he says Odysseus borrowed the rags and put them on . . . whereas Aristarchus takes the word to mean "a beggar."

10 Scholiast on the *Odyssey*, "and brought back much *phronis*"

The post-Homeric writers take *phronis* to mean "booty."[39]

11 Hesychius, *Lexicon*

"Diomedian compulsion": a proverbial expression. Clearchus explains . . . The author of the *Little Iliad* connects it with the theft of the Palladion.

[38] That is, he allowed himself to be wounded for the sake of his disguise. On this escapade see *Odyssey* 4.242–264.

[39] The context is the same expedition of the disguised Odysseus into Troy. The inference is that in the Cyclic poem he returned to the Greek camp with some booty.

Paus. Att. δ 14

Διομήδειος ἀνάγκη· παροιμία . . . οἱ δέ, ὅτι Διομήδης καὶ Ὀδυσσεὺς τὸ Παλλάδιον κλέψαντες νυκτὸς ἐκ Τροίας ἐπανήιεσαν, ἑπόμενος δὲ ὁ Ὀδυσσεὺς τὸν Διομήδην ἐβουλήθη ἀποκτεῖναι· ἐν τῆι σελήνηι δὲ ἰδὼν τὴν σκιὰν τοῦ ξίφους ὁ Διομήδης, ἐπιστραφεὶς καὶ βιασάμενος τὸν Ὀδυσσέα ἔδησε καὶ προάγειν ἐποίησε παίων αὐτοῦ τῶι ξίφει τὸ μετάφρενον. τάττεται δὲ ἐπὶ τῶν κατ' ἀνάγκην τι πραττόντων.

Cf. Conon. *FGrHist* 26 F 1.34.

12 Apollod. epit. 5.14

εἰς τοῦτον Ὀδυσσεὺς εἰσελθεῖν πείθει πεντήκοντα τοὺς ἀρίστους, ὡς δὲ ὁ τὴν Μικρὰν γράψας Ἰλιάδα φησί, ιγ´.

ιγ´ Severyns: τρισχιλίους (sc. ͵γ) libri.

13 Schol. *Od.* 4.285

ὁ Ἄντικλος ἐκ τοῦ κύκλου.

14 Schol. Eur. *Hec.* 910

Καλλισθένης ἐν β´ τῶν Ἑλληνικῶν (*FGrHist* 124 F 10a)

---

[40] Conon tells a version of the story in which Diomedes is helped over the Trojan city wall by Odysseus but then leaves him outside and gets the Palladion by himself. On the way back, afraid that Odysseus will deprive him of it and of the credit for obtaining

Pausanias, *Collected Attic Words*

"Diomedian compulsion": a proverbial expression . . . Others say that Diomedes and Odysseus were on their way back from Troy at night after stealing the Palladion, and Odysseus, who was behind Diomedes, intended to kill him; but in the moonlight Diomedes saw the shadow of his sword, turned round, overpowered Odysseus, tied him up, and forced him to go ahead by beating his back with his sword. The expression is applied to people who do something under compulsion.[40]

12 Apollodorus, *The Library*

Odysseus persuaded the fifty best men to get inside the horse, or as the writer of the *Little Iliad* says, thirteen.[41]

13 Scholiast on the *Odyssey*

Anticlus comes from the Cycle.[42]

14 Scholiast on Euripides, *Hecuba*

Callisthenes in Book 2 of his *Greek History* writes: "Troy was

it, he pretends that the image he has brought out is not the true Palladion. Odysseus, however, sees it twitch in indignation and realizes that it is the true one. He then makes his abortive attempt to kill Diomedes. He refrains when Diomedes draws his own sword, but it is then Odysseus who drives Diomedes along with blows on the back, not vice versa.

41 "Thirteen" is a paleographically plausible emendation of the incredible "three thousand" given by the manuscripts.

42 In the *Odyssey* passage, which Aristarchus suspected was not genuine, Anticlus is one of the men in the horse. Odysseus had to restrain him from responding when Helen went round the horse calling the heroes' names and mimicking their wives' voices (4.271–289).

οὕτως γράφει· "ἑάλω μὲν ἡ Τροία Θαργηλιῶνος μηνός, ὡς μέν τινες τῶν ἱστορικῶν, ιβʹ ἱσταμένου, ὡς δὲ ὁ τὴν Μικρὰν Ἰλιάδα, ηʹ φθίνοντος· διορίζει γὰρ αὐτὸς τὴν ἅλωσιν, φάσκων συμβῆναι τότε τὴν κατάληψιν, ἡνίκα

νὺξ μὲν ἔην μέσση, λαμπρὰ δ' ἐπέτελλε σελήνη.

μεσονύκτιος δὲ μόνον τῆι ὀγδόηι φθίνοντος ἀνατέλλει, ἐν ἄλληι δὲ οὔ."

Cf. Clem. *Strom.* 1.104.1, ubi νὺξ μὲν ἔην μεσάτα, λαμπρὰ δ' ἐπέτελλε σελάνα; Tzetz. in Lyc. 344 ὁ Σίνων, ὡς ἦν αὐτῶι συντεθειμένον, φρυκτὸν ὑποδείξας τοῖς Ἕλλησιν, ὡς ὁ Λέσχης φησίν, ἡνίκα "νὺξ - σελήνη." Cf. eund. *Posthom.* 719–721; 773.

15–27 Paus. 10.25.5–27.2

(**15**) πλησίον δὲ τοῦ Ἑλένου Μέγης ἐστί· τέτρωται δὲ τὸν βραχίονα ὁ Μέγης, καθὰ δὴ καὶ Λέσχεως ὁ Αἰσχυλίνου Πυρραῖος ἐν Ἰλίου περσίδι ἐποίησε· τρωθῆναι δὲ ὑπὸ τὴν μάχην τοῦτον ἣν ἐν τῆι νυκτὶ ἐμαχέσαντο οἱ Τρῶες, ὑπὸ Ἀδμήτου φησὶ τοῦ Αὐγείου. (**16**) γέγραπται δὲ καὶ Λυκομήδης παρὰ τὸν Μέγητα ὁ Κρέοντος, ἔχων τραῦμα ἐπὶ τῶι καρπῶι· Λέσχεως οὕτω φησὶν αὐτὸν ὑπὸ Ἀγήνορος τρωθῆναι. δῆλα οὖν ὡς ἄλλως γε οὐκ ἂν ὁ Πολύγνωτος ἔγραψεν οὕτω τὰ ἕλκη σφίσιν, εἰ μὴ ἐπελέξατο τὴν ποίησιν τοῦ Λέσχεω . . . (**17**) Λέσχεως δὲ ἐς τὴν Αἴθραν

[43] This calculation goes back to Damastes of Sigeum (fr. 7 Fowler) and Ephorus (*FGrHist* 70 F 226).

taken in the month of Thargelion, on the 12th, as some historians say, but according to the author of the *Little Iliad* on the 23rd. For he defines the date by saying that the capture occurred when

It was the middle of the night, and the bright moon was rising.

It rises at midnight on the 23rd of the month, and on no other day."[43]

Cf. Tzetzes, commentary on Lycophron: Sinon, as arranged, showed the Greeks a torch signal, as Lesches says, when "it was the middle of the night, and the bright moon was rising."

15–27 Pausanias, *Geography of Greece*[44]

(**15**) Near Helenus there is Meges. He has a wound in the arm, just as Lescheos the son of Aeschylinus from Pyrrha says in his *Sack of Ilion*; he says he got the wound from Admetus the son of Augeas in the battle that the Trojans fought in the night. (**16**) Beside Meges there is also painted Lycomedes the son of Creon, with a wound in his wrist: Lescheos says he was so wounded by Agenor. So clearly Polygnotus would not otherwise have depicted their wounds in this way, if he had not read Lescheos' poem . . . (**17**) Lescheos wrote of Aethra[45] that

[44] In this passage Pausanias describes the great murals painted by Polygnotus in the Cnidian Lesche at Delphi, and comments on their relationship to the epic sources. Besides Homer and Lesches (whom he calls Lescheos), he refers to Stesichorus' *Sack of Ilion*, and this explains his slip in naming Lesches' poem as the *Sack of Ilion* instead of the *Little Iliad*.

[45] The mother of Theseus; she had been at Troy as a servant of Helen (*Iliad* 3.144). See the *Sack of Ilion*, fr. 6.

ἐποίησεν, ἡνίκα ἡλίσκετο Ἴλιον, ὑπεξελθοῦσαν ἐς τὸ στρατόπεδον αὐτὴν ἀφικέσθαι τὸ Ἑλλήνων καὶ ὑπὸ τῶν παίδων γνωρισθῆναι τῶν Θησέως, καὶ ὡς παρ' Ἀγαμέμνονος αἰτῆσαι Δημοφῶν αὐτήν· ὃ δὲ ἐκείνωι μὲν ἐθέλειν χαρίζεσθαι, ποιήσειν δὲ οὐ πρότερον ἔφη πρὶν Ἑλένην πεῖσαι· ἀποστείλαντι δὲ αὐτῶι κήρυκα ἔδωκεν Ἑλένη τὴν χάριν . . . (**18**) *γέγραπται μὲν Ἀνδρομάχη, καὶ ὁ παῖς οἱ προσέστηκεν ἑλόμενος τοῦ μαστοῦ. τούτωι Λέσχεως ῥιφέντι ἀπὸ τοῦ πύργου συμβῆναι λέγει τὴν τελευτήν, οὐ μὴν ὑπὸ δόγματός γε τῶν Ἑλλήνων, ἀλλ' ἰδίαι Νεοπτόλεμον αὐτόχειρα ἐθελῆσαι γενέσθαι* (cf. fr. 29) . . . (**19**) *Λέσχεως δὲ καὶ ἔπη τὰ Κύπρια* (fr. 28) *διδόασιν Εὐρυδίκην γυναῖκα Αἰνείαι.* (**20**) *γεγραμμέναι δὲ ἐπὶ κρήνης ὑπὲρ ταύτας Δηϊνόμη τε καὶ Μητιόχη καὶ Πεῖσίς ἐστι καὶ Κλεοδίκη. τούτων ἐν Ἰλιάδι καλουμένηι Μικρᾶι μόνης ἐστὶ τὸ ὄνομα τῆς Δηϊνόμης . . .* (**21**) *Ἀστύνοον δέ, οὗ δὴ ἐποιήσατο καὶ Λέσχεως μνήμην, πεπτωκότα ἐς γόνυ ὁ Νεοπτόλεμος ξίφει παίει . . .* (**22**) *Λέσχεως δὲ τετρωμένον τὸν Ἑλικάονα ἐν τῆι νυκτομαχίαι γνωρισθῆναί τε ὑπὸ Ὀδυσσέως καὶ ἐξαχθῆναι ζῶντα ἐκ τῆς μάχης φησίν . . .* (**23**) *νεκροὶ δὲ ὁ μὲν γυμνὸς Πῆλις ὄνομα ἐπὶ τὸν νῶτόν ἐστιν ἐρριμμένος, ὑπὸ δὲ τὸν Πῆλιν Ἠιονεύς τε κεῖται καὶ Ἄδμητος, ἐνδεδυκότες ἔτι τοὺς θώρακας. καὶ αὐτῶν Λέσχεως Ἠιονέα ὑπὸ Νεοπτολέμου, τὸν δὲ ὑπὸ Φιλοκτήτου φησὶν ἀποθανεῖν τὸν Ἄδμητον . . .* (**24**) *ἀφίκετο μὲν δὴ ἐπὶ τὸν Κασσάνδρας ὁ Κόροιβος γάμον· ἀπέθανε δέ, ὡς μὲν ὁ πλείων λόγος, ὑπὸ Νεοπτολέμου, Λέσχεως δὲ ὑπὸ Διομήδους ἐποίησεν.* (**25**) *εἰσὶ δὲ καὶ ἐπάνω τοῦ Κοροιβου Πρίαμος καὶ Ἀξίων τε*

when Ilion was being taken, she got out and made her way to the Greek camp and was recognized by the sons of Theseus; and that Demophon asked Agamemnon if he could have her. He said he was willing to grant him this, but only if he had Helen's agreement. He sent a herald, and Helen granted the favor . . . (**18**) Andromache is depicted, with her son standing beside her; he has taken hold of her breast. Lescheos says that his end came about when he was thrown from the fortifications, not by a decision of the Greeks but from a private desire of Neoptolemus to be his slayer . . . (**19**) Lescheos and the epic *Cypria* give Aeneas Eurydice as wife. (**20**) Above these women, at a fountain, are depicted Deïnome, Metioche, Peisis, and Cleodice. Of these, only Deïnome's name appears in the so-called *Little Iliad* . . . (**21**) Astynous, whom Lescheos too mentions, has sunk to his knees and Neoptolemus is striking him with his sword . . . (**22**) Lescheos says that Helicaon[46] was wounded in the night fighting, recognized by Odysseus, and brought out of the battle alive . . . (**23**) Of the dead, there is one naked, Pelis by name, flung on his back, and below Pelis lie Eïoneus and Admetus, still wearing their cuirasses. Of these Lescheos says that Eïoneus was killed by Neoptolemus, and Admetus by Philoctetes . . . (**24**) Coroebus had come in order to marry Cassandra; he was killed by Neoptolemus in the majority version, but Lescheos makes it by Diomedes. (**25**) Above Coroebus are Priam, Axion, and Agenor. As

[46] One of the sons of Antenor, who had saved Odysseus and Menelaus from death; see the Argument to the *Cypria*.

καὶ Ἀγήνωρ. Πρίαμον δὲ ‹οὐκ› ἀποθανεῖν ἔφη Λέσχεως ἐπὶ τῆι ἐσχάραι τοῦ Ἑρκείου, ἀλλὰ ἀποσπασθέντα ἀπὸ τοῦ βωμοῦ πάρεργον τῶι Νεοπτολέμωι πρὸς ταῖς τῆς οἰκίας γενέσθαι θύραις . . . (**26**) *Ἀξίονα δὲ παῖδα εἶναι Πριάμου Λέσχεως καὶ ἀποθανεῖν αὐτὸν ὑπὸ Εὐρυπύλου τοῦ Εὐαίμονός φησι.* (**27**) *τοῦ Ἀγήνορος δὲ κατὰ τὸν αὐτὸν ποιητὴν Νεοπτόλεμος αὐτόχειρ ἐστί.*

25 cf. Pocula Homerica MB 27–29 (~ 30) (pp. 94–96 Sinn) *κατὰ ποιητὴν Λέσχην ἐκ τῆς Μικρᾶς Ἰλιάδος· καταφυγόντος τοῦ Πριάμου ἐπὶ τὸν βωμὸν τοῦ Ἑρκείου Διός, ἀποσπάσας ὁ Νεοπτόλεμος ἀπὸ τοῦ βωμοῦ πρὸς τῆ(ι) οἰκίαι κατέσφαξεν.*

27 cf. *IG* 14.1285 ii = Tabula Veronensis II p. 57 Sadurska [*Νεοπτόλεμος ἀ*]*π*[*οκ*]*τείνει Πρίαμον καὶ Ἀγήνορα, Πολυποίτης Ἐχεῖον, Θρασυμήδης Νι‹κ›αίνετον, Φιλοκτήτης Διοπ(ε)ίθην, Διο*[*μήδης . . .*

28 Schol. Ar. *Lys.* 155, "*ὁ γῶν Μενέλαος τᾶς Ἑλένας τὰ μᾶλά παι* | *γυμνᾶς παραυιδὼν ἐξέβαλ᾿, οἰῶ, τὸ ξίφος*"

ἡ ἱστορία παρὰ Ἰβύκωι (*PMGF* 296)· *τὰ δὲ αὐτὰ καὶ Λέσχης ὁ Πυρραῖος ἐν τῆι Μικρᾶι Ἰλιάδι.*

29–30 Tzetz. in Lyc. 1268 (cf. 1232)

Λέσχης δὲ ὁ τὴν Μικρὰν Ἰλιάδα πεποιηκὼς Ἀνδομάχην καὶ Αἰνείαν αἰχμαλώτους φησὶ δοθῆναι τῶι Ἀχιλλέως υἱῶι Νεοπτολέμωι, καὶ ἀπαχθῆναι σὺν αὐτῶι εἰς Φαρσαλίαν τὴν Ἀχιλλέως πατρίδα. φησὶ δὲ οὑτωσί·

regards Priam, Lescheos says he was not killed at the hearth altar of Zeus of the Courtyard, but was pulled away from the altar and dealt with in passing by Neoptolemus at the doors of the house[47] . . . (**26**) As for Axion, Lescheos says that he was a son of Priam, and killed by Eurypylus the son of Euhaemon. (**27**) Agenor's slayer, according to the same poet, was Neoptolemus.[48]

28 Scholiast on Aristophanes, *Lysistrata*, "At any rate, when Menelaus glimpsed Helen's bare apples, he dropped his sword, I believe"

The story is found in Ibycus; Lesches of Pyrrha too tells the same in the *Little Iliad*.

29–30 Tzetzes, commentary on Lycophron

Lesches, the author of the *Little Iliad*, says that Andromache and Aeneas were captured and given to Achilles' son Neoptolemus, and taken away with him to Pharsalia, Achilles' homeland. These are his words:

47 One group of the Homeric Cups, where Lesches' *Little Iliad* is named as the source, has the caption "When Priam had fled to the altar of Zeus of the Hearth, Neoptolemus tore him away from the altar and slaughtered him beside his house."

48 One of the Augustan plaques has the caption "[Neoptolemus] kills Priam and Agenor, Polypoites kills Echios, Thrasymedes Nicaenetus, Philoctetes Diopeithes, Dio[medes . . ." But it is not certain that the artist was here following the *Little Iliad*.

αὐτὰρ Ἀχιλλῆος μεγαθύμου φαίδιμος υἱός
Ἑκτορέην ἄλοχον κάταγεν κοίλας ἐπὶ νῆας,
παῖδα δ' ἑλὼν ἐκ κόλπου ἐϋπλοκάμοιο τιθήνης
ῥῖψε ποδὸς τεταγὼν ἀπὸ πύργου, τὸν δὲ πεσόντα
ἔλλαβε πορφύρεος θάνατος καὶ μοῖρα κραταιή
. . .

(**30**) *ἐκ δ' ἕλετ' Ἀνδρομάχην, ἠΰζωνον παράκοιτιν*
Ἕκτορος, ἥν τέ οἱ αὐτῶι ἀριστῆες Παναχαιῶν
δῶκαν ἔχειν ἐπίηρον ἀμειβόμενοι γέρας ἀνδρί·
αὐτόν τ' Ἀγχίσαο κλυτὸν γόνον ἱπποδάμοιο
Αἰνείαν ἐν νηυσὶν ἐβήσατο ποντοπόροισιν
ἐκ πάντων Δαναῶν ἀγέμεν γέρας ἔξοχον ἄλλων.

Fr. 30 Simiae *Gorgoni* trib. schol. Eur. *Andr.* 14.

Schol. (A) *Il.* 24.735a (Aristonici)

ὅτι ἐντεῦθεν κινηθέντες οἱ μεθ' Ὅμηρον ποιηταὶ ῥιπτόμενον κατὰ τοῦ τείχους ὑπὸ τῶν Ἑλλήνων εἰσάγουσι τὸν Ἀστυάνακτα.

31 Ath. 73e

σικυός . . . καὶ Λέσχης·

ὡς δ' ὅτ' ἀέξηται σικυὸς δροσερῶι ἐνὶ χώρωι.

Λέσχης Kaibel: λευχης, λάχης codd.

But great-hearted Achilles' glorious son led Hector's wife back to the hollow ships; her child he took from the bosom of his lovely-haired nurse and, holding him by the foot, flung him from the battlement, and crimson death and stern fate took him at his fall. . . .

(**30**) He took from the spoils Andromache, Hector's fair-girt consort, whom the chiefs of all the Achaeans gave him as a welcome reward and mark of honor. And Aeneas himself, the famous son of Anchises the horse-tamer, he embarked on his seagoing ships, to take as a special prize for himself out of all the Danaans.[49]

Scholiast on the *Iliad* (Aristonicus)

(The critical sign is) because from this passage (*Iliad* 24.735) the post-Homeric poets have introduced Astyanax being thrown down from the wall by the Greeks.

31 Athenaeus, *Scholars at Dinner*

The cucumber . . . And Lesches mentions it:

And as when a cucumber grows big in a well-watered spot.

[49] Tzetzes quotes two passages that were not consecutive in the epic. The first is about Neoptolemus' actions during the sack of the city; the second refers to the subsequent distribution of booty in the Achaean camp.

32* Aeschin. 1.128

εὑρήσετε καὶ τὴν πόλιν ἡμῶν καὶ τοὺς προγόνους Φήμης ὡς θεοῦ μεγίστης βωμὸν ἱδρυμένους, καὶ τὸν Ὅμηρον πολλάκις ἐν τῆι Ἰλιάδι λέγοντα πρὸ τοῦ τι τῶν μελλόντων γενέσθαι·

φήμη δ᾽ εἰς στρατὸν ἦλθε.

ΙΛΙΟΥ ΠΕΡΣΙΣ

TESTIMONIA

IG 14.1286 = Tabula Iliaca B p. 49 Sadurska

[Ἰλιάδα καὶ Ὀ]δύσσειαν ῥαψωιδιῶν μη̄· Ἰλίου πέρσ[ιδα

Dion. Hal. *Ant. Rom.* 1.68.2

παλαιότατος δὲ ὧν ἡμεῖς ἴσμεν <*ὁ*> *ποιητὴς Ἀρκτῖνος.*

De Arctino v. etiam ad *Aethiopidem.*

ARGUMENTUM

Proclus, *Chrestomathia*, suppleta ex Apollod. epit. 5.16–25

ἕπεται δὲ τούτοις Ἰλίου πέρσιδος βιβλία δύο Ἀρκτίνου Μιλησίου περιέχοντα τάδε·

32* Aeschines, *Against Timarchus*

You will find that our city and our forefathers have established an altar to Rumor, as a most mighty goddess, and that Homer often says in the *Iliad*, before something happens,

Rumor came to the war host.[50]

THE SACK OF ILION

TESTIMONIA

Augustan–Tiberian relief plaque

[The *Iliad* and] *Odyssey*, in 48 rhapsodies; the *Sack of Ilion* [

Dionysius of Halicarnassus, *Roman Antiquities*

And, most ancient of all the sources we know of, the poet Arctinus.

On Arctinus see also the testimonia to the *Aethiopis*.

ARGUMENT

Proclus, *Chrestomathy*, with additions and variants from Apollodorus, *The Library*

This is succeeded by the two books of the *Sack of Ilion* by Arctinus of Miletus, with the following content:

[50] This half-line does not occur in the *Iliad* or *Odyssey*. Aeschines was perhaps thinking of the *Little Iliad*.

(1) †ὡς† τὰ περὶ τὸν ἵππον οἱ Τρῶες ὑπόπτως ἔχοντες περιστάντες βουλεύονται ὅ τι χρὴ ποιεῖν. καὶ <Κασσάνδρας λεγούσης ἔνοπλον ἐν αὐτῶι δύναμιν εἶναι, καὶ προσέτι Λαοκόωντος τοῦ μάντεως, Ap.> τοῖς μὲν δοκεῖ κατακρημνίσαι αὐτόν, τοῖς δὲ καταφλέγειν, οἳ δὲ ἱερὸν αὐτὸν ἔφασαν δεῖν τῆι Ἀθηνᾶι ἀνατεθῆναι· καὶ τέλος νικᾶι ἡ τούτων γνώμη. τραπέντες δὲ εἰς εὐφροσύνην εὐωχοῦνται ὡς ἀπηλλαγμένοι τοῦ πολέμου. ἐν αὐτῶι δὲ τ<ούτωι> <Ἀπόλλων αὐτοῖς σημεῖον ἐπιπέμπει· Ap.> δύο δράκοντες ἐπιφανέντες <διανηξάμενοι διὰ τῆς θαλάσσης ἐκ τῶν πλησίον νήσων Ap.> τόν τε Λαοκόωντα καὶ τὸν ἕτερον τῶν παίδων διαφθείρουσιν. ἐπὶ δὲ τῶι τέρατι δυσφορήσαντες οἱ περὶ τὸν Αἰνείαν ὑπεξῆλθον εἰς τὴν Ἴδην.

(2) καὶ Σίνων τοὺς πυρσοὺς ἀνίσχει τοῖς Ἀχαιοῖς, πρότερον εἰσεληλυθὼς προσποίητος· οἳ δὲ ἐκ Τενέδου προσπλεύσαντες, καὶ οἱ ἐκ τοῦ δουρείου ἵππου, ἐπιπίπτουσι τοῖς πολεμίοις. <ὡς δὲ ἐνόμισαν κοιμᾶσθαι τοὺς πολεμίους, ἀνοίξαντες σὺν τοῖς ὅπλοις ἐξήιεσαν· καὶ πρῶτος μὲν Ἐχίων Πορθέως ἀφαλλόμενος ἀπέθανεν· οἱ δὲ λοιποὶ σειρᾶι ἐξάψαντες ἑαυτοὺς ἐπὶ τὰ τείχη παρεγένοντο, καὶ τὰς πύλας ἀνοίξαντες ὑπεδέξαντο τοὺς ἀπὸ Τενέδου καταπλεύσαντας. Ap.> καὶ πολλοὺς ἀνελόντες τὴν πόλιν κατὰ κράτος λαμβάνουσι. καὶ Νεοπτόλεμος μὲν ἀποκτείνει Πρίαμον ἐπὶ τὸν τοῦ Διὸς τοῦ ἑρκείου βωμὸν καταφυγόντα· Μενέλαος δὲ ἀνευρὼν Ἑλένην ἐπὶ τὰς ναῦς κατάγει, Δηΐφοβον φονεύσας.

(1) The Trojans are suspicious in the matter of the horse, and stand round it debating what to do: <with Cassandra saying that it contained an armed force, and the seer Laocoon likewise,> some want to push it over a cliff, and some to set fire to it, but others say it is a sacred object to be dedicated to Athena, and in the end their opinion prevails. They turn to festivity and celebrate their deliverance from the war. But in the middle of this <Apollo sends them a sign:> two serpents appear, <swimming across the sea from the nearby islands,> and they kill Laocoon and one of his two sons. Feeling misgivings at the portent, Aeneas and his party slip away to Ida.

(2) Sinon holds up his firebrands for the Achaeans, having first entered the city under a pretence. They sail in from Tenedos, and with the men from the wooden horse they fall upon the enemy. <When they reckoned the enemy were asleep, they opened the horse and came out with their weapons. First Echion, the son of Portheus, jumped out, and was killed; the rest let themselves down with a rope, and reached the walls and opened the gates to let in those who had sailed back from Tenedos.> They put large numbers to death and seize the city. And Neoptolemus kills Priam, who has fled to the altar of Zeus of the Courtyard; Menelaus finds Helen and takes her to the ships after slaying Deiphobus.[51]

[51] Compare *Odyssey* 8.517 f.

(3) Κασσάνδραν δὲ Αἴας ὁ Ἰλέως πρὸς βίαν ἀποσπῶν συνεφέλκεται τὸ τῆς Ἀθηνᾶς ξόανον· ἐφ' ὧι παροξυνθέντες οἱ Ἕλληνες καταλεῦσαι βουλεύονται τὸν Αἴαντα· ὁ δὲ ἐπὶ τὸν τῆς Ἀθηνᾶς βωμὸν καταφεύγει, καὶ διασώιζεται ἐκ τοῦ ἐπικειμένου κινδύνου· ἐπεὶ δὲ ἀποπλέουσιν οἱ Ἕλληνες, φθορὰν αὐτῶι[7] ἡ Ἀθηνᾶ κατὰ τὸ πέλαγος μηχανᾶται.

(4) καὶ Ὀδυσσέως Ἀστυάνακτα ἀνελόντος, Νεοπτόλεμος Ἀνδρομάχην γέρας λαμβάνει, καὶ τὰ λοιπὰ λάφυρα διανέμονται. Δημοφῶν δὲ καὶ Ἀκάμας Αἴθραν εὑρόντες ἄγουσι μεθ' ἑαυτῶν. ἔπειτα ἐμπρήσαντες τὴν πόλιν Πολυξένην σφαγιάζουσιν ἐπὶ τὸν τοῦ Ἀχιλλέως τάφον.

FRAGMENTA

1 Schol. Monac. in Verg. *Aen.* 2.15, "instar montis equum"

Arctinus dicit fuisse in longitudine pedes C et in latitudine pedes L; cuius caudam et genua mobilia fuisse tradidit.

Servius auctus in Verg. *Aen.* 2.150, "immanis equi"

Hunc tamen equum quidam longum centum uiginti ‹pedes›, latum triginta fuisse tradunt, cuius cauda genua oculi mouerentur.

(3) Ajax the son of Ileus, in dragging Cassandra away by force, pulls Athena's wooden statue along with her. The Greeks are angry at this, and deliberate about stoning Ajax. But he takes refuge at Athena's altar, and so saves himself from the immediate danger. However, when the Greeks sail home, Athena contrives his destruction at sea.

(4) Odysseus kills Astyanax, Neoptolemus receives Andromache as his prize, and they divide up the rest of the booty. Demophon and Acamas find Aethra and take her with them. Then they set fire to the city, and slaughter Polyxena at Achilles' tomb.

FRAGMENTS

1 Scholiast on Virgil, "a horse like a mountain"

Arctinus says that it was 100 feet long and 50 feet wide, and that its tail and knees could move.

Servius auctus on Virgil, "the huge horse"

Some record that this horse was 120 feet long and 30 wide, and that its tail, knees, and eyes could move.

---

[7] *ἐπεὶ δὲ . . . φθορὰν αὐτῶι* West: *ἔπειτα . . . καὶ φθορὰν αὐτοῖς* cod.

2 Schol. (T) *Il.* 11.515, "ἰούς τ' ἐκτάμνειν"

ἔνιοι δέ φασιν ὡς οὐδὲ ἐπὶ πάντας τοὺς ἰατροὺς ὁ ἔπαινος οὗτός ἐστι κοινός, ἀλλ' ἐπὶ τὸν Μαχάονα, ὃν μόνον χειρουργεῖν τινες λέγουσι· τὸν γὰρ Ποδαλείριον διαιτᾶσθαι νόσους . . . τοῦτο ἔοικε καὶ Ἀρκτῖνος ἐν Ἰλίου πορθήσει νομίζειν, ἐν οἷς φησι·

αὐτὸς γάρ σφιν ἔδωκε πατὴρ <γέρας> Ἐννοσίγαιος
ἀμφοτέροις· ἕτερον δ' ἑτέρου κυδίον' ἔθηκεν·
τῶι μὲν κουφοτέρας χεῖρας πόρεν ἔκ τε βέλεμνα
σαρκὸς ἑλεῖν τμῆξαί τε καὶ ἕλκεα πάντ' ἀκέσασθαι,
τῶι δ' ἄρ' ἀκριβέα πάντα ἐνὶ στήθεσσιν ἔθηκεν
ἄσκοπά τε γνῶναι καὶ ἀναλθέα ἰήσασθαι·
ὅς ῥα καὶ Αἴαντος πρῶτος μάθε χωομένοιο
ὄμματά τ' ἀστράπτοντα βαρυνόμενόν τε νόημα.

3 Schol. Eur. *Andr.* 10

<οἳ δέ> φασιν ὅτι <οὐκ ἔμελλεν> ὁ Εὐριπίδης Ξάνθωι προσέχειν περὶ τῶν Τρωϊκῶν μύθων, τοῖς δὲ χρησιμωτέροις καὶ ἀξιοπιστοτέροις· Στησίχορον μὲν γὰρ (*PMGF* 202) ἱστορεῖν ὅτι τεθνήκοι, καὶ τὸν τὴν Πέρσιδα συντεταχότα κυκλικὸν ποιητὴν ὅτι καὶ ἀπὸ τοῦ τείχους ῥιφθείη, ὧι ἠκολουθηκέναι Εὐριπίδην.

2 Scholiast on the *Iliad*, "a doctor is worth many others when it comes to cutting arrows out"

But some say that this commendation does not apply generally to all doctors, but specially to Machaon, who certain people say was the only one to do surgery, as Podalirius tended illnesses . . . This seems to be the view also of Arctinus in the *Sack of Ilion*, where he says:

For their father the Earth-shaker[52] himself gave them both the healing gift; but he made one higher in prestige than the other. To the one he gave defter hands, to remove missiles from flesh and cut and heal all wounds, but in the other's heart he placed exact knowledge, to diagnose what is hidden and to cure what does not get better. He it was who first recognized the raging Ajax's flashing eyes and burdened spirit.

3 Scholiast on Euripides, *Andromache*

But others say that Euripides was not likely to pay attention to Xanthus on the myths about Troy, but only to the more serviceable and trustworthy sources: Stesichorus records that Astyanax was dead, and the Cyclic poet who composed the *Sack* that he was in fact hurled from the wall, and Euripides has followed him.

[52] Poseidon. But elsewhere Machaon and Podalirius are the sons of Asclepius.

4 Dion. Hal. *Ant. Rom.* 1.69.3

Ἀρκτῖνος δέ φησιν ὑπὸ Διὸς δοθῆναι Δαρδάνωι Παλλάδιον ἓν καὶ εἶναι τοῦτο ἐν Ἰλίωι τέως ἡ πόλις ἡλίσκετο, κεκρυμμένον ἐν ἀβάτωι· εἰκόνα δ' ἐκείνου κατεσκευασμένην ὡς μηδὲν τῆς ἀρχετύπου διαφέρειν ἀπάτης τῶν ἐπιβουλευόντων ἕνεκεν ἐν φανερῶι τεθῆναι, καὶ αὐτὴν Ἀχαιοὺς ἐπιβουλεύσαντας λαβεῖν.

5* Schol. (D) *Il.* 18.486a, "Πληϊάδες"

ἑπτὰ ἀστέρες . . . φασὶν δὲ Ἠλέκτραν οὐ βουλομένην τὴν Ἰλίου πόρθησιν θεάσαθαι διὰ τὸ κτίσμα τῶν ἀπογόνων καταλιπεῖν τὸν τόπον οὗ κατηστέριστο, διόπερ οὔσας πρότερον ἑπτὰ γενέσθαι ἕξ. ἡ ἱστορία παρὰ τοῖς κυκλικοῖς.

6 Schol. Eur. *Tro.* 31, "τὰς δὲ Θεσσαλὸς λεώς | εἴληχ' Ἀθηναίων τε Θησεῖδαι πρόμοι"

ἔνιοι ταῦτά φασι πρὸς χάριν εἰρῆσθαι, μηδὲν γὰρ εἰληφέναι τοὺς περὶ Ἀκάμαντα καὶ Δημοφῶντα ἐκ τῶν λαφύρων ἀλλὰ μόνην τὴν Αἴθραν, δι' ἣν καὶ ἀφίκοντο εἰς Ἴλιον Μενεσθέως ἡγουμένου. Λυσίμαχος δὲ (*FGrHist* 382 F 14) τὸν τὴν Πέρσιδα πεποιηκότα φησὶ γράφειν οὕτως·

> Θησείδαις δ' ἔπορεν δῶρα κρείων Ἀγαμέμνων
> ἠδὲ Μενεσθῆϊ μεγαλήτορι ποιμένι λαῶν.

4 Dionysius of Halicarnassus, *Roman Antiquities*

Arctinus says that a single Palladion was given by Zeus to Dardanus, and that this remained in Ilion while the city was being taken, concealed in an inner sanctum; an exact replica had been made of it and placed in the public area to deceive any who had designs on it, and it was this that the Achaeans schemed against and took.[53]

5* Scholiast on the *Iliad*, "the Pleiades"

Seven stars . . . They say that Electra, being unwilling to watch the sack of Ilion because it was a foundation of her descendants,[54] left the place where she had been set as a star, so that whereas they had previously been seven, they became six. The story is found in the Cyclic poets.

6 Scholiast on Euripides, *Trojan Women*, "and others the Thessalian host has received, and Theseus' sons, the lords of Athens"

Some say that this is said to please the audience, as Acamas and Demophon took nothing from the booty but only Aethra, on whose account they went to Ilion in the first place under Menestheus' leadership. But Lysimachus says that the author of the *Sack* writes as follows:

To the sons of Theseus the lord Agamemnon gave gifts,
and to great-hearted Menestheus, shepherd of peoples.

[53] This fragment has been suspected of reflecting a Roman claim to possess the true Palladion; see Nicholas Horsfall, *CQ* 29 (1979), 374 f. But the same claim may have been made in Arctinus' time by the Aineiadai in the Troad.

[54] She was the mother of Dardanus by Zeus, and so ancestor of Laomedon.

Ps.-Demosth. 60.29

ἐμέμνηντ᾽ Ἀκαμαντίδαι τῶν ἐπῶν ἐν οἷς Ὅμηρος ἕνεκα τῆς μητρός φησιν Αἴθρας Ἀκάμαντ᾽ εἰς Τροίαν στεῖλαι· ὃ μὲν οὖν παντὸς ἐπειρᾶτο κινδύνου τοῦ σῶσαι τὴν ἑαυτοῦ μητέρ᾽ ἕνεκα.

ΝΟΣΤΟΙ. ΑΤΡΕΙΔΩΝ ΚΑΘΟΔΟΣ

TESTIMONIA

Schol. Pind. *Ol.* 13.31a, see below, Testimonia to Eumelus.

Hesychius Milesius, *Vita Homeri* 6

ἀναφέρεται δὲ εἰς αὐτὸν καὶ ἄλλα τινὰ ποιήματα· Ἀμαζονία, Ἰλιὰς Μικρά, Νόστοι, κτλ.

Suda ν 500

νόστος· ἡ οἴκαδε ἐπάνοδος . . . καὶ οἱ ποιηταὶ δὲ οἱ τοὺς Νόστους ὑμνήσαντες ἕπονται τῶι Ὁμήρωι ἐς ὅσον εἰσὶ δυνατοί.

φαίνεται ὅτι οὐ μόνος εἷς εὑρισκόμενος ἔγραψε Νόστον Ἀχαιῶν ἀλλὰ καί τινες ἕτεροι ex marg. add. codd. GM.

Eust. *Od.* 1796.52

ὁ δὲ τοὺς Νόστους ποιήσας Κολοφώνιος . . . (*Telegonia* fr. 6).

Pseudo-Demosthenes, *Funeral Oration*

The Acamantids recalled the verses in which Homer says that Acamas went to Troy on account of his mother Aethra. He, then, experienced every danger for the sake of rescuing his own mother.[55]

THE RETURNS

TESTIMONIA

Scholiast on Pindar, *Olympian* 13.31a, see the testimonia to Eumelus.

Hesychius of Miletus, *Life of Homer*

Certain other poems are also attributed to him: the *Amazonia*, the *Little Iliad*, the *Returns*, etc.

The *Suda*

nostos: a return home. . . . And the poets who have celebrated *The Returns* follow Homer as far as they are able.

Two manuscripts add from the margin: It appears that it was not one poet alone who wrote *The Return of the Achaeans*, but several others too.

Eustathius, commentary on the *Odyssey*

The Colophonian poet of the *Returns* . . .

[55] Actually his grandmother. The orator has made a mistake.

ARGUMENTUM

Proclus, *Chrestomathia*, suppleta ex Apollod. epit. 6.1–30

συνάπτει δὲ τούτοις τὰ τῶν Νόστων βιβλία πέντε Ἁγίου Τροιζηνίου περιέχοντα τάδε·

(1) Ἀθηνᾶ Ἀγαμέμνονα καὶ Μενέλαον εἰς ἔριν καθίστησι περὶ τοῦ ἔκπλου. Ἀγαμέμνων μὲν οὖν τὸν τῆς Ἀθηνᾶς ἐξιλασόμενος χόλον ἐπιμένει· Διομήδης δὲ καὶ Νέστωρ ἀναχθέντες εἰς τὴν οἰκείαν διασώιζονται. μεθ' οὓς ἐκπλεύσας ὁ Μενέλαος, <χειμῶνι περιπεσών, Ap.> μετὰ πέντε νεῶν εἰς Αἴγυπτον παραγίνεται, τῶν λοιπῶν διαφθαρεισῶν νεῶν ἐν τῶι πελάγει.

(2) οἱ δὲ περὶ Κάλχαντα καὶ Λεοντέα καὶ Πολυποίτην πεζῆι πορευθέντες εἰς Κολοφῶνα Τειρεσίαν <Κάλχαντα Ap.> ἐνταῦθα τελευτήσαντα θάπτουσι.

(3) τῶν δὲ περὶ τὸν Ἀγαμέμνονα ἀποπλεόντων Ἀχιλλέως εἴδωλον ἐπιφανὲν πειρᾶται διακωλύειν προλέγον τὰ συμβησόμενα. <Ἀγαμέμνων δὲ θύσας ἀνάγεται, καὶ Τενέδωι προσίσχει· Νεοπτόλεμον δὲ πείθει Θέτις ἀφικομένη ἐπιμεῖναι δύο ἡμέρας καὶ θυσιάσαι, καὶ ἐπιμένει. οἱ δὲ ἀνάγονται, καὶ περὶ Τῆνον χειμάζονται· Ἀθηνᾶ γὰρ ἐδεήθη Διὸς τοῖς Ἕλλησι χειμῶνα ἐπιπέμψαι· καὶ πολλαὶ νῆες βυθίζονται. Ap.> εἶθ' ὁ περὶ τὰς Καφηρίδας πέτρας δηλοῦται χειμὼν καὶ ἡ Αἴαντος φθορὰ τοῦ Λοκροῦ. <καὶ ἐκβρασθέντα θάπτει Θέτις ἐν Μυκόνωι. Ap.>

RETURNS

ARGUMENT

Proclus, *Chrestomathy*, with additions and variants from Apollodorus, *The Library*

Connecting with this are the five books of the *Returns* by Agias of Troezen, with the following content:

(1) Athena sets Agamemnon and Menelaus in dispute about the voyage away. Agamemnon, to appease Athena's anger, waits behind; Diomedes and Nestor put out to sea and reach their homes safely.[56] After them Menelaus sails out, <encounters a storm, and> arrives in Egypt with five ships, the rest having been destroyed at sea.[57]

(2) The group around Calchas, Leonteus, and Polypoites[58] make their way on foot to Colophon; Teiresias[59] dies there and they bury him.

(3) When Agamemnon's party is preparing to sail, Achilles' ghost appears and tries to prevent them by foretelling what will happen. <Agamemnon sets out after making a sacrifice, and puts in at Tenedos, but Thetis comes to Neoptolemus and persuades him to wait for two days and make sacrifice, which he does. The others set sail, and meet with a storm near Tenos, for Athena had besought Zeus to send a storm on the Greeks; and many ships sink.> Then the storm around the Kapherian rocks[60] is described, and how the Locrian Ajax perished <and his body was washed up and buried by Thetis on Myconos>.

56 See *Odyssey* 3.130–183.

57 See *Odyssey* 3.276–300.

58 Apollodorus adds Amphilochus and Podalirius.

59 Apollodorus says Calchas, which makes much better sense.

60 The east-facing promontory at the southern end of Euboea. On the death of Ajax see *Odyssey* 4.499–510.

(4) Νεοπτόλεμος δὲ Θέτιδος ὑποθεμένης πεζῆι ποιεῖται τὴν πορείαν· καὶ παραγενόμενος εἰς Θράικην Ὀδυσσέα καταλαμβάνει ἐν τῆι Μαρωνείαι. καὶ τὸ λοιπὸν ἀνύει τῆς ὁδοῦ, καὶ τελευτήσαντα Φοίνικα θάπτει· αὐτὸς δὲ εἰς Μολοσσοὺς ἀφικόμενος ἀναγνωρίζεται Πηλεῖ.

(5) <ἔπει>τα Ἀγαμέμνονος ὑπὸ Αἰγίσθου καὶ Κλυταιμήστρας ἀναιρεθέντος ὑπ' Ὀρέστου καὶ Πυλάδου τιμωρία, καὶ Μενελάου εἰς τὴν οἰκείαν ἀνακομιδή.

FRAGMENTA

1 Paus. 10.28.7

ἡ δὲ Ὁμήρου ποίησις ἐς Ὀδυσσέα καὶ ἡ Μινυάς τε καλουμένη καὶ οἱ Νόστοι (μνήμη γὰρ δὴ καὶ ἐν ταύταις Ἅιδου καὶ τῶν ἐκεῖ δειμάτων ἐστίν) ἴσασιν οὐδένα Εὐρύνομον δαίμονα.

2* *Et. Gen.*, *Magn.*, *Gud.* s.v. νεκάδες

παρὰ μὲν τοῖς κυκλικοῖς αἱ ψυχαὶ νεκάδες λέγονται.

3 Ath. 281b

φιλήδονον δὲ οἱ ποιηταὶ καὶ τὸν ἀρχαῖόν φασι γενέσθαι Τάνταλον. ὁ γοῦν τὴν τῶν Ἀτρειδῶν ποιήσας κάθοδον ἀφικόμενον αὐτὸν λέγει πρὸς τοὺς θεοὺς καὶ συνδιατρίβοντα ἐξουσίας τυχεῖν παρὰ τοῦ Διὸς αἰτήσασθαι ὅτου ἐπιθυμεῖ· τὸν δέ, πρὸς τὰς ἀπολαύσεις ἀπλήστως διακεί-

(4) Neoptolemus, following Thetis' advice, makes his way by land. On coming to Thrace he finds Odysseus at Maronea. He completes the rest of his journey, and when Phoenix dies he buries him. He goes on as far as the Molossians, and is recognized by Peleus.[61]

(5) Then follow Orestes' and Pylades' avenging of Agamemnon's murder by Aegisthus and Clytaemestra, and Menelaus' return to his kingdom.[62]

FRAGMENTS

1 Pausanias, *Description of Greece*

But Homer's poem about Odysseus and the so-called *Minyas* and the *Returns* (for in these too there is mention of Hades and the terrors in it) know of no demon Eurynomus.

2 *Etymologicum Genuinum*

In the Cyclic poets the souls of the dead are called *nekades.*

3 Athenaeus, *Scholars at Dinner*

The poets say that old Tantalus too was a voluptuary. At any rate the author of the *Return of the Atreidai* tells that when he came to the gods and spent some time with them, and was granted the liberty by Zeus to ask for whatever he wanted, he,

[61] Apollodorus says that he became king of the Molossians after winning a battle and that Andromache bore him a son, Molossus.

[62] See *Odyssey* 3.303–312.

μενον, ὑπὲρ αὐτῶν τε τούτων μνείαν ποιήσασθαι καὶ τοῦ ζῆν τὸν αὐτὸν τρόπον τοῖς θεοῖς. ἐφ' οἷς ἀγανακτήσαντα τὸν Δία τὴν μὲν εὐχὴν ἀποτελέσαι διὰ τὴν ὑπόσχεσιν, ὅπως δὲ μηδὲν ἀπολαύηι τῶν παρακειμένων ἀλλὰ διατελῆι ταραττόμενος, ὑπὲρ τῆς κεφαλῆς ἐξήρτησεν αὐτῶι πέτρον, δι' ὃν οὐ δύναται τῶν παρακειμένων <ἡδονῆς> τυχεῖν οὐδενός.

4 Paus. 10.29.6

ἔστι δὲ πεποιημένα ἐν Νόστοις Μινύου μὲν τὴν Κλυμένην θυγατέρα εἶναι, γήμασθαι δὲ αὐτὴν Κεφάλωι τῶι Δηίονος, καὶ γενέσθαι σφίσιν Ἴφικλον παῖδα.

5 Paus. 10.30.5

ὑπὲρ τούτους Μαῖρά ἐστιν ἐπὶ πέτραι καθεζομένη. περὶ δὲ αὐτῆς πεποιημένα ἐστὶν ἐν Νόστοις ἀπελθεῖν μὲν παρθένον ἔτι ἐξ ἀνθρώπων, θυγατέρα δὲ αὐτὴν εἶναι Προίτου τοῦ Θερσάνδρου, τὸν δὲ εἶναι Σισύφου.

6 Argum. Eur. *Med.*

περὶ δὲ τοῦ πατρὸς αὐτοῦ (Ἰάσονος) Αἴσονος ὁ τοὺς Νόστους ποιήσας φησὶν οὕτως·

αὐτίκα δ' Αἴσονα θῆκε φίλον κόρον ἡβώοντα,
γῆρας ἀποξύσασα ἰδυίῃσι πραπίδεσσιν,
φάρμακα πόλλ' ἕψουσα ἐνὶ χρυσέοισι λέβησιν.

3 *ἐνὶ* Schneidewin: *ἐπὶ* codd.

being insatiably devoted to sensual pleasures, spoke of these, and of living in the same style as the gods. Zeus was angry at this, and fulfilled his wish, because of his promise, but so that he should get no enjoyment from what was set before him but suffer perpetual anxiety, he suspended a boulder over his head. Because of this he is unable to get <pleasure from> anything set before him.

4 Pausanias, *Description of Greece*

It is written in the poem *Returns* that Clymene was the daughter of Minyas, that she married Cephalus the son of Deion, and that their child was Iphiclus.

5 Pausanias, *Description of Greece*

Above these[63] is Maira, sitting on a rock. Concerning her it is written in the poem *Returns* that she departed from mankind still a virgin, and that she was the daughter of Proitos son of Thersander, and that he was a son of Sisyphus.

6 Argument of Euripides, *Medea*

About Jason's father Aison the poet of the *Returns* says:

And straightway she [Medea] made Aison a nice young lad, stripping away his old skin by her expertise, boiling various drugs in her golden cauldrons.

63 In Polygnotus' mural; see above on the *Little Iliad* (p. 135).

7 Clem. *Strom.* 6.12.7

Ἀντιμάχου τε τοῦ Τηΐου εἰπόντος· (*Epigoni* fr. 2) "ἐκ γὰρ δώρων πολλὰ κάκ' ἀνθρώποισι πέλονται," Ἀγίας ἐποίησεν·

δῶρα γὰρ ἀνθρώπων νόον ἤπαφεν ἠδὲ καὶ ἔργα.

Ἀγίας Thiersch: Αὐγ⟦ε⟧ίας cod.

8* Schol. *Od.* 2.120

Μυκήνη Ἰνάχου θυγάτηρ καὶ Μελίας τῆς Ὠκεανοῦ· ἧς καὶ Ἀρέστορος Ἄργος, ὡς ἐν τῶι κύκλωι φέρεται.

9 Philod. *De pietate* B 4901 Obbink

τὸν Ἀσκλ[ηπιὸν δ' ὑ]πὸ Διὸς κα[τακταν]θῆναι γεγρ[άφασιν Ἡ]σίοδος . . . λ[έγεται] δὲ καὶ ἐν τọ[ῖς Νόσ]τοις.

10 Poculum Homericum MB 36 (p. 101 Sinn)

[κατὰ τὸν ποιητὴν] Ἀ[γίαν] ἐκ τῶν [Νό]στωṿ Ἀχα[ι]ῶν. θάνατος Ἀγαμέμ[νο]νος. Comites Agamemnonis Ṇ ̣ị̣α̣ς, Ἀλκμέων, Μήστωρ Αἴαντος, quos aggrediuntur Ἀντίοχος et Ἀργεῖος.

7 Clement of Alexandria, *Miscellanies*

And where Antimachus of Teos had said "For from gifts much ill comes to mankind," Agias wrote:

For gifts delude people's minds and (corrupt) their actions.[64]

8* Scholiast on the *Odyssey*

Mycene was the daughter of Inachus and the Oceanid Melia. She and Arestor were the parents of Argos, as it is related in the Cycle.

9 Philodemus, *On Piety*

He]siod has written that Ascl[epius] was killed by Zeus . . . [It is sai]d also in t[he *Ret*]*urns*.

10 Caption to vase relief (third–second century BC)

[After the poet] A[gias], from the [*Re*]*turns of the Achaeans*: the death of Agamemnon.

The vase shows followers of Agamemnon named Alcmeon and Mestor son of Ajax, and a third whose name is illegible, reclining at a feast and being attacked by men called Antiochus and Argeios.

64 Probably an allusion to the bribing of Eriphyle.

11 Apollod. *Bibl.* 2.1.5

ἔγημεν (Ναύπλιος), ὡς μὲν οἱ τραγικοὶ λέγουσι, Κλυμένην τὴν Κατρέως, ὡς δὲ ὁ τοὺς Νόστους γράψας, Φιλύραν . . . καὶ ἐγέννησε Παλαμήδην Οἴακα Ναυσιμέδοντα.

12 Ath. 399a, "ψύαι"

ὁ τὴν τῶν Ἀτρειδῶν κάθοδον πεποιηκὼς ἐν τῶι τρίτωι φησίν·

Ἶσον δ' Ἑρμιονεὺς ποσὶ καρπαλίμοισι μετασπών
ψύας ἔγχεϊ νύξε.

2 ψοίας Kaibel.

13 Schol. *Od.* 4.12, "ἐκ δούλης"

αὕτη, ὡς μὲν Ἀλεξίων . . . ὡς δὲ ὁ τῶν Νόστων ποιητής, Γέτις.

11 Apollodorus, *The Library*

Nauplius married Clymene the daughter of Catreus, according to the tragedians, but according to the author of the *Returns* he married Philyra . . . and he fathered Palamedes, Oeax, and Nausimedon.[65]

12 Athenaeus, *Scholars at Dinner*

The poet of the *Return of the Atreidai* says in Book 3:

Hermioneus chased swiftly after Isus and stabbed him in the groin with his spear.[66]

13 Scholiast on the *Odyssey*

She[67] was, as Alexion says, . . . but as the poet of the *Returns* says, a Getic.[68]

65 Nauplius' sons came to assist Aegisthus and were killed by Orestes and Pylades (Pausanias 1.22.6, after a painting on the Acropolis).

66 Hermioneus was perhaps a son of Menelaus who assisted Orestes in the battle against Aegisthus' men.

67 The slave by whom Menelaus fathered Megapenthes (*Odyssey* 4.12).

68 The meaning may be that her name was Getis. But the poet had probably said ἐκ δούλης Γέτιδος, meaning "from a Getic slave." This is the earliest reference to the Getae, a Thracian tribe.

ΤΗΛΕΓΟΝΙΑ. ΘΕΣΠΡΩΤΙΣ

TESTIMONIA

Clem. *Strom.* 6.25.1

αὐτοτελῶς γὰρ τὰ ἑτέρων ὑφελόμενοι ὡς ἴδια ἐξ-ήνεγκαν, καθάπερ Εὐγάμμων ὁ Κυρηναῖος ἐκ Μουσαίου τὸ περὶ Θεσπρωτῶν βιβλίον ὁλόκληρον.

Phot. *Bibl.* 319a26

καὶ περατοῦται ὁ ἐπικὸς κύκλος ἐκ διαφόρων ποιητῶν συμπληρούμενος μέχρι τῆς ἀποβάσεως Ὀδυσσέως τῆς εἰς Ἰθάκην, ἐν ἧι καὶ ὑπὸ τοῦ παιδὸς Τηλεγόνου ἀγνοοῦντος κτείνεται.

Euseb. *Chron.*

Ol. 4.1: (v. ad Cinaethonem).

Ol. 53.2: Eugammon Cyrenaeus qui Telegoniam fecit agnoscitur.

Choerob.(?) περὶ ποσότητος, *An. Ox.* ii.299.26 (Herodian. i.249.9, ii.451.20 Lentz)

τὰ ἐπὶ πραγματείας ἤγουν συγγράμματος διὰ τῆς ει διφθόγγου γράφονται, οἷον Ὀδύσσεια ἡ κατὰ Ὀδυσσέα, Ἡράκλεια ἡ κατὰ Ἡρακλέα, Τηλεγόνεια ἡ κατὰ Τηλέγονον.

Cf. Eust. *Il.* 785.21.

TELEGONY. THESPROTIS

TESTIMONIA

Clement of Alexandria, *Miscellanies*

For on their own initiative (the Greeks) have stolen other people's works and brought them out as their own; as Eugammon of Cyrene stole from Musaeus his entire book about the Thesprotians.

Photius, *Library*

And the Epic Cycle is completed by being filled up from various poets as far as Odysseus' landing at Ithaca, where he is killed in ignorance by his son Telegonus.

Eusebius, *Chronicle*

Ol. 4.1: (see on Cinaethon).

Ol. 53.2 (567/566): Eugammon the Cyrenaean, who composed the *Telegony*, is recognized.

Choeroboscus(?), *On Syllabic Quantity*

Those that refer to a work (a written composition) are spelled with the diphthong *ei*, for example *Odysseia* for the work about Odysseus, *Herakleia* for that about Heracles, *Telegoneia* for that about Telegonus.

ARGUMENTUM

Proclus, *Chrestomathia*, suppleta ex Apollod. epit. 7.34–37

μετὰ ταῦτά ἐστιν Ὁμήρου Ὀδύσσεια· ἔπειτα Τηλεγονίας βιβλία δύο Εὐγάμμωνος Κυρηναίου περιέχοντα τάδε·

(1) οἱ μνήστορες ὑπὸ τῶν προσηκόντων θάπτονται. καὶ Ὀδυσσεὺς θύσας Νύμφαις εἰς Ἦλιν ἀποπλεῖ ἐπισκεψόμενος τὰ βουκόλια, καὶ ξενίζεται παρὰ Πολυξένωι δῶρόν τε λαμβάνει κρατῆρα, καὶ ἐπὶ τούτωι τὰ περὶ Τροφώνιον καὶ Ἀγαμήδην καὶ Αὐγέαν. ἔπειτα εἰς Ἰθάκην καταπλεύσας τὰς ὑπὸ Τειρεσίου ῥηθείσας τελεῖ θυσίας.

(2) καὶ μετὰ ταῦτα εἰς Θεσπρωτοὺς ἀφικνεῖται <καὶ κατὰ τὰς Τειρεσίου μαντείας θυσιάσας ἐξιλάσκεται Ποσειδῶνα, Ap.> καὶ γαμεῖ Καλλιδίκην βασιλίδα τῶν Θεσπρωτῶν. ἔπειτα πόλεμος συνίσταται τοῖς Θεσπρωτοῖς πρὸς Βρύγους, Ὀδυσσέως ἡγουμένου. ἐνταῦθα Ἄρης τοὺς περὶ τὸν Ὀδυσσέα τρέπεται, καὶ αὐτῶι εἰς μάχην Ἀθηνᾶ καθίσταται· τούτους μὲν Ἀπόλλων διαλύει. μετὰ δὲ τὴν Καλλιδίκης τελευτὴν τὴν μὲν βασιλείαν διαδέχεται Πολυποίτης Ὀδυσσέως υἱός, αὐτὸς δὲ εἰς Ἰθάκην ἀφικνεῖται. <καὶ εὑρίσκει ἐκ Πηνελόπης Πολιπόρθην αὐτῶι γεγεννημένον. Ap.>

(3) κἀν τούτωι Τηλέγονος <παρὰ Κίρκης μαθὼν ὅτι παῖς Ὀδυσσέως ἐστὶν Ap.> ἐπὶ ζήτησιν τοῦ πατρὸς

TELEGONY

ARGUMENT

Proclus, *Chrestomathy*, with additions and variants from Apollodorus, *The Library*

After this comes Homer's *Odyssey*, and then the two books of the *Telegony* by Eugammon of Cyrene, with the following content:

(1) The suitors are buried by their families. Odysseus, after sacrificing to the Nymphs, sails off to Elis to inspect his herds. He is entertained by Polyxenus, and receives the gift of a mixing bowl, on which is represented the story of Trophonius, Agamedes, and Augeas.[69] Then he sails back to Ithaca and performs the sacrifices specified by Teiresias.

(2) After this he goes to the land of the Thesprotians ‹and appeases Poseidon by making sacrifice in accord with Teiresias' prophecies›,[70] and marries the Thesprotian queen Callidice. Then war breaks out between the Thesprotians, led by Odysseus, and the Bryges. Ares turns Odysseus' forces to flight, and Athena faces him in combat, but Apollo pacifies them. After Callidice's death the kingdom passes to Polypoites, Odysseus' son, and he himself returns to Ithaca. ‹There he finds that Ptoliporthes has been born to him from Penelope.›

(3) Meanwhile Telegonus, ‹having learned from Circe that he is Odysseus' son,› has sailed in search of his father,

[69] Agamedes and Trophonius were commissioned by Augeas (Polyxenus' grandfather) to build him a treasure house. They made a secret door in it, which they made use of to enter and steal the treasure. Augeas set a trap, and Agamedes was caught in it; but Trophonius cut off his accomplice's head to conceal his identity, and escaped. Herodotus' story of Rhampsinitus (2.121) is another version of the same folk tale.

[70] See *Odyssey* 11.121–131.

πλέων ἀποβὰς εἰς τὴν Ἰθάκην τέμνει τὴν νῆσον· ἐκβοηθήσας δὲ Ὀδυσσεὺς ὑπὸ τοῦ παιδὸς ἀναιρεῖται κατ᾽ ἄγνοιαν. <καὶ Ὀδυσσέα βοηθοῦντα τῶι μετὰ χεῖρας δόρατι τρυγόνος κέντρον τὴν αἰχμὴν ἔχοντι τιτρώσκει, καὶ Ὀδυσσεὺς θνήισκει. Ap.>

(4) *Τηλέγονος δὲ ἐπιγνοὺς τὴν ἁμαρτίαν τό τε τοῦ πατρὸς σῶμα καὶ τὸν Τηλέμαχον καὶ τὴν Πηνελόπην πρὸς τὴν μητέρα μεθίστησιν· ἣ δὲ αὐτοὺς ἀθανάτους ποιεῖ <εἰς Μακάρων νήσους ἀποστέλλει* Ap.>, *καὶ συνοικεῖ τῆι μὲν Πηνελόπηι Τηλέγονος, Κίρκηι δὲ Τηλέμαχος.*

FRAGMENTA

1* Ath. 412d

γέρων τε ὢν (*Ὀδυσσεὺς*)

ἤσθιεν ἁρπαλέως κρέα τ᾽ ἄσπετα καὶ μέθυ ἡδύ.

2* Synes. *Epist.* 148

οὐ γὰρ σφᾶς ἐκ νυκτὸς ἐγείρει κῦμ᾽ ἐπιθρῶισκον.

Telegoniae ascripsit E. Livrea, *ZPE* 122 (1998) 3.

3 Paus. 8.12.5

καὶ ἐν δεξιᾶι τῆς ὁδοῦ γῆς χῶμα ὑψηλόν· Πηνελόπης δὲ εἶναι τάφον φασίν, οὐχ ὁμολογοῦντες τὰ ἐς αὐτὴν ποιήσει <τῆι> Θεσπρωτίδι ὀνομαζομένηι. ἐν ταύτηι μέν γέ

and after landing at Ithaca he is ravaging the island. Odysseus comes out to defend it and is killed by his son in ignorance. ‹And when Odysseus comes to defend it, he wounds him with the spear he carries, which has the barb of a sting ray as its point, and Odysseus dies.›[71]

(4) Telegonus, realizing his mistake, transports his father's body and Telemachus and Penelope to his mother. She makes them immortal ‹sends them to the Isles of the Blest›, and Telegonus sets up with Penelope, and Telemachus with Circe.

FRAGMENTS

1* Athenaeus, *Scholars at Dinner*

And Odysseus in his old age

ate heartily of abundant meat and sweet wine.

2* Synesius, *Epistles*

For they are not awakened at night by the crashing waves.

3 Pausanias, *Description of Greece*

And on the right of the road there is a high mound; they say it is the grave of Penelope, not agreeing in her regard with the poem called the *Thesprotis*. In this poem it is stated that

[71] This was taken as the fulfilment of Teiresias' prophecy in *Odyssey* 11.134 that death would come to Odysseus in a mild form and "from the sea." Others, however, rejecting the Telegonus story, held that the expression meant "away from the sea."

ἐστι τῆι ποιήσει ἐπανήκοντι ἐκ Τροίας Ὀδυσσεῖ τεκεῖν τὴν Πηνελόπην Πτολιπόρθην παῖδα.

4 Eust. *Od.* 1796.48

ὁ δὲ τὴν Τηλεγόνειαν γράψας Κυρηναῖος ἐκ μὲν Καλυψοῦς Τηλέγονον υἱὸν Ὀδυσσεῖ ἀναγράφει ἢ Τηλέδαμον, ἐκ δὲ Πηνελόπης Τηλέμαχον καὶ Ἀρκεσίλαον.

5 Schol. *Od.* 11.134, "θάνατος δέ τοι ἐξ ἁλός"

ἔξω τῆς ἁλός· οὐ γὰρ οἶδεν ὁ ποιητὴς τὰ κατὰ τὸν Τηλέγονον καὶ τὰ κατὰ τὸ κέντρον τῆς τρυγόνος.

ἔνιοι δέ . . . φασιν ὡς ἐντεύξει τῆς Κίρκης Ἥφαιστος κατεσκεύασε Τηλεμάχωι δόρυ ἐκ τρυγόνος θαλασσίας, ἣν Φόρκυς ἀνεῖλεν ἐσθίουσαν τοὺς ἐν τῆι Φορκίδι λίμνηι ἰχθῦς· οὗ τὴν μὲν ἐπιδορατίδα ἀδαμαντίνην, τὸν δὲ στύρακα χρυσοῦν εἶναι· ὧι τὸν Ὀδυσσέα ἀνεῖλεν.

οἱ νεώτεροι τὰ περὶ Τηλέγονον ἀνέπλασαν τὸν Κίρκης καὶ Ὀδυσσέως, ὃς δοκεῖ κατὰ ζήτησιν τοῦ πατρὸς εἰς Ἰθάκην ἐλθὼν ὑπ' ἀγνοίας τὸν πατέρα διαχρήσασθαι τρυγόνος κέντρωι.

6 Eust. *Od.* 1796.52

ὁ δὲ τοὺς Νόστους ποιήσας Κολοφώνιος Τηλέμαχον μέν φησι τὴν Κίρκην ὕστερον γῆμαι, Τηλέγονον δὲ τὸν ἐκ Κίρκης ἀντιγῆμαι Πηνελόπην.

after Odysseus returned from Troy Penelope bore him a son Ptoliporthes.

4 Eustathius, commentary on the *Odyssey*

The Cyrenaean author of the *Telegony* records Telegonus (or Teledamus) as Odysseus' son from Calypso, and Telemachus and Arcesilaus as his sons from Penelope.[72]

5 Scholia on the *Odyssey*, "and death will come to you from the sea"

Meaning away from the sea; the poet does not know the story about Telegonus and the barb of the sting ray.

But some . . . say that on a visit to Circe Hephaestus made Telegonus a spear from a sting ray that Phorcys had killed when it was eating the fish in Phorcys' lake. Its head was of adamant, and its shaft of gold. With it he killed Odysseus.

Post-Homeric writers invented the story of Telegonus the son of Circe and Odysseus, who is supposed to have gone to Ithaca in search of his father and killed him in ignorance with the barb of a sting ray.

6 Eustathius, commentary on the *Odyssey*

The Colophonian poet of the *Returns* says that Telemachus afterwards married Circe, while Telegonus, the son from Circe, married Penelope.[73]

[72] "Calypso" is an error for Circe. "Telegonus or Teledamus" is Eustathius' characteristic way of noting variants he found in his manuscripts. Arcesilaus is probably an alternative name for Ptoliporthes. [73] This time Eustathius has got Telegonus' mother right but made a mistake about the poem.

POEMS ON HERACLES AND THESEUS

ΚΡΕΩΦΥΛΟΥ ΟΙΧΑΛΙΑΣ ΑΛΩΣΙΣ

TESTIMONIA

Strabo 14.1.18

Σάμιος δ' ἦν καὶ Κρεώφυλος, ὅν φασι δεξάμενον ξενίαι ποτὲ Ὅμηρον λαβεῖν δῶρον τὴν ἐπιγραφὴν τοῦ ποιήματος ὃ καλοῦσιν Οἰχαλίας ἅλωσιν. Καλλίμαχος δὲ τοὐναντίον ἐμφαίνει δι' ἐπιγράμματός τινος, ὡς ἐκείνου μὲν ποιήσαντος, λεγομένου δ' Ὁμήρου διὰ τὴν λεγομένην ξενίαν (Call. *Epigr.* 6 Pf.)·

τοῦ Σαμίου πόνος εἰμί, δόμωι ποτὲ θεῖον ἀοιδόν
　δεξαμένου, κλείω δ' Εὔρυτον ὅσσ' ἔπαθεν
καὶ ξανθὴν Ἰόλειαν· Ὁμήρειον δὲ καλεῦμαι
　γράμμα. Κρεωφύλωι, Ζεῦ φίλε, τοῦτο μέγα.

τινὲς δὲ διδάσκαλον Ὁμήρου τοῦτόν φασιν· οἱ δ' οὐ τοῦτον ἀλλ' Ἀριστέαν τὸν Προκοννήσιον.

Clem. *Strom.* 6.25.1, see below, Testimonia to Panyassis.

POEMS ON HERACLES AND THESEUS

CREOPHYLUS, *THE CAPTURE OF OICHALIA*

TESTIMONIA

Strabo, *Geography*

Another Samian was Creophylus, who they say once received Homer as his guest and was rewarded with the attribution of the poem known as the *Capture of Oichalia*. But Callimachus indicates the converse in an Epigram, that Creophylus composed it but that it was called Homer's as a result of the said hospitality:

> I am the work of the Samian, who once received in his house the divine bard, and I celebrate Eurytus' misfortunes and the flaxen-haired Iole; but I am known as a writing of Homer's—dear Zeus, a great compliment to Creophylus!

And some say this man was Homer's teacher, though others say it was not he but Aristeas of Proconnesus.

Clement of Alexandria, *Miscellanies*: see below, Testimonia to Panyassis.

Proclus, *Vita Homeri* 5

λέγουσιν οὖν αὐτὸν εἰς Ἴον πλεύσαντα διατρῖψαι μὲν παρὰ Κρεωφύλωι, γράψαντα δὲ Οἰχαλίας ἅλωσιν τούτωι χαρίσασθαι· ἥτις νῦν ὡς Κρεωφύλου περιφέρεται.

Hesychius Milesius, *Vita Homeri* 6

ἀναφέρεται δὲ εἰς αὐτὸν καὶ ἄλλα τινὰ ποιήματα· Ἀμαζονία, Ἰλιὰς Μικρά . . . Οἰχαλίας ἅλωσις . . .

Suda κ 2376 (ex Hesychio Milesio)

Κρεώφυλος Ἀστυκλέους, Χῖος ἢ Σάμιος, ἐποποιός. τινὲς δὲ αὐτὸν ἱστόρησαν Ὁμήρου γαμβρὸν ἐπὶ θυγατρί, οἱ δὲ φίλον μόνον γεγονέναι αὐτὸν Ὁμήρου λέγουσι, καὶ ὑποδεξάμενον Ὅμηρον λαβεῖν παρ᾽ αὐτοῦ τὸ ποίημα τὴν τῆς Οἰχαλίας ἅλωσιν.

Cf. schol. Plat. *Resp.* 600b; Phot. *Lex.* s.v. Κρεόφυλος.

FRAGMENTA

1 *Epimerismi Homerici* o 96 Dyck

τοῦτο δὲ εὑρήσομεν καὶ ἐν τῆι <Οἰ>χαλίας ἁλώσει, ἣ εἰς Ὅμηρον ἀναφέρεται, ἔστι δὲ Κρεώφυλος ὁ ποιήσας· Ἡρακλῆς δ᾽ ἐστιν ὁ λέγων πρὸς Ἰόλην·

> "ὦ γύναι, <αὐτὴ> ταῦτά γ᾽ ἐν ὀφθαλμοῖσιν
> ὅρηαι."

αὐτὴ suppl. Köchly *γ᾽* Peppmüller: *τ᾽* cod.

CREOPHYLUS

Proclus, *Life of Homer*

So they say he sailed to Ios and spent time with Creophylus, and when he wrote the *Capture of Oichalia*, he gave it to him, and it is now current under Creophylus' name.

Hesychius of Miletus, *Life of Homer*

Certain other poems are also attributed to him: the *Amazonia*, the *Little Iliad* . . . the *Capture of Oichalia* . . .

The *Suda* (from Hesychius of Miletus, *Index of Famous Authors*)

Creophylus son of Astycles, from Chios or Samos, epic poet. Some relate that he was Homer's son-in-law, while others say that he was just Homer's friend, and that after giving Homer hospitality he received from him the poem *The Capture of Oichalia*.

FRAGMENTS

1 *Homeric Parsings*

We shall find this form (ὄρηαι) also in the *Capture of Oichalia*, which is attributed to Homer, though Creophylus is its author. Heracles is addressing Iole:

"Lady, you can see this with your <own> eyes."

2 Strabo 9.5.17

τὴν δ' Οἰχαλίαν πόλιν Εὐρύτου λεγομένην ἔν τε τοῖς τόποις τούτοις ἱστοροῦσι καὶ ἐν Εὐβοίαι καὶ ἐν Ἀρκαδίαι . . . περὶ δὲ τούτων ζητοῦσι, καὶ μάλιστα τίς ἦν ἡ ὑπὸ Ἡρακλέους ἁλοῦσα, καὶ περὶ τίνος συνέγραψεν ὁ ποιήσας τὴν Οἰχαλίας ἅλωσιν.

Paus. 4.2.3

Θεσσαλοὶ δὲ καὶ Εὐβοεῖς (ἥκει γὰρ δὴ ἐς ἀμφισβήτησιν τῶν ἐν τῆι Ἑλλάδι <τὰ> πλείω) λέγουσιν, οἳ μὲν ὡς τὸ Εὐρύτιον - χωρίον δὲ ἔρημον ἐφ' ἡμῶν ἐστι τὸ Εὐρύτιον - πόλις τὸ ἀρχαῖον ἦν καὶ ἐκαλεῖτο Οἰχαλία· τῶι δὲ Εὐβοέων λόγωι Κρεώφυλος ἐν Ἡρακλείαι πεποίηκεν ὁμολογοῦντα.

3 Schol. Soph. *Trach.* 266

διαφωνεῖται δὲ ὁ τῶν Εὐρυτιδῶν ἀριθμός· Ἡσίοδος μὲν γὰρ δ' φησιν (fr. 26.27–31) . . . *Κρεώφυλος δὲ β', Ἀριστοκράτης δὲ* (*FGrHist* 591 F 6) *γ', Τοξέα Κλυτίον Δηίονα.*

ΠΕΙΣΑΝΔΡΟΥ ΗΡΑΚΛΕΙΑ

TESTIMONIA

Theocritus, *Epigr.* 22

τὸν τοῦ Ζανὸς ὅδ' ὑμὶν υἱὸν ὡνήρ

2 Strabo, *Geography*

They locate Oichalia, famed as the city of Eurytus, both in these parts[1] and in Euboea and in Arcadia . . . They investigate these questions, and above all which was the Oichalia taken by Heracles, and which one the author of the *Capture of Oichalia* wrote about.

Pausanias, *Description of Greece*

The Thessalians and Euboeans (most things in Greece being controversial) say, in the latter case that Eurytion, a deserted site in my time, was anciently a city and was called Oichalia; and Creophylus in his *Heraclea*[2] has written things in agreement with the Euboeans' story.

3 Scholiast on Sophocles, *Trachiniae*

There is disagreement about the number of Eurytus' sons: Hesiod says there were four . . ., Creophylus two, and Aristocrates three, Toxeus, Clytius, and Deion.

PISANDER, *HERACLEA*

TESTIMONIA

Theocritus, epigram for a statue

This man first of the poets of old, Pisander of Camirus,

[1] The Thessalian Hestiaiotis.
[2] Evidently Pausanias' name for *The Capture of Oichalia*.

τὸν λεοντομάχαν, τὸν ὀξύχειρα,
πρᾶτος τῶν ἐπάνωθε μουσοποιῶν
Πείσανδρος συνέγραψεν οὑκ Καμίρου
χὤσσους ἐξεπόνασεν εἶπ' ἀέθλους.

Strabo 14.2.13

καὶ Πείσανδρος δ' ὁ τὴν Ἡράκλειαν γράψας ποιητὴς Ῥόδιος.

Steph. Byz. s.v. *Κάμιρος*

Πείσανδρος δὲ ὁ διασημότατος ποιητὴς Καμιρεὺς ἦν.

Quintil. *Inst. or.* 10.1.56

Quid? Herculis acta non bene Pisandros?

Clem. *Strom.* 6.25.1

αὐτοτελῶς γὰρ τὰ ἑτέρων ὑφελόμενοι ὡς ἴδια ἐξήνεγκαν, καθάπερ Εὐγάμμων . . . καὶ Πείσανδρος ‹ὁ› Καμιρεὺς Πεισίνου τοῦ Λινδίου τὴν Ἡράκλειαν.

Anon. frag. de musica, *Gramm. Lat.* vi.607 Keil (ex Aristoxeno, fr. 92 Wehrli)

Prior est musicá inventione metrica; cum sint enim antiquissimi poetarum Homerus, Hesiodus, Pisander, hos secuti elegiarii . . .

wrote up the son of Zeus, the lion-battler, the fierce of hand, and told of all the labors he worked his way through.

Strabo, *Geography*

Pisander too, the poet who wrote the *Heraclea*, was a Rhodian.

Stephanus of Byzantium, *Geographical Lexicon*

And Pisander the celebrated poet was from Camirus.

Quintilian, *Training in Oratory*

Did Pisander not treat well of the deeds of Hercules?

Clement of Alexandria, *Miscellanies*

For on their own initiative (the Greeks) have stolen other people's works and brought them out as their own; as Eugammon . . . and Pisander of Camirus stole the *Heraclea* from Pisinous of Lindos.

Anonymous fragment on music (from Aristoxenus)

The invention of music was preceded by that of meter. For whereas the most ancient poets are Homer, Hesiod, and Pisander, and they were followed by the elegiac poets, etc.

Proclus, *Vita Homeri* 1

ἐπῶν ποιηταὶ γεγόνασι πολλοί· τούτων δ' εἰσὶ κράτιστοι Ὅμηρος, Ἡσίοδος, Πείσανδρος, Πανύασσις, Ἀντίμαχος.

Cf. eiusdem *Chrestomathiam* ap. Phot. *Bibl.* 319a.

Suda π 1465 (ex Hesychio Milesio)

Πείσανδρος Πείσωνος καὶ Ἀρισταίχμας, Καμιραῖος ἀπὸ Ῥόδου· Κάμιρος γὰρ ἦν πόλις Ῥόδου. καί τινες μὲν αὐτὸν Εὐμόλπου (Εὐμήλου?) τοῦ ποιητοῦ σύγχρονον καὶ ἐρώμενον ἱστοροῦσι, τινὲς δὲ καὶ Ἡσιόδου πρεσβύτερον, οἱ δὲ κατὰ τὴν λγ' ὀλυμπιάδα (= 648/5) τάττουσι. ἔσχε δὲ καὶ ἀδελφὴν Διόκλειαν. ποιήματα δὲ αὐτοῦ Ἡράκλεια ἐν βιβλίοις β'· ἔστι δὲ τὰ Ἡρακλέους ἔργα· ἔνθα πρῶτος Ἡρακλεῖ ῥόπαλον περιτέθεικε. τὰ δὲ ἄλλα τῶν ποιημάτων νόθα αὐτοῦ δοξάζεται, γενόμενα ὑπό τε ἄλλων καὶ Ἀριστέως τοῦ ποιητοῦ.

FRAGMENTA

1 [Eratosth.] *Catast.* 12

Λέων· οὗτός ἐστι μὲν τῶν ἐπιφανῶν ἄστρων. δοκεῖ δ' ὑπὸ Διὸς τιμηθῆναι τοῦτο τὸ ζώδιον διὰ τὸ τῶν τετραπόδων ἡγεῖσθαι. τινὲς δέ φασιν ὅτι Ἡρακλέους πρῶτος οὗτος ἆθλος ἦν εἰς τὸ μνημονευθῆναι· φιλοδοξῶν γὰρ μόνον

Proclus, *Life of Homer*

There have been many hexameter poets; the chief among them are Homer, Hesiod, Pisander, Panyassis, and Antimachus.[3]

The *Suda* (from Hesychius of Miletus, *Index of Famous Authors*)

Pisander son of Piso and Aristaechma, a Camirian from Rhodes. (Camirus was a city of Rhodes.) Some make him the contemporary and the loved one of the poet Eumolpus (Eumelus?), but some date him even before Hesiod, and others place him in the 33rd Olympiad [= 648/645 BC]. He had a sister Dioclea. His poetry consists of the *Heraclea*, in two books, an account of Heracles' deeds, in which he was the first to equip Heracles with a club.[4] His other poems are considered spurious, the work of others including the poet Aristeus.[5]

FRAGMENTS

1 Pseudo-Eratosthenes, *Catasterisms*

Leo: this is one of the conspicuous constellations. It is held that this zodiacal animal was honored by Zeus[6] because of its being the first among the beasts. But some say that this was the first of Heracles' Labors to be commemorated; for this was the

[3] This canonical list of five epic poets is repeated by Tzetzes in several places. [4] Compare fr. 1. According to Megaclides, Stesichorus (*PMGF* 229, compare S16) was the first to represent Heracles as wearing a lionskin and carrying a bow and club.

[5] Aristeas of Proconnesus may be meant.

[6] That is, in being set among the stars.

τοῦτον οὐχ ὅπλοις ἀνεῖλεν, ἀλλὰ συμπλακεὶς ἀπέπνιξεν. λέγει δὲ περὶ αὐτοῦ Πείσανδρος ὁ Ῥόδιος. ὅθεν καὶ τὴν δορὰν αὐτοῦ ἔσχεν, ὡς ἔνδοξον ἔργον πεποιηκώς.

Cf. Hygin. *Astr.* 2.24; schol. German. *Arat.* pp. 71 et 131 Breysig.

Strabo 15.1.8

τῶν δὲ κοινωνησάντων αὐτῶι τῆς στρατείας ἀπογόνους εἶναι τοὺς Σίβας, σύμβολα τοῦ γένους σώιζοντας τό τε δορὰς ἀμπέχεσθαι καθάπερ τὸν Ἡρακλέα καὶ τὸ σκυταληφορεῖν καὶ ἐπικεκαῦσθαι βουσὶ καὶ ἡμιόνοις ῥόπαλον . . . (9) καὶ ἡ τοῦ Ἡρακλέους δὲ στολὴ ἡ τοιαύτη πολὺ νεωτέρα τῆς Τρωϊκῆς μνήμης ἐστί, πλάσμα τῶν τὴν Ἡράκλειαν ποιησάντων, εἴτε Πείσανδρος ἦν εἴτ᾽ ἄλλος τις· τὰ δ᾽ ἀρχαῖα ξόανα οὐχ οὕτω διεσκεύασται.

2 Paus. 2.37.4

κεφαλὴν δὲ εἶχεν ἐμοὶ δοκεῖν μίαν καὶ οὐ πλείονας, Πείσανδρος δὲ ὁ Καμιρεύς, ἵνα τὸ θηρίον τε δοκοίη φοβερώτερον καὶ αὐτῶι γίνηται ἡ ποίησις ἀξιόχρεως μᾶλλον, ἀντὶ τούτων τὰς κεφαλὰς ἐποίησε τῆι ὕδραι τὰς πολλάς.

3 Schol. Pind. *Ol.* 3.50b

θήλειαν δὲ εἶπε καὶ χρυσοκέρων ἀπὸ ἱστορίας· ὁ γὰρ <τὴν> Θησηΐδα γράψας (fr. 2) τοιαύτην αὐτὴν <λέγει>, καὶ Πείσανδρος ὁ Καμιρεὺς καὶ Φερεκύδης (fr. 71 Fowler).

only creature that in his eagerness for fame he did not kill with weapons but wrestled with and throttled. Pisander of Rhodes tells about it. That was why he got its skin, because he had accomplished a famous deed.

Strabo, *Geography*

They say that the Sibai[7] are descendants of those who accompanied Heracles on this expedition, and that as a token of their lineage they wear skins like Heracles, carry staves, and brand their cattle and mules with the device of a club . . . This manner of equipping Heracles, too, is much more recent than the Trojan saga, a fiction of whoever wrote the *Heraclea*, whether it was Pisander or someone else; the old wooden statues of him are not fashioned like this.

2 Pausanias, *Description of Greece*

In my opinion the Hydra had one head, not more, but Pisander of Camirus, desiring to make the creature more frightful and his own poem more noteworthy, gave it its many heads for these reasons.

3 Scholiast on Pindar, *Olympians*

He made it [the Cerynian Hind] female and gold-horned on the basis of legend; for the author of the *Theseis* describes it like that, as do Pisander of Camirus and Pherecydes.

[7] An Indian tribe.

4 Paus. 8.22.4

Πείσανδρος δὲ αὐτὸν ὁ Καμιρεὺς ἀποκτεῖναι τὰς ὄρνιθας οὔ φησιν, ἀλλὰ ὡς ψόφωι κροτάλων ἐκδιώξειεν αὐτάς.

5 Ath. 469c

Πείσανδρος ἐν δευτέρωι Ἡρακλείας τὸ δέπας ἐν ὧι διέπλευσεν ὁ Ἡρακλῆς τὸν Ὠκεανὸν εἶναι μέν φησιν Ἡλίου, λαβεῖν δ' αὐτὸ παρ' Ὠκεαν<οῦ τ>ὸν Ἡρακλέα.

6 Schol. Pind. *Pyth.* 9.185a

ὄνομα δὲ αὐτῆι Ἀλκηΐς, ὥς φησι Πείσανδρος ὁ Καμιρεύς.

7 Schol. Ar. *Nub.* 1051a

οἳ δέ φασιν ὅτι τῶι Ἡρακλεῖ πολλὰ μογήσαντι περὶ Θερμοπύλας ἡ Ἀθηνᾶ θερμὰ λουτρὰ ἐπαφῆκεν, ὡς Πείσανδρος·

τῶι δ' ἐν Θερμοπύληισι θεὰ γλαυκῶπις Ἀθήνη
ποίει θερμὰ λοετρὰ παρὰ ῥηγμῖνι θαλάσσης.

Cf. Zenob. vulg. 6.49; Diogenian. 5.7; Harpocr. Θ 11.

8* Stob. 3.12.6

Πεισάνδρου·

οὐ νέμεσις καὶ ψεῦδος ὑπὲρ ψυχῆς ἀγορεύειν.

4 Pausanias, *Description of Greece*

Pisander of Camirus says that (Heracles) did not kill the (Stymphalian) birds, but scared them off with the noise of clappers.

5 Athenaeus, *Scholars at Dinner*

Pisander in Book 2 of the *Heraclea* says that the cup in which Heracles sailed across Oceanus belonged to the Sun god, but that Heracles got it from Oceanus.

6 Scholiast on Pindar, *Pythians*

The name of Antaeus' daughter was Alceïs, according to Pisander of Camirus.

7 Scholiast on Aristophanes, *Clouds*

Some say that when Heracles had toiled strenuously in the neighborhood of Thermopylae Athena sent forth hot springs for him, as Pisander has it:

For him at Thermopylae the steely-eyed goddess Athena
made hot bathing-places beside the seashore.

8* Stobaeus, *Anthology*

Pisander:

There is no blame in telling a lie to save one's life.

9* Hesych. ν 683

νοῦς οὐ παρὰ Κενταύροισι·

παροιμιῶδες. ἔστι δὲ Πεισάνδρου κομμάτιον, ἐπὶ τῶν ἀδυνάτων ταττόμενον.

Cf. Diogenian. 6.84; Macar. 6.12; Apostol. 12.12; Phot. s.v., *Suda* ν 525.

οὐ παρὰ Hesych. etc.: οὐκ ἔνι Phot., *Suda*.

10 Ath. 783c

Πείσανδρος δέ φησιν Ἡρακλέα Τελαμῶνι τῆς ἐπὶ Ἴλιον στρατείας ἀριστεῖον ἄλεισον δοῦναι.

11 *Epimerismi Homerici* A 52B Dyck

ἔστι δὲ καὶ

ἀέ

παρὰ Πεισάνδρωι τῶι Καμειρεῖ.

Cf. *Et. Gud.* s.v. ἀεί.

12 Plut. *De Herodoti malignitate* 857f

καίτοι τῶν παλαιῶν καὶ λογίων ἀνδρῶν οὐχ Ὅμηρος, οὐχ Ἡσίοδος, οὐκ Ἀρχίλοχος, οὐ Πείσανδρος, οὐ Στησίχορος, οὐκ Ἀλκμάν, οὐ Πίνδαρος Αἰγυπτίου λόγον ἔσχον Ἡρακλέους ἢ Φοίνικος, ἀλλ᾽ ἕνα τοῦτον ἴσασι πάντες Ἡρακλέα τὸν Βοιώτιον ὁμοῦ καὶ Ἀργεῖον.

9* Hesychius, *Lexicon*

There is no sense with the Centaurs.

A proverbial saying. It is a phrase from Pisander, applied to impossible situations.

10 Athenaeus, *Scholars at Dinner*

Pisander says that Heracles gave Telamon a goblet as a prize for heroism in the campaign against Ilion.

11 *Homeric Parsings* (on the forms of the word *aiei*, "always")

There is also *ae* in Pisander of Camirus.

12 Plutarch, *On the Malice of Herodotus*

Yet of the ancient men of letters neither Homer nor Hesiod, Archilochus, Pisander, Stesichorus, Alcman, or Pindar took note of an Egyptian or Phoenician Heracles: all of them know only this one Heracles, the Boeotian and Argive one.

ΠΑΝΥΑΣΣΙΔΟΣ ΗΡΑΚΛΕΙΑ

TESTIMONIA

Suda π 248 (ex Hesychio Milesio)

Πανύασις Πολυάρχου Ἁλικαρνασσεύς, τερατοσκόπος καὶ ποιητὴς ἐπῶν, ὃς σβεσθεῖσαν τὴν ποιητικὴν ἐπανήγαγε. Δοῦρις δὲ (*FGrHist* 76 F 64) Διοκλέους τε παῖδα ἀνέγραψε καὶ Σάμιον, ὁμοίως δὲ καὶ Ἡρόδοτον Θούριον. ἱστόρηται δὲ Πανύασις Ἡροδότου τοῦ ἱστορικοῦ ἐξάδελφος· γέγονε γὰρ Πανύασις Πολυάρχου, ὁ δὲ Ἡρόδοτος Λύξου τοῦ Πολυάρχου ἀδελφοῦ. τινὲς δὲ οὐ Λύξην ἀλλὰ Ῥοιὼ τὴν μητέρα Ἡροδότου Πανυάσιδος ἀδελφὴν ἱστόρησαν. ὁ δὲ Πανύασις γέγονε κατὰ τὴν οη´ ὀλυμπιάδα· κατὰ δέ τινας πολλῶι πρεσβύτερος· καὶ γὰρ ἦν ἐπὶ τῶν Περσικῶν. ἀνῃρέθη δὲ ὑπὸ Λυγδάμιδος τοῦ τρίτου τυραννήσαντος Ἁλικαρνασσοῦ. ἐν δὲ ποιηταῖς τάττεται μεθ᾽ Ὅμηρον, κατὰ δέ τινας καὶ μετὰ Ἡσίοδον καὶ Ἀντίμαχον. ἔγραψε δὲ καὶ Ἡράκλειαν ἐν βιβλίοις ιδ´ εἰς ἔπη ͵θ´, Ἰωνικὰ ἐν πενταμέτρωι (ἔστι δὲ τὰ περὶ Κόδρον καὶ Νηλέα καὶ τὰς Ἰωνικὰς ἀποικίας) εἰς ἔπη ͵ζ´.

Merkelbach–Stauber, *Steinepigramme aus dem griechischen Osten* 01/12/01 = *IG* 12(1).145

κοὺ] μὴν Ἡροδότου γλύκιον στόμα καὶ Πανύασσιν

PANYASSIS, *HERACLEA*

TESTIMONIA

The *Suda* (from Hesychius of Miletus, *Index of Famous Authors*)

Panyassis the son of Polyarchus, from Halicarnassus, interpreter of prodigies and hexameter poet, who restored the art of verse from extinction. Duris, however, registers him as the son of Diocles and as a Samian, just as he makes Herodotus come from Thurii.[8] Panyassis is recorded as being the cousin of the historian Herodotus, for Panyassis was the son of Polyarchus, and Herodotus of Polyarchus' brother Lyxes. Some, however, relate that it was not Lyxes but Herodotus' mother Rhoio that was Panyassis' sister. Panyassis is dated to about the 78th Olympiad (= 468/465 BC); or according to some, considerably earlier, as he lived at the time of the Persian Wars. He was put to death by Lygdamis, the third tyrant of Halicarnassus. As a poet he is ranked after Homer, and by some authorities also after Hesiod and Antimachus. He wrote a *Heraclea* in fourteen books, to the sum of 9,000 verses; *Ionica* in elegiacs, dealing with Codrus, Neleus, and the Ionian colonies, to the sum of 7,000 verses.

Hellenistic verse inscription from Halicarnassus

Nor was it ancient Babylon that nurtured Herodotus'

[8] The point is that Duris denied Halicarnassus' claims to both of its major authors.

ἡ̣[δυ]ε̣π̣ῆ Βαβυλὼν ἔτρεφεν ὠγυγίη,
ἀλλ᾽ Ἁλικαρνασσοῦ κραναὸν πέδον· ὧν διὰ μολπάς
κλειτὸν ἐν Ἑλλήνων ἄστεσι κῦδος ἔχει.

Ibid. 01/12/02 de Halicarnasso

ἔσπειρεν Πανύασσιν ἐπῶν ἀρίσημον ἄνακτα,
Ἰλιακῶν Κυπρίαν τίκτεν ἀοιδοθέτην.

Inscr. in poetae effigie, Mus. Neapol. inv. 6152 (I. Sgobbo, *Rendiconti dell'Accademia Archeologica di Napoli* 46 [1971] 115 sqq.)

Πανύασσις ὁ ποιητὴς {ς´} λυπηρότατός ἐστι.

Dion. Hal. *De imitatione* fr. 6.2.2–4

Ἡσίοδος μὲν γὰρ ἐφρόντισεν ἡδονῆς δι᾽ ὀνομάτων λειότητος καὶ συνθέσεως ἐμμελοῦς· Ἀντίμαχος δὲ εὐτονίας καὶ ἀγωνιστικῆς τραχύτητος καὶ τοῦ συνήθους τῆς ἐξαλλαγῆς· Πανύασις δὲ τάς τε ἀμφοῖν ἀρετὰς εἰσηνέγκατο, καὶ αὐτὸς πραγματείαι καὶ τῆι κατ᾽ αὐτὸν οἰκονομίαι διήνεγκεν.

Cf. Quintil. *Inst. Or.* 10.1.52–54.

Clem. *Strom.* 6.25.1

αὐτοτελῶς γὰρ τὰ ἑτέρων ὑφελόμενοι ὡς ἴδια ἐξ-

honeyed voice and sweet-versing Panyassis, but Halicarnassus' rocky soil; through their music it enjoys a proud place among Greek cities.

Another

(This city) sowed the seed of Panyassis, famous master of epic verse; it gave birth to Cyprias, the poet of Trojan epic.

Inscription on a statue of the poet

Panyassis the poet is a severe pain.

Dionysius of Halicarnassus, *On imitation*

For Hesiod aimed at pleasing by smoothness of names and melodious construction; Antimachus at well-toned, athletic toughness and departure from the familiar; while Panyassis brought the virtues of both, he in turn excelling by his treatment of his material and its disposition.

Clement of Alexandria, *Miscellanies*

For on their own initiative (the Greeks) have stolen other

ἤνεγκαν, καθάπερ Εὐγάμμων . . . Πανύασίς *τε* ὁ Ἁλικαρνασσεὺς *παρὰ* Κρεωφύλου *τοῦ* Σαμίου *τὴν* Οἰχαλίας *ἅλωσιν*.

Euseb. *Chron.*

Ol. 72.3: Pannyasis poeta habetur inlustris.

Proclus, *Vita Homeri* 1, v. ad Pisandrum.

FRAGMENTA

1 Paus. 9.11.2

ἐπιδεικνύουσι δὲ (*οἱ* Θηβαῖοι) Ἡρακλέους *τῶν παίδων τῶν ἐκ* Μεγάρας *μνῆμα, οὐδέν τι ἀλλοίως τὰ ἐς τὸν θάνατον λέγοντες ἢ* Στησίχορος ὁ Ἱμεραῖος (*PMGF* 230) *καὶ* Πανύασσις *ἐν τοῖς ἔπεσιν ἐποίησαν*.

2 Paus. 10.8.9

Πανύασσις *δὲ* ὁ Πολυάρχου *πεποιηκὼς ἐς* Ἡρακλέα *ἔπη θυγατέρα* Ἀχελώιου *τὴν* Κασταλίαν *φησὶν εἶναι. λέγει γὰρ δὴ περὶ τοῦ* Ἡρακλέους·

> Παρνησσὸν *νιφόεντα θοοῖς διὰ ποσσὶ περήσας*
> *ἵκετο* Κασταλίης Ἀχελωΐδος *ἄμβροτον ὕδωρ*.

people's works and brought them out as their own; as Eugammon . . . and Panyassis of Halicarnassus stole the *Capture of Oichalia* from Creophylus of Samos.

Eusebius *Chronicle*

Ol. 72.3 (490/489): the poet Panyassis is celebrated.

For Panyassis in the canon of epic poets, see above on Pisander.

FRAGMENTS

1 Pausanias, *Description of Greece*

The Thebans also display a memorial to Heracles' children by Megara, telling no different story about their death from what Stesichorus of Himera and Panyassis related in their verses.[9]

2 Pausanias, *Description of Greece*

Panyassis the son of Polyarchus, the author of a Heracles epic, makes Castalia a daughter of Achelous. For he says of Heracles:

Crossing snowy Parnassus with swift feet, he came to Acheloian Castalia's immortal water.

9 The reference is to Heracles' killing his children in a fit of insanity, a story best known to us from Euripides' tragedy *Heracles*. The next fragment may refer to his visit to Delphi to seek purification. According to Apollodorus, *Library* 2.4.12, the oracle told him to go to Tiryns and serve Eurystheus, who would make him undertake a series of difficult tasks.

3 Clem. *Protr.* 2.35.3

Πανύασσις γὰρ πρὸς τούτοις καὶ ἄλλους παμπόλλους ἀνθρώποις λατρεῦσαι θεοὺς ἱστορεῖ, ὧδέ πως γράφων·

"τλῆ μὲν Δημήτηρ, τλῆ δὲ κλυτὸς Ἀμφιγυήεις,
τλῆ δὲ Ποσειδάων, τλῆ δ᾽ ἀργυρότοξος Ἀπόλλων
ἀνδρὶ παρὰ θνητῶι θητευσέμεν εἰς ἐνιαυτόν,
τλῆ δὲ <καὶ> ὀβριμόθυμος Ἄρης ὑπὸ πατρὸς
ἀνάγκης,"

καὶ τὰ ἐπὶ τούτοις.

3 *θητευέμεν* Sylburg: *θῆσαι μέγαν* Meineke.

4 Apollod. *Bibl.* 1.5.2

Πανύασις δὲ Τριπτόλεμον Ἐλευσῖνος λέγει· φησὶ γὰρ Δήμητρα πρὸς αὐτὸν ἐλθεῖν.

Cf. Hygin. *Fab.* 147.

5 Sext. Emp. *Adv. math.* 1.260

οἱ ἱστορικοὶ τὸν ἀρχηγὸν ἡμῶν τῆς ἐπιστήμης Ἀσκληπιὸν κεκεραυνῶσθαι λέγουσιν . . . Στησίχορος μὲν ἐν Ἐριφύλῃ (*PMGF* 194) εἰπὼν ὅτι τινὰς τῶν ἐπὶ Θήβαις πεσόντων ἀνιστᾶι . . . Πανύασις δὲ διὰ τὸ νεκρὸν Τυνδάρεω ἀναστῆσαι.

Cf. schol. Eur. *Alc.* 1; Apollod. *Bibl.* 3.10.3; Philod. *De pietate* B 4906 Obbink; schol. Pind. *Pyth.* 3.96.

3 Clement of Alexander, *Protreptic*

For Panyassis relates that a whole number of other gods beside these were in service to mortals, writing as follows:

"Demeter put up with it, renowned Hephaestus put up with it, Poseidon put up with it, silverbow Apollo put up with menial service with a mortal man for the term of a year; grim-hearted Ares too put up with it, under compulsion from his father,"

and so on.[10]

4 Apollodorus, *The Library*

But Panyassis makes Triptolemus a son of Eleusis, for he says that Demeter came to the latter.[11]

5 Sextus Empiricus, *Against the Professors*

The antiquarians say that the author of our science, Asclepius, was struck by the thunderbolt . . . Stesichorus in the *Eriphyle* saying that it was because he resurrected some of those who fell at Thebes . . . but Panyassis that it was for resurrecting the dead Tyndareos.[12]

[10] Someone, perhaps Athena, is consoling Heracles, recalling various mythical episodes of gods who submitted to servitude under mortal masters. The allusions were probably explained more fully in what followed, and fragments 4 and 5 fit well in this context.

[11] That is, the king in whose house she served as nurse was called Eleusis, not Keleos as in the *Hymn to Demeter.*

[12] Apollo, upset at the destruction of his son Asclepius, killed the Cyclopes, the manufacturers of the thunderbolt. It was to atone for this that he was made to serve Admetus for a year.

6 Steph. Byz. s.v. Βέμβινα

κώμη τῆς Νεμέας . . . Πανύασις ἐν Ἡρακλείας πρώτηι·

δέρμά τε θήρειον Βεμβινήταο λέοντος.

καὶ ἄλλως·

7

καὶ Βεμβινήταο πελώρου δέρμα λέοντος.

8 [Eratosth.] *Catast.* 11

Καρκίνος· οὗτος δοκεῖ ἐν τοῖς ἄστροις τεθῆναι δι᾽ Ἥραν, ὅτι μόνος, Ἡρακλεῖ τῶν ἄλλων συμμαχούντων ὅτε τὴν ὕδραν ἀνήιρει, ἐκ τῆς λίμνης ἐκπηδήσας ἔδακεν αὐτοῦ τὸν πόδα, καθάπερ φησὶ Πανύασις ἐν Ἡρακλείαι· θυμωθεὶς δ᾽ ὁ Ἡρακλῆς δοκεῖ τῶι ποδὶ συνθλάσαι αὐτόν, ὅθεν μεγάλης τιμῆς τετύχηκε καταριθμούμενος ἐν τοῖς ιβ´ ζωιδίοις.

Cf. Hygin. *Astr.* 2.23; schol. Arat. 147; schol. German. *Arat.* pp. 70 et 128 Breysig.

9 Ath. 498d

Πανύασσις τρίτωι Ἡρακλείας φησίν·

τοῦ κεράσας κρητῆρα μέγαν χρυσοῖο φαεινόν
σκύπφους αἰνύμενος θαμέας πότον ἡδὺν ἔπινεν.

1 φαεινοῦ Kinkel.

6 Stephanus of Byzantium, *Geographical Lexicon*

Bembina: a village in the territory of Nemea . . . Panyassis in Book 1 of the *Heraclea*:

and the animal skin from the lion of Bembina,

and again:

7

and the skin of Bembina's monster lion.

8 Pseudo-Eratosthenes, *Catasterisms*

Cancer (The Crab): it is held that this was placed among the stars by Hera because it alone, when all the others were helping Heracles when he was killing the Hydra, leaped out of the lake and bit him in the foot, as Panyassis says in the *Heraclea*; and Heracles in anger is held to have crushed it with his foot. Hence it has been highly honored by being numbered among the twelve creatures of the Zodiac.

9 Athenaeus, *Scholars at Dinner*

Panyassis says in Book 3 of the *Heraclea*:

Mixing some of it in a great shining golden bowl, he took cup after cup and enjoyed a fine bout of drinking.[13]

[13] This may refer to Heracles' entertainment by the centaur Pholos as he was on his way to capture the Erymanthian Boar (Apollodorus, *Library* 2.5.4). Compare Stesichorus, *Geryoneis*, *PMG* 181 = S19.

10 Schol. Pind. *Pyth.* 3.177b

ἔνιοι δὲ τὴν Θυώνην ἑτέραν τῆς Σεμέλης φασὶν εἶναι, τροφὸν τοῦ Διονύσου, ὥσπερ Πανύασις ἐν τρίτωι Ἡρακλείας·

καί ῥ᾽ ὃ μὲν ἐκ κόλποιο τροφοῦ θόρε ποσσὶ Θυώνης.

11 Ath. 172d

πεμμάτων δὲ πρῶτόν φησι μνημονεῦσαι Πανύασσιν Σέλευκος (*FGrHist* 634 F 2) *ἐν οἷς περὶ τῆς παρ᾽ Αἰγυπτίοις ἀνθρωποθυσίας διηγεῖται, πολλὰ μὲν ἐπιθεῖναι λέγων πέμματα, πολλὰς δὲ νοσσάδας ὄρνις.*

πέμματα πόλλ᾽ ἐπιθείς, πολλὰς δέ τε νοσσάδας ὄρνις.

Versum restituit Meineke.

12 Ath. 469d

Πανύασις δ᾽ ἐν †πρώτωι Ἡρακλείας παρὰ Νηρέως φησὶ τὴν τοῦ Ἡλίου φιάλην κομίσασθαι τὸν Ἡρακλέα καὶ διαπλεῦσαι εἰς Ἐρύθειαν.

πρώτωι cod.: *τετάρτωι* Dübner: *πέμπτωι* Robert: *ια´* Wilamowitz

10 Scholiast on Pindar, *Pythians*

But some say that Thyone is different from Semele, being Dionysus' nurse, as Panyassis does in Book 3 of the *Heraclea*:

And he jumped out from the bosom of his nurse Thyone.

11 Athenaeus, *Scholars at Dinner*

As for cakes, Seleucus says that Panyassis was the first to mention them, in his account of the Egyptians' human sacrifice, saying that (Busiris)

placed many cakes on top, and many fledgling birds.

12 Athenaeus, *Scholars at Dinner*

Panyassis says in Book 1(?) of the *Heraclea* that Heracles got the Sun's goblet from Nereus and sailed over to Erythea in it.[14]

[14] It is very unlikely that this came as early as Book 1. Fragment 13 suggests that it may have appeared in book 4 or 5.

13 "Ammonius" in *Il.* 21.195 (P. Oxy. 221 ix 8; v.93 Erbse)

[Σέλ]ευκος δὲ ‹τὸν αὐτὸν Ὠκεανῶι τὸν Ἀχελῶιον εἶναι Πανύασσιν ἀποφαίνει λέγοντα› ἐν ε´ [Ἡρ]ακλείας·

"πῷ[ς] δ' ἐπορ[εύθ]ῃς ῥεῦμ' Ἀ[χ]ε̣λ̣[ω]ΐου
ἀργυ[ρο]δίνα,
Ὠκεανοῦ ποταμοῖο̣ [δι'] εὐρέος ὑγ[ρ]ὰ κέλευθ̣α;"

‹τὸν αὐτὸν - λέγοντα› suppl. West.

14* Schol. Nic. *Ther.* 257a, "ὅτ' ἄνθεσιν εἴσατο χαλκοῦ"

γράφεται δὲ καὶ "ἄνθεσι χάλκης" . . . ἔστι δὲ ἡ χάλκη ἄνθος, ἀφ' οὗ καὶ τὴν πορφύραν ὠνόμασαν. ὁμοίως τὸ ἐμφερὲς τὸ ἐν τῆι Ἡρακλείαι·

φολὶς δ' ἀπέλαμπε φαεινή·
ἄλλοτε μὲν κυάνου, τοτὲ δ' ἄνθεσιν εἴσατο
χαλκοῦ.

15 Hygin. *Astr.* 2.6.1

Engonasin: hunc Eratosthenes Herculem dicit supra draconem conlocatum, de quo ante diximus, eumque paratum ut ad decertandum, sinistra manu pellem leonis dextra clauam tenentem. Conatur interficere draconem Hesperidum custodem, qui numquam oculos operuisse somno coactus existimatur, quo magis custos adpositus esse demonstratur. De hoc etiam Panyasis in Heraclea dicit.

13 "Ammonius," commentary on *Iliad* 21

Seleucus <points out that Panyassis identified Achelous with Oceanus> in Book 5 of the *Heraclea*:

"And how did you travel the stream of silver-eddying Achelous, over the watery ways of the broad river Oceanus?"[15]

14* Scholiast on Nicander, *Theriaca*, "sometimes he looks like flowers of copper"

There is a variant reading "flowers of *chalke*" . . . *chalke* is a (purple) flower, from which the name is applied to the purple fish. Likewise the simile in the *Heraclea*:

And its shining scale glittered; sometimes it looked like blue enamel, and sometimes like flowers of copper.[16]

15 Hyginus, *Astronomy*

The Kneeler:[17] Eratosthenes says that this is Heracles stationed over the aforementioned serpent, ready for the battle, holding his lionskin in his left hand and his club in his right. He is endeavoring to kill the Hesperides' guardian serpent, which is held never to have closed its eyes under compulsion of sleep, a proof of its guardian status. Panyassis tells of this in his *Heraclea*.

[15] The addressee is Heracles, the speaker perhaps Geryon.

[16] Meaning perhaps green like verdigris. The lines probably come from a description of the serpent that guarded the Golden Apples.

[17] The modern constellation Hercules.

Cf. [Eratosth.] *Catast.* 4; schol. German. *Arat.* pp. 61 et 118 Breysig.

Avienius, *Phaen.* 172–187

Illa laboranti similis succedet imago
protinus, expertem quam quondam dixit Aratus (63–66)
nominis et cuius lateat quoque causa laboris.
Panyasi sed nota tamen . . .
nam dura immodici memorat sub lege tyranni
Amphitryoniaden primaeuo in flore iuuentae,
qua cedunt medii longe secreta diei
Hesperidum uenisse locos atque aurea mala,
inscia quae lenti semper custodia somni
seruabat, carpsisse manu, postquam ille nouercae
insaturatae odiis serpens uictoris ab ictu
spirarumque sinus et fortia uincula laxans
occubuit: sic membra genu subnixa sinistro
sustentasse ferunt, sic insidisse labore
deuictum fama est.

16 Schol. *Od.* 12.301

Νυμφόδωρος ὁ τὴν Σικελίαν περιηγησάμενος (*FGrHist* 572 F 3) καὶ Πολύαινος (639 F 7) καὶ Πανύασις φύλακα τῶν Ἡλίου βοῶν Φάλακρόν φησι γενέσθαι.

Φάλακρον Meineke: φυλάκιον, φυλάϊκον, φύλαιον codd.

Avienius, *Phaenomena*

Next you will see a figure as of one exerting himself. Aratus said of old that it had no name and that the reason of its exertion was obscure; but it was known to Panyassis . . . He relates that Amphitryon's son in the first flower of his youth, being subject to the harsh rule of an immoderate tyrant, came where the unknown South retreats into the distance, to the regions of the Hesperides,[18] and plucked the golden apples guarded by a custodian ignorant of sluggish sleep, after that serpent, the creature of a stepmother insatiable in her hatred,[19] succumbed to the victor's blow, slackening its sinuous coils that barred the way. Thus, they say, he held his body supported on his left knee, and thus the tale is that he rested, overcome by his exertions.

16 Scholiast on the *Odyssey*

Nymphodorus the author of the *Description of Sicily*, Polyaenus, and Panyassis say that the guardian of the Sun's cattle was Phalacrus.

[18] Panyassis apparently located the Hesperides to the far south of Africa. Pherecydes was to transfer them to the far north (fr. 17 Fowler ~ Apollodorus, *Library* 2.5.11). See *JHS* 99 (1979), 145.

[19] Hera, Heracles' implacable enemy.

17 Paus. 10.29.9

Πανύασσις δὲ ἐποίησεν ὡς Θησεὺς καὶ Πειρίθους ἐπὶ τῶν θρόνων παράσχοιντο σχῆμα οὐ κατὰ δεσμώτας, προσφυῆ δὲ ἀπὸ τοῦ χρωτὸς ἀντὶ δεσμῶν σφισιν ἔφη τὴν πέτραν.

Cf. Apollod. epit. 1.24; schol. Ar. *Eq.* 1368.

18 Comm. in Antim. p.442 Matthews, "Στυγὸς ὕδωρ"

ὑποτίθεται ἐν Ἅιδου, καθάπερ καὶ Πανύασσ[ις λέγων περὶ τ]οῦ Σισ[ύ]φου ἐν Ἅιδου [ὄ]ντος φησίν·

ὣς ἄρα μιν εἰπόντα κατασ[τέγασε Στυγὸς] ὕδωρ.

19 Stob. 3.18.21 (Πανυάσσιδος); 12–19 cit. etiam Ath. 37a, 12–13 et *Suda* οι 135

"ξεῖν', ἄγε δὴ καὶ πῖν'· ἀρετή νύ τίς ἐστι καὶ αὕτη,
ὅς κ' ἀνδρῶν πολὺ πλεῖστον ἐν εἰλαπίνηι μέθυ πίνηι
εὖ καὶ ἐπισταμένως, ἅμα τ' ἄλλον φῶτα κελεύηι.
ἶσον δ' ὅς τ' ἐν δαιτὶ καὶ ἐν πολέμωι θοὸς ἀνήρ,
ὑσμίνας διέπων ταλαπενθέας, ἔνθά τε παῦροι
θαρσαλέοι τελέθουσι μένουσί τε θοῦρον ἄρηα.
τοῦ κεν ἐγὼ θείμην ἶσον κλέος, ὅς τ' ἐνὶ δαιτί
τέρπηται παρεὼν ἅμα τ' ἄλλον λαὸν ἀνώγηι.
οὐ γάρ μοι ζώειν γε δοκεῖ βροτὸς οὐδὲ βιῶναι

17 Pausanias, *Description of Greece*

Panyassis wrote that Theseus and Pirithous on their chairs did not give the appearance of being bound there, but that instead of bonds the rock had grown onto their flesh.[20]

18 Commentary on Antimachus, *Thebaid*, "the Water of Shuddering"

He places it in Hades, in the same way as Panyassis, speaking of Sisyphus in Hades, says:

After he had spoken thus, the Water [of Shuddering cover]ed him over.

19 Stobaeus, *Anthology*; lines 12–19 also Athenaeus, *Scholars at Dinner*

"Come on, friend, drink! This too is a virtue, to drink the most wine at the banquet in expert fashion, and to encourage your fellow. It's just as good to be sharp in the feast as in battle, busy amid the grievous slaughter, where few men are brave and withstand the furious fight. I should count his glory equal, who enjoys being at the feast, and encourages other folk to as well. A man doesn't seem to me to be really alive, or to live the life of a hardy mortal, if he sits out

[20] They were detained in the Underworld after they went down with the aim of securing Persephone as Pirithous' wife. Heracles saw them when he went down to capture Cerberus.

ἀνθρώποιο βίον ταλασίφρονος, ὅστις ἀπ᾽ οἴνου
θυμὸν ἐρητύσας μείνηι πότον, ἀλλ᾽ ἐνεόφρων.
οἶνος γὰρ πυρὶ ἶσον ἐπιχθονίοισιν ὄνειαρ,
ἐσθλὸν ἀλεξίκακον, πάσης συνοπηδὸν ἀοιδῆς.
ἐν μὲν γὰρ θαλίης ἐρατὸν μέρος ἀγλαΐης τε,
ἐν δὲ χοροιτυπίης, ἐν δ᾽ ἱμερτῆς φιλότητος,
ἐν δέ τε μενθήρης καὶ δυσφροσύνης ἀλεωρή.
τώ σε χρὴ παρὰ δαιτὶ δεδεγμένον εὔφρονι θυμῶι
πίνειν, μηδὲ βορῆς κεκορημένον ἠΰτε γῦπα
ἧσθαι πλημύροντα, λελασμένον εὐφροσυνάων."

4 *δ᾽ ὅς τ᾽* West: *τ᾽ ὃς* codd. 7 *κεν* Nauck: *μὲν* codd. 11 *μείνηι* West: *πίνει* codd. 13 *πάσηι συνοπηδὸν ἀνίηι* Ath., *Suda* 14 *ἐρατὸν* Ath.: *ἱερὸν* Stob. 16 *ἀλεωρή* Hense: *ἀλεγεινῆς* codd.

20 Ath. 36d

Πανύασις δ᾽ ὁ ἐποποιὸς τὴν μὲν πρώτην πόσιν ἀπονέμει Χάρισιν, Ὥραις καὶ Διονύσωι, τὴν δὲ δευτέραν Ἀφροδίτηι καὶ πάλιν Διονύσωι, Ὕβρει δὲ καὶ Ἄτηι τὴν τρίτην. Πανύασίς φησι·

"*πρῶται μὲν Χάριτές τ᾽ ἔλαχον καὶ ἐΰφρονες Ὧραι*
μοῖραν καὶ Διόνυσος ἐρίβρομος, οἵ περ ἔτευξαν·
τοῖς δ᾽ ἔπι Κυπρογένεια θεὰ λάχε καὶ Διόνυσος,
ἔνθά τε κάλλιστος πότος ἀνδράσι γίνεται οἴνου·
εἴ τις μέ<τρα> πίοι καὶ ὑπότροπος οἴκαδ᾽ ἀπέλθοι

the party restraining his appetite for the wine: he's an idiot. Wine is as much of a blessing as fire for us on earth: a good shield against harm, accompaniment to every song, for it has in it a delightful element of the festive, of luxury, of dancing, of entrancing love, and a refuge from care and depression. So you must take the toasts at the feast and drink merrily, and not sit costive like a vulture after you have fed your face, oblivious of good cheer."[21]

20 Athenaeus, *Scholars at Dinner*

The epic poet Panyassis assigns the first round of drinks to the Graces, the Horai, and Dionysus, the second to Aphrodite and Dionysus again, but the third to Hybris and Ate. He says:

"The Graces and the cheerful Horai take the first portion, and Dionysus the mighty roarer, the ones who created it. After them the goddess born in Cyprus takes her share, and Dionysus, at the stage where the wine session is at its most perfect for men: if you drink in measure and go back

[21] The speaker is perhaps Eurytus at Oichalia, encouraging his guest Heracles to drink more deeply. I take fragments 20–22 to be from Heracles' reply as he tries to restrain his too bibulous host. This temperate Heracles, the counterpart of the moral hero represented by Pindar and Prodicus, would be a modification of the older tradition.

δαιτὸς ἄπο γλυκερῆς, οὐκ ἄν ποτε πήματι κύρσαι·
ἀλλ' ὅτε τις μοίρης τριτάτης πρὸς μέτρον ἐλαύνοι
πίνων ἀβλεμέως, τότε δ' Ὕβριος αἶσα καὶ Ἄτης
γίνεται ἀργαλέη, κακὰ δ' ἀνθρώποισιν ὀπάζει.
ἀλλὰ πέπον, μέτρον γὰρ ἔχεις γλυκεροῖο ποτοῖο,
στεῖχε παρὰ μνηστὴν ἄλοχον, κοίμιζε δ' ἑταίρους·
δείδια γὰρ τριτάτης μοίρης μελιηδέος οἴνου
πινομένης, μή σ' Ὕβρις ἐνὶ φρεσὶ θυμὸν ἀέρσηι,
ἐσθλοῖς δὲ ξενίοισι κακὴν ἐπιθῆσι τελευτήν.
ἀλλὰ πιθοῦ καὶ παῦε πολὺν πότον.

5 suppl. West ὑπότροπος Peppmüller: ἀποτρ- codd. 14 δὲ Meineke: ἐν codd. 15 ἀλλὰ πιθοῦ Meineke: ἀλλ' ἄπιθι codd.

21 Ath. 37a (post fr. 19)

καὶ πάλιν·

οἶνος ‹ › θνητοῖσι θεῶν πάρα δῶρον ἄριστον
ἀγλαός· ὧι πᾶσαι μὲν ἐφαρμόζουσιν ἀοιδαί,
πάντες δ' ὀρχησμοί, πᾶσαι δ' ἐραταὶ φιλότητες.
πάσας δ' ἐκ κραδίης ἀνίας ἀνδρῶν ἀλαπάζει
πινόμενος κατὰ μέτρον· ὑπὲρ μέτρον δὲ χερείων.

1 et 5 cit. Clem *Strom.* 6.11.6 5 ὑπέρμετρος Clem.

home from the feast, you will never run into anything bad. But when someone drinks heavily and presses to the limit of the third round, then Hybris and Ate take their unlovely turn, which brings trouble. Now, pal, you've had your ration of the sweet liquor, so go and join your wedded wife, and send your comrades to bed. With the third round of the honey-sweet wine being drunk, I'm afraid of Hybris stirring up your spirits and bringing your good hospitality to a bad end. So do as I say, and stop the excess drinking."

21 Athenaeus, *Scholars at Dinner* (after fr. 19)

And again:

Wine is mortals' finest gift from the gods, glorious wine: every song harmonizes with it, every dance, every delightful love. And every pain it expels from men's hearts, so long as it is drunk in due measure; but beyond the measure, it is not so good.

22 Ath. 36d (post fr. 20)

καὶ ἑξῆς περὶ ἀμέτρου οἴνου·

> *ἐν γάρ οἱ Ἄτης τε καὶ Ὕβριος αἶσ' <ἅμ'>*
> *ὀπηδεῖ.*

ἐν West: *ἐκ* codd. *ἅμ'* add. Naeke.

23 Schol. (T) *Il.* 24.616b, "*αἵ τ' ἀμφ' Ἀχελώϊον*"

τινὲς "αἵ τ' ἀμφ' Ἀχελήσιον"· ποταμὸς δὲ Λυδίας, ἐξ οὗ πληροῦται ὁ Ὕλλος· καὶ Ἡρακλέα νοσήσαντα ἐπὶ τῶν τόπων, ἀναδόντων αὐτῶι θερμὰ λουτρὰ τῶν ποταμῶν, τοὺς παῖδας Ὕλλον καλέσαι καὶ τὸν ἐξ Ὀμφάλης Ἀχέλητα, ὃς Λυδῶν ἐβασίλευσεν. εἰσὶ δὲ καὶ νύμφαι Ἀχελήτιδες, ὥς φησι Πανύασσις.

Schol. Ap. Rhod. 4.1149/50

Πανύασις δέ φησιν ἐν Λυδίαι τὸν Ἡρακλέα νοσήσαντα τυχεῖν ἰάσεως ὑπὸ Ὕλλου τοῦ ποταμοῦ, ὅς ἐστι τῆς Λυδίας· διὸ καὶ τοὺς δύο υἱοὺς αὐτοῦ Ὕλλους ὀνομασθῆναι.

24 Steph. Byz. s.v. *Τρεμίλη*

ἡ Λυκία ἐκαλεῖτο οὕτως. οἱ κατοικοῦντες Τρεμιλεῖς. ἀπὸ Τρεμίλου, ὡς Πανύασις·

> *ἔνθα δ' ἔναιε μέγας Τρεμίλης καί ῥ' ἤγαγε*
> *κούρην,*

22 Athenaeus, *Scholars at Dinner* (after fr. 20)

And following that, about immoderate wine:

For with it the turn of Ate and Hybris comes along.[22]

23 Scholiast on the *Iliad*, "the nymphs who dance about the Achelous"

Some read "about the Achelesius"; this is a river in Lydia, a tributary of the Hyllus, and (they say) that after Heracles fell sick in these parts, and the rivers provided him with warm bathing, he named his sons Hyllus, and the one born to Omphale Acheles—he became king of Lydia. There are also Achelesian nymphs, as Panyassis says.

Scholiast on Apollonius of Rhodes

Panyassis says that Heracles fell sick in Lydia and obtained therapy from the river Hyllus, which is in Lydia; and this is why his two sons were both named Hyllus.

24 Stephanus of Byzantium, *Geographical Lexicon*

Tremile: Lycia was so called. The inhabitants are Tremileis. The name is from Tremiles, as in Panyassis:

And there dwelt great Tremiles, and he married a maid, an

[22] This line may have directly followed fragment 21.

νύμφην Ὠγυγίην, ἣν Πρηξιδίκην καλέουσιν,
Σίβρωι ἔπ' ἀργυρέωι, ποταμῶι πάρα δινήεντι·
τῆς δ' ὀλοοὶ παῖδες Τλῶος {Ξάνθος τε} Πίναρός
  ‹τ' ἐγένοντο›
καὶ Κράγος, ὃς κρατέων πάσας ληΐζετ' ἀρούρας.

1 Τρεμίλης Meineke: τρεμύλ(ι)ος codd. ῥ' ἤγαγε κούρην West: ἔγημε θύγατρα codd. 3 Σίρβει? 4 ita West: ξανθὸς Πίναρός τε Salmasius.

25 Steph. Byz. s.v. Ἀσπίς

πόλις Λιβύης . . . ἔστι καὶ νῆσος πρὸς τῆι Λυκίαι. ἔστι καὶ νῆσος ἄλλη μεταξὺ Λεβέδου καὶ Τέω . . . ἔστι καὶ νῆσος ἄλλη Ψύρων ἐγγύς. ἔστι καὶ ἄλλη, ὡς Κλέων ὁ Συρακούσιος ἐν τῶι περὶ τῶν λιμένων, ἄδενδρος οὖσα. ἔστι καὶ πέραν Πίσης, ὡς Πανύασις ἐν Ἡρακλείας ἑνδεκάτηι.

26 Clem. *Protr.* 2.36.2

ναὶ μὴν καὶ τὸν Ἀϊδωνέα ὑπὸ Ἡρακλέους τοξευθῆναι Ὅμηρος λέγει (*Il.* 5.395), καὶ τὸν Ἠλεῖον Ἅιδην Πανύασσις ἱστορεῖ· ἤδη δὲ καὶ τὴν Ἥραν τὴν ζυγίαν ἱστορεῖ ὑπὸ τοῦ αὐτοῦ Ἡρακλέους ὁ αὐτὸς οὗτος Πανύασις

ἐν Πύλωι ἠμαθόεντι.

Ἅιδην Matthews: Αὐγέαν cod. (et schol.).

Ogygian nymph, whom they call Praxidice, at the silvery Sibrus, beside that swirling river. And from her ‹were born› baleful sons, Tloos, Pinaros, and Cragus, who in his might plundered all the plowlands.[23]

25 Stephanus of Byzantium, *Geographical Lexicon*

Aspis: a town in Libya . . . Also an island off Lycia. Also another island between Lebedos and Teos . . . Also another island near Psyra. Also another, as Cleon of Syracuse writes in his work *On Harbors*, a treeless one. Also one beyond Pisa,[24] mentioned by Panyassis in the *Heraclea*, Book 11.

26 Clement, *Protreptic*

Aye, and Homer says that Aïdoneus was shot by Heracles, and Panyassis records that the Elean Hades was; and this same Panyassis also records that Conjugal Hera was shot by the same Heracles

in sandy Pylos.

[23] Tremileis represents a native tribal name that appears in Lycian inscriptions. The Sibrus or Sirbis is the Xanthus; the familiar name has intruded as a gloss in the next line. Tloos and Pinaros are the eponyms of the Lycian hill towns Tlos and Pinara, and Cragus of the mountain to the west of the Xanthus valley.

[24] Presumed to be in southern Asia Minor.

Arnob. *Adv. nationes* 4.25

Non ex uobis Panyassis unus est, qui ab Hercule Ditem patrem et reginam memorat sauciatam esse Iunonem?

27 *Et. Gen.* (A) s.v. *μῦθος*

ἡ στάσις . . . καὶ Πανύασσις·

διχθάδιός ποτε μῦθος †ἄλλα δὲ† μετεμέμβ<λ>ετο λαῶν,

ἀντὶ τοῦ στάσις.

28 Apollod. *Bibl.* 3.14.4

Ἡσίοδος δὲ (fr. 139) *αὐτὸν Φοίνικος καὶ Ἀλφεσιβοίας λέγει*, Πανύασις δέ *φησι Θείαντος βασιλέως Ἀσσυρίων, ὃς ἔσχε θυγατέρα Σμύρναν. αὕτη κατὰ μῆνιν Ἀφροδίτης (οὐ γὰρ αὐτὴν ἐτίμα) ἴσχει τοῦ πατρὸς ἔρωτα, καὶ σύνεργον λαβοῦσα τὴν τροφὸν ἀγνοοῦντι τῶι πατρὶ νύκτας δώδεκα συνευνάσθη. ὁ δὲ ὡς ᾔσθετο, σπασάμενος ξίφος ἐδίωκεν αὐτήν, ἡ δὲ περικαταλαμβανομένη θεοῖς ηὔξατο ἀφανὴς γενέσθαι. θεοὶ δὲ κατοικτίραντες αὐτὴν εἰς δένδρον μετήλλαξαν ὃ καλοῦσι σμύρναν. δεκαμηνιαίωι δὲ ὕστερον χρόνωι τοῦ δένδρου ῥαγέντος γεννηθῆναι τὸν λεγόμενον Ἄδωνιν· ὃν Ἀφροδίτη διὰ κάλλος ἔτι νήπιον κρύφα θεῶν εἰς λάρνακα κρύψασα Περσεφόνηι παρίστατο· ἐκείνη δὲ ὡς ἐθεάσατο, οὐκ ἀπεδίδου. κρίσεως δὲ ἐπὶ Διὸς γενομένης εἰς τρεῖς μοίρας διηρέθη ὁ ἐνιαυτός, καὶ μίαν μὲν παρ' ἑαυτῶι μένειν τὸν Ἄδωνιν, μίαν δὲ παρὰ*

Arnobius, *Against the Heathens*

Is Panyassis not one of you, who records that Hades and the queen Hera were wounded by Heracles?[25]

27 *Etymologicum Genuinum*

mythos [lit. words]: dissension . . . And in Panyassis:

Divided words once [. . .][26] of the peoples had repented,

that is, dissension.

28 Apollodorus, *The Library*

But Hesiod says Adonis was the son of Phoenix and Alphesiboea, while Panyassis makes him the son of Theias, a king of Assyria, who had a daughter Smyrna. She, through the anger of Aphrodite (whom she failed to honor), conceived a desire for her father, and with her nurse as accomplice she lay with him for twelve nights without his realizing it. When he became aware of it, he drew a sword and chased her, and she as she was being overtaken prayed to the gods to disappear. They took pity on her and changed her into the tree called *smyrna* (myrrh). Ten months later the tree split open, and the said Adonis was born from it. Because of his beauty Aphrodite concealed him from the gods, still a baby, in a chest, and placed it with Persephone; but when she saw him, she refused to give him back. An adjudication was made by Zeus, and the year was divided into three parts. He ordained that Adonis should stay by himself for one part, stay for one with

[25] Compare *Iliad* 5.392–397.
[26] Text corrupt and unintelligible.

Περσεφόνηι προσέταξε, τὴν δὲ ἑτέραν παρ' Ἀφροδίτηι· ὁ δὲ Ἄδωνις ταύτηι προσένειμε καὶ τὴν ἰδίαν μοῖραν. ὕστερον δὲ θηρεύων Ἄδωνις ὑπὸ συὸς πληγεὶς ἀπέθανε.

Cf. Philod. *De pietate* B 7553 Obbink; schol. Lyc. 829; Ant. Lib. 34.

29 Hesych. η 652

Ἠοίην·

τὸν Ἄδωνιν. Πανύασις.

30 Schol. (h *B) *Il.* 1.591 = *Et. Magn.* s.v. βηλός

καὶ ὁ Πανύασις δὲ τὰ πέδιλα

βηλά

λέγει.

ΘΗΣΗΪΣ

TESTIMONIUM

Arist. *Poet.* 1451a19

διὸ πάντες ἐοίκασιν ἁμαρτάνειν ὅσοι τῶν ποιητῶν Ἡρακληΐδα, Θησηΐδα, καὶ τὰ τοιαῦτα ποιήματα πεποιήκασιν· οἴονται γάρ, ἐπεὶ εἷς ἦν ὁ Ἡρακλῆς, ἕνα καὶ τὸν μῦθον εἶναι προσήκειν.

Persephone, and the other with Aphrodite. But Adonis gave Aphrodite his own time too. Later, while hunting, he was gored by a boar and died.[27]

29 Hesychius, *Lexicon*

Eoies [He of the Dawn]: Adonis. Panyassis.

30 Scholiast on the *Iliad*; *Etymologicum Magnum*

And Panyassis calls sandals "platforms" (*bēla*).

THESEIS

TESTIMONIUM

Aristotle, *Poetics*

So all those poets appear to go wrong who have composed a *Heracleis*, a *Theseis*, and poems of that kind; they suppose that because Heracles was one person, it ought to be one myth.

[27] It is not clear how much of the story stood in Panyassis, or in what context. Fragment 29 must belong with it.

FRAGMENTA

1 Plut. *Thes.* 28.1

ἣν γὰρ ὁ τῆς Θησηΐδος ποιητὴς Ἀμαζόνων ἐπανάστασιν γέγραφε, Θησεῖ γαμοῦντι Φαίδραν τῆς Ἀντιόπης ἐπιτιθεμένης καὶ τῶν μετ' αὐτῆς Ἀμαζόνων ἀμυνομένων καὶ κτείνοντος αὐτὰς Ἡρακλέους, περιφανῶς ἔοικε μύθωι καὶ πλάσματι.

2 Schol. Pind. *Ol.* 3.50b

θήλειαν δὲ εἶπε καὶ χρυσοκέρων ἀπὸ ἱστορίας· ὁ γὰρ ‹τὴν› Θησηΐδα γράψας τοιαύτην αὐτὴν ‹λέγει›, καὶ Πείσανδρος ὁ Καμιρεὺς (fr. 3) καὶ Φερεκύδης (fr. 71 Fowler).

THESEIS

FRAGMENTS

1 Plutarch, *Life of Theseus*

For the Amazon uprising that the poet of the *Theseis* has written of, in which, when Theseus was celebrating his wedding to Phaedra, Antiope attacked him and the Amazons with her gave support and Heracles killed them, obviously bears the marks of a mythical fiction.[28]

2 Scholiast on Pindar, *Olympians*

He made it [the Cerynian Hind] female and gold-horned on the basis of legend; for the author of the *Theseis* describes it like that, as do Pisander of Camirus and Pherecydes.

[28] Antiope was an Amazon whom Theseus had previously brought to Athens and married. See Apollodorus, epitome 1.16–17.

GENEALOGICAL AND ANTIQUARIAN EPICS

ΕΥΜΗΛΟΣ

TESTIMONIA

Clem. *Strom.* 1.131.8

Σιμωνίδης μὲν οὖν κατὰ Ἀρχίλοχον φέρεται, Καλλῖνος δὲ πρεσβύτερος οὐ μακρῶι . . . Εὔμηλος δὲ ὁ Κορίνθιος πρεσβύτερος ὢν ἐπιβεβληκέναι Ἀρχίαι τῶι Συρακούσας κτίσαντι.

Id. 6.26.7

τὰ δὲ Ἡσιόδου μετήλλαξαν εἰς πεζὸν λόγον καὶ ὡς ἴδια ἐξήνεγκαν Εὔμηλός τε καὶ Ἀκουσίλαος οἱ ἱστοριογράφοι.

Euseb. *Chron.*

Ol. 5.1: Eumelus poeta, qui Bugoniam et Europiam . . . agnoscitur.

GENEALOGICAL AND ANTIQUARIAN EPICS

EUMELUS

TESTIMONIA

Clement of Alexandria, *Miscellanies*

Simonides is said to have been contemporary with Archilochus, and Callinus a little older . . . and Eumelus of Corinth, who was older, to have overlapped with Archias the founder of Syracuse.

Clement of Alexandria, *Miscellanies*

And Hesiod's poetry was turned into prose and brought out as their own work by the historians Eumelus and Acusilaus.

Eusebius, *Chronicle*

Ol. 5.1 (760/759): the poet Eumelus, who composed the *Bougonia* and *Europia*, is recognized.

Ol. 9.1: Eumelus Corinthius uersificator agnoscitur et Sibylla Erythraea.

Cf. Cyrill. *Contra Iulian.* 1.12 (Patrol. Gr. lxxvi. 520D).

Schol. Pind. *Ol.* 13.31a, "ἐν δὲ Μοῖσ' ἁδύπνοος"

τοῦτο δὲ διὰ τὸν Εὔμηλον ὄντα Κορίνθιον καὶ γράψαντα Νόστον τῶν Ἑλλήνων.

Εὔμηλον Gyraldus: Εὔμολπον codd.

Paus. 4.4.1

ἐπὶ δὲ Φίντα τοῦ Συβότα πρῶτον Μεσσήνιοι τότε τῷ Ἀπόλλωνι ἐς Δῆλον θυσίαν καὶ ἀνδρῶν χορὸν ἀποστέλλουσι· τὸ δέ σφισιν ᾆσμα προσόδιον ἐς τὸν θεὸν ἐδίδαξεν Εὔμηλος, εἶναί τε ὡς ἀληθῶς Εὐμήλου νομίζεται μόνα τὰ ἔπη ταῦτα.

Cf. Paus. 4.33.2 (*PMG* 696), 5.19.10.

FRAGMENTS

1. (Εὐμήλου ἢ Ἀρκτίνου) Τιτανομαχία

1 Philod. *De pietate* B 4677 Obbink

ὁ δὲ τὴν Τι[τανο]μαχίαν γρά[ψας ἐξ] Αἰθέρος φη[σίν (sc. τὰ πάντα).

Ol. 9.1 (744/3): Eumelus the Corinthian poet is recognized, and the Erythraean Sibyl.

Cyril of Alexandria also dates Eumelus to the ninth Olympiad.

Scholiast on Pindar, *Olympians*, "Among them (the Corinthians) the sweet-breathed Muse blooms"

He says this because of Eumelus, who was a Corinthian and wrote *The Return of the Greeks*.

Pausanias, *Description of Greece*

In the time of Sybotas' son Phintas the Messenians first sent a sacrifice and men's chorus to Delos for Apollo; their processional song for the god was produced by Eumelus, and this poem alone is thought to be genuinely by Eumelus.[1]

FRAGMENTS

1. Eumelus or Arctinus, *Titanomachy*

1 Philodemus, *On Piety*

Whereas the author of the *Titanomachy* says that everything came from Aither.

[1] Pausanias later quotes a fragment of the processional; see the Loeb *Greek Lyric*, ii.290.

Epimerismi Homerici α 313 Dyck (from Methodius)

ἄκμων· . . . οἱ δὲ Ἄκμονα τὸν αἰθέρα· Αἰθέρος δὲ υἱὸς Οὐρανός, ὡς ὁ τὴν Τιτανομαχίαν γράψας, ὁ δὲ αἰθὴρ ἀκάματος, ἐπεὶ καὶ τὸ πῦρ ἀκάματον.

2 Lydus *De mensibus* 4.71

Εὔμηλος δὲ ὁ Κορίνθιος τὸν Δία ἐν τῆι καθ' ἡμᾶς Λυδίαι τεχθῆναι βούλεται.

3 Schol. Ap. Rhod. 1.1165c

Εὔμηλος δὲ ἐν τῆι Τιτανομαχίαι τὸν Αἰγαίωνα Γῆς καὶ Πόντου φησὶ παῖδα, κατοικοῦντα δὲ ἐν τῆι θαλάσσηι τοῖς Τιτᾶσι συμμαχεῖν.

Virg. *Aen.* 10.565

Aegaeon qualis, centum cui bracchia dicunt | centenasque manus, quinquaginta oribus ignem | pectoribusque arsisse, Iouis cum fulmina contra | tot paribus streperet clipeis, tot stringeret ensis.

Servius auctus ad *Aen.* 6.287, "*centumgeminus Briareus*"

Qui ut nonnulli tradunt pro diis aduersus Gigantes bella gessit; ut uero alii adfirmant, contra deos pugnauit, eo maxime tempore quo inter Iouem et Saturnum de caelesti regno

Homeric Parsings (from Methodius)

Others understand Akmon as the air (*aithēr*), Ouranos being Aither's son according to the author of the *Titanomachy*; the air is tireless (*akamatos*), because fire is.[2]

2 Lydus, *On the Months*

Eumelus of Corinth would have it that Zeus was born in the country that is now Lydia.[3]

3 Scholiast on Apollonius of Rhodes

Eumelus in the *Titanomachy* says that Aigaion was the son of Earth and Sea, lived in the sea, and fought on the side of the Titans.[4]

Virgil, *Aeneid*

Like Aigaion, who they say had a hundred arms and a hundred hands and blazed fire from fifty mouths and in fifty breasts, when he raged against Jupiter's thunderbolt with the same number of matching shields and bared the same number of swords.

Servius auctus on the *Aeneid*, "centuplet Briareus"

Who, as some record, waged war on the gods' behalf against the Giants; but as others affirm, he fought against the gods, above all on the occasion when Jupiter and Saturn were con-

[2] The author is reporting explanations of why some poets called Ouranos (Heaven) the son of Akmon. [3] Probably on Mt. Sipylos; see Aristides, *Orations* 17.3, 18.2, 21.3.

[4] Compare Antimachus, fr. 14 Matthews.

certamen fuit, unde eum a Ioue fulmine ad inferos tradunt esse trusum.

Id. ad *Aen.* 10.565

Alii hunc ex Terra et Ponto natum dicunt, qui habuit Coeum (Cottum *Thilo*) et Gygen fratres. Hic contra Titanas Ioui adfuisse dicitur, uel ut quidam uolunt Saturno.

4* Serv. ad *Aen.* 6.580 (de Titanomachia)

De his autem solus Sol abstinuisse narratur ab iniuria numinum, unde et caelum meruit.

5* Hesych. ι 387

Ἴθας· ὁ τῶν Τιτήνων κήρυξ, Προμηθεύς. τινὲς Ἴθαξ.

6* Apollod. *Bibl.* 1.2.1

μεθ' ὧν Ζεὺς τὸν πρὸς Κρόνον καὶ Τιτᾶνας ἐξήνεγκε πόλεμον. μαχομένων δὲ αὐτῶν ἐνιαυτοὺς δέκα ἡ Γῆ τῶι Διὶ ἔχρησε τὴν νίκην, τοὺς καταταρταρωθέντας ἂν ἔχηι συμμάχους· ὁ δὲ τὴν φρουροῦσαν αὐτῶν τὰ δεσμὰ Κάμπην ἀποκτείνας ἔλυσε. καὶ Κύκλωπες τότε Διὶ μὲν διδόασι βροντὴν καὶ ἀστραπὴν καὶ κεραυνόν, Πλούτωνι δὲ κυνέην, Ποσειδῶνι δὲ τρίαιναν. οἱ δὲ τούτοις ὁπ-

testing for the kingship of heaven. Hence they record that he was driven down by Jupiter to the underworld with a thunderbolt.

Others say he was born from Earth and Sea, and had Coeus[5] and Gyges as his brothers. He is said to have assisted Jupiter against the Titans; or as some would have it, to have assisted Saturn.

4* Servius on the *Aeneid*

Of these (the Titans), the Sun god alone[6] is related to have abstained from assaulting the gods; hence he earned a place in heaven.

5* Hesychius, *Lexicon*

Ithas: the Titans' herald, Prometheus. Some write "Ithax."

6* Apollodorus, *The Library*

With them [his brothers and sisters] Zeus unleashed the war against Kronos and the Titans. When they had been fighting for ten years, Ge prophesied to Zeus that he would be victorious if he had those who had been consigned to Tartarus[7] as his allies; so he killed their prison warder Kampe (Worm) and freed them. Then the Cyclopes gave thunder, lightning, and the thunderbolt to Zeus, the cap of invisibility to Pluto, and the trident to Poseidon. Armed with this equipment they

[5] Thilo emends to "Cottus" to accord with Hesiod and other sources. Coeus was a Titan, the father of Leto.

[6] The Titan Hyperion may be meant. In Hesiod he is the father of Helios, but the name often stands for the sun.

[7] The Cyclopes and Hundred-Handers.

λισθέντες κρατοῦσι Τιτάνων, καὶ καθείρξαντες αὐτοὺς ἐν τῶι Ταρτάρωι τοὺς Ἑκατόγχειρας κατέστησαν φύλακας. αὐτοὶ δὲ διακληροῦνται περὶ τῆς ἀρχῆς· καὶ λαγχάνει Ζεὺς μὲν τὴν ἐν οὐρανῶι δυναστείαν, Ποσειδῶν δὲ τὴν ἐν θαλάσσηι, Πλούτων δὲ τὴν ἐν Ἅιδου.

7* Apollod. *Bibl.* 1.2.3

Ἰαπετοῦ δὲ καὶ Ἀσίας Ἄτλας, ὃς ἔχει τοῖς ὤμοις τὸν οὐρανόν, καὶ Προμηθεὺς καὶ Ἐπιμηθεύς, καὶ Μενοίτιος, ὃν κεραυνώσας ἐν τῆι τιτανομαχίαι Ζεὺς κατεταρτάρωσεν.

8 Ath. 22c

Εὔμηλος δὲ ὁ Κορίνθιος ⌊ἢ Ἀρκτῖνος⌋ τὸν Δία ὀρχούμενόν που παράγει λέγων·

μέσσοισιν δ' ὠρχεῖτο πατὴρ ἀνδρῶν τε θεῶν τε.

9 Philod. *De pietate* B 5731 Obbink

καὶ τὰς Ἁρπυίας τὰ μῆ[λα φ]υλάττειν Ἀκο[υσί]λ̣αος (fr. 10 Fowler), Ἐπιμεν[ί]δης δὲ (fr. 9 F.) καὶ τοῦτο καὶ τὰς αὐτὰς εἶναι ταῖς Ἑσπερίσιν· ὁ δὲ τὴν Τι<τα>νομαχίαν <γράψας φησὶν τὰ> μὲν μῆλα φυλάτ[τειν . . .

---

8 The division of the universe by lot, also referred to in *Iliad* 15.187–192, is an old Babylonian motif; see M. L. West, *The East Face of Helicon* (Oxford, 1997), 109–110. The poet perhaps lo-

overcame the Titans, imprisoned them in Tartarus, and set the Hundred-Handers to be their warders. They themselves cast lots for government, and Zeus got power in heaven, Poseidon in the sea, and Pluto in the underworld.[8]

7* Apollodorus, *The Library*

Iapetos' sons by Asia were Atlas, who holds the heaven on his shoulders, Prometheus and Epimetheus, and Menoitios, whom Zeus thunderbolted in the battle with the Titans and consigned to Tartarus.[9]

8 Athenaeus, *Scholars at Dinner*

Eumelus of Corinth[10] portrays Zeus as dancing, when he says

And in their midst danced the father of gods and men.

9 Philodemus, *On Piety*

And Acusilaus says the Harpies guarded the (golden) apples; Epimenides agrees, while identifying them with the Hesperides. The author of the *Titanomachy* says the apples were guarded by [. . .

cated the event at Mekone, as does Callimachus, fr. 119. Mekone, often identified with Sicyon, was the place where according to Hesiod (*Theogony* 535–557) gods and mortals parted and determined their respective portions.

9 Compare Hesiod, *Theogony* 509–516.

10 One manuscript adds in the margin "or Arctinus." The fragment probably refers to celebrations following the defeat of the Titans: compare Diodorus, *Histories* 6.4; Dionysius of Halicarnassus, *Roman Antiquities* 7.72.7; Tibullus 2.5.9; Seneca, *Agamemnon* 333.

10 Ath. 470b

Θεόλυτος δὲ ἐν δευτέρωι Ὥρων (*FGrHist* 478 F 1) *ἐπὶ λέβητός φησιν αὐτὸν διαπλεῦσαι, τοῦτο πρῶτον εἰπόντος τοῦ τὴν Τιτανομαχίαν ποιήσαντος.*

11 Schol. (T) *Il.* 23.295b

καὶ ὁ τὴν Τιτανομαχίαν δὲ γράψας δύο ἄρρενάς φησιν Ἡλίου καὶ δύο θηλείας.

Hyg. *Fab.* 183 (equorum Solis et Horarum nomina)

Eo<u>s: per hunc caelum uerti solet. Aeth{i}ops: quasi flammeus est, qui coquit fruges. Hi funales sunt mares; feminae iugariae, Bronte, quae nos tonitrua appellamus, Steropeque, quae fulgitrua. Huic rei auctor est Eumelus Corinthius.

12 Schol. Ap. Rhod. 1.554, "Χείρων Φιλλυρίδης"

ὁ δὲ τὴν Γιγαντομαχίαν ποιήσας φησὶν ὅτι Κρόνος μεταμορφωθεὶς εἰς ἵππον ἐμίγη Φιλύραι τῆι Ὠκεανοῦ, διόπερ καὶ ἱπποκένταυρος ἐγεννήθη Χείρων. τούτου δὲ γυνὴ Χαρικλώ.

Cf. Pherec. fr. 50 F.; Ap. Rhod. 2.1231–1241; Apollod. *Bibl.* 1.2.4.

13 Clem. *Strom.* 1.73.3

ὁ δὲ Βηρύτιος Ἕρμιππος Χείρωνα τὸν Κένταυρον σοφὸν

10 Athenaeus, *Scholars at Dinner*

Theolytus in Book 2 of his *Annals* says that the Sun sails across (Oceanus) on a cauldron, the first to say this being the author of the *Titanomachy*.

11 Scholiast on the *Iliad*

The author of the *Titanomachy* likewise says that the Sun's horses were two males and two females.

Hyginus, *Legends*, on the names of the Sun's horses

Eous; through him the sky revolves. Aethops: more or less "flaming," the one that ripens produce. These trace horses are males; the yoke pair are females, Bronte, that we call thunder, and Sterope, that we call lightning. The source for this is Eumelus of Corinth.

12 Scholiast on Apollonius of Rhodes

The author of the *Gigantomachy*[11] says that Kronos changed into a horse when he made love to the Oceanid Philyra, which is why Chiron was born a horse-centaur. His wife was Chariklo.

13 Clement of Alexandria, *Miscellanies*

Hermippus of Beirut calls the centaur Chiron wise. Referring

[11] Assumed to be an error for *Titanomachy*.

καλεῖ· ἐφ' οὗ καὶ ὁ τὴν Τιτανομαχίαν γράψας φησὶν ὡς πρῶτος οὗτος

εἴς τε δικαιοσύνην θνητῶν γένος ἤγαγε δείξας
ὅρκους καὶ θυσίας ἱλαρὰς καὶ σχήματ' Ὀλύμπου.

14 Ath. 277d

οἶδα ὅτι ὁ τὴν Τιτανομαχίαν ποιήσας, εἴτ' Εὔμηλός ἐστιν ὁ Κορίνθιος ἢ Ἀρκτῖνος ἢ ὅστις δήποτε χαίρει ὀνομαζόμενος, ἐν τῶι δευτέρωι οὕτως εἴρηκεν·

ἐν δ' αὐτῆι πλωτοὶ χρυσώπιδες ἰχθύες ἐλλοί
νήχοντες παίζουσι δι' ὕδατος ἀμβροσίοιο.

ἔχαιρε δὲ Σοφοκλῆς τῶι ἐπικῶι κύκλωι, ὡς καὶ ὅλα δράματα ποιῆσαι κατακολουθῶν τῆι ἐν τούτωι μυθοποιίαι.

2. Κορινθιακά

15 Schol. Ap. Rhod. 4.1212–1214b

Ἐφύρα ἡ Κόρινθος, ἀπὸ Ἐφύρας τῆς Ἐπιμηθέως θυγατρός· Εὔμηλος δὲ ἀπὸ Ἐφύρας τῆς Ὠκεανοῦ καὶ Τηθύος, γυναικὸς δὲ γενομένης Ἐπιμηθέως.

to him the author of the *Titanomachy* too says that he first

led the human race to righteousness by instructing them in oath-taking and cheerful sacrifices and the patterns of Olympus.[12]

14 Athenaeus, *Scholars at Dinner*[13]

I know that the author of the *Titanomachy*, whether it is Eumelus of Corinth or Arctinus or however he likes to be identified, has said this in Book 2:

And in it[14] there float fish with golden scales, that swim and sport through the ambrosial water.

Sophocles liked the Epic Cycle, to the extent of composing whole plays in accordance with the mythology it contains.

2. *Corinthiaca*

15 Scholiast on Apollonius of Rhodes

"Ephyra" is Corinth, from Ephyra the daughter of Epimetheus; Eumelus, however, says from Ephyra the daughter of Oceanus and Tethys, who became Epimetheus' wife.[15]

12 Olympus here must stand for heaven. The reference will be to astronomical or meteorological lore. Chiron was known in myth as an educator of heroes. A didactic poem ascribed to Hesiod, the *Precepts of Chiron*, purported to embody his teaching to Achilles.

13 The question under discussion is where Sophocles found the word ἐλλός "scaly" that he applies to fish in *Ajax* 1297.

14 Probably a lake or pool.

15 Compare Hyginus, *Legends* 275.6.

Paus. 2.1.1

ἡ δὲ Κορινθία χώρα μοῖρα οὖσα τῆς Ἀργείας ἀπὸ Κορίνθου τὸ ὄνομα ἔσχηκε. Διὸς δὲ εἶναι Κόρινθον οὐδένα οἶδα εἰπόντα πω σπουδῆι πλὴν Κορινθίων τῶν πολλῶν, ἐπεὶ Εὔμηλός γε ὁ Ἀμφιλύτου τῶν Βακχιαδῶν καλουμένων, ὃς καὶ τὰ ἔπη λέγεται ποιῆσαι, φησὶν ἐν τῆι Κορινθίαι συγγραφῆι—εἰ δὴ Εὐμήλου γε ἡ συγγραφή—Ἐφύραν Ὠκεανοῦ θυγατέρα οἰκῆσαι πρῶτον ἐν τῆι γῆι ταύτηι. Μαραθῶνα δὲ κτλ. (fr. 19).

16* Favorin. *Corinth.* 11

(τῆς πόλεως) ὑπὲρ ἧς τοὺς δύο θεούς φασιν ἐρίσαι, Ποσειδῶνα καὶ τὸν Ἥλιον . . . ἐρίσαντε δὲ καὶ τὴν δίαιταν ἐπιτρέψαντε τρίτωι θεῶι πρεσβυτέρωι, οὗ

πλεῖσται μὲν κεφαλαί, πλεῖσται δέ τε χεῖρες,

τούτωι τὴν δίαιταν ἐπιτρέψαντες ἀμφότεροι τήνδε τὴν πόλιν καὶ τὴν χώραν ἔχουσιν.

Paus. 2.1.6

λέγουσι δὲ καὶ οἱ Κορίνθιοι Ποσειδῶνα ἐλθεῖν Ἡλίωι περὶ τῆς γῆς ἐς ἀμφισβήτησιν, Βριάρεων δὲ διαλλακτὴν γενέσθαι σφίσιν, ἰσθμὸν μὲν καὶ ὅσα ταύτηι δικάσαντα εἶναι Ποσειδῶνος, τὴν δὲ ἄκραν Ἡλίωι δόντα τὴν ὑπὲρ τῆς πόλεως. Cf. 2.4.6.

Pausanias, *Description of Greece*

The Corinthian territory, being a part of the Argive, has its name from Korinthos. That he was a son of Zeus, I do not know that anyone has stated seriously apart from most of the Corinthians; for Eumelus the son of Amphilytus, one of the so-called Bacchiadai, and the reputed author of the poetry, says in the *Corinthian History*—if it is by Eumelus—that Ephyra, a daughter of Oceanus, first dwelt in this land; and that subsequently Marathon, etc. (see fr. 19).

16* Favorinus, *Corinthian Oration*

(The city) over which they say two gods contested, Poseidon and Helios . . . and after referring their dispute for arbitration to a third, more senior god, who had

very many heads, and very many arms,[16]

they both occupy this city and territory.

Pausanias, *Description of Greece*

The Corinthians too say that Poseidon got into dispute with Helios over the land, and that Briareos acted as their arbitrator, who decreed that the Isthmus and that whole area should belong to Poseidon, but gave Helios the heights above the city.

[16] Anonymous verse attributed to Eumelus by Wilamowitz.

17 Schol. Pind. *Ol.* 13.74f (exscripsit schol. Eur. *Med.* 9)

διὰ τί Μηδείας ἐμνημόνευσεν; ὅτι ἡ Κόρινθος πατρῷιον αὐτῆς κτῆμα γέγονε τούτωι τῶι λόγωι· . . . διδάσκει δὲ τοῦτο Εὔμηλός τις ποιητὴς ἱστορικὸς εἰπών·

ἀλλ᾽ ὅτε δὴ Αἰήτης καὶ Ἀλωεὺς ἐξεγένοντο
Ἠελίου τε καὶ Ἀντιόπης, τότε δ᾽ ἄνδιχα χώρην
δάσσατο παισὶν ἑοῖς Ὑπερίονος ἀγλαὸς υἱός·
ἣν μὲν ἔχ᾽ Ἀσωπός, ταύτην πόρε δίωι Ἀλωεῖ·
ἣν δ᾽ Ἐφύρη κτεάτισσ᾽, Αἰήτηι δῶκεν ἅπασαν.
Αἰήτης δ᾽ ἄρ᾽ ἑκὼν Βούνωι παρέδωκε φυλάσσειν,
εἰς ὅ κεν αὐτὸς ἵκοιτ᾽ ἢ᾽ ἐξ αὐτοῖό τις ἄλλος,
ἢ παῖς ἢ᾽ υἱωνός· ὃ δ᾽ ἵκετο Κολχίδα γαῖαν.

Βοῦνος δὲ Ἑρμοῦ καὶ νύμφης τινὸς παῖς. Cf. Tzetz. in Lyc. 174.

1 δὴ West: δ᾽ codd.

Paus. 2.3.10

Εὔμηλος δὲ Ἥλιον ἔφη δοῦναι τὴν χώραν Ἀλωεῖ μὲν τὴν Ἀσωπίαν, Αἰήτηι δὲ τὴν Ἐφυραίαν. καὶ Αἰήτην ἀπιόντα ἐς Κόλχους παρακαταθέσθαι Βούνωι τὴν γῆν, Βοῦνον δὲ Ἑρμοῦ καὶ Ἀλκιδαμείας εἶναι.

17 Scholiast on Pindar, *Olympians*

Why does he mention Medea? Because Corinth was her ancestral possession according to this account . . . And this we learn from Eumelus, a historical poet, who says:

But when Aietes and Aloeus were born from Helios and Antiope, then Hyperion's glorious son divided the country in two between his sons. The Asopus riverland he awarded to noble Aloeus, while all that Ephyra had settled he gave to Aietes. Aietes chose to entrust it to Bounos, until such time as he himself should return, or someone of his blood, a child or grandchild, and he went off to the Colchian land.[17]

Bounos was the child of Hermes and a nymph.[18]

Pausanias, *Description of Greece*

Eumelus said that Helios gave Aloeus the Asopus land and Aietes the Ephyraean; and that Aietes when he went away to Colchis entrusted the country to Bounos, Bounos being the child of Hermes and Alcidamea.

[17] Another scholium on the same passage (74d) adds that Aietes went to Colchis because of an oracle that instructed him to found there a city named after himself, that is, Aia.

[18] Bounos is a stopgap figure derived from Hera's local cult title Bounaia (Pausanias 2.4.7).

18 pergit Paus.

καὶ ἐπεὶ Βοῦνος ἐτελεύτησεν, οὕτως Ἐπωπέα τὸν Ἀλωέως καὶ τὴν Ἐφυραίων σχεῖν ἀρχήν.

19 Paus. 2.1.1 (post fr. 15)

Μαραθῶνα δὲ ὕστερον τὸν Ἐπωπέως τοῦ Ἀλωέως τοῦ Ἡλίου, φεύγοντα ἀνομίαν καὶ ὕβριν τοῦ πατρός, ἐς τὰ παραθαλάσσια μετοικῆσαι τῆς Ἀττικῆς· ἀποθανόντος δὲ Ἐπωπέως ἀφικόμενον ἐς Πελοπόννησον καὶ τὴν ἀρχὴν διανείμαντα τοῖς παισίν, αὐτὸν ἐς τὴν Ἀττικὴν αὖθις ἀναχωρῆσαι. καὶ ἀπὸ μὲν Σικυῶνος τὴν Ἀσωπίαν, ἀπὸ δὲ Κορίνθου τὴν Ἐφυραίαν μετονομασθῆναι.

20 Paus. 2.3.10 (post fr. 17/18)

Κορίνθου δὲ ὕστερον τοῦ Μαραθῶνος οὐδένα ὑπολειπομένου παῖδα, τοὺς Κορινθίους Μήδειαν μεταπεμψαμένους ἐξ Ἰωλκοῦ παραδοῦναί οἱ τὴν ἀρχήν.

Schol. Eur. Med. 9 (= 19)

ὅτι δὲ βεβασίλευκε τῆς Κορίνθου ἡ Μήδεια, Εὔμηλος ἱστορεῖ καὶ Σιμωνίδης (*PMG* 545).

18 Pausanias, *Description of Greece* (continued from fr. 17)

And that when Bounos died, Aloeus' son Epopeus acquired power over the Ephyraeans too.

19 Pausanias, *Description of Greece* (continued from fr. 15)

And that subsequently Marathon, son of Epopeus, son of Aloeus the son of Helios, to escape his father's lawlessness and violence, migrated to the coastal region of Attica; and that after Epopeus' death he went to the Peloponnese and divided his realm between his sons, and himself returned to Attica; and that Sikyon gave his name to the Asopus land, and Korinthos gave his to Ephyraea.[19]

20 Pausanias, *Description of Greece* (continued from fr. 18)

And that subsequently, as Marathon's son Korinthos left no child, the Corinthians sent for Medea from Iolcus and handed over the sovereignty to her.

Scholiast on Euripides, *Medea*

That Medea was queen of Corinth, Eumelus and Simonides record.

[19] In other words the historical cities of Sicyon and Corinth got their names from the two sons of Marathon.

21 Schol. Ap. Rhod. 3.1354–1356a, "οἳ δ' ἤδη κατὰ πᾶσαν ἀνασταχύεσκον ἄρουραν | γηγενέες· φρῖξεν δὲ περὶ στιβαροῖς σακέεσσι | δούρασί τ' ἀμφιγύοις κορύθεσσί τε λαμπομένῃσιν | Ἄρηος τέμενος φθεισιμβρότου"

οὗτος καὶ οἱ ἑξῆς στίχοι εἰλημμένοι εἰσὶ παρ' Εὐμήλου, παρ' ὧι φησι Μήδεια πρὸς Ἴδμονα· < >.

22* Favorin. *Corinth.* 14

καὶ γάρ τοι καὶ ἀγῶνα πρῶτον ἐνταυθοῖ τεθῆναί φασιν ὑπὸ τῶν δύο θεῶν, καὶ νικῆσαι Κάστορα μὲν στάδιον, Κάλαϊν δὲ δίαυλον . . . Ὀρφεὺς κιθάραι, Ἡρακλῆς πάμμαχον, πυγμὴν Πολυδεύκης, πάλην Πηλεύς, δίσκον Τελαμών, ἐνόπλιον Θησεύς. ἐτέθη δὲ καὶ ἵππων ἀγών, καὶ ἐνίκα κέλητι μὲν Φαέθων, τεθρίππωι δὲ Νηλεύς. ἐγένετο δὲ καὶ νεῶν ἅμιλλα, καὶ Ἀργὼ ἐνίκα. καὶ μετὰ ταῦτα οὐκ ἔπλευσεν, ἀλλ' αὐτὴν ἀνέθηκεν ὁ Ἰάσων ἐνταῦθα τῶι Ποσειδῶνι.

---

[20] These are Apollonius' lines about the growth of warriors from the earth after Jason sowed the dragon's teeth. The scholiast should not be understood to mean that they were taken verbatim from Eumelus, but that some lines in Eumelus, spoken by Medea to the seer Idmon, appeared to be the model. The actual quotation has fallen out, but it no doubt used the "bristling" image, for which a Sophoclean parallel is also adduced.

21 Scholiast on Apollonius of Rhodes, "But now the earthborn ones were springing up all over the plowland; the murderous War god's acre bristled with stout shields and two-edged spears and shining helmets."[20]

This and the following lines are taken from Eumelus, in whom Medea says to Idmon: <" . ">.

22* Favorinus, *Corinthian Oration*

For indeed they say that games were first established here by the two gods,[21] and that the victors were

> Castor in the single straight race, Calais in the double[22] . . .

Orpheus with the lyre, Heracles as pancratiast, in the boxing Polydeuces, in the wrestling Peleus, with the discus Telamon, in the race in armor Theseus. A competition for horses was also arranged, and Phaethon won in the saddle, and Neleus with the four-horse chariot. There was also a boat race, and the Argo won it. And after that it sailed no more: Jason dedicated it there to Poseidon.[23]

21 Poseidon and Helios. This provides a mythical origin for the Isthmian Games, which were in honor of Poseidon.

22 This looks like a verse fragment. Apart from Phaethon, the son of Helios, all the victors named were Argonauts. They had brought Medea to Corinth.

23 The Argo's voyage to the Isthmus and its dedication there by Jason are mentioned also by Diodorus 4.53.2; Aristides, *Oration* 46.29; Apollodorus, *Library* 1.9.27.

23 Paus. 2.3.11 (post fr. 20)

βασιλεύειν μὲν δὴ δι᾽ αὐτὴν Ἰάσονα ἐν Κορίνθωι. Μηδείαι δὲ παῖδας μὲν γίνεσθαι, τὸ δὲ ἀεὶ τικτόμενον κατακρύπτειν αὐτὴν ἐς τὸ ἱερὸν φέρουσαν τῆς Ἥρας, κατακρύπτειν δὲ ἀθανάτους ἔσεσθαι νομίζουσαν. τέλος δὲ αὐτήν τε μαθεῖν ὡς ἡμαρτήκοι τῆς ἐλπίδος, καὶ ἅμα ὑπὸ τοῦ Ἰάσονος φωραθεῖσαν—οὐ γὰρ αὐτὸν ἔχειν δεομένηι συγγνώμην, ἀποπλέοντα <δὲ> ἐς Ἰωλκὸν οἴχεσθαι—τούτων δὴ ἕνεκα ἀπελθεῖν καὶ Μήδειαν, παραδοῦσαν Σισύφωι τὴν ἀρχήν. τάδε μὲν οὕτως ἔχοντα ἐπελεξάμην.

24 Paus. 2.2.2

<τάφους δὲ> Σισύφου καὶ Νηλέως—καὶ γὰρ Νηλέα ἀφικόμενον ἐς Κόρινθον νόσωι τελευτῆσαί φασι καὶ περὶ τὸν ἰσθμὸν ταφῆναι—οὐκ ἂν οἶδ᾽ εἰ ζητοίη τις, ἐπιλεξάμενος τὰ Εὐμήλου. Νηλέως μὲν γὰρ οὐδὲ Νέστορι ἐπιδειχθῆναι τὸ μνῆμα ὑπὸ τοῦ Σισύφου φησί, χρῆναι γὰρ ἄγνωστον τοῖς πᾶσιν ὁμοίως εἶναι· Σίσυφον δὲ ταφῆναι μὲν ἐν τῶι ἰσθμῶι, τὸν δέ οἱ τάφον καὶ τῶν ἐφ᾽ αὐτοῦ Κορινθίων ὀλίγους εἶναι τοὺς εἰδότας.

(Σισύφου) φησί Bekker: φασί codd.

23 Pausanias, *Description of Greece* (continued from fr. 20)

So because of her Jason was king at Corinth. Medea had children, but as each one was born she would take it into the shrine of Hera and bury it, in the belief that they would be made immortal. But in the end she realized that her hopes were in vain, and she was detected by Jason, who had no sympathy with her pleas but sailed off back to Iolcus; so Medea departed too, transferring the sovereignty to Sisyphus. That is the story as I have read it.[24]

24 Pausanias, *Description of Greece*

As for tombs of Sisyphus and Neleus—for Neleus too they say came to Corinth and died there of an illness, and was buried at the Isthmus—I do not know if one should look for them, after my reading of Eumelus. For he says that Neleus' tomb was not even shown to Nestor by Sisyphus, as it had to be unknown to his sons as to everyone else; and that Sisyphus was buried in the Isthmus, but his tomb was known to few of the Corinthians even of his own time.

[24] The story of Medea's children's death and her separation from Jason takes a different form from that familiar from Euripides' *Medea*. The underlying fact is a Corinthian cult of the dead children, whose tomb was situated in the precinct of Hera. See Euripides, *Medea* 1378–1383; Parmeniscus in schol. Eur. *Medea* 264; Pausanias 2.3.7; M. P. Nilsson, *Griechische Feste von religiöser Bedeutung* (Leipzig, 1906), 57–60. Probably the dead children of the cult were originally sons of a local goddess Medea who had no connection with the Medea of the Argonautic legend. The coincidence of name then led to Aietes' and Jason's introduction into the Corinthian story.

25 Schol. Ap. Rhod. 1.146–149a

Γλαύκου δὲ αὐτὴν (Ledam) τοῦ Σισύφου εἶναι πατρὸς ἐν Κορινθιακοῖς λέγει Εὔμηλος καὶ Παντειδυίας μητρός, ἱστορῶν ὅτι τῶν ἵππων ἀπολομένων ἦλθεν εἰς Λακεδαίμονα ὁ Γλαῦκος καὶ ἐκεῖ ἐμίγη Παντειδυίαι· ἣν ὕστερον γήμασθαι Θεστίωι φασὶ (v.l. φησὶ) <καὶ τεκεῖν> τὴν Λήδαν, γόνωι μὲν οὖσαν Γλαύκου, λόγωι δὲ Θεστίου.

3. Εὐρωπία

26 Philod. *De pietate* B 7262 Obbink

ὁ̣ δὲ̣ [τὴν Εὐ]ρώπειαν γράψα[ς] κα̣ὶ̣ α̣ὐ̣τῆς τ̣ὸ̣ν̣ α[ὐ]τὸν ἐρασθῆνα̣[ί] φησιν, καὶ διὰ τ[ὸ] μὴ ὑπομεῖνα[ι μι]χθῆναι̣ Δ̣ι̣ὶ̣ α̣ὐ̣τ̣[ὸν] αὐτὴ̣ν̣ [τὸν] Δ̣ί̣α̣ [πα]ρηι̣ρ̣ῆ̣σ̣[θαι

27 Schol. (D) *Il.* 6.131

Διόνυσος ὁ Διὸς καὶ Σεμέλης παῖς, ἐν Κυβέλοις τῆς Φρυγίας ὑπὸ τῆς Ῥέας τυχὼν καθαρμῶν καὶ διδαχθεὶς τὰς τελετὰς καὶ λαβὼν πᾶσαν παρὰ τῆς θεοῦ τὴν διασκευήν, ἀνὰ πᾶσαν ἐφέρετο τὴν γῆν χορεύων καὶ τελετὰς ποιούμενος, καὶ τιμῶν τυγχάνων προηγεῖτο πάντων τῶν ἀνθρώπων. παραγενόμενον δὲ αὐτὸν εἰς τὴν Θράικην Λυκοῦργος ὁ Δρύαντος, λυπήσας Ἥρας μίσει, μύωπι ἀπελαύνει τῆς γῆς, καὶ καθάπτεται τῶν τούτου τιθηνῶν· ἐτύγχανον γὰρ αὐτῶι συνοργιάζουσαι· θεηλάτωι δὲ ἐλαυνόμενος μάστιγι τὸν θεὸν ἔσπευδε τιμωρήσασθαι. ὁ δὲ ὑπὸ δέους εἰς τὴν θάλασσαν καταδύνει, καὶ ὑπὸ Θέτιδος ὑπολαμβάνεται καὶ Εὐρυνόμης. ὁ οὖν Λυκοῦργος οὐκ

25 Scholiast on Apollonius of Rhodes

But Eumelus in the *Corinthiaca* says that Leda's father was Glaucus the son of Sisyphus and her mother Panteidyia; he records that when his horses were missing Glaucus went to Lacedaemon, and there made love to Panteidyia, who they say [variant: he says] subsequently married Thestius <and bore> Leda, so that she was biologically the child of Glaucus, though officially of Thestius.

3. *Europia*

26 Philodemus, *On Piety*

The author of the *Europia* says that the same god fell in love with her [Europa?] too, and that because she would not submit to intercourse with Zeus, Zeus himself abducted her.

27 Scholiast on the *Iliad*

Dionysus the son of Zeus and Semele, having received purification from Rhea at Mt. Kybela in Phrygia and been taught the rites and acquired all the paraphernalia from the goddess, roamed all over the world, dancing and celebrating the rites and receiving honors, and all the people followed him. But when he came to Thrace, Lycurgus the son of Dryas, made vexatious by Hera's hatred, tried to drive him out of the country with an ox-goad, and assaulted his nurses, who were participating in his revels; driven on by a divine scourge, he was set on punishing the god. Dionysus plunged into the sea in his fear, and was taken in by Thetis and Eurynome. Well,

ἀμισθὶ δυσσεβήσας ἔδωκε τὴν ἐξ ἀνθρώπων δίκην· ἀφηιρέθη γὰρ πρὸς τοῦ Διὸς τοὺς ὀφθαλμούς. τῆς ἱστορίας πολλοὶ ἐμνήσθησαν, προηγουμένως δὲ ὁ τὴν Εὐρωπίαν πεποιηκὼς Εὔμηλος.

28 Clem. *Strom.* 1.164.3

ἀλλὰ καὶ ὁ τὴν Εὐρωπίαν ποιήσας ἱστορεῖ τὸ ἐν Δελφοῖς ἄγαλμα Ἀπόλλωνος κίονα εἶναι διὰ τῶνδε·

> ὄφρα θεῶι δεκάτην ἀκροθίνιά τε κρεμάσαιμεν
> σταθμῶν ἐκ ζαθέων καὶ κίονος ὑψηλοῖο.

29 Schol. Ap. Rhod. 2.946–954c, "Σινώπην | θυγατέρ' Ἀσωποῖο"

πόλις τοῦ Πόντου ἡ Σινώπη, ὠνομασμένη ἀπὸ τῆς Ἀσωποῦ θυγατρὸς Σινώπης, ἣν ἁρπάσας Ἀπόλλων ἀπὸ Ὑρίας ἐκόμισεν εἰς Πόντον . . . ἐν δὲ τοῖς Ὀρφικοῖς (fr. 45 Kern) Ἄρεως καὶ Αἰγίνης γενεαλογεῖται, κατὰ δέ τινας Ἄρεως καὶ Παρνάσσης, κατ' Εὔμηλον καὶ Ἀριστοτέλην (fr. 581) Ἀσωποῦ.

30 Paus. 9.5.8

ὁ δὲ τὰ ἔπη τὰ ἐς Εὐρώπην ποιήσας φησὶν Ἀμφίονα χρήσασθαι λύραι πρῶτον, Ἑρμοῦ διδάξαντος· πεποίηκε δὲ καὶ <τὰ περὶ> λίθων καὶ θηρίων, ὅτι καὶ ταῦτα ἄιδων ἦγε.

Cf. Apollod. *Bibl.* 3.5.5.

Lycurgus paid for his impiety with mortal punishment: he was deprived of his eyesight by Zeus. Many authors refer to the story, and in the first instance Eumelus, the author of the *Europia*.

28 Clement of Alexandria, *Miscellanies*

The author of the *Europia*, too, records that Apollo's image at Delphi was a pillar, in these verses:

So that we might hang up for the god a tithe and first fruits from his holy steading and tall pillar.

29 Scholiast on Apollonius of Rhodes, "Sinope, daughter of Asopus"

Sinope is a Pontic town, named after Asopus' daughter Sinope, whom Apollo carried off from Hyria and took to the Black Sea . . . In the Orphic poems she is made the daughter of Ares and Aegina; according to some, of Ares and Parnassa; according to Eumelus and Aristotle, of Asopus.

30 Pausanias, *Description of Greece*

The author of the Europa epic says that Amphion was the first to use the lyre, Hermes having instructed him. And he has told the tale of the stones and animals that Amphion drew by his singing.[25]

[25] Amphion and his brother Zethus built the walls of Thebes (*Odyssey* 11.262–265). Amphion's lyre music made the stones move into place of their own accord ("Hesiod," fr. 182). According to Asius (fr. 1) the two brothers were the sons of the Sicyonian Epopeus.

4. Incertae Sedis

31 Apollod. *Bibl.* 3.8.2

Εὔμηλος δὲ καί τινες ἕτεροι λέγουσι Λυκάονι καὶ θυγατέρα Καλλιστὼ γενέσθαι.

32 Apollod. *Bibl.* 3.9.1

Ἀρκάδος δὲ καὶ Λεανείρας τῆς Ἀμύκλου ἢ Μετανείρας τῆς Κρόκωνος, ὡς δὲ Εὔμηλος λέγει, νύμφης Χρυσοπελείας, ἐγένοντο παῖδες Ἔλατος καὶ Ἀφείδας.

33 Apollod. *Bibl.* 3.11.1

Μενέλαος μὲν οὖν ἐξ Ἑλένης Ἑρμιόνην ἐγέννησε . . . ἐκ Κνωσσίας δὲ νύμφης κατὰ Εὔμηλον Ξενόδαμον.

34 Clem. *Strom.* 6.11.1

Εὐμήλου γὰρ ποιήσαντος

Μνημοσύνης καὶ Ζηνὸς Ὀλυμπίου ἐννέα κοῦραι,

Σόλων τῆς ἐλεγείας ὧδε ἄρχεται· “Μνημοσύνης καὶ Ζηνὸς Ὀλυμπίου ἀγλαὰ τέκνα” (fr. 13.1 West).

4. Unplaced Fragments

31 Apollodorus, *The Library*

Eumelus and certain others say that Lycaon also had a daughter, Callisto.[26]

32 Apollodorus, *The Library*

From Arcas and Leaneira the daughter of Amyclus, or Metaneira the daughter of Crocon, or, as Eumelus says, a nymph Chrysopeleia, were born Elatos and Apheidas.

33 Apollodorus, *The Library*

Menelaus fathered Hermione from Helen . . . and from a Cnossian nymph, according to Eumelus, Xenodamus.

34 Clement of Alexandria, *Miscellanies*

For when Eumelus had written

O daughters nine of Mnemosyne and Olympian Zeus,

Solon begins his elegy thus: "O glorious children of Mnemosyne and Olympian Zeus."

[26] Eumelus must have told the story of how Zeus made love to Callisto and changed her into a bear. Artemis killed her, but Zeus saved her child, who was Arcas (fr. 32), the eponym of the Arcadians.

35 Tzetz. in Hes. *Op.* p.23 Gaisford

ἀλλ᾽ Εὔμηλος μὲν ὁ Κορίνθιος τρεῖς φησιν εἶναι Μούσας θυγατέρας Ἀπόλλωνος· Κηφισοῦν, Ἀπολλωνίδα, Βορυσθενίδα.

ΚΙΝΑΙΘΩΝ

TESTIMONIA

Plut. *De Pyth. orac.* 407b

Ὀνομάκριτοι δ᾽ ἐκεῖνοι καὶ Πρόδικοι καὶ Κιναίθωνες ὅσην αἰτίαν ἠνέγκαντο <ἐπὶ> τῶν χρησμῶν, ὡς τραγωιδίαν αὐτοῖς καὶ ὄγκον οὐδὲν δεομένοις προσθέντες, ἐῶ λέγειν.

Πρόδικοι καὶ Κιναίθωνες Botzon: προδόται καὶ κινέσωνες codd.

Euseb. *Chron.*

Ol. 4.1: Cinaethon Lacedaemonius poeta, qui Telegoniam scripsit agnoscitur.

Telegoniam] Genealogias *Scaliger.*

IG 14.1292 ii 11 = Tabula Iliaca K (Borgiae) p. 61 Sadurska

τ]ὴν Οἰδιπόδειαν τὴν ὑπὸ Κιναίθωνος τοῦ [Λακεδαιμονίου λεγομένην πεποιῆσθαι παραλιπόν]τες, ἐπῶν

35 Tzetzes, commentary on Hesiod

But Eumelus of Corinth says there are three Muses, daughters of Apollo: Cephiso, Apollonis, and Borysthenis.[27]

CINAETHON

TESTIMONIA

Plutarch, *On the Pythia's Oracles*

As for all the blame those people such as Onomacritus, Prodicus, and Cinaethon have incurred in respect of oracles by adding unnecessary pomp and drama to them, I pass over it.

Eusebius, *Chronicle*

Ol. 4.1 (764/763): Cinaethon the Lacedaemonian poet, who wrote the *Telegony*,[28] is recognized.

Borgia plaque

. . . passing over t]he *Oedipodea*, which [they say was composed] by Cinaethon the [Lacedaemonian] in 6,600 verses,

[27] Borysthenis is from Borysthenes, the river Dnieper; Cephiso is also from a river, there being several Greek rivers Cephisus. Perhaps Apollonis is a mistake for another river-derived name such as Achelois (Hermann) or Asopis.

[28] Perhaps an error for *Genealogies*.

οὖσαν ͵ϝχʹ, ὑποθήσομεν Θηβαΐδα [

[Λακεδαιμονίου - παραλιπόν]τες e.g. suppl. Wilamowitz.

Schol. Eur. *Tro.* 822

. . . τῶι τὴν Μικρὰν Ἰλιάδα πεποιηκότι, ὃν οἱ μὲν Θεστορίδην Φωκ<αι>έα φασίν, οἱ δὲ Κιναίθωνα Λακεδαιμόνιον, ὡς Ἑλλάνικος (fr. 202C Fowler, Hellan. gramm. fr. 6* Montanari), οἱ δὲ Διόδωρον Ἐρυθραῖον.

Ἑλλάνικος Hermann: μελάνικος cod.

FRAGMENTA

1 Paus. 8.53.5

Κιναίθων δὲ ἐν τοῖς ἔπεσιν ἐποίησεν <ὡς> Ῥαδάμανθυς μὲν Φαίστου, Φαῖστος δὲ εἴη Τάλω, Τάλων δὲ εἶναι Κρητὸς παῖδα.

Φαίστου, Φαῖστος Malten: Ἡφαίστου, Ἥφαιστος codd.

2 Paus. 2.3.9

Κιναίθων δὲ ὁ Λακεδαιμόνιος, ἐγενεαλόγησε γὰρ καὶ οὗτος ἔπεσι, Μήδειον καὶ θυγατέρα Ἐριῶπιν Ἰάσονι εἶπεν ἐκ Μηδείας γενέσθαι· πέρα δὲ ἐς τοὺς παῖδας οὐδὲ τούτωι πεποιημένα ἐστίν.

we will put down the *Thebaid* [. . .

Scholiast on Euripides, *Trojan Women*

. . . the author of the *Little Iliad*, whom some say was Thestorides of Phocaea, others Cinaethon of Lacedaemon, as Hellanicus says,[29] and others Diodorus of Erythrae.

FRAGMENTS

1 Pausanias, *Description of Greece*

Cinaethon in his verses made Rhadamanthys the son of Phaestus, Phaestus the son of Talos, and Talos the son of Cres.[30]

2 Pausanias, *Description of Greece*

Cinaethon the Lacedaemonian (for he too wrote genealogies in verse) said that Jason had Medeios and a daughter Eriopis by Medea; but there is nothing further about the children in his work either.

[29] It is uncertain whether the fifth-century mythographer or the Hellenistic grammarian is meant.

[30] Phaestus (emended from "Hephaestus") is the eponym of the Cretan town of that name, and Cres the eponym of the island.

3 Porphyrius ap. schol. (D) *Il.* 3.175

Ἑλένης τε καὶ Μενελάου ἱστορεῖ Ἀρίαιθος (*FGrHist* 316 F 6) παῖδα Μαράφιον, ἀφ' οὗ τὸ τῶν Μαραφίων γένος ἐν Πέρσαις· ὡς δὲ Κιναίθων, Νικόστρατον.

4 Paus. 2.18.6

Ὀρέστου δὲ ἀποθανόντος ἔσχε Τεισαμενὸς τὴν ἀρχήν, Ἑρμιόνης τῆς Μενελάου καὶ Ὀρέστου παῖς. τὸν δὲ Ὀρέστου νόθον Πενθίλον Κιναίθων ἔγραψεν <ἐν> τοῖς ἔπεσιν Ἠριγόνην τὴν Αἰγίσθου τεκεῖν.

5 Paus. 4.2.1

πυθέσθαι δὲ σπουδῆι πάνυ ἐθελήσας, οἵτινες παῖδες Πολυκάονι ἐγένοντο ἐκ Μεσσήνης, ἐπελεξάμην τάς τε Ἠοίας καλουμένας καὶ τὰ ἔπη τὰ Ναυπάκτια, πρὸς δὲ αὐτοῖς ὁπόσα Κιναίθων καὶ Ἄσιος ἐγενεαλόγησαν· οὐ μὴν ἔς γε ταῦτα ἦν σφισιν οὐδὲν πεποιημένον.

ΑΣΙΟΣ

1 Paus. 2.6.4

καὶ ἔπη <ἐπὶ> τούτωι πεποίηκεν Ἄσιος ὁ Ἀμφιπτολέμου·

Ἀντιόπη δ' ἔτεκε Ζῆθον κἀμφίονα δῖον
Ἀσωποῦ κούρη ποταμοῦ βαθυδινήεντος,
Ζηνί τε κυσαμένη καὶ Ἐπωπέϊ ποιμένι λαῶν.

3 Porphyry, *Homeric Questions*

From Helen and Menelaus Ariaithos records a son Maraphius, from whom the Maraphians of Persia descend; or as Cinaethon says, Nicostratus.[31]

4 Pausanias, *Description of Greece*

When Orestes died, Tisamenus became ruler, the son of Menelaus' daughter Hermione and of Orestes. As for Orestes' bastard son Penthilus, Cinaethon in his verses wrote that he was born to Aegisthus' daughter Erigone.

5 Pausanias, *Description of Greece*

Wanting very much to find out what children Polycaon had by Messene, I read the so-called *Ehoiai* and the *Naupactia*, and besides them all the genealogies of Cinaethon and Asius; but on this point they had not said anything.

ASIUS

1 Pausanias, *Description of Greece*

And Asius the son of Amphiptolemus has composed verses on this:

Antiope, daughter of Asopus the deep-swirling river, bore Zethus and noble Amphion, after conceiving to Zeus and Epopeus, shepherd of peoples.

31 For Nicostratus see "Hesiod," fr. 175.

2 Strab. 6.1.15

καὶ Ἄσιον τὸν ποιητὴν φήσαντα ὅτι τὸν Βοιωτὸν

Δίου ἐνὶ μεγάροις τέκεν εὐειδὴς Μελανίππη.

3 Paus. 9.23.6

εἶναι δὲ Ἀθάμαντος καὶ Θεμιστοῦς παῖδα τὸν Πτῶον, ἀφ' οὗ τῶι τε Ἀπόλλωνι ἐπίκλησις καὶ τῶι ὄρει τὸ ὄνομα ἐγένετο, Ἄσιος ἐν τοῖς ἔπεσιν εἴρηκε.

4 Paus. 5.17.8

Ἄσιος δὲ ἐν τοῖς ἔπεσι καὶ Ἀλκμήνην ἐποίησε θυγατέρα Ἀμφιαράου καὶ Ἐριφύλης εἶναι.

5 Paus. 2.29.4

Φώκωι δὲ Ἄσιος ὁ τὰ ἔπη ποιήσας γενέσθαι φησὶ Πανοπέα καὶ Κρῖσον. καὶ Πανοπέως μὲν ἐγένετο Ἐπειὸς ὁ τὸν ἵππον τὸν δούρειον, ὡς Ὅμηρος ἐποίησεν (*Od.* 8.493), ἐργασάμενος· Κρίσου δὲ ἦν ἀπόγονος τρίτος Πυλάδης, Στροφίου τε ὢν τοῦ Κρίσου καὶ Ἀναξιβίας ἀδελφῆς Ἀγαμέμνονος.

6 Paus. 3.13.8

γεγόνασι δὲ οἱ Τυνδάρεω παῖδες τὰ πρὸς μητρὸς ἀπὸ τοῦ Πλευρῶνος· Θέστιον γὰρ τὸν Λήδας πατέρα Ἄσιός φησιν ἐν τοῖς ἔπεσιν Ἀγήνορος παῖδα εἶναι τοῦ Πλευρῶνος.

2 Strabo, *Geography*

. . . and the poet Asius, who said that Boeotus

was born in Dius' house to fair Melanippe.

3 Pausanias, *Description of Greece*

That Ptous, from whom Ptoian Apollo got his title and Mt. Ptoion its name, was the son of Athamas and Themisto, Asius has said in his verses.

4 Pausanias, *Description of Greece*

Asius in his verses made Alcmena too the daughter of Amphiaraus and Eriphyle.

5 Pausanias, *Description of Greece*

Phocus' sons, according to Asius the verse-writer, were Panopeus and Crisus.[32] And from Panopeus was born Epeios, the man who constructed the wooden horse, as Homer wrote, while Crisus' grandson was Pylades, who was the son of Crisus' son Strophios and Agamemnon's sister Anaxibia.

6 Pausanias, *Description of Greece*

The sons of Tyndareus are of Pleuron's stock on their mother's side, for Asius in his verses says that Leda's father Thestius was the son of Agenor the son of Pleuron.

[32] Phocus is the eponym of Phocis, and his sons the eponyms of the Phocian towns Panopeus and Crisa. Compare "Hesiod," fr. 58.

7 Paus. 7.4.1

Ἄσιος δὲ ὁ Ἀμφιπτολέμου Σάμιος ἐποίησεν ἐν τοῖς ἔπεσιν ὡς Φοίνικι ἐκ Περιμήδης τῆς Οἰνέως γένοιτο Ἀστυπάλαια καὶ Εὐρώπη, Ποσειδῶνος δὲ καὶ Ἀστυπαλαίας εἶναι παῖδα Ἀγκαῖον, βασιλεύειν δὲ αὐτὸν τῶν καλουμένων Λελέγων· Ἀγκαίωι δὲ τὴν θυγατέρα τοῦ ποταμοῦ λαβόντι τοῦ Μαιάνδρου Σαμίαν γενέσθαι Περίλαον καὶ Ἔνουδον καὶ Σάμον καὶ Ἁλιθέρσην καὶ θυγατέρα ἐπ᾽ αὐτῶι Παρθενόπην· Παρθενόπης δὲ τῆς Ἀγκαίου καὶ Ἀπόλλωνος Λυκομήδην γενέσθαι. Ἄσιος μὲν ἐς τοσοῦτο ἐν τοῖς ἔπεσιν ἐδήλωσε.

8 Paus. 8.1.4

πεποίηται δὲ καὶ Ἀσίωι τοιάδε ἐς αὐτόν·

> ἀντίθεον δὲ Πελασγὸν ἐν ὑψικόμοισιν ὄρεσσιν
> γαῖα μέλαιν᾽ ἀνέδωκεν, ἵνα θνητῶν γένος εἴη.

9 Apollod. *Bibl.* 3.8.2

Εὔμηλος δὲ (fr. 31) καί τινες ἕτεροι λέγουσι Λυκάονι καὶ θυγατέρα Καλλιστὼ γενέσθαι. <ἄλλοι δὲ οὔ φασιν αὐτὴν τούτου γενέσθαι·> Ἡσίοδος μὲν γὰρ αὐτὴν (fr. 163) μίαν εἶναι τῶν νυμφῶν λέγει, Ἄσιος δὲ Νυκτέως, Φερεκύδης δὲ (fr. 157 Fowler) Κητέως.

7 Pausanias, *Description of Greece*

Asius of Samos, the son of Amphiptolemus, wrote in his verses that to Phoenix from Oineus' daughter Perimede were born Astypalaea and Europa, and that Poseidon and Astypalaea had a son Ancaeus, who was king of the people called Leleges; and that to Ancaeus, who married Samia, the daughter of the river Maeander, were born Perilaus, Enoudos, Samos, Halitherses, and a daughter Parthenope in addition; and that from Ancaeus' daughter Parthenope and Apollo, Lycomedes was born. This much Asius made clear in his verses.

8 Pausanias, *Description of Greece*

Asius too has written about him as follows:

And godlike Pelasgus the dark earth put forth in the wooded mountains, so that there might be a mortal race.[33]

9 Apollodorus, *The Library*

Eumelus and some others say that Lycaon also had a daughter, Callisto. <But others say she was not his daughter,> for Hesiod says she was one of the nymphs, Asius makes her the daughter of Nycteus, and Pherecydes the daughter of Ceteus.

[33] In Arcadian myth Pelasgus was the first man, who grew from the earth like a tree. Compare "Hesiod," fr. 160.

10 Schol. *Od.* 4.797, "δέμας δ' ἤϊκτο γυναικί, | Ἰφθίμηι, κούρηι μεγαλήτορος Ἰκαρίοιο"

οὕτως ἐκαλεῖτο κυρίως ἡ ἀδελφὴ τῆς Πηνελόπης. Ἄσιος δέ φησι·

κοῦραί τ' Ἰκαρίοιο Μέδη καὶ Πηνελόπεια.

Ἄνδρων δὲ (fr. 12 Fowler) Ὑψιπύλην λέγει.

11 Paus. 2.6.5

Σικυῶνα δὲ οὐ Μαραθῶνος τοῦ Ἐπωπέως, Μητίονος δὲ εἶναι τοῦ Ἐρεχθέως φασίν· ὁμολογεῖ δέ σφισι καὶ Ἄσιος.

12 Paus. 4.2.1, see Cinaethon fr. 5.

13 Ath. 525e

περὶ δὲ τῆς Σαμίων τρυφῆς Δοῦρις ἱστορῶν (*FGrHist* 76 F 60) παρατίθεται Ἀσίου ποιήματα, ὅτι ἐφόρουν χλίδωνας περὶ τοῖς βραχίοσιν καὶ τὴν ἑορτὴν ἄγοντες τῶν Ἡραίων ἐβάδιζον κατεκτενισμένοι τὰς κόμας ἐπὶ τὸ μετάφρενον καὶ τοὺς ὤμους . . . ἔστι δὲ τὰ τοῦ Ἀσίου ἔπη οὕτως ἔχοντα·

οἳ δ' αὔτως φοίτεσκον, ὅπως πλοκάμους κτενίσαιντο,
εἰς Ἥρης τέμενος, πεπυκασμένοι εἵμασι καλοῖς,
χιονέοισι χιτῶσι †πέδον χθονὸς εὐρέος εἶχον†·

10 Scholiast on the *Odyssey*, "and in form she resembled a woman, Iphthime, the daughter of the heroic Icarius"

This was the proper name of Penelope's sister. But Asius says:

And the daughters of Icarius, Meda and Penelope.

And Andron calls her Hypsipyle.

11 Pausanias, *Description of Greece*

As for Sikyon, they say he was not the son of Epopeus' son Marathon,[34] but of Erechtheus' son Metion; and Asius agrees with them.

12 Pausanias, *Description of Greece*: see above, Cinaethon fr. 5.

13 Athenaeus, *Scholars at Dinner*

On the subject of the Samians' luxury, Duris adduces poetry of Asius to the effect that they wore bangles round their arms, and that when they celebrated the Heraia festival they paraded with their hair combed back over the nape and shoulders . . . Asius' lines are as follows:

And they would go like that, when they had combed their locks, to Hera's precinct, wrapped in fine garments, in snowy tunics reaching down to the ground(?);[35] there were

[34] As in the version of Eumelus, fr. 19.
[35] The Greek is corrupt.

χρύσειαι δὲ κορύμβαι ἐπ' αὐτῶν τέττιγες ὥς·
χαῖται δ' <ἠι>ωρέο<ν>τ' ἀνέμωι χρυσέοις ἐνὶ δεσμοῖς·
δαιδάλεοι δὲ χλίδωνες ἄρ' ἀμφὶ βραχίοσιν ἦσαν
<   >τες ὑπασπίδιον πολεμιστήν.

ΗΓΗΣΙΝΟΥ ΑΤΘΙΣ

Paus. 9.29.1

θῦσαι δὲ ἐν Ἑλικῶνι Μούσαις πρώτους καὶ ἐπονομάσαι τὸ ὄρος ἱερὸν εἶναι Μουσῶν Ἐφιάλτην καὶ Ὦτον λέγουσιν, οἰκίσαι δὲ αὐτοὺς καὶ Ἄσκρην. καὶ δὴ καὶ Ἡγησίνους ἐπὶ τῶιδε ἐν τῆι Ἀτθίδι ἐποίησεν·

Ἄσκρηι δ' αὖ παρέλεκτο Ποσειδάων ἐνοσίχθων,
ἣ δή οἱ τέκε παῖδα περιπλομένων ἐνιαυτῶν
Οἴοκλον, ὃς πρῶτος μετ' Ἀλωέος ἔκτισε παίδων
Ἄσκρην, ἥ θ' Ἑλικῶνος ἔχει πόδα πιδακόεντα.

ταύτην τοῦ Ἡγησίνου τὴν ποίησιν οὐκ ἐπελεξάμην, ἀλλὰ πρότερον ἄρα ἐκλελοιπυῖα ἦν πρὶν ἢ ἐμὲ γενέσθαι· Κάλλιππος *δὲ* Κορίνθιος *ἐν τῆι ἐς* Ὀρχομενίους *συγγραφῆι* (*FGrHist* 385 F 1) *μαρτύρια ποιεῖται τῶι λόγωι τὰ ἔπη, ὡσαύτως δὲ καὶ ἡμεῖς πεποιήμεθα παρ' αὐτοῦ* {Καλλίππου} *διδαχθέντες.*

gold brooches on them, like crickets;[36] their hair floated in the wind, bound in gold; round their arms there were ornate bracelets; [. . .] a shield-covered warrior.

HEGESINOUS, *ATTHIS*

Pausanias, *Description of Greece*

They say that the first to sacrifice to the Muses on Helicon and to pronounce the mountain to be sacred to the Muses were Ephialtes and Otus; and that they also founded Ascra. And indeed Hegesinous composed verses on this in his *Atthis*:

As for Ascra, Poseidon the earth-shaker lay with her, and she bore him a son in the course of time: Oioklos, the original founder, with the sons of Aloeus, of Ascra, which occupies Helicon's well-watered foot.

This poem of Hegesinous I have not read; it had gone out of circulation before my time; but Callippus of Corinth in his work addressed to the Orchomenians quotes the verses in support of his argument, and we have done likewise, as apprised by him.

36 See A. W. Gomme's commentary on Thucydides 1.6.3.

ΧΕΡΣΙΑΣ

TESTIMONIA

Plut. *Sept. sap. conv.* 156e

εἰπόντος δὲ ταῦτα τοῦ Μνησιφίλου, Χερσίας ὁ ποιητής (ἀφεῖτο γὰρ ἤδη τῆς αἰτίας καὶ διήλλακτο τῶι Περιάνδρωι νεωστί, Χίλωνος δεηθέντος) "ἆρ᾽ οὖν," ἔφη, κτλ.

Plut. *Sept. sap. conv.* 163f

ἐπὶ δὲ τούτοις ὁ ποιητὴς Χερσίας ἄλλων τε σωθέντων ἀνελπίστως ἐμέμνητο καὶ Κυψέλου τοῦ Περιάνδρου πατρός . . . διὸ καὶ τὸν οἶκον ἐν Δελφοῖς κατεσκεύασεν ὁ Κύψελος . . . καὶ ὁ Πιττακὸς προσαγορεύσας τὸν Περίανδρον, "εὖ γ'" ἔφη "Περίανδρε Χερσίας ἐποίησε μνησθεὶς τοῦ οἴκου· πολλάκις γὰρ ἐβουλόμην ἐρέσθαι σε τῶν βατράχων τὴν αἰτίαν ἐκείνων, τί βούλονται περὶ τὸν πυθμένα τοῦ φοίνικος ἐντετορευμένοι τοσοῦτοι . . ." τοῦ δὲ Περιάνδρου τὸν Χερσίαν ἐρωτᾶν κελεύσαντος, εἰδέναι γὰρ ἐκεῖνον καὶ παρεῖναι τῶι Κυψέλωι καθιεροῦντι τὸν οἶκον, ὁ Χερσίας μειδιάσας κτλ.

CHERSIAS

TESTIMONIA

Plutarch, *Banquet of the Seven Sages*

When Mnesiphilus had spoken, the poet Chersias (for he had now been acquitted of the charge against him and recently reconciled with Periander on Chilon's pleading) said, etc.

Whereupon the poet Chersias recalled other cases of unexpected salvation, and that of Cypselus, Periander's father . . . which was why Cypselus constructed the building at Delphi . . . And Pittacus, addressing Periander, said, "It's good that Chersias has mentioned the building, Periander, because I've often wanted to ask you the explanation of those frogs, why they are carved in such numbers round the base of the palm-tree . . ." When Periander told him to ask Chersias, as he knew that he had actually been present when Cypselus consecrated the building, Chersias smiled and said, etc.

FRAGMENTUM

Paus. 9.38.9

Ἀσπληδόνα δὲ ἐκλιπεῖν τοὺς οἰκήτοράς φασιν ὕδατος σπανίζοντας· γενέσθαι δὲ τὸ ὄνομα ἀπὸ Ἀσπληδόνος τῆι πόλει, τοῦτον δὲ εἶναι νύμφης τε Μιδείας καὶ Ποσειδῶνος. ὁμολογεῖ δὲ καὶ ἔπη σφίσιν ἃ ἐποίησε Χερσίας ἀνὴρ Ὀρχομένιος·

> ἐκ δὲ Ποσειδάωνος ἀγακλειτῆς τε Μιδείης
> Ἀσπληδὼν γένεθ' υἱὸς ἀν' εὐρύχορον πτολίεθρον.

οὐδὲ τοῦ Χερσίου τῶν ἐπῶν οὐδεμία ἦν ἔτι κατ' ἐμὲ μνήμη, ἀλλὰ καὶ τάδε ἐπηγάγετο ὁ Κάλλιππος (*FGrHist* 385 F 2) ἐς τὸν αὐτὸν λόγον τὸν ἔχοντα ἐς Ὀρχομενίους. τούτου δὲ τοῦ Χερσίου καὶ ἐπίγραμμα οἱ Ὀρχομένιοι τὸ ἐπὶ τῶι Ἡσιόδου τάφωι μνημονεύουσιν.

ΔΑΝΑΙΣ

TESTIMONIUM

IG 14.1292 ii 10 = Tabula Iliaca K (Borgiae) p. 61 Sadurska

] ἔπεσιν, καὶ Δαναΐδας ͵Ϝφ´ ἐπῶν, καὶ τὸν [

FRAGMENTA

1 Clem. *Strom.* 4.120.4

> καὶ τότ' ἄρ' ὡπλίζοντο θοῶς Δαναοῖο θύγατρες
> πρόσθεν ἐϋρρεῖος ποταμοῦ Νείλοιο ἄνακτος.

DANAIS

FRAGMENT

Pausanias, *Description of Greece*

They say that its founders abandoned Aspledon for lack of water; and that the town got its name from Aspledon, who was the son of a nymph Midea and Poseidon. They find agreement in the verses composed by Chersias, an Orchomenian:

And from Poseidon and renowned Midea a son Aspledon
was born in the broad-arena'd township.

Of Chersias' verses too[37] there was no longer any record in my time: they too were adduced by Callippus in that same discourse bearing on the Orchomenians. Of this Chersias the Orchomenians also record an epigram, the one on Hesiod's tomb.[38]

DANAIS

TESTIMONIUM

Borgia plaque

. . . and the *Danaids*, in 6,500 verses, and the [. . .

FRAGMENTS

1 Clement of Alexandria, *Miscellanies*

And then swiftly the daughters of Danaus armed themselves in front of the fair-flowing river, the lord Nile.

[37] Like those of Hegesinous, which Pausanias quoted a few pages earlier.

[38] For this epigram see *Certamen* 14. Pausanias has quoted it a page earlier (9.38.4).

2 Harpocr. A 272

ὁ δὲ Πίνδαρος (fr. 253) καὶ ὁ τὴν Δαναΐδα πεποιηκώς φασιν Ἐριχθόνιον καὶ Ἥφαιστον ἐκ γῆς φανῆναι.

3 Philod. *De pietate* B 5818 Obbink

πα]ρὰ δὲ τῶι ποή[σαν]τι τὴν Δανα[ΐδα] μητρὸς τῶν θ[εῶν θ]εράπον[τ]ες [οἱ Κου]ρῆτες.

ΜΙΝΥΑΣ

1 Paus. 10.28.2

ἐπηκολούθησε δὲ ὁ Πολύγνωτος ἐμοὶ δοκεῖν ποιήσει Μινυάδι· ἔστι γὰρ δὴ ἐν τῆι Μινυάδι ἐς Θησέα ἔχοντα καὶ Πειρίθουν·

> ἔνθ᾽ ἤτοι νέα μὲν νεκυάμβατον, ἣν ὁ γεραιός
> πορθμεὺς ἦγε Χάρων, οὐκ ἔλλαβον ἔνδοθεν ὅρμου.

ἐπὶ τούτωι οὖν καὶ Πολύγνωτος γέροντα ἔγραψεν ἤδη τῆι ἡλικίαι τὸν Χάρωνα.

2 Paus. 10.28.7

ἡ δὲ Ὁμήρου ποίησις ἐς Ὀδυσσέα καὶ ἡ Μινυάς τε καλουμένη καὶ οἱ Νόστοι (μνήμη γὰρ δὴ καὶ ἐν ταύταις Ἅιδου καὶ τῶν ἐκεῖ δειμάτων ἐστίν) ἴσασιν οὐδένα Εὐρύνομον δαίμονα.

2 Harpocration, *Lexicon to the Orators*

Pindar and the author of the *Danais* say that Erichthonius and Hephaestus appeared out of the earth.[39]

3 Philodemus, *On Piety*

And according to the author of the *Danais*, the Kouretes are servants of the Mother of the Gods.

MINYAS

1 Pausanias, *Geography of Greece*

Polygnotus in my opinion followed the poem *Minyas*. For in the *Minyas* there is this, referring to Theseus and Pirithous:

There they did not find the boat that the dead board, which the old ferryman Charon guided, at its berth.

On this basis, then, Polygnotus too painted Charon as already advanced in age.

2 Pausanias, *Geography of Greece*

But Homer's poem about Odysseus and the so-called *Minyas* and the *Returns* (for in these too there is mention of Hades and the terrors in it) know of no demon Eurynomus.

39 "And Hephaestus" may be corrupt. The usual story is that Hephaestus, in trying to rape Athena, spilt his semen on the ground, which then gave birth to Erichthonius.

3 Paus. 9.5.8

λέγεται δὲ καὶ ὡς ἐν Ἅιδου δίκην δίδωσιν Ἀμφίων ὧν ἐς Λητὼ καὶ τοὺς παῖδας καὶ αὐτὸς ἀπέρριψε· καὶ τὰ ἐς τὴν τιμωρίαν τοῦ Ἀμφίονός ἐστι ποιήσεως Μινυάδος, ἔχει δὲ ἐς Ἀμφίονα κοινῶς καὶ ἐς τὸν Θρᾶικα Θάμυριν.

4 Paus. 4.33.7

Πρόδικος δὲ Φωκαεύς, εἰ δὴ τούτου τὰ ἐς τὴν Μινυάδα ἔπη, προσκεῖσθαί φησι Θαμύριδι ἐν Ἅιδου δίκην τοῦ ἐς τὰς Μούσας αὐχήματος.

5 Paus. 10.31.3

αἱ δὲ Ἠοῖαί τε καλούμεναι (Hes. fr. 25.12–13) καὶ ἡ Μινυὰς ὡμολογήκασιν ἀλλήλαις· Ἀπόλλωνα γὰρ δὴ αὗταί φασιν αἱ ποιήσεις ἀμῦναι Κούρησιν ἐπὶ τοὺς Αἰτωλοὺς καὶ ἀποθανεῖν Μελέαγρον ὑπὸ Ἀπόλλωνος.

6 Philod. *De pietate* B 4922 Obbink

Ὠ]ρίωνα δὲ θ̣νη̣[τὸν] λέγει καὶ ὁ τὴ[ν Μι]ν̣υάδα γράψ[ας, ἀποθανεῖν δ' ὑ]π' Ἀ[ρτέμιδος.

7* P. Ibscher col. i

[“ οὐ δύνατ' οὔ τις]
ἀνθρώπων ὀλ]έσαι με βίηφί τε δ̣ουρ̣ί̣ τ̣ε̣ μακρῶι,
ἀλλά με Μοῖρ' ὀλο]ὴ̣ καὶ Λητοῦς ὤλεσ̣ε̣[ν υἱός.
ἀλλ' ἄγε δή μοι ταῦτα δι]α̣μπερέως ἀγό̣[ρευσον·

3 Pausanias, *Geography of Greece*

It is also said that Amphion is punished in Hades for his insults towards Leto and her children; the reference to Amphion's punishment is in the poem *Minyas*, and it refers jointly to Amphion and the Thracian Thamyris.

4 Pausanias, *Geography of Greece*

Prodicus of Phocaea (if he is the author of the epic on the *Minyas*)[40] says that punishment has been imposed on Thamyris in Hades for his boast to the Muses.

5 Pausanias, *Geography of Greece*

But the so-called *Ehoiai* and the *Minyas* are in agreement with each other: these poems say that Apollo assisted the Kouretes against the Aetolians, and that Meleager was killed by Apollo.

6 Philodemus, *On Piety*

And the writer of the *Minyas* says that Orion was mor[tal, and killed by Artemis].

7* Ibscher papyrus (first century BC)[41]

"No man was able] to slay me by his strength and long spear; [it was dread Fate and the son] of Leto who destroyed [me. But come, tell [me this] from the beginning:

[40] An odd expression. Possibly *Minyas* here means the country of the Minyans. For Thamyris and his boast see *Iliad* 2.594–600.

[41] Meleager in Hades is speaking to Theseus.

τίπτ᾽ ἄρ᾽ ὁδὸν τοσσή]ν̣δε κατήλ̣υθες [εἰς Ἀΐδαο,
τίπτε δὲ Πειρίθοός τοι] ἅμ᾽ ἕσπετο π̣ι̣σ̣[τὸς] ἑ̣[ταῖρος;
]ε̣ι̣ τί κατὰ χρ<ε>ὼ̣ ζ̣ω[ὸς ἱκάνε]ι̣ς̣;"
τὸν δ᾽ αὖτε προσέφη π]ρ̣ότερό[ς] τ̣᾽ ἀ̣π̣[ὸ] μ̣ῦ̣θον ἔειπε[ν
Θησεὺς Αἰγείδης]ας ἐς ποιμένα λ̣αῶν·
"διογεν]ὲ̣ς̣ [Μελ]έ̣α̣γ̣[ρε, δαΐ]φρονος Οἰνέο̣ς̣ υ̣ἱ̣έ̣,
τοιγὰρ ἐγώ τοι] τ̣αῦτ̣[α μ]ά̣λ̣᾽ ἀτρεκέως κ̣αταλ̣έξω.
9 Πειρίθοον μεγάλ᾽ ἆσε θ]εὰ δασπλῆτις Ἐρ̣ι̣νύς·
12].ε̣ν̣ω̣ε̣υ̣δ̣ε̣[ ]ἀγαυὴν Φερσεφό̣ν̣ειαν
]. . . .α̣ς̣ φὰς ν̣[εῦσ]α̣ι̣ Δ[ία] τερπικέ̣ραυ̣νον
ἀθανά]των τε νό̣μ̣ο̣ις, ἵνα ἑδνώσειε̣ν̣ ἄ̣κ[ο]ιτιν·
καὶ γὰρ] ἐκείνους φασὶ κασιγνήτας μεγ̣[ακ]υ̣δ̣εῖς
μνησ]τ̣εύειν, γαμέειν δὲ φίλων ἀ̣π̣ά̣ν̣[ευθε τοκήων.
ὧδε κ]α̣ὶ ἐκ̣ μακ̣ά̣ρων γάμον ὄρνυται ἑδ̣ν̣ώ̣σασθαι
αὐτοκ]ασιγνήτην ὁμοπάτριον· ἐγγυτέρω γάρ
φῆσ᾽ εἶ]ν̣αι γεγαὼς αὐτὸς μεγάλου Ἀΐδαο
Φερσεφ]ό̣νηι κούρηι Δημήτερος ἠϋκόμ̣ο̣ι̣ο̣·
αὐτὸς] μὲν γάρ φ̣η̣σι κασίγνητος καὶ ὄπατρος
τῆς ἔμ]εν<αι>, Ἀΐδην δὲ φίλον πάτρωα τ̣ε̣τ̣ύχθαι·
τοῦ δ᾽ ἕν]εκε̣ν̣ φ̣ά̣το βῆμεν ὑπὸ ζόφον ἠερόε̣ν̣τ̣α̣."
ὣς ἔφατ᾽·] Οἰνε̣ί̣δ̣η̣ς̣ δ̣ὲ κατέστυγε μῦθον ἀκού̣σ̣α̣ς̣,
τὸν δ᾽ ἀπ]α̣μ̣[ειβό]μενος προσεφώνει μειλιχίοισιν·
"Θησεῦ Ἀθην]α̣ί̣ων βουληφόρε θωρηκ̣τ̣άων,
ἦ ῥ᾽ οὐχ Ἱππο]δάμεια περίφρων ἦν παρ̣ά̣[κοι]τ̣ι̣ς̣
μ]εγαθύμου Πειριθόοιο;
θερ]ά̣π̣οντ̣α̣[

[why] have you come [all this way to Hades? And why has Pirithous] your trusty comrade come with you? [. . .] What need had you to [come here a]live?"

[Theseus the son of Aegeus spoke] first and answered him, [ ]ing at the shepherd of peoples:

"[Noble Mel]eager, son of the wise Oineus, I will tell you exactly. [Pirithous has been greatly misled by] the grim goddess Erinys: [he has come to seek] illustrious Persephone, saying that Zeus whose sport is the thunderbolt [has given approval, and according to the go]ds' customs, to contract for her as his wife. For they too are said to woo their glorious sisters, and make love to them out of sight of their dear [parents. So] he is eager to contract a marriage from among the blessed ones—his own sister from the same father; for he [claims] he is closer kin than great Hades to Persephone, the daughter of lovely-haired Demeter. For he says he is her brother, of one father, while Hades is her dear uncle. It was for that he said he was going down to the misty dark."

[So he spoke,] and Oineus' son shuddered on hearing what he said, and addressed him in answer with soothing words:

"[Theseus], counsellor of the warrior Athe[nians, was not prudent [Hippo]dameia the wife [. . .] of great-spirited Pirithous? . . . "

(fragments of four more lines, and of 22 in the following column)

4, 6 suppl. Page; 15 fin., 18, 19 Latte; 16 fin., 23 Maas; cetera Merkelbach, West   9 post 11 transp. West.

8* Pausimachus ap. Philod. *De poematis* 1 col. 123.6 Janko

ἢ [δὲ με]τὰ φθιμένοισι πολυ[λ]λίστη βασίλεια

ΝΑΥΠΑΚΤΙΑ

TESTIMONIUM

Paus. 10.38.11

τὰ δὲ ἔπη τὰ Ναυπάκτια ὀνομαζόμενα ὑπὸ Ἑλλήνων ἀνδρὶ ἐσποιοῦσιν οἱ πολλοὶ Μιλησίωι· Χάρων δὲ ὁ Πυθέω (*FGrHist* 262 F 4) φησὶν αὐτὰ ποιῆσαι Ναυπάκτιον Καρκίνον. ἑπόμεθα δὲ καὶ ἡμεῖς τῆι τοῦ Λαμψακηνοῦ δόξηι· τίνα γὰρ καὶ λόγον ἔχοι ἂν ἔπεσιν ἀνδρὸς Μιλησίου πεποιημένοις ἐς γυναῖκας τεθῆναί σφισιν ὄνομα Ναυπάκτια;

FRAGMENTA

1 Schol. (T) *Il.* 15.336c

ὁμοίως τῶι ποιητῆι καὶ Ἑλλάνικος (fr. 121 Fowler) Ἐριώπην τὴν μητέρα Αἴαντός φησιν· Φερεκύδης δὲ ἐν ε′ (fr.

(Fragments of four more lines, and of 22 in the following column.)

8* Pausimachus of Miletus

[But] she among the dead, the Queen much prayed to.[42]

CARMEN NAUPACTIUM

TESTIMONIUM

Pausanias, *Description of Greece*

As for the epic which the Greeks call the *Naupactia*, most father it on a man from Miletus, but Charon the son of Pythes says that a Naupactian, Carcinus, composed it. We too follow the Lampsacene historian's opinion, for what sense would it have for a poem by a Milesian, on the subject of women, to be entitled *Naupactia*?

FRAGMENTS

1 Scholiast on the *Iliad*

Like Homer, Hellanicus says that Eriope was Ajax's mother. But Pherecydes in Book 5 and Mnaseas in Book 8 say it was

[42] Persephone. Pausimachus, known only from Philodemus, wrote on euphonious composition, perhaps around 200 BC.

24 F.) καὶ Μνασέας ἐν η′ (*FHG* iii.153 fr. 19) Ἀλκιμάχην· ὁ δὲ τῶν Να<υ>πακτίδων ποιητὴς διώνυμον αὐτήν φησι·

τὴν δὲ μέθ' ὁπλοτάτην <τίκτεν περικαλλέα κούρην,
τὴν δὴ μητροπάτωρ> Ἐριώπην ἐξονόμαζεν,
Ἀλκιμάχην δὲ πατήρ τε καὶ Ἄδμητος καλέεσκεν.

< > e.g. suppl. West.

2 Herodian. π. μον. λέξ. 15 (ii.922.1 Lentz)

καὶ τὸ ῥήν . . . ἐν συνθέσει πολύρρην παρὰ τῶι τὰ Ναυπακτικὰ ποιήσαντι·

ἀλλ' ὃ μὲν οὖν ἀπάνευθε θαλάσσης εὐρυπόροιο
οἰκία ναιετάασκε πολύρρην πο<υ>λυβοώτης.

1 ἀπάνευθε Lobeck: ἐπινευσὶ cod.: ἐπὶ θινὶ Cramer.

3 Schol. Ap. Rhod. 2.299, "κευθμῶνα Κρήτης"

ὁ <δὲ> τὰ Ναυπακτικὰ ποιήσας καὶ Φερεκύδης ἐν ϛ′ (fr. 29 Fowler) φασὶν εἰς τὸ σπέος αὐτὰς (sc. τὰς Ἁρπυίας) φυγεῖν τῆς Κρήτης τὸ ὑπὸ τῶι λόφωι τῶι Ἀργινοῦντι.

4 Schol. Ap. Rhod. 3.515–21

ὁ μὲν Ἀπολλώνιος τούτους φησὶ προαιρεῖσθαι ζεῦξαι τοὺς βόας, ὁ δὲ τὰ Ναυπακτικὰ ποιήσας πάντας ἀριθμεῖ τοὺς ὑπ' αὐτοῦ φερομένους ἀριστεῖς.

Alcimache, while the poet of the *Naupactids* [sic] says she had a double name:

And after her, as the youngest, <she bore a fair daughter, whom her maternal grandfather> called Eriope, but her father and Admetus called her Alcimache.

2 Herodian, *On Peculiar Words*

. . . and *rhēn* . . . In a compound, *polyrrhēn* in the author of the *Naupactica*:

But he had his home apart from the broad-wayed sea, a man rich in sheep and rich in cattle.

3 Scholiast on Apollonius of Rhodes

The author of the *Naupactica* and Pherecydes in Book 6 say that they [the Harpies] fled into the cave in Crete which is below the hill of Arginous.[43]

4 Scholiast on Apollonius of Rhodes

Apollonius says that these individuals volunteered to yoke the oxen, whereas the author of the *Naupactica* lists all the heroes recognized by him.

[43] Unknown. The Harpies were pursued by the Boreads; compare "Hesiod," frs. 150–156.

5 Schol. Ap. Rhod. 3.523–524

ἐν δὲ τοῖς Ναυπακτικοῖς Ἴδμων ἀναστὰς Ἰάσονι κελεύει ὑποστῆναι τὸν ἆθλον.

6 Schol. Ap. Rhod. 4.66a, 86 (cf. 3.240)

παρὰ δὲ τῶι τὰ Ναυπακτικὰ πεποιηκότι οὐκ ἔστι κατὰ τὴν ἰδίαν προαίρεσιν ἐξιοῦσα ἡ Μήδεια, ἀλλ' ἐφ' ἑστία<σι>ν καλουμένων τῶν Ἀργοναυτῶν κατ' ἐπιβουλήν, ἐνστάντος τοῦ τῆς ἀναιρέσεως αὐτῶν καιροῦ, προτραπομένου δὲ τοῦ Αἰήτου ἐπὶ τὴν Εὐρυλύτης τῆς γυναικὸς συνουσίαν, Ἴδμονος ὑποθεμένου τοῖς Ἀργοναύταις ἀποδιδράσκειν, καὶ Μήδεια συνεκπλεῖ.

(86) *ὁ τὰ Ναυπακτικὰ πεποιηκὼς ὑπὸ Ἀφροδίτης φησὶ τὸν Αἰήτην κατακοιμηθῆναι . . . δεδειπνηκότων παρ' αὐτῶι τῶν Ἀργοναυτῶν καὶ κοιμωμένων, διὰ τὸ βούλεσθαι αὐτὸν τὴν ναῦν ἐμπρῆσαι·*

> *δὴ τότ' ἄρ' Αἰήτηι πόθον ἔμβαλε δῖ' Ἀφροδίτη*
> *Εὐρυλύτης φιλότητι μιγήμεναι, ἧς ἀλόχοιο,*
> *κηδομένη φρεσὶν ἧισιν, ὅπως μετ' ἄεθλον Ἰήσων*
> *νοστήσηι οἶκόνδε σὺν ἀγχεμάχοις ἑτάροισιν.*

ὁ δὲ Ἴδμων συνῆκε τὸ γεγονὸς καί φησι·

7

> *"φευγέμεναι μεγάροιο θοὴν διὰ νύκτα μέλαιναν."*

5 Scholiast on Apollonius of Rhodes

In the *Naupactica* Idmon stands up and tells Jason to undertake the task.[44]

6 Scholiast on Apollonius of Rhodes

In the author of the *Naupactica* we do not find Medea going out on her own initiative: the Argonauts were invited to a dinner as part of a plot, and when the moment for their destruction was impending, but Aietes turned to make love to his wife Eurylyte, Idmon advised the Argonauts to escape, and Medea sailed off with them.

The author of the *Naupactica* says that Aietes was put to sleep by Aphrodite . . . after the Argonauts had dined with him and were going to bed, and she did this because he intended to set fire to the ship:

Then high-born Aphrodite cast desire upon Aietes to unite in love with Eurylyte his wife; she was concerned in her mind that after his great trial Jason should come safe home with his combative comrades.

Idmon understood what had happened, and said:

7

"Flee from the hall, swift through the dark night!"

[44] As in fr. 4, the task is that of yoking Aietes' fire-breathing oxen.

τὴν δὲ Μήδειαν τὴν ποδοψοφίαν ἀκούσασαν ἀναστᾶσαν συνεξορμῆσαι.

φευγέμεν ἐκ Meineke.

8 Schol. Ap. Rhod. 4.87

ὁ μὲν Ἀπολλώνιος μετὰ τὸ φυγεῖν τὴν Μήδειαν ἐκ τοῦ Αἰήτου οἴκου πεποίηται ὑπισχνουμένην τὸ κῶας τῶι Ἰάσονι· ὁ δὲ τὰ Ναυπακτικὰ γράψας συνεκφέρουσαν αὐτὴν τὸ κῶας κατὰ τὴν φυγήν, κατὰ τὸν αὐτοῦ οἶκον κείμενον {τοῦ Αἰήτου}.

9 Paus. 2.3.9

ἔπη δέ ἐστιν ἐν Ἕλλησι Ναυπάκτια ὀνομαζόμενα, πεποίηται δὲ ἐν αὐτοῖς Ἰάσονα ἐξ Ἰωλκοῦ μετὰ τὸν Πελίου θάνατον ἐς Κόρκυραν μετοικῆσαι· καί οἱ Μέρμερον μὲν τὸν πρεσβύτερον τῶν παίδων ὑπὸ λεαίνης διαφθαρῆναι θηρεύοντα ἐν τῆι πέραν ἠπείρωι· Φέρητι δὲ οὐδέν ἐστιν ἐς μνήμην προσκείμενον.

10 Philod. *De pietate* B 6736 Obbink

Ἀσκληπιὸ̣[ν δὲ Ζ]ε̣ὺς ἐκεραύνωσ[εν, ὡς μ]ὲν ὁ τὰ Ναυπα[κτι]α̣κὰ συγγράψας [ἔν τ]ε̣ Ἀσκληπιῶ[ι Τελ]έστης (*PMG* 807) *καὶ Κινη[σίας] ὁ μελοποιός* (*PMG* 774), *ὅ[τι τὸ]ν Ἱππόλυτον [παρα]κληθεὶς ὑπ' Ἀρ[τέμι]δος ἀνέστ[η]σε[ν, κτλ.*

Cf. ibid. B 4912; Apollod. *Bibl.* 3.10.3 (interp.).

And Medea, hearing the noise of feet, got up and set off with them.

8 Scholiast on Apollonius of Rhodes

Apollonius has made Medea promise the Fleece to Jason after her flight from Aietes' house, whereas the writer of the *Naupactica* had her bring it out with her as she fled, as it had been lying in his house.

9 Pausanias, *Description of Greece*

There is an epic called *Naupactia* among the Greeks, and it is written in it that Jason migrated from Iolcus after Pelias' death to Corcyra; and that Mermerus, the elder of his sons, was killed by a lioness as he was hunting on the mainland opposite, but nothing further is recorded about Pheres.[45]

10 Philodemus, *On Piety*

Asclepius was thunderbolted by Zeus: as the author of the *Naupactiaca* and Telestes in his *Asclepius* and Cinesias the lyricist say, because he raised Hippolytus from the dead at Artemis' pleading.[46]

[45] An Epirotic son of Mermerus is mentioned in *Odyssey* 1.259. He was probably originally an independent figure of local saga who was made a son of Jason when the latter was brought into Corcyraean legend.

[46] Others gave other reasons for Asclepius' suffering this fate. Compare "Hesiod," fr. 51; Stesichorus, *PMG* 194; Panyassis, fr. 5; Pherecydes, fr. 35 Fowler; Pindar, *Pyth.* 3.54–58; Orph. fr. 40.

11 Paus. 4.2.1, see Cinaethon fr. 5.

ΦΟΡΩΝΙΣ

1 Clem. *Strom.* 1.102.6

Ἀκουσίλαος γὰρ (fr. 23a Fowler) Φορωνέα πρῶτον ἄνθρωπον γενέσθαι λέγει· ὅθεν καὶ ὁ τῆς Φορωνίδος ποιητὴς εἶναι αὐτὸν ἔφη

πατέρα θνητῶν ἀνθρώπων.

πατέρα Clem.: πατὴρ fort. poeta.

2 Schol. Ap. Rhod. 1.1126–1131b, "Δάκτυλοι Ἰδαῖοι"

ὁ δὲ τὴν Φορωνίδα συνθεὶς γράφει οὕτως·

ἔνθα γόητες
Ἰδαῖοι, Φρύγες ἄνδρες, ὀρέστερα οἰκί᾽ ἔναιον,
Κέλμις Δαμναμενεύς τε μέγας καὶ ὑπέρβιος Ἄκμων,
εὐπάλαμοι θεράποντες ὀρείης Ἀδρηστείης,
οἳ πρῶτοι τέχνηις πολυμήτιος Ἡφαίστοιο
εὗρον ἐν οὐρείῃσι νάπαις ἰόεντα σίδηρον
ἐς πῦρ τ᾽ ἤνεγκαν καὶ ἀριπρεπὲς ἔργον ἔδειξαν.

2 ὀρέστερα West: ὀρέστεροι codd. 5 τέχνηις West: τέχνην codd.

11 Pausanias, *Description of Greece*: see above, Cinaethon fr. 5.

PHORONIS

1 Clement, *Miscellanies*

For Acusilaus says that Phoroneus was the first human; hence the poet of the *Phoronis* said he was

the father of mortal men.

2 Scholiast on Apollonius of Rhodes, "Idaean Dactyls'

And the composer of the *Phoronis* writes as follows:

. . . where the wizards of Ida, Phrygian men, had their mountain homes: Kelmis, great Damnameneus, and haughty Akmon, skilled servants of Adrastea of the mountain, they who first, by the arts of crafty Hephaestus, discovered dark iron in the mountain glens, and brought it to the fire, and promulgated a fine achievement.

3 Strab. 10.3.19

ὁ δὲ τὴν Φορωνίδα γράψας αὐλητὰς καὶ Φρύγας τοὺς Κουρῆτας λέγει.

4 Clem. *Strom.* 1.164.1

πρὶν γοῦν ἀκριβωθῆναι τὰς τῶν ἀγαλμάτων σχέσεις, κίονας ἱστάντες οἱ παλαιοὶ ἔσεβον τούτους ὡς ἀφιδρύματα τοῦ θεοῦ. γράφει γοῦν ὁ τὴν Φορωνίδα ποιήσας·

Καλλιθόη, κληιδοῦχος Ὀλυμπιάδος βασιλείης,
Ἥρης Ἀργείης, ἣ στέμμασι καὶ θυσάνοισιν
πρώτη ἐκόσμησεν πέρι κίονα μακρὸν ἀνάσσης.

5 *Et. Gen./Magn.* s.v. ἐριούνιος

ἐπίθετον Ἑρμοῦ . . . παρὰ τὸ ἐρι ἐπιτατικὸν καὶ τὴν ὄνησιν . . . καὶ γὰρ ὁ τὴν Φορωνίδα γράψας φησίν·

Ἑρμείαν δὲ πατὴρ ἐριούνιον ὠνόμασ᾽ αὐτόν·
πάντας γὰρ μάκαράς τε θεοὺς θνητούς τ᾽ ἀνθρώπους
κέρδεσι κλεπτοσύνῃσί τ᾽ ἐκαίνυτο τεχνηέσσαις.

6 P. Oxy. 2260 i 3

καὶ ὁ τὴν Φορ[ωνίδα] πεποιηκώς, ἐν ο[ἷς φη]σιν·

οὐδέ τι κούρ[η
ἀρκέσει ἐγρεμάχη [δο]λιχάορος ἀγρομέ[νοισιν.

3 Strabo, *Geography*

The writer of the *Phoronis* says that the Kouretes are pipers and Phrygians.

4 Clement, *Miscellanies*

Certainly, before the qualities of statues were refined, the ancients used to set up pillars and revere them as images of God. At any rate, the author of the *Phoronis* writes:

Callithoe, keyholder of the Olympian queen, Argive Hera; she who first decorated the Lady's tall pillar round about with wreaths and tassels.[47]

5 *Etymologicum Genuinum* and *Magnum*

Eriounios: an epithet of Hermes . . . from the intensive prefix *eri-* and *onêsis* (profit) . . . For the writer of the *Phoronis* too says:

And his father named him Hermes *eriounios*, because he surpassed all the blessed gods and mortal men in profiteering and artful thievery.

6 Oxyrhynchus papyrus (second century AD)

And so the composer of the *Phoronis*, where he says:

Nor will the battle-rousing maiden of the long sword[48] be enough to save them when they gather(?).

[47] Callithoe or Callithyessa, identified with Io, was the first priestess of Hera at Argos.

[48] Athena.

EPICA ADESPOTA

1 Amphora picta, Mus. Brit. E 270 (Kretschmer, *Die griech. Vaseninschriften* 90)

hôδέ ποτ' ἐν Τύρινθι

2 Simonides *PMG* 564

(Μελέαγρος,) ὃς δουρὶ πάντας νίκασε νέους, δινάεντα βαλὼν Ἄναυρον ὕπερ πολυβότρυος ἐξ Ἰωλκοῦ· οὕτω γὰρ Ὅμηρος ἰδὲ Στασίχορος ἄεισε λαοῖς.

3 Hippocr. *De articulis* 8

καλῶς γὰρ Ὅμηρος καταμεμαθήκει ὅτι πάντων τῶν προβάτων βόες μάλιστα ἀτονέουσι ταύτην τὴν ὥρην (sc. τοῦ χειμῶνος τελευτῶντος) . . . τὰ μὲν γὰρ ἄλλα πρόβατα δύναται βραχεῖαν τὴν ποίην βόσκεσθαι, βοῦς δὲ οὐ μάλα, πρὶν βαθεῖα γένηται . . . διὰ τοῦτο οὖν ἐποίησεν τάδε τὰ ἔπη·

ὡς δ' ὁπότ' ἀσπάσιον ἔαρ ἤλυθε βουσὶν ἕλιξιν,

ὅτι ἀσμενωτάτη αὐτοῖσιν ἡ βαθεῖα ποίη φαίνεται.

Cf. eund. *Vectiarius* 5.

UNPLACED FRAGMENTS[1]

1 Red-figure vase by the Cleophrades Painter (early fifth century)

Even so once in Tiryns . . .[2]

2 Simonides, lyric fragment

(Meleager,) who surpassed all the young men with the javelin, hurling it across the eddying Anauros from Iolcus rich in vines: so Homer and Stesichorus sang to the peoples.[3]

3 "Hippocrates," *Dislocations*

For Homer well understood that of all grazing animals it is oxen that are most out of condition at the end of winter . . . For other animals can crop the grass when it is short, but the ox cannot until it is long . . . This is why he composed this passage:

And as when spring comes welcome to curly-horned oxen,[4]

because the long grass is a most welcome sight to them.

[1] Mostly ascribed to "Homer." [2] The vase shows a rhapsode performing, with these words coming out of his mouth.

[3] "Homer" is here cited as the author of an account of the funeral games for Pelias at Iolcus.

[4] Perhaps from the account of Agamemnon's or Menelaus' homecoming in the *Nostoi*. That epic may also have been the source of the ox simile at *Odyssey* 4.535 and 11.411.

4 Arist. *Eth. Nic.* 1116b26

ἰτητικώτατον γὰρ ὁ θυμὸς πρὸς τοὺς κινδύνους· ὅθεν καὶ Ὅμηρος "σθένος ἔμβαλε θυμῶι" (cf. *Il.* 11.11, 14.151, 16.529) καὶ "μένος καὶ θυμὸν ἔγειρε" (cf. *Il.* 15.594) καὶ "δριμὺ δ' ἀνὰ ῥῖνας μένος" (cf. *Od.* 24.318 sq.) καὶ

ἔζεσεν αἷμα.

5 Arist. *Pol.* 1338a22

ἣν γὰρ οἴονται διαγωγὴν εἶναι τῶν ἐλευθέρων, ἐν ταύτηι (sc. ἐν σχολῆι) τάττουσιν. διόπερ Ὅμηρος οὕτως ἐποίησεν·

ἀλλ' οἷον †μέν† ἐστι καλεῖν ἐπὶ δαῖτα θάλειαν.

μόνον ἐστὶ Newman.

6 Schol. (T) *Il.* 24.420b

ἀδύνατον νεκρῶν τραύματα μύειν, ὥς φησιν Ἀριστοτέλης (fr. 167) εἰρηκέναι Ὅμηρον·

μύσεν δὲ πέρι βροτόεσσ' ὠτειλή.

τοῦτο δὲ τὸ ἡμιστίχιον οὐδὲ φέρεται.

4 Aristotle, *Nicomachean Ethics*

For the *thymos* (heart, spirit) is most go-for-it in the face of danger; hence Homer says "(the god) put strength in his *thymos*," and "roused his fury and *thymos*," and "acid fury in his nostrils," and

his blood boiled.[5]

5 Aristotle, *Politics*

For it is to leisure that they assign what they consider the life-style of free men. This is why Homer wrote:

but (he is?) the sort of man one can invite to the banquet.

6 Scholiast on the *Iliad*

It is impossible for dead men's wounds to close up, as Aristotle says Homer described:

and the bloody wound closed up round the edges.

This half-line does not in fact occur in Homer.

[5] None of the phrases quoted occurs exactly in the *Iliad* or *Odyssey*, but the first three are probably distorted or conflated recollections of expressions that do.

7 Clearchus fr. 90 W. (– ὄχλον); Philod. *De pietate* A 1679 Obbink (– σκεδάσεις); Diog. Laert. 2.117

οὐκ ἀπ᾽ ἐμοῦ σκεδάσεις ὄχλον, ταλαπείριε
πρέσβυ;

Fort. ἀπό μοι.

8 Plut. *Thes.* 32.6

Ἡρέας δὲ (*FGrHist* 486 F 2) ὑπὸ Θησέως αὐτοῦ περὶ Ἀφίδνας ἀποθανεῖν τὸν Ἁλυκὸν ἱστόρηκε, καὶ μαρτύρια ταυτὶ τὰ ἔπη παρέχεται περὶ τοῦ Ἁλυκοῦ·

τὸν ἐν εὐρυχόρωι ποτ᾽ Ἀφίδνηι
μαρνάμενον Θησεὺς Ἑλένης ἕνεκ᾽ ἠϋκόμοιο
κτεῖνεν.

9 Chrysippus, *SVF* ii.251.28

ὅτι μὲν γὰρ τὸ λογιστικόν ἐστιν ἐνταῦθα, διὰ τούτων ἐμφαίνεται (ὁ ποιητής)·

ἄλλο δ᾽ ἐνὶ στήθεσσι νόος καὶ μῆτις ἀμύμων.

Fort. ἄλλος ἐνὶ - ἀμείνων

10 Id. ii.253.20

πρῆσεν ἐνὶ στήθεσσιν ἐρισθενέος Διὸς ἀλκήν
γνώμεναι.

7 Clearchus, *On Riddles*; Philodemus, *On Piety*; Diogenes Laertius, *Lives of the Philosophers*

"Will you not disperse this throng from me, long-suffering old sir?"[6]

8 Plutarch, *Life of Theseus*

Hereas[7] has recorded that Halycus was killed by Theseus himself at Aphidnae, and as evidence he adduces these verses about Halycus:

whom once in broad-arena'd Aphidna Theseus killed as he fought over lovely-haired Helen.

9 Chrysippus, *On the Soul*

That the reasoning faculty is located there (around the heart), Homer indicates in these verses:

Then another thing in his breast his mind and good ingenuity (conceived).

10 Chrysippus, *On the Soul*

Made flare in his breast the awareness of mighty Zeus' aid.

[6] The sources report various wits and philosophers (Charmus, Socrates, Bion) as having used this verse for their own purposes. It is conjectured that Menelaus spoke it to Nestor in the *Cypria* when he went to consult him, distraught over the loss of Helen. See Dirk Obbink, *Philodemus On Piety, Part 1* (Oxford, 1996), 544–548.

[7] A fourth-century Megarian historian. Halycus was a Megarian local hero.

11 Strabo 1.2.4

ἀλλὰ μὴν ταῦτά γε πάντα ὁ ποιητὴς Ὀδυσσεῖ προσῆψεν . . . οὗτος γὰρ αὐτῶι "πολλῶν δ' ἀνθρώπων ἴδεν ἄστεα καὶ νόον ἔγνω" (*Od.* 1.3), *οὗτός τε . . . οὗτος δὲ ὁ "πτολίπορθος" ἀεὶ λεγόμενος καὶ τὸ Ἴλιον ἑλὼν*

βουλῆι καὶ μύθοισι καὶ ἠπεροπηΐδι τέχνηι.

Cf. eund.13.1.41; Polyaen. 1 prooem. 8; Stob. 4.13.48.

12 "Ammonius" in *Il.* 21.195 (P.Oxy. 221 ix 1; v.93 Erbse)

κ]ῦμασ[ιν] ἐγκατέλεξα Ἀχελω[ΐου] ἀργυροδ[ί]νεω, ἐξ οὗ πᾶσα θάλασσα.

13 Ps.-Plut. *De Homero* 2.20

εἰσὶ δὲ καὶ παρ' αὐτῶι μεταφοραὶ ποικίλαι, αἳ μὲν ἀπὸ ἐμψύχων ἐπὶ ἔμψυχα, οἷον

φθέγξατο δ' ἡνίοχος νηὸς κυανοπρώιροιο

ἀντὶ τοῦ ναύτης.

Cf. Anon. *De tropis*, iii.228.24 Spengel.

14 Ps.-Plut. *De Homero* 2.55

καὶ τοὐναντίον τὸ ἐνεργητικὸν ἀντὶ τοῦ παθητικοῦ·

δωρήσω τρίποδα χρυσούατον,

ἀντὶ τοῦ δωρήσομαι.

11 Strabo, *Geography*

But Homer connected all of this with Odysseus . . . For this is the hero that he has "seeing many men's cities and learning their mind', this is the one . . . and this is the one always called "city-sacker," who took Ilion

by his counsel and persuasion and art of deception.

12 "Ammonius," commentary on *Iliad* 21

"I laid (him?) in the [wat]ers of silver-eddying Achelous, from which is the whole sea."

13 Pseudo-Plutarch, *On Homer*

He also has complex metaphors, some from animate to animate things, as in

Then spoke the charioteer of the dark-prowed ship,

instead of "the sailor."

14 Pseudo-Plutarch, *On Homer*

And conversely the active instead of the passive:

"I will gift a tripod with gold handles,"

with δωρήσω instead of δωρήσομαι

15 Ammon. in Porph. *Isag.*, *CAG* iv(3).9

ἐκεῖνοι σοφὸν ὠνόμαζον τὸν ἡντιναοῦν μετιόντα τέχνην . . . καὶ ὁ ποιητής·

ἐπεὶ σοφὸς ἤραρε τέκτων.

Cf. Clem. *Strom.* 1.25.1 Ὅμηρος δὲ καὶ τέκτονα σοφὸν καλεῖ.

16 Ath. 137e

Σόλων δὲ τοῖς ἐν πρυτανείωι σιτουμένοις μᾶζαν παρέχειν κελεύει, ἄρτον δὲ ταῖς ἑορταῖς προσπαρατιθέναι, μιμούμενος τὸν Ὅμηρον· καὶ γὰρ ἐκεῖνος τοὺς ἀριστεῖς συνάγων πρὸς τὸν Ἀγαμέμνονα

φύρετο δ᾽ ἄλφιτα

φησίν.

17 Schol. (T) *Il.* 9.668b

εἷλε δὲ τὴν Σκῦρον ὅτε εἰς Αὐλίδα ἐστρατολόγουν, διὰ τὸ εἶναι ἐκεῖ Δόλοπας ἀποστάντας τῆς Πηλέως ἀρχῆς·

ἔπλεον εἰς Σκῦρον Δολοπηΐδα.

τότε δὲ καὶ τὸν Νεοπτόλεμον ἐπαιδοποιήσατο.

15 Ammonius, commentary on Porphyry's *Introduction to Aristotle's Categories*

They applied the term *sophos* (wise, clever) to anyone who pursued any kind of skill . . . So Homer:

when the clever builder had constructed it.[8]

16 Athenaeus, *Scholars at Dinner*

Solon says that barley bread should be given to those who take meals in the town hall, with the addition of wheaten bread on festival days; he is copying Homer, for he too, when he brings the heroes together at Agamemnon's quarters, says

and barley meal was mixed.

17 Scholiast on the *Iliad*

(Achilles) took Scyros at the time when they were recruiting for Aulis, because there were Dolopes there who had revolted from Peleus' rule:

They sailed to Dolopian Scyros.

That was also when he fathered Neoptolemus.[9]

[8] The wooden horse?

[9] The scholiast's story is not in accord with the *Cypria* or *Little Iliad*. The verse fragment, however, may come from one of these epics.

18 Schol. Lyc. 86, "*γρυνόν*"

γρυνὸς γάρ ἐστιν ὁ κορμός. Ὅμηρος·

γρυνοὶ μὲν δαίοντο, μέγας δ' ἥφαιστος ἀνέστη.

19 *Suda θ* 448

θωΰσσοντες· ὑλακτοῦντες. Ὅμηρος·

βαρύβρομα θωΰσσοντες.

18 Scholiast on Lycophron

A "stegg" is a log. Homer:

The steggs burned, and a great blaze arose.

19 The *Suda*

Hallooing: barking. Homer:

With deep-roaring halloos they . . .

COMPARATIVE NUMERATION

OEDIPODEA

West	Kinkel	Allen	Davies	Bernabé
1	1	1	2	2
2	–	–	–	–
3	2	2	1	1

THEBAID

West	Kinkel	Allen	Davies	Bernabé
1–3	1–3	1–3	1–3	1–3
4	–	–	–	11
5	6	6	8	5
6	5	5	7	10
7	–	–	–	–
8	–	–	"Hom." 3	4
9	–	–	5	9
10	7	7	4	6
11	4	4	6	7–8

EPIGONI

West	Kinkel	Allen	Davies	Bernabé
1	1	1	1	1
2	Antim. 2	–	Antim. 2	4
3	2	2	p.74	5
4	4	4	3	3
5	3	3	2	2

COMPARATIVE NUMERATION

ALCMEONIS

West	Kinkel	Davies	Bernabé
1–4	1–4	1–4	1–4
5	5	6	5
6	6	5	6
7	7	7	7

CYPRIA

West	Kinkel	Allen	Bethe	Davies	Bernabé
1	1	1	1	1	1
2	–	2	2	2	2
3	–	–	E1	–	–
4	2	3	3	3	3
5	3	4	4	4	4
6	4	5	5	5	5
7	–	–	5A	dub. 1	6
8	–	–	D3	–	37
9	5	6	6	6	8
10	6	7	7	7	9
11	–	–	8	8	10
12	–	10	C2	12	13
13	–	–	5B	dub. 2	7
14	8	12	10	11	14
15	7	8	9	9	11
16	9	11	11	13	15
17	–	–	11	14	15
18	10	13	12	15	17
19	11	14	13	16/p.75	19, 21
20	12	15	14	17	24
21	13	16	B2	adesp. 4	25
22	14	17	15	18	26
23	15	18	18	21	27
24	16	19	19	22	28
25	24	–	D4	–	41

West	Kinkel	Allen	Bethe	Davies	Bernabé
26	17	20	17	19	29
27	18	21	16	20	30
28	19	22	20	23	31
29	20	23	22	24	18
30	21	24	21	26	32
31	22	25	23	25	33

AETHIOPIS

West	Kinkel	Allen	Bethe	Davies	Bernabé
1	1	1	1	spur.	1
2	–	–	3	dub.	2
3	–	–	–	–	3
4	–	–	C6	p.74	4
5	*Il. Pers.*	*Il. Pers.*	*Il. Pers.*	Arct.	*Il. Pers.*
	4	6	16	spur. 1	7
6	2	2	2	1	5

LITTLE ILIAD

West	Kinkel	Allen	Bethe	Davies	Bernabé
1	1	1	1	1	28
2	2	2	3	2	2
3	3	3	4	3	3
4	4	4	5	4	24
5	5	5	2	5	5
6	6	6	6	6	29
7	7	7	7	7	30
8	8	8	8	8	7
9	–	11	C3	–	6
10	–	–	–	–	–
11	9	9	9	9	25
12	–	22	10	10	8
13	10	10	C4	–	26

West	Kinkel	Allen	Bethe	Davies	Bernabé
14	11	12	11	11	9
15	12	13	*Il. Pers.* 4	12	10
16	12	13	*Il. Pers.* 5	12	11
17	17	18	*Il. Pers.* 14	23	20
18	18	*Il. Pers.* 2	*Il. Pers.* 15	21	21
19	19	20	*Il. Pers.* 6	22	22
20	19	20	12	22	31
21	14	15	*Il. Pers.* 7	14	13
22	13	14	*Il. Pers.* 8	13	12
23	15	16	*Il. Pers.* 9	15	14
24	15	16	*Il. Pers.* 10	16	15
25	15	16	*Il. Pers.* 11	17	16
26	15	16	*Il. Pers.* 12	18	17
27	15	16	*Il. Pers.* 13	18	18
28	16	17	14	19	19
29	18	19	13	20	21
30	–	19/21	13	20	21
31	–	–	15	dub. 3	23
32	dub. 1	p.148	A3	"Hom." 1	27

SACK OF ILION

West	Kinkel	Allen	Bethe	Davies	Bernabé
1	–	–	–	2	2
2	*Aeth.* 3	5	2	1	4
3	2	2	15	3	5
4	1	1	1	dub	1
5	–	–	C7	p.74	*Titanom.* 14
6	3	3/4	3	4	6

COMPARATIVE NUMERATION

RETURNS

West	Kinkel	Allen	Bethe	Davies	Bernabé
1	3	3	3	3	3
2	p.59	11	C8	p.75	12
3	10	10	*Atreidai* 2	9	4
4	4	4	4	4	5
5	5	5	5	5	6
6	6	6	6	6	7
7	8	8	7	7	8
8	p.58	12	C5	p.75	9
9	–	–	–	–	–
10	–	–	–	test. 2	10
11	1	1	1	1	1
12	–	–	*Atreidai* 1	8	11
13	2	2	2	2	2

TELEGONY

West	Kinkel	Allen	Bethe	Davies	Bernabé
1	–	–	–	"Hom." 10	1
2	–	–	–	–	–
3	–	–	1	1	–
4	1	1	2	2	3
5	–	–	D7	–	4
6	*Nostoi* 9	1	2	2	5

PISANDER

West	Kinkel	Davies	Bernabé
1	1	1/2	1
2	2	3	2
3	3	4	3
4	4	5	4
5	5	6	5
6	6	7	6

West	Kinkel	Davies	Bernabé
7	7	9	7
8	8	dub. 1	8
9	9	dub. 2	9
10	–	8	11
11	11	10	12
12	test.	11	test. 6

PANYASSIS

West	(Kinkel) Matthews	Davies	Bernabé
1	22	20	1
2	15	15	2
3	16	16	3
4	24	21	13
5	19	19	26
6	1	1	4
7	2	2	5
8	3	3	6
9	4	4	7
10	5	5	8
11	26	23	12
12	7	7	9
13	28 M.	dub. 3	31
14	32 M.	dub. 2	33
15	10	10	11
16	8	8	10
17	9	9	14
18	30 M.	26	15
19	12	12	16
20	13	13(i)	17
21	14	14	19
22	14.6	13(ii)	18
23	17	17	20

West	(Kinkel) Matthews	Davies	Bernabé
24	18	18	23
25	11	11	22
26	6/20/21	6	21/24/25
27	29 M.	dub. 1	30
28	25	22ab	27
29	25	22c	28
30	23	25	29

EUMELUS: *Titanomachy*

West	Kinkel	Allen	Davies	Bernabé
1	1	1	1	1/2
2	18	–	Eum. dub. 4	18
3	2	2	3	3
4	–	–	–	–
5	–	–	–	–
6	–	–	–	–
7	–	–	–	–
8	5	5	5	6
9	9	8	10	9
10	8	7	7	8
11	3	3	4	7
12	7	(9)	9	10
13	6	6	6	11
14	4	4	8	4

EUMELUS: *Corinthiaca, Europia,* incerta

West	Kinkel	Jacoby 451 F	Davies	Bernabé	Fowler
15	1	1	*Cor.* 1	1	1
16	–	–	*Cor.* 12	2	–
17	2	2	*Cor.* 2	3	3
18	3	2	*Cor.* 3a	3	3

West	Kinkel	Jacoby 451 F	Davies	Bernabé	Fowler
19	4	1	*Cor.* 5	4	1
20	3	2	*Cor.* 3a	5	3
21	9	3	*Cor.* 4	19	–
22	–	–	*Cor.* 12	8	–
23	3	2	*Cor.* 3a	5	3
24	5	4	*Cor.* 6	6	4
25	6	6	*Cor.* 8	7	2
26	–	–	–	–	–
27	10	–	*Eur.* 1	11	–
28	11	–	*Eur.* 2	12	–
29	8	5	*Cor.* 7	10	5
30	12	–	*Eur.* 3	13	–
31	14	8	*Cor.* 10	14	7
32	15	9	*Cor.* 11	15	8
33	7	7	*Cor.* 9	9	6
34	16	–	dub. 2	16	–
35	17	–	dub. 2	17	9

MINYAS

West	Kinkel	Davies	Bernabé
1–2	1–2	1–2	1–2
3	3	4	3
4	4	4	4
5	5	3	5
6	6	5	6
7–8	–	–	7,–

CARMEN NAUPACTIUM

West	Kinkel	Davies	Bernabé
1–3	1–3	1–3	1–3
4	5	4	4
5	6	5	5

West	Kinkel	Davies	Bernabé
6	4/7	6/7	6
7	8	7	7
8	9	8	8
9	10	9	9
10	11/12	10	10/11
11	13	test. 3	12

PHORONIS

West	Kinkel	Davies	Bernabé
1–2	1–2	1–2	1–2
3	3	2A	3
4	4	3	4
5	5	4	5
6	–	5	6

ADESPOTA

West	Kinkel	Allen pp.147–151	Bethe pp. 42–44	Davies "Homerus"	Bernabé *Cypria*
1	–	p. 151		–	
2	–	–		29	
3	2	1/2	A2A	14	
4	–	11		5d	
5	4	–		7	
6	8	7		8	
7	–	–		Adesp. 5	16
8	–	–		Adesp. 8	
9	–	14		11	
10	–	12		12	
11	10	–		25	
12	–	–		–	
13	12	16		19	
14	13	17		22	

West	Kinkel	Allen pp.147–151	Bethe pp. 42–44	Davies "Homerus"	Bernabé *Cypria*
15	–	22		3	
16	–	–	A4	9	38
17	–	–		–	40
18	14	18		27	
19	17	25		26	

For the *Capture of Oichalia*, *Theseis*, *Danais*, Asius, and Cinaethon my numerations are the same as those of Kinkel, Davies, and Bernabé.

INDEX

Composed in ZephGreek and ZephText by
Technologies 'N Typography, Merrimac, Massachusetts.
Printed and bound by Edwards Brothers, Ann Arbor, Michigan
on acid-free paper made by Glatfelter, Spring Grove, Pennsylvania.